Narrow Seas

Alaric Bond

Narrow Seas
Copyright © 2024 by Alaric Bond
Published by Old Salt Press LLC

Paperback: ISBN: 978-1-943404-49-0
E.book: ISBN: 978-1-943404-50-6

The cover artwork shows a detail from artwork by Jim Rae. Jim Rae served in both the Merchant and Royal Navy. Further examples of his work can be seen at Fidra Fine Art: www.fidrafineart.co.uk

Publisher's Note: This is a work of historical fiction. Certain characters and their actions may have been inspired by historical individuals and events. The characters in the novel, however, represent the work of the author's imagination. Any resemblance to actual persons, living or dead, is entirely coincidental. Published by Old Salt Press. Old Salt Press, LLC is based in Jersey City, New Jersey with an affiliate in New Zealand. For more information about Old Salt Press titles go to www.oldsaltpress.com

Thanks are due to Fred, Joan, Antoine, George, Tony, and Rick for their support, Tessa for copy editing and Kitty for keeping me sane.

For Alie

Other novels by Alaric Bond

The Fighting Sail series
His Majesty's Ship
The Jackass Frigate
True Colours
Cut and Run
The Patriot's Fate
The Torrid Zone
The Scent of Corruption
HMS Prometheus
The Blackstrap Station
Honour Bound
Sealed Orders
Sea Trials
Lone Escort
The Seeds of War
On the Barbary Coast

and

Turn a Blind Eye
The Guinea Boat

The Coastal Forces series
Hellfire Corner
Glory Boys

Contents

Narrow Seas

Chapter One

"Same again, Patty," Frank Thompson told the barmaid, "but hold the port an' lemon." The girl gave a quizzical look but did begin to pump his beer.

"When we going to get something to eat, Frank?"

Thompson looked round to see Joyce had joined him at the bar.

"In a minute, doll," he said, though his attention quickly turned to where his mates were gathered at the back of the smoke-filled room. There were nine – a reasonable turnout – and they had dragged two tables together to make a cosy little group. Apart from them, the pub was almost empty although Thompson had grown up nearby and this was his local; the serious drinkers would not show until much later.

"This was only supposed to be just the one round." Joyce considered the row of foaming mugs forming up along the counter.

"One round or two," Thompson shrugged, "don't make much difference either way. And it seems to be going down well with the boys. Sure you don't want another port an' lemon?"

"I'm fine, really."

"Where'd you get that dress?"

"It's a suit and real tweed," she said. "Don't tell me this is the first time you've noticed."

He turned away. "Must have cost a pretty penny," he said. "And a fair number of coupons."

"It's borrowed, Frank." She was pressing up against him now; resting her face against his arm. "Girl I know at the café; it were a present from her mother. I got to give it back first thing."

1

"Shame your mother couldn't make the wedding; or any of your friends."

She pulled away and looked at him, though her hand remained on his arm. "Weren't convenient, you know that. Most've got kids or are on the day shift. We could've had the reception there; Mr Burrows was all in favour."

"A Lyons Corner House's no place for a weddin' reception," he said.

"An' a pub is, I suppose?"

He pulled a face. "That don't explain why your mum ain't here; she ain't workin'," he said, adding, "not that I'm objecting, mind."

"She don't like this sort of thing."

"This sort of thing...or me?"

"She don't dislike you, Frank, but you know how it is. With Dad gone and Pete up north, I'm all she's got."

"And I'm not good enough?"

"Don't start." She released his arm. "Not on our weddin' day."

He considered her again; it was a smart suit, and she must have paid special attention to her hair; there were definitely lighter strands amongst the brown and, now that he looked, he could see curls. Yet there remained something in Joyce's manner, something he did not like. Something that had been absent during their brief period of courting.

"Aye, it's our weddin' day," he agreed. "So you won't begrudge a man a bit of a wet."

"Of course not, Frank." She spoke quickly, lowering her head as she did. "Though you got a long journey tomorrow, and we still 'ave to book in at the 'otel."

"Won't take long to get settled," he said, "and hardly worth unpacking. I'll be off first thing."

"I don't know why we had to book anywhere," she said. "Mother's place is only round the corner; we could have saved ourselves a fortune."

"Your mother didn't bother showing up." He gave a brief sigh and raised his eyes to heaven. "Here we go again!"

"What's keepin' the beer?" The voice was loud and belonged to a corporal in the RASC who breathed fumes from his last.

2

"Coming, Alfie," Thompson assured him, before turning back to the barmaid. "That it, Patty?"

"Ten pints," the girl confirmed.

"What about the chasers?"

"You had all our Scotch with the last."

"But it's me weddin' day!"

The barmaid shrugged. "That's your problem; can't serve what we ain't got."

"Alright, put it on the slate." With the skill acquired from long practice, Thompson collected two mugs in each paw. "Give us an' 'and with the rest, Alfie," he told the soldier, "then you may as well order in the next."

"But Frank, we have to eat!"

He stopped and considered the woman again. Yes, she had definitely worked on her appearance but that didn't excuse any lip.

"I told you, we're havin' a few bevvies first," he said. "Then, an' when I feels like it, we might think about some grub."

Joyce didn't speak though her expression revealed a mixture of surprise and disappointment. For a moment Thompson wondered if he had gone too far; they'd only been married a matter of hours, and he really hardly knew the girl. More to the point, she hardly knew him. Yet, with the war now well into its third year, there was nothing unusual in short engagements. And besides, no one had forced her to marry him.

"That's the way, Frankie old boy," Alfie told him when they were halfway back to joining the lads. "Don't do to give up the whip hand; got to treat 'em firm right from the start..."

"Too right," Thompson agreed.

Their arrival was greeted by a chorus of cheers from those at the tables.

"Thought you were brewin' the stuff," Charlie said as he helped himself to a pint.

"And where's the neckers?" Ted asked. "Your bint bringing 'em, is she?"

Thompson looked back at the bar where Joyce now stood alone. That tweed definitely suited her and did nothing to hide what was a truly impressive figure. All things considered, he reckoned he'd done all right in the wife department. Once she got to know the rules, they'd get along splendidly.

3

"Old girl seems as good as ever." Lieutenant Commander Harris' voice rose above the roar of engines and, though Lieutenant Anderson nodded in reply, he was not in total agreement.

It was a bright June morning that looked likely to improve further. Slightly less than a mile out and riding on the plane, MGB*194* was cutting a straight path across the grey-blue waters, bows rising high above the placid surface as her triple Packards powered her on. The gunboat had been handed back from the Wellington Dock three days before, but this was the first time they had taken her to sea. And yes, despite repairs that saw major sections of her hull replaced, to say nothing of two engines and a substantial portion of deck, he supposed she was very much as before.

However, there remained one major difference. Anderson didn't hold with any rubbish about ships having souls or even personalities and certainly had no truck with anything supernatural: "We're not at home to Mr Superstition," as his mother would say. But he did believe in people; it was the crew that gave a vessel personality, and the wounds *194* suffered in her last engagement were by no means confined to her material.

He glanced back to where a brand new 20mm Oerlikon sat, heavily shrouded, and still packed in grease and carriage corks. The gun had yet to be commissioned but would probably perform in much the same way as its predecessor. However, without the unlikely pairing of Smith and Godliman in control, Anderson doubted it would prove as efficient. Though differing in size and temperament, the two had worked as one, seemingly knowing the other's thoughts and expectations and turning what was light ordnance into a formidable weapon. Having such a team manning their main armament had been a definite advantage and probably accounted for the vessel's continued existence, yet one single long-range barrage from an E-boat ended their perfect synergy.

And they weren't the only absentees. Below, in the cramped confines of *194*'s engine room, their former chief motor mechanic was also missing. Les Carter had sailed with Anderson and Harris from the start and, though now replaced by Bill Newman – another long-standing shipmate – his quiet competence would be missed.

The gunboat was running parallel to the heavily defended beach. In the current conditions it would take slightly longer to raise Dover although, after nearly two months on shore, he had no wish to be home. And neither, he guessed, did Harris.

On such a tiny bridge no one could ever be far away, but as Anderson considered the nearby figure of his captain – eyes slit and oilskins pressed tight by the oncoming gale – Lieutenant Commander Harris could have been in a completely different world. Anderson was only a temporary officer, to be released at the end of hostilities, yet even he had missed the sea, so how would a career man such as Harris be feeling? Not only had his captain been stuck on the beach for several weeks, but much of that time was spent in one hospital or another as he recovered from his wounds. Anderson decided the old boy deserved a bit of a blow.

Standing slightly forward was the wiry figure of Nolan, another newcomer. Their previous coxswain had been young and, for one who shared his working space with two commissioned officers, rather too fond of the odd sassy comment. Phillips handled the boat well, however, and had been showing all the makings of a fine warrant officer when he met with the enemy shell that could easily have written off all on the bridge.

Nolan, his replacement, was a carpenter before the war and only a leading hand now, whereas the post of coxswain usually fell to a petty officer. Yet the Navy was changing all the time and a general lack of manpower meant quite junior men being given responsible tasks. Several lower in rank than himself were in command of Coastal Forces vessels so Anderson should not be surprised. Nolan had served aboard a destroyer and his report claimed him to be a natural when handling small craft, however, the Liverpudlian had already created quite a different impression aboard *194*.

On his first day he attempted to smuggle a ginger tom into the ratings' dormitory. That might have been excused but when word got out of his intentions to take the poor beast on regular patrols, the captain – every inch a straight striper – stepped in. That, and a minor altercation in the mess when they ran out of powdered egg, suggested Nolan would become one of *194*'s 'characters'. Anderson could only hope his skills as a helmsman proved as impressive.

But not all the new hands were replacing casualties; in the

W/T office David Jelly, their former telegraphist, had taken up a shore posting and was currently being inducted into the mysteries of RDF – what many were starting to call radar. His place was taken by Harvey, a former apprentice electrician who'd spent the best part of a year aboard a cruiser. He seemed confident enough, and Anderson was never one to make broad assumptions, yet it would be hard to match his predecessor's innate skills.

Fortunately there were old faces as well; in the starboard turret, Seaman Gunner John Daly was taking a casual interest in the boat's progress. This was only a brief coastal jaunt, and his matched pair of Vickers machine guns were pointing at nothing more hostile than a clear blue sky, but Anderson knew from experience the Irishman could be depended upon.

At that moment Daly was responsible for *194*'s total armament as the port turret lay empty. Gibson, who once occupied it, was also missing and one of the few able to leave the ship in apparent good health. It turned out to be a brief reprieve, however. Gibson was arrested shortly after that last, disastrous, operation and currently awaited civil trial for a murder that would probably end in his execution.

The memory naturally drew Anderson's thoughts to *194*'s last outing; one that had seemed positively commonplace after the horrors they experienced at St Nazaire only a few months before. Within seconds they went from leading a successful raid on an enemy convoy to fighting for their very lives and, with the captain wounded, only one able man in the engine room and a boat leaking like the proverbial colander, Anderson still wondered quite how they made it back.

Yet he had sailed in high-speed launches long enough to realise the scenario was not uncommon. Though dedicated to Coastal Forces and, specifically, the senior officer standing next to him, Anderson knew the score. And when light wooden craft driven by powerful petrol engines were sent to fight a superior enemy, he really should expect nothing less.

* * *

Bill Newman unconsciously flexed the fingers of his left hand as he considered the massive Packards before him. All three had been running at just under two thousand revs for over an hour and, apart from a minor leak in the oil pump of one – something he, or one of his mechanics, could address easily enough once the engine cooled – there were no problems. Not that he expected any; each of the mills were brought up to temperature more than once while *194* was moored at the Pens. But the still waters of a harbour berth could not compare with the rough and tumble of the Channel and, as this was his first posting as a Chief Motor Mechanic (Temporary Acting), Newman was taking no chances.

At the port engine, Pickering made a small adjustment to one of the Holley carburettors that currently sucked much of the oxygen from the dark, cramped space. Until recently both men had been of equal rank, it was only when Carter, their former governor, bought it during the last trip that Newman was made up to take his place. Geoff Pickering showed no resentment at this sudden promotion; the very reverse in fact and they worked together better now than before.

His other mechanic, Kipling, was standing by the starboard mill. This was the first time Newman had seen the new hand at sea and was reasonably satisfied. But then, however well he might perform on land, the real test of any marine engineer was his ability to work when travelling at speed. Feeling Newman's eyes upon him, Kipling looked round and gave a childlike grin that matched his short stature. Kipling's size was a distinct advantage in the engine room's restricted space, but that smile gave away what was perhaps his only potential failing.

Though no fool, the lad alternated from being slavishly eager to knowing it all. Much could be put down to nerves, of course, and the boy was still in his teens. This was also his first active service posting and Coastal Forces was not the easiest of billets. Newman gave a brief nod in reply; Kipling may mellow, though a few more years of growing was what he really needed.

He flexed his fingers again. It was a habit acquired after the cast from his forearm was removed. The bone had been broken the same night Carter met his end, and, as the pair were within inches of the other, Newman counted himself lucky to get away with just a wounded arm. The medics predicted a perfect mend, and his muscles should soon be back to full strength, yet he remained cautious about using the limb and guessed he always would be.

One of the bulkhead lamps flickered and went out. Pickering reached up and gave the housing a solid thump to no effect. The mechanic glanced back at Newman who shook his head. It would probably just be the bulb and, though possible to replace at sea, this was only supposed to be a short trip. They would also need to check the voltage but both that, and the change of pump, should be done in little more than an hour once back in harbour.

He glanced at the luminous dial of his watch; yes, they should be heading back shortly and then, as if in response, the boat did begin a slow turn to starboard. All three waited expectantly; it might just be the skipper manoeuvring or perhaps the start of their run home. Those living in such a sheltered environment soon became good at guessing the craft's position and, as the seconds mounted, Newman became increasingly certain this would be a full one-eighty.

Also recognising this, Pickering gave a grin and Kipling said something no one heard, but it was clear the pair were pleased to be returning. As was Newman, who flexed his fingers once more.

* * *

It never failed to amaze Anderson that, whatever the state of the tide or current, a homeward leg often felt faster than the journey out. They had only turned back half an hour before, yet Dover was in sight, if only as a distant blur. A trio of minesweepers had passed out of the harbour entrance and were coming up on their port bow.

"They're running late," Anderson bellowed.

"Probably an additional check," the captain replied.

That was likely; the previous night had been ideal for laying mines: there may have been too many suspect areas for the regular early morning patrol to deal with.

"Bring her down to sixteen hundred," Harris ordered, and Anderson could not contain a sigh as the din dropped to a more manageable level. Even at the lower revs, the boat remained firmly on the plane, however, her bows scudding above the gentle waves, and they must still be making close on thirty knots. At that rate they should be back before two, with every chance of hot food waiting for them. "No sense in rushing," the captain added in a slightly softer voice, "and we don't want to make too much wash for your former friends."

The trio were growing nearer with every second and Anderson watched them with professional interest. Until volunteering for Coastal Forces, he had been the first officer in a converted trawler carrying out a similar task on the east coast. These more modern vessels were specifically designed for the work, though it was every bit as dangerous. It also lacked any form of glamour, although the same might be said of minelayers. Those concerned with sea mines in any way were commonly considered inferior to the crews of battleships or aircraft carriers, yet the small but deadly packages had already accounted for more tonnage sunk than all the shells, torpedoes and bombs put together. And Anderson, for one, did not doubt the value of such frail craft.

"Looks like they're in business," he said.

That was certainly the case; the three had taken up the customary vic formation and their sweeps were definitely out.

"So I see." Harris sounded pensive. "There's been no alert, but maybe we should drop it down a notch further?"

At his captain's command, Nolan lowered the speed by two hundred revs, and there was a further, pleasurable, reduction in noise. Anderson watched but said nothing; this was probably the only area where he had greater expertise than Harris. Providing the mines had been dropped by air, which would seem to be the case, running a knot or two slower would make little difference.

"We've sweepers about, Tel'." Harris was now leaning forward to the W/O office speaking tube. "See if you can make contact; ask them if they're on an exercise."

Anderson said nothing, although he could see the active pennant on all three vessels.

"'Parrently there was enemy aircraft activity in the area," Harvey, the telegraphist, duly reported. "They've been sent to check to be on the safe side."

"Very good," Harris replied, but Harvey had more to add.

"They said we should let them know if we run into anything loud."

Harris closed the speaking tube cover and turned to Anderson. "I suppose that sort of wit is encouraged in minesweeping circles?"

"There is a fair amount of gallows humour," Anderson admitted.

9

And then it wasn't funny anymore. With a blinding flash that easily overpowered the midday sun, the sea rose up between two of the craft. Both began to bob and thrash in the boiling waters while a few seconds later the ear-splitting crack reached *194*, deafening all on deck.

"That hurt!" Harris rubbed at both ears. "Though probably worse for the sweepers."

Anderson knew that for a fact. All three were still being tossed about like corks in a maelstrom while a seemingly constant deluge of water rained down.

"Let's send them a message," Harris said when there was relative peace. "Make, 'that was a big one!'"

Anderson collected the Aldis and began to send the signal.

"Does that sort of thing make you regret leaving the service?" Harris enquired as Anderson worked.

"I think it might even be safer in Coastal Forces," he said.

A flickering answer came from one of the minesweepers.

"What are they saying?" Harris asked as Anderson's smile deepened.

"They said, 'what was?'"

* * *

The mean little room was lit by a single, yellowed, bulb.

"Poky lookin' drum," Thompson announced as he led the way in.

"An' it could do with a decent airing," Joyce agreed, following. "Maybe open a window or two?"

"Leave it out, place is barely warm."

"Just as you like." She closed the curtains again and moved away from the window, adding, "Nice lot of cupboards."

"Not much use to us," Thompson smirked. "It's the bed we wants."

Joyce gave an automatic smile; from the look of the hotel and, more specifically, the old man at its front desk, they wouldn't be the first guests with similar intentions.

"Right, khazi's only next door; I'm off for a Jimmy." He tossed his grip on the bed where it raised a cloud of dust. "Make yourself comfortable; be back before you knows it."

She lowered herself next to Thompson's bag as the door

clicked shut, closing her mind to the noises that followed through the light partition.

It had been quite a day. Much of the morning was spent in the only house Joyce had known and, though little more than a two-up, two-down terrace, the place was important to her. She remembered it when her father was alive; she and her younger brother used to play in the alley behind and, though cramped and with countless draughts, there was always a fire burning inside in winter.

Much had changed since. With Dad dying and Pete signing for the Air Force, Joyce's mum had been relying on her income, so it was natural she should take against any man who swept her away. And it was equally understandable that Frank might not appear the ideal catch. There were no airs and graces in her family, though Joyce was brought up properly and did well at school; at one point they even thought she would matriculate.

But though he might appear on the rough side, there was a lot of good in her new husband. Before the war Frank had done all right for himself working for Mr Granger and, when his call-up papers came, did well with his basic training. So much so that he was given the chance to become a gunner – one of the more responsible seagoing positions, or so he'd told her.

Her mother was still not happy but then Joyce doubted anyone would be good enough for her little girl. And without her own friends, the ceremony was a pretty lonely affair, although Frank's pals did their best to make things go with a swing.

The house was no more than a quarter of a mile from the registry office, yet Mr Granger sent one of Frank's mates around with a car which was a nice touch, even if Ted was already the worse for wear and smelled of beer. Then they'd needed to wait for their spot as the couple before had some sort of emergency with the woman, who looked like she might pop at any moment, being taken off in an ambulance. But it was done in the end, with Ted burping his way through as one of the witnesses and Mr Granger – someone Frank obviously respected and even seemed oddly frightened of – the other.

They'd stayed longer in *The Crown* than she'd expected, but Frank and his mates were more than happy, and she was only going to get married once. Besides, their food, when it came, was all right. Not as good as what her friends could have done at the

Corner House but there'd been a cake of sorts with plaster icing that looked just like the real thing.

Now though, as she glanced around the gloomy room and rested her hands on the worn eiderdown, she was less certain. There were still a few mysteries of wedded bliss to discover, and she didn't want to let Frank down; he always seemed to know more than her and was bound to be an expert. There would also be that early start; he had to report to his base on the south coast by noon so needed to be at St Pancras first thing and they'd have to cross London first. But before then it would be down to her, as far as the marriage bed was concerned. No time for false starts, she'd have to get everything right first go.

"All right, doll?"

She jumped slightly as Frank's head appeared around the door. He was grinning and had taken off his jacket and shirt. The vest was holed in places and his trousers were stained. It was the first time she'd seen him so and always assumed him to be well built, yet that body did look slightly flabby. The round face was also flushed and there was a trace of saliva running from the side of his mouth.

"Thought you'd be ready for me," he said, though there was something other than disappointment in those dark eyes. "Well, come on then, make me welcome."

Chapter Two

"All things considered, I think we can call that a success," Harris said.

"Just the small matter of the port engine," Anderson agreed as he gathered the pile of papers together and slipped them into a folder.

"Which should be relatively simple, or so Newman thinks."

The port Packard began to play up just as they were approaching harbour. Newman shut it down, suspecting a broken valve. Which proved correct, once the head was removed.

"It might turn out a good test for his team," Harris continued, "and lucky it popped as we were coming in, and not when putting out for the next exercise."

Anderson sealed the folder of ship's papers, then collected his own jotter and leafed through the closely written notes. *194* had been back in her berth for several hours but the rest of their afternoon and much of that evening was spent checking over what remained to be done before returning her to active service. Even after serving under Harris for so long, Anderson was still learning. The programme they finally agreed upon was extensive, but nothing stood out as impossible and all should be achieved in the time they were allowed.

"It's cold in here," Harris said, stating a truth that had been creeping up on them both for the last few hours. Indeed, their tiny wardroom was only meant for the occasional overnight stay and possibly sheltering wounded. There was a fine layer of damp on the deckhead and scantlings while increasingly large clouds of condensation appeared when each man spoke.

"Armourers are attending first thing," Anderson reminded, and Harris rose.

"Indeed, so we may as well call it a day; I'm supposed to be meeting Laura when she comes off shift at nine. Come on we can walk back to *Wasp* together."

It was a crisp, clear night and as Anderson opened the wheelhouse door and stepped out on deck, he gave an involuntary shiver.

"Think we should check on Newman and his lot?" he asked as Harris joined him, but the captain shook his head.

"He won't thank us for it. When I looked in an hour ago, they still had the lid off and there were parts spread about everywhere: a distraction's the last thing they need."

The pair stepped off the boat and onto the wharf; soon they were striding towards the dark and vaguely forbidding building that was their base.

"So you reckon *194*'s a goer, materially I mean," Harris said.

"I'd say so," Anderson had picked up on the inference. "Materially..."

"The men are a different matter, and not so easy to assess." Harris paused in the act of opening the Pen gate and considered for a moment. "Must say, I'll miss young Jelly."

"So will I, but he'd had it: worn out." Anderson remembered the quiet but capable telegraphist and what had become of him. "I guess none of us realised quite how St Nazaire had affected the poor bugger."

"You're probably right." They were off the wharf and making directly for the former hotel that was now HMS *Wasp*. "A few years ago they'd have called that sort of thing shell shock."

"And probably dealt with it very differently," Anderson agreed.

That his captain was so aware of Jelly's condition came as a mild surprise. At the time the rating was transferred, Harris had been in hospital having shrapnel removed from his chest. Anderson glanced across to the figure striding next to him. Harris was a straight striper: a professional seaman – very different from himself, a volunteer who had been happily teaching geography until hostilities began. Much could be said for both types of officer, but there was no doubting who was the more qualified.

"Maybe a spell ashore will put him right," Harris said.

"I hope so," Anderson added with less certainty.

"Still, Harvey seems efficient enough," the older man continued. "Might not have Jelly's skills when it comes to stripping down a set, but he handles the comms well enough. And then there's the new chap in the engine room."

"Kipling?"

Harris nodded.

"Newman seems to like him," Anderson continued, "as does Pickering, though I must say he looks little more than a child."

"Maybe, but old enough to serve."

Newman's team of three would have total charge of 194's engines and, consequently, her safety. Providing they worked together all would be well, and the indications were good. But Anderson was right, the boy looked more suited to the schoolroom.

"And then there is Nolan..." Harris left a significant pause.

"He would appear to be a competent helmsman," Anderson added hopefully.

"Maybe so, but there are other aspects I'm not so sure about."

They were nearing *Wasp* now so Harris would have to be quick, and both knew Nolan was not an easy subject.

"Take that incident with the cat..."

"Cats are quite common aboard larger warships," Anderson said. "Some even have dogs and I heard of a skipper who let his for'ard mess breed rabbits."

"That might be fine in battlewagons or the occasional destroyer; not a seventy-foot gunboat."

"Much might be put down to inexperience?"

"And I'm prepared to," Harris was quick to assure. "But will be keeping my eye on that one and suggest you should also."

Anderson decided a change of tack was in order. "There're three more new men due shortly," he said. "All gunners."

"Excellent. As soon as they arrive, we can start working up."

"I guess so," Anderson agreed. "It'll be interesting to see how they all get on together though I gather the Oerlikon pair are already a team."

"As were the last lot; what were their names?"

"Smith and Godliman."

"That's right, and damned efficient," Harris said. "Let's hope the new chaps prove as good."

"They came from a destroyer so there's every likelihood. And we're getting another man for the port Vickers, he'll be replacing Gibson."

"Gibson, yes; I certainly won't be forgetting *that* name in a hurry..."

They had reached *Wasp*'s outer perimeter now and both paused beyond the sentries' earshot.

"Do you know anything about the new Vickers gunner?"

"Not much," Anderson confessed. "Names Frank Thompson and this is his first posting."

"A greenhorn?" Harris sighed. "But hang on, wasn't he due in yesterday?"

"Applied to get married," Anderson said. "So they allowed an extra two days' leave."

"Newlywed?" This time Harris shook his head. "It just gets better and better."

* * *

"Funny, it's the same boat," Pickering, one of *194*'s mechanics, mused, "though she feels different."

"To be sure," Daly, the gunboat's starboard Vickers gunner, agreed. "But then I fancy it's the men that make a ship."

"An' there ain't many of us old sods left," Pickering grinned.

They were in the washroom, which was conveniently placed next to the dormitory *194*'s ratings shared at HMS *Wasp*. Some months before, Pickering had received serious burns to his face and neck and, though the scars were healing, shaving remained a painful and lengthy business best faced at night when there was less need to rush. And Daly, who had served with him the longest, was accustomed to sharing the time with his shipmate.

"What would you be thinking of the new lot?" he asked.

"Those that have arrived seem canny enough." The Geordie was tackling the area above his upper lip, which was badly pitted and needed extra care. "In a week's time it'll be like they've always been there." Pickering shook the razor in the basin of water and then addressed his chin.

"That's how it usually works," Daly agreed. "And more'll be coming soon."

"Hope so." Pickering glanced sideways at his mate. "Else you'll be on your tod as our only gunner!"

16

"Did you ever think of growing a beard?" the Irishman asked. "They're mighty relaxed about such things, and it'd save a ton of time."

Pickering was leaning over the sink for a final, careful, rinse.

"Can't abide all that fur," he said, reaching for his towel. "Rather keep a clean face."

"As you like," Daly agreed. "What say we get to know the new folk better?"

The room they returned to held ten beds but only five were in use and, even when they were up to full complement, there would be a spare. Appropriately enough, Harvey, their new telegraphist, had taken his predecessor's berth while Nolan, the Scouser coxswain, unintentionally opted for Gibson's. Pickering wondered what he would say if he knew his bed had belonged to a murderer.

"Well, aren't we a merry lot, then?" Daly enquired as he followed the mechanic in. "How'd you like your first trip to sea aboard a gunboat?"

"Wasn't the first for me," Nolan replied over his newspaper. "Dozens of 'em at *St Christopher*'s."

"Not like *194*." Pickering settled on his own bunk. "She's a Yank, an' there's none to touch her."

"I don't see much of a difference myself," Harvey, the telegraphist, said.

"Well so, you wouldn't," Daly said. "Sure, everything will feel the same when you're cooped up in a cupboard."

"Must have been a hell of a mess." Nolan lowered his paper. "The boat I'm meaning. To have spent so long in dock – they could have made a new one in half the time."

"It were," Pickering agreed. "Thought we was for it, happened so fast; by rights, we should ne'er have made it back."

"Lost a lot of good men an' all," Daly added.

"Never mind, you got us now." Nolan returned to his reading. "An' there'll be a load more comin' before long."

"That's right," Daly agreed. "Ain't we the lucky ones?"

* * *

17

"And it just blew up?"

Laura was impressed, as Harris hoped she would be. But even though her post at Dover Command was important, and came with the rank of second officer, Wrens never went to sea, and she was delightfully naïve when it came to combat matters. He could probably make up any old story and Laura would believe it, although that was not the kind of relationship he wanted.

The restaurant was empty and should have closed long ago, but they were regular customers, so allowed some leeway.

"Mines are funny old things," he said. "Properly laid, they're a menace to the other side but, however much care is taken, one can always come adrift, while any laid by air must be dropped with pinpoint accuracy."

He had been about to describe the various types in more detail, but Laura's expression was becoming fixed.

"In any case, this was a loose one and didn't do any damage, though it probably gave the sweepers a bit of a thrill."

"I would think that's putting it mildly," she said. "But how are you finding the boat?"

"More or less as before," he said. "As soon as we integrate the new men we can start to work up."

"How long will that take?"

Harris pursed his lips. "No more than a few days, after that she'll be ready for active service."

"And is that what you want?" She was looking at him with those liquid eyes that even her heavy tortoiseshell spectacles did little to defuse.

"It's why I joined the Navy," he said.

"And, once your boat is operational, you'll be satisfied?"

"I don't think I'll ever be satisfied," Harris replied. "It kills ambition and is not in my nature. I'll be a darn sight happier, though, that's for certain."

"But you'll still want more?"

"Oh yes." There was no hesitation. "I want my flotilla back, though nothing's been said."

"I thought you'd come to terms with serving under Lieutenant Commander Johnston; as I recall he did rather pull you out of a hole."

Harris nodded. "There's no doubting that, though I'd still prefer to be my own boss."

18

"And maybe the boss of others?"

He grinned. "If you like."

"But fresh boats are coming through." She lowered her voice while looking around, though the staff had all retreated into the kitchen and none of the neighbouring tables were even made up. "They're hoping to deliver a new MkV every four days."

"Maybe so, but they're not coming our way," Harris said. "And until they do, I'll have to be happy with what I've got – or can get," he added quickly. For a moment, their eyes met, and she gave a knowing smile.

"I take it your ambitions are not confined to motor gunboats and the command of a flotilla," she said.

"Something along those lines," he agreed.

At a time when most relationships were short and intense, theirs had yet to progress beyond eating in restaurants and the occasional walk. But Harris now wanted more and, from the look in those eyes, sensed Laura might also.

"We'll have to see about that," she said, though her expression was not totally negative. "You know what they say, some things are worth waiting for."

* * *

The deed was done, Frank Thompson rolled over in the narrow bed and yawned. There was room for improvement and exactly why Joyce had held out until now was beyond him; it wasn't as if she'd been keeping anything special. Yet he was moderately satisfied and, with a few tips, she would improve. At least there was now a guaranteed bed waiting for him when leave came up; something that strongly influenced his decision to bag a wife.

In civilian life it was so much easier; women were accessible, and time less precious. He used to brag about bedding any girl he wanted, which was pretty close to the truth. But as soon as his call-up papers arrived everything changed and, in his brief but hectic time at HMS *Ganges*, there was no opportunity to mix with anyone other than his fellow recruits. Once installed at his new base that was unlikely to change; from what he'd heard of HMS *Wasp*, it was verging on a monastery. There would be Wrens, of course, but if they were like those he'd already met, most would have their eyes firmly fixed on officers. Consequently, Joyce, who had been in the background for so long, became the obvious solution – for now at least; he could do better in time, that was for certain.

And it would be useful having her down at Dover; once she found herself a place, and preferably a job, he could be looked after properly when free time was available. Having an address outside the base would be handy in other ways: Mr Granger was planning on extending his empire to the south coast. Being able to put up any of his men would do Thompson no harm at all. Of course, once the war was sorted, she'd have to be gone; there would be places to go, people to see and no need for hangers on.

He felt the bed move slightly and wondered if she was still awake. It seemed likely, there was a gentle regular movement, almost as if she were crying. But then that wasn't to be surprised at – it had been a busy day, and women were emotional creatures.

He rolled over and reached for the travel clock. Its luminous hands glowed in the darkened room; almost one, he'd be lucky to get more than five hours kip before they had to be up. He might grab a wink or two on the train down from London though. And then, HMS *Wasp*...

On volunteering for Coastal Forces, Thompson had little idea of what the work actually entailed, yet figured that, with Granger moving south, being based nearby should mean he did not lose his position. Since then he'd discovered rather more and now wondered if dashing about in high-speed launches was really his sort of thing. And he could certainly expect casualties; the press were being coy with statistics, but it was clearly not the safe number he anticipated. Well, he'd find out for sure soon enough and wasn't afraid to act if things didn't fit in with his plans. If there was one thing Frank Thompson prided himself on, it was looking after himself.

* * *

It should not have taken more than an hour, Newman decided, probably less. They'd already been working all afternoon replacing a valve in one of the port Packard's heads and, thinking the oil pump would be a simple matter, he'd sent Pickering off to get some shut eye.

"Make sure the pressure relief valve is the right way up."

"I did that before," Kipling replied.

"No, you did not," Newman drew breath, "otherwise we wouldn't be having to take it to pieces again."

"But we ain't!" Kipling protested. "I'm doing all the work!"

"You're doing nothing but wasting my time."

Kipling may have pulled a face, but Newman decided to let it go. It wasn't that the lad lacked skill, he was simply too impulsive, too inclined to dash ahead without checking properly. And then, when he made mistakes, too keen to try and argue his way out.

"Come on, I'm not going to do it for you," Newman added.

Once more the boy set to with too small a screwdriver, only changing it on hearing another sharp intake of breath. Newman shook his head; what had been a tiring day was in danger of turning into a long night.

Chapter Three

"Alright, Bob, you've won," Commander Brooks told him.

"Won?" Harris was confused.

"As soon as *194* finishes working up, you'll have your flotilla."

Having endured the slow suffocation of being under another's command, Harris felt free to breathe deeply once more and a long-held sigh escaped.

"So, no more serving under Johnston?" he asked.

Brooks gave a grim smile. "I'm not even going to answer that; Johnston's a fine officer and I think you owe him more than you know."

Harris nodded; that might have been the case, but being back in charge of a squadron of gunboats was the only thing that mattered now.

"You won't have an impressive force," Brooks continued. "The MkVs are coming through but still in small quantities; we can't let you have any of those. But there'll be a couple of the older British Power Boat seventy footers, at least one Vosper and two former MASBs."

"MASBs?" That came as a surprise. His first command had been a converted Motor Anti-Submarine Boat, but that was some time ago; surely they'd pretty much died out?

"Yes, they've been doing sterling work at *St Christopher*'s, but the new intake need to train on something more up to date so it was time to let them go."

"And put them into active service?" It seemed ironic in the extreme.

"Bob, I think I'd better make a few things clear." The base captain leant back in his chair. "There's no flotilla without boats and I've moved heaven and earth to get you this posting. These former MASBs are well armed and can keep up to some extent, though it will be down to you how they are used. Frankly, you can take them, and their crews, who are also fresh from training, or stick it out under Johnston."

Harris knew when he was beaten. "I'll take them," he said.

"I'm glad to hear it, now let's move on to the work ahead." Brooks looked up. "Which won't be very different, I'm afraid. I'm not sure how much you've been keeping up with things since your injury, but not much has changed. Germans are still sending regular convoys north, which we do our best to intercept, and there's been no let up in their mine-laying operations." He grinned suddenly, "As I believe you may have noticed."

Harris nodded. "It was well away from any recognised field."

"So I understand," Brooks agreed. "Basically it's just as dangerous as ever out there and, with better weather and the longer summer days, likely to grow more so."

"But are we winning?" Harris chanced.

"Winning?" Brooks considered for less than a second. "In general, yes. With the Yanks at our side it's probably just a matter of time. But if you're asking about Coastal Forces, I'd say not. We think the Germans have a new marque of E-boat, though that has yet to be confirmed, but even without that we're outgunned, outnumbered and, far too often, outclassed. We had hoped the steam-powered gunboats would prove more effective against larger enemy escorts but that's not the case. And you'll still be facing an enemy that is better armed and carries a positive arsenal of heavy weaponry."

"These new E's, are they faster?"

Brooks gave a grim smile. "Hard to say," he said, "we've yet to catch one."

Harris raised his eyes. "Then I doubt my MASBs will."

"Maybe not, but they'll have other uses and I expect you to exploit them to the full. Now, when do you expect to finish working up?"

"We're not scheduled to even start until tomorrow," Harris said, "though I'm not anticipating any problems."

"And are you happy with the new men?"

This took slightly more thought. "They look fine, though the Oerlikon crew only reported last night."

"Then they've got a bit of catching up to do," Brooks said. "And I suppose it's hard to judge anyone until they've worked together at sea."

23

"And preferably in action," Harris agreed.

"Ideally I'd like your flotilla operational by the end of the month, though if it takes longer so be it: there's no point in rushing. Get to know your new COs and try a few combined exercises but, more to the point, make sure they know their own boats. And, of course, decide how best to use what you have to the best effect."

"Even if a couple are pretty much obsolete?"

Brooks gave a grim smile. "Even then."

* * *

Anderson had been visiting the same telephone box for several months and, though the cardboard used to replace some of the broken glass made it dark and smell strongly of damp, he could usually get a line. And this time was no exception, although no one appeared to be answering. He tapped his pennies against the Bakelite cabinet as the ringing tone reverberated in his ear, and was about to replace the receiver when there was a loud click followed by a pause. He swallowed and began feeding in the coppers.

"This is Lieutenant Ian Anderson; I wish to speak with Mulberry."

It was ludicrous, of course. He had no idea of Eve's official alias but was darn sure it wasn't Mulberry. An organisation such as SOE was allowed secrets, however, and he would jump through any number of hoops if it meant talking to her.

"Hold the line."

He glanced at his watch. There had been coins enough for five minutes though outside calls were limited to three; he hoped she wouldn't be long.

"Hello, Ian?"

"Hi there." He spoke with care. In the past he had said her true name, and the line immediately went dead. "How are things?"

"Well," she paused, and he could almost see her smile, "you know how it is..."

Yes, he knew, and was equally aware there would be no substance to the conversation, at least from her side. Though it would be little different with him. Since they last met and spent those three heady days in London, much had happened, yet he

24

would only be able to share the most inane details.

"I'm looking forward to July," he said, hoping it would be permitted.

"Ah, that might be a problem..."

He was expecting her to say something similar.

"But you are still coming?" That really was stretching it.

"I can't tell you more now," she said, "but have written."

He pursed his lips; her letters were spectacular and worth reading a dozen times, yet for a different reason and they rarely gave any actual information.

"Alright," he said. "I should get that soon and will ring again then."

"No don't," she said. "Better I call you in future, you see I may be being transferred."

Despite his disappointment, Anderson found time to marvel. This was proper news.

"I'll try and get a message to you but don't expect me to be reachable for a few weeks."

"You are alright?" he asked.

"I'm fine and will be quite safe."

Eve's definition of safe was questionable, yet he was slightly reassured.

"And I'll be in contact – somehow."

"That's fine," he said.

"And know that I love you," she added. "And always will."

There was a click, they had been cut off, and Anderson replaced the receiver.

Outside, the sun seemed unusually bright as he made his way back to *Wasp*. It was disappointing of course but when Eve volunteered for SOE, neither of them expected anything less. Besides, she had said all he really needed to hear.

* * *

"Name's Harris, I understand you'll be joining my flotilla."

Brooks had already pointed the youngsters out, so Harris had no hesitation in approaching when he noticed them leaving the officers' mess.

"That's right, sir." The taller of the two was first to reply and eagerly shook Harris' hand, his face alight with all the innocence of youth. "Maddox, Joe Maddox, and this is Mike Penrose."

Penrose was slightly shorter and looked more serious; he also had a firmer grip.

"You're down from *St Christopher*'s?" Harris asked.

"Yes indeed." Again it was Maddox. "Trained on our boats for six weeks and did so well they let us keep them!"

Harris gave a more serious nod. "So I've heard." He glanced about; *Wasp*'s entrance foyer was hardly the place for a private conversation and the mess itself would still be crowded with diners. "Let's take a walk, you can fill me in on your commands."

The morning had blossomed into a hot summer day. Harris, who expected different first thing, wore a sleeveless jumper under his tunic and, on passing out of the large glass doors, immediately felt the heat.

"They're sixty footers," Maddox said as they left the sentry post behind and began a leisurely walk towards the Camber. "Though excellent sea boats."

"I had one myself," Harris confessed. Both youngsters wore full uniform yet appeared far cooler, even in the blazing sun. They were also following the RNVR habit of leaving the top right button undone. The affectation was supposed to indicate the cavalier attitude of their service, though Harris always found it ridiculous. Maddox gave a slight whistle but, again, Penrose was more serious.

"I heard yours was a Rolls boat, sir," he said.

"Indeed," Harris agreed, impressed with the lad's knowledge. "Supercharged Merlins."

Penrose went to speak again, but Maddox got in first. "We have Napiers," he said. "Though they can still move."

Harris paused. "Twenty-five knots tops, or so I gather." Penrose wasn't the only one to have carried out research.

"My CMM thinks he can squeeze a little more," Penrose said.

"Especially downhill," Maddox grinned.

"I don't doubt it," Harris said. The small harbour was relatively crowded and someone was carrying out engine tests in the nearby Wellington Dock; he had no intention of being deafened. "And how are you armed?" he asked, moving on once

26

more.

"Two 303s and a single Oerlikon." Penrose again. "And they left us a couple of depth charges."

"Only two?" Harris had hoped for more. Originally a MASB would have carried upwards of twelve and, though they were unlikely to encounter enemy submarines, the high explosives could be equally effective when used against surface craft.

"They may have been considering our overall speed, sir," Penrose suggested, and Harris knew he was right. Even such a short time in the sun was becoming uncomfortable but he would still rather talk in the open, and informally, than some stuffy briefing room.

"Very well. You are happy with your crews?"

"Been with us throughout training," Maddox beamed.

That was good on one point; it meant all should have melded into a team. But much could be learned from more experienced hands, to say nothing of the officers. The likelihood was each boat would be manned by amateurs unlikely to have seen an enemy, let alone been under fire.

"I have yet to start my own boat's working up exercises though there should be no problems," Harris said. "Consequently, I've already scheduled our first group sea trial for the beginning of next week. Eight o'clock at the Camber, make sure you're warmed up and ready to be off."

It would be an early start, but necessary as he intended to cram as much into the day as possible.

"The morning will be mainly flotilla manoeuvres," he added, "but I propose to inspect each of your craft later."

At this Penrose's face grew more serious still, although Maddox's grin remained intact.

"Eight o'clock it is, sir. See you on the water!"

* * *

"So that's the new tub!" Seaman Gunner Alec Bridger announced as he surveyed the moored gunboat. She looked workmanlike enough and probably just back from refit as several panels showed evidence of fresh paint. "*194*," he mused, "must be an early one."

"Not necessarily," John Mitchel, Bridger's loader, said. "A lot of non-standard boats are given numbers out of sequence."

"And this is non-standard?"

"I'd say. Yank built for a start." Mitchel's dark brown eyes continued to assess the miniature warship. "Probably one of the first to come over."

They had arrived the night before and already met with most of the gunboat's crew but waited for morning to see the vessel in daylight. And really, she was no disappointment. Despite being considerably smaller than the destroyer they'd only just left, there was no doubting *194* meant business.

To begin with, she almost shouted speed. Neither man had been in the Navy longer than eighteen months and both knew relatively nothing about ship design while, moored to the pontoon as she was, her lower lines were hidden. But what they could see was impressive and they had already been around warships long enough to sense what worked. At anything above tick-over, much of the forward hull would rise onto the plane, at which point raw energy from three adapted aircraft engines could bring her to a speed that more than matched their previous vessel.

Of course, there was a downside to such power; even bright sunshine could not disguise the fact that she lacked solidity. Rather than steel plates and iron bulkheads, this would be a matchwood job with little of the frame being built of anything heavier than what might grace a garden shed. And though likely to be first on the scene, a pair of half-inch machine guns and an Oerlikon hardly competed with the four-point-sevens of a *Tribal* class destroyer.

Actually, it was the armament that bothered both men the most, although neither felt confident enough to voice their fears. Bridger and Mitchel had acquired something of a reputation aboard HMS *Makua*. Despite manning only a small part of the destroyer's secondary armament, they quickly proved themselves and, when the old girl went in for a major refit, held the record for downing the most enemy planes. Their pride in this came mainly from the fact their Oerlikon was not the most powerful gun on board, but all that would change when they joined *194*. From being very much in the chorus, and responsible for a minor fraction of a warship's ordnance, they would be taking centre stage. Apart from their own weapon, there were only machine guns, so all eyes would be watching them and expecting much.

"There's not a lot of point standing and looking." Mitchel,

the older and larger of the pair, had a heavy jaw that was rarely without stubble, however often he shaved. "May as well get aboard and see what we'll be handling."

It turned out to be a standard 20mm Oerlikon and far newer than they were used to – the piece could only have been fired a couple of times in test. Bridger flexed the slide experimentally.

"She'll need loosening up," he said. "And a decent scrape off."

Mitchel was looking at the magazine receiver – his own particular area of expertise – but did not disagree. Though paint might be the perfect protector for ordnance in storage, it would not do for a working unit and a good deal of rubbing down, followed by careful and regular greasing, would be necessary to make this a proper, functioning weapon.

"Not so sure about the position." Bridger, who would be aiming the beast, was standing back now and considering the gunboat's aft deck in general. "We have a pretty wide arc but it's mainly to the rear; train forward and we hit the guard."

"That's so," Mitchel agreed, "and somehow I don't see this baby reversing into action."

"Might mean we're not in the thick of it." Bridger's fair skin still bore the marks of recent acne, while his teeth were decidedly crooked and, when he brought his thin lips back in a smile, appeared more so. "According to the lads we met last night, we're the third Oerlikon crew; the rest only lasted a matter of months."

"A matter of months seems to be par for the course in gunboats," Mitchel mused. "Apart from the officers, there's only a couple of her original crew left."

"Aye, but they weren't all killed," Bridger pointed out.

"That's right," Mitchel agreed. The rest were either wounded or went bonkers."

"And that's ignoring the bloke they arrested for murder," Bridger added. "Ask me, we were better off aboard the old *Maka*."

"Probably," Mitchel agreed, "but then we knew what we'd be getting into when they offered us gunboats."

* * *

"See you on the water?" Anderson repeated, and Harris clearly found his disbelief reassuring.

"That's what he said," he confirmed. "Almost as if we were a bunch of pals setting off for a May Week regatta."

Anderson rolled his eyes; the image of his captain as part of a university pleasure cruise was hard to imagine. They were due to start *194*'s working up exercises the following morning and, until Harris mentioned the other gunboat commanders, Anderson had been feeling quite optimistic.

"Do they have any small boat experience?" he asked.

"Maddox learned to sail dinghies with the sea scouts, but Penrose keeps a half-ton yawl at Chichester – your old stamping ground, I believe?" Harris looked up expectantly, but Anderson shook his head.

"Can't say the name's familiar."

"Maybe not but he could have possibilities; Penrose is the older of the two and a darn sight more serious. I also checked on the report from *St Christopher*'s: they rated him quite highly."

"That's something, I suppose, but what about the other – Maddox, wasn't it?"

Harris settled back on the tiny wardroom sofa. "Not as good. Seems proficient enough when it comes to ship handling and knows his basic seamanship but several of the instructors had concerns about inconsistencies when dealing with the men."

"Inconsistencies?"

"One moment he's a tough and demanding commander, the next he wants to be their best friend."

"I'd say that shows a measure of immaturity," Anderson said.

"And is a darn sight worse than being consistently lax," Harris agreed.

"Yet they've still seen fit to release him for active service." Anderson had only seen the pair from a distance, and both appeared far too young, even for the single stripe on their sleeves. But of late he'd noticed several sub-lieutenants who'd have looked more at home in a school uniform, and it was probably more a sign of advancing age in himself.

"I suppose with a couple of boats coming close to obsoletion, there wasn't much to lose," Harris said.

"What about their first officers?" Anderson asked.

"Both midshipmen, one has a good deal of small boat experience, the other was intending to join the RNVR at university."

"Not a seasoned man amongst them?"

"Maddox's chief motor mechanic's a regular who's served aboard MTBs," Harris said. "Apart from him, they're all fresh from basic training. Frankly, I can't see how they can survive with only a bunch of amateurs in command."

As an RNVR officer himself, Anderson could have taken exception to that last remark, although he knew Harris well enough, and was even inclined to agree. "I guess they'll need a good deal of watching," he said, and Harris nodded in agreement.

"I think you may be right."

* * *

Frank Thompson glanced about the crowded mess hall. It was the following evening and, until then he had eaten most of his meals at *Wasp* alone, instinctive wariness making him choose the company of strangers to those of his shipmates. But the first day of *194*'s sea trials had been longer and more taxing than he expected, and Thompson felt the need to be with others who had shared the experience.

"This taken, is it?" he asked, lowering his tray onto a table where two from the gunboat already sat.

"Help yourself, fella," one told him, moving his own plate to give more room.

Thompson nodded brief thanks; the Irishman was his oppo on the starboard Vickers and seemed a regular sort though, for the moment, his name escaped him.

"So, how'd you find the start of our working up?" the other asked. This was Pickering, one of the grease monkeys and a Geordie. Pickering had old burn marks to his face and neck that did not bode well, but at least made him more memorable.

"Sure, an' wouldn't it have been your first time at sea aboard the old barge?" the Irishman grinned. "Enjoy yourself, did you?"

"It were right enough," Thompson replied guardedly. "Though she tips about a bit..."

Both men laughed. "Think you so? That wasn't anything

more'n a gentle swell," Pickering said.

"Sure, wait till we're punchin' the tide with a headwind, then you'll know all about it!"

"Don't listen to Paddy," Pickering told him. "The chop's something you gets used to. And it's a powerful sight worse down below."

That rang true; even in the security of his turret, Thompson had been thrown about like the only apple in a barrel; how anyone coped amid the hazards of a cramped engine room was beyond him.

"To be sure, an' there'll be the odd distraction from time to time," the Irish gunner continued. "Run into Jerry, and the last thing you'll be thinking of is the state of the water."

That sounded right as well, although even without being called upon to use his guns, the exercises were violent enough. For much of the time their skipper seemed dead set on tearing the boat to pieces, throwing her into impossible turns and accelerating, then lying cut, with little or no notice; the idea of meeting an enemy in anything other than a calm was inconceivable.

"Cheering up the new man are you, Daly?"

It was another from *194*; the wireless op. this time. Thompson knew his name; Harvey, and now he was reminded of the Irishman's as well.

"I'm only tellin' it like it is," Daly said.

"Thompson, isn't it?" Harvey enquired.

"That's right."

"Not had the chance to speak properly before." He gave a friendly nod. "Where you from?"

"East End of London." The answer came without a great deal of thought; Thompson was more interested in his dinner and poked at a sausage experimentally.

"Know it well," Harvey said. "I'm from Birmingham myself but my old man used to trade cars with a bloke near Bethnal Green. We were always going back an' forth."

Now Thompson was not only wary about the food; Harvey's line of questioning had become dangerous.

"So, what did you do, before this lot, I mean?" the telegraphist persisted.

Thompson took longer to finish his first mouthful than was necessary. Anyone familiar with the used car trade in his manor

32

would know of Granger and that dealing in motors was just one of many sidelines. In line with a good few businessmen, his old boss was taking full advantage of the relaxed laws and a limited police force to expand into most forms of illicit trade.

"This and that, whatever I could get me hands on." He took another hasty mouthful and was careful not to meet anyone's eye.

Harvey and Daly might have exchanged glances, but Thompson was keeping his head down. And he would continue to do so, he decided, for as long as was necessary.

"Howay, marra!"

The call from Pickering made him look up and he saw a short, skinny, red-haired seaman standing at the table.

"Room for a little one?" the man asked, squeezing in between Daly and Harvey.

"Three bangers, Nolan?" Harvey enquired, glancing over at the Liverpudlian's plate.

"Told her at the counter I needed building up; she offered to take us home an' give me a proper meal." Nolan displayed a fine set of teeth. "Reckon I'm in there."

"Gob like yours could butter up Goebbels," Pickering said but Nolan continued to grin.

"Just got to know the right words an' when to say 'em."

"A veggie could eat these bangers," Harvey said, although he continued to eat, but Thompson was considering his food more carefully. He'd been allowed two rather meagre specimens, as had the others, and neither came close to the smallest of Nolan's three.

For a man used to being in control, his brief time at HMS *Wasp* had been disconcerting; there was so much he didn't know or understand that he'd vowed to keep a low profile. And until then he had barely considered their provisions, but such blatant unfairness touched a nerve and he spoke without thinking.

"This ain't right," he said. "No one should get better grub just 'cause they chat up one of the servin' bints."

"It's not better, just more," Harvey corrected.

"If you think you need a fillin' go back an' ask," Daly advised. "There's usually a bit put by."

"Pad's right," Harvey confirmed. "They can't do much about the quality, but we're on active service; no one goes hungry."

"I may do that an' all," Thompson said.

Nolan contemplated him for a moment, then took a hearty

bite out of one of his own sausages.

"Thompson, ain't it?" he asked through the food.

"That's right."

"And you work the larboard Vickers?"

"Port," Thompson corrected.

"That's what I said," Nolan informed him. "I'm the cox'n."

"I know, I seen you." Thompson was meeting, and matching, the steady gaze. "What of it?"

"What of it?" Nolan seemed to relax and gave what appeared to be a genuine smile.

"That's what I said." Thompson remained serious. Then Nolan's fork dropped on his plate with a sudden clatter.

"What say you keep your neb out of my business, an' I'll do the same for you?" Nolan reached across and gave Thompson a gentle pat on the cheek. "That way, you and I'll get along stunning."

* * *

"Well, you got what you wanted," Laura told him.

Harris blinked. "Whatever do you mean?"

She poked him painfully in the ribs. "Your flotilla, stupid."

It was the first time they'd met up since he got the news and, after a busy day at sea, Harris had not expected the evening to end in such a way. Yet, now it had, he was not sorry.

"I was thinking more of *194*," he said. "We began working up today."

"I don't believe you," she said.

"No?"

"No, you've captained her before and will do so again. Your mind was on your new flotilla."

He turned and looked at her. "Not totally," he said.

"So go on, spill the beans," she urged.

"Nothing to say for now, I've yet to find out how the other boats behave at sea."

"And some might not be all you wished for?"

Harris smiled and rested his hands behind his head. Her bed was small, and hard, with a slight dip in the middle, but he had rarely been as comfortable.

"A couple are close to obsolete, though I still think they'll

34

do; it's their captains that give me the willies."

"Much can be done with practice," Laura said, "and remember, this is going to be a new experience for them; they'll have to adapt." She paused. "As will you."

He turned to her and smiled; she really was very beautiful; he was quite undeserving.

"And I'm not the best at adapting?" he asked.

"Something like that."

"But you're right." He returned to staring up at the ceiling. "Practice does much, and it's not just the captains that have to settle. No gunboat is more than the sum of her parts; everything, each member of her crew, all the equipment, every fitting has to work together. Until that happens, there'll never be an improvement.

"Surely you could say the same about a ship, or any size of vessel?"

"Probably," he said. "Though the smaller it is, the more important everyone becomes."

"You mean a battleship can afford to carry a bit of fat?"

"Exactly, but there's no room for passengers aboard a high-speed launch." He paused and thought on. "And in the same way, a flotilla needs all her boats to be on the top line. Or if not the top, at least able to work together. Without that, there is nothing."

She was leaning on one shoulder and had begun to trace her finger over his top lip; a new experience for Harris and one he found delightful.

"Though I doubt any Flotilla Senior Officer is ever satisfied," he said at last. "Even if they gave me a dozen MkVs, with crews of battle-hardened veterans, I'd find something to gripe about. The finger continued, and he half closed his eyes to enjoy it fully.

"Is that all Flotilla SOs?" she asked, and he could just make out her wicked smile. "Or just you?"

Chapter Four

They were at sea once more, and Daly liked it fine. Whatever he might have told the new man, he rarely felt uncomfortable in his tiny turret and, though the boat could buck and rear like any frisky racehorse, she remained a thoroughbred. *194* might have accounted for several former shipmates, often in front of his eyes, but the old girl had never done him any harm and neither did he expect her to.

They were currently mid-Channel, with the dark line of France prominent off the starboard beam, and travelling at a moderate speed just on the plane. Behind, their two MASBs were stationed on either quarter. After finishing his own sea trials, the skipper resumed his rightful place as a flotilla leader and since then they'd been exercising the new force. Which was going well enough, as far as the Irishman was concerned, although for this particular exercise the pair now in their wake were being singled out for special treatment.

After a flicker of light from the first officer, equally secure in the bridge a few feet from where Daly sat, *194* began a gentle turn to starboard. Her speed increased with the change in direction until she was travelling close to her maximum, with the enemy coast growing visibly nearer. Daly glanced back; the followers had also straightened up and were maintaining station, seemingly physically connected to their leader. It was only when *194*'s superior speed began to tell that either started to fall behind. The Irishman glanced across to the bridge, where it was clear both officers had noticed this. The skipper shouted something and there was another flicker of light.

This time *194* flew into as tight a turn to port as Daly had ever experienced and, caught off guard, he was flung against the turret wall, while the hydraulic mount of his twin machine guns spun wildly. The manoeuvre also tipped the hull, bringing him closer to the grey water speeding beneath. He glanced left; Thompson, the new man, had equally been taken by surprise and was sprawled half out of his nest, gloved hands seeking purchase on anything solid while his face bore the expression of a child tricked into riding a rollercoaster. Daly flashed him a grin, then looked aft.

One of the trailing gunboats had followed and was heeling just as dramatically as it clung to the mother ship's starboard quarter; the other was out of sight and must be in a similar position to port. And then, as if driven by some unearthly power, it blasted across their stern, having avoided a collision by a matter of inches while probably endangering the other craft.

Daly watched as the errant boat reduced speed and took a wider turn to port and then, when *194* slowed also, began a self-conscious passage back towards her leader. Daly was trained in signals and knew how easily the flashes of an Aldis could be missed, or misinterpreted, and supposed it better to happen on exercise than in the pell-mell of action. Yet it was obvious that, unless that particular gunboat was given more practice, they'd be as dangerous to their own side as any enemy.

* * *

From their position at the Oerlikon, Bridger and Mitchel also noticed the errant boat cross *194*'s stern but it came as no surprise. As soon as they were thrown into the turn it was clear the following boat had either missed the signal or been too slow to respond. At one point, collision seemed inevitable.

"Strewth!" Bridger exclaimed, while Mitchel simply closed his eyes in anticipation. Even ignoring ammunition and depth charges, both boats were carrying enough high-octane petrol to blow them into a thousand pieces.

But, either by word of command or the reaction of an attentive helmsman, the oncoming boat missed them by a matter of feet and less than a second. That did not rule out the next danger, however. The starboard boat had been obedient in her turn and was the next to be threatened. Too close for considered action, her escape owed more to raw fortune and, as the wayward gunboat continued on her oblique course, both gunners inwardly gave thanks to whatever they considered holy.

"Didn't expect that," Mitchel said when the danger had passed.

"You're not the only one," Bridger agreed. "Reckon there'll be a few further for'ard who'll have been taken by surprise an all," he added, nodding towards the nearby bridge. "I wouldn't care to be skipper of that boat when it comes to the de-brief."

"Guess that's why they have exercises," Mitchel supposed. "Though somehow you assume they're gonna be safer than combat."

"Aye," Bridger agreed. "After that little lot, mixing it with the Germans will seem like a doddle."

* * *

Maddox's failure to note their turn had taken place over two hours before. Since then, Harris had carried out several similar manoeuvres and each time the trailing boats followed obediently. And they were equally prompt in forming lines abreast or ahead, testing all weapons or lying suddenly cut as if they'd been born to it, yet still he was not content.

"We'll have to try again tomorrow," he shouted, and Anderson gave a brief nod in reply. It was still relatively early, darkness would not come for several hours yet that night's service boats would soon be waking up for the evening's work. It would be better to see themselves safely berthed before the nighttime patrols put out.

"Take us back to Dover, 'Swain," he ordered, adding, "and you'd better signal that to our friends, Number One; don't want them getting any funny ideas."

"It was probably only a momentary lapse," Anderson said when their speed had reduced to a more social fifteen hundred revs.

"Oh, I don't doubt it," Harris agreed. "But it's just the sort of thing that'll see them lost in a ruck, that or ploughing into the side of an enemy coaster."

There was no arguing that one. In fact, Anderson had only spoken in the newcomer's defence out of habit; essentially, he was just as concerned by the lack of attention as his captain.

"So, what do you think?" Harris continued. "Do it all over again tomorrow and hope they perform better?"

That was probably unfair, Anderson decided. It was only Maddox who'd missed the signal, and just the once; Penrose

38

performed faultlessly throughout. However, they joined the flotilla at the same time and commanded very similar craft; it was inevitable an old salt horse like Harris should group them together.

Although in some ways he was correct; both had undergone the same amount of training and were similar in other respects, Maddox could have displayed a fault that was just as present in Penrose.

"Another day's exercise is needed," he said eventually.

"Absolutely," Harris agreed. "And if they can't get it right, they'll have to go."

Anderson nodded in reply although he was uncomfortably aware that, without the two craft, Harris' new flotilla would not be viable, and they might have to make an ignominious return to Johnston's lot.

A brief whistle sounded over the rumble of engines and Anderson leant forward to the W/T office speaking tube.

"What is it, Tel'?"

"General alert from Dover Command." It was still a surprise to hear any other voice than Jelly's, but Harvey was proving every bit as capable. "A flyboy's gone down near our sector and all available boats are being vectored in to search."

Anderson glanced at Harris. Neither were aware of any air activity in the last few hours, but then their minds had been elsewhere; arguably *194*'s officers had been guilty of the same inattention as Maddox.

"Very well," Anderson said, turning back to the speaking tube.

"Let's have the coordinates and we'll start a box-pattern search."

* * *

Two hours later, *194* and her companions were still apparently crossing the same patch of choppy water with only Anderson, who had responsibility for navigation, being fully aware of how the area had grown. And Maddox's boat performed perfectly throughout while having it, and Penrose's craft, to command increased the scope and size of their search considerably, yet of the downed airman there was no sign.

"What do you reckon, Number One. Can't stay out here for ever."

"Maybe some of the others will have had more luck?" Anderson suggested.

That was certainly a possibility. Earlier in the search they were joined by aircraft from both Coastal Command and, it was presumed, the pilot's own squadron. But for the last hour or so the skies had been empty and the only other vessels nearby – minesweepers to the south and what could have been fishers in the north and northeast – had extended their searches to the extent they were almost invisible.

"If we don't head back soon, we'll hit rush hour at the Pens," Harris said. "Though extending the time does seems to have done Penrose and Maddox a bit of good."

Anderson opened his mouth to reply when a whistle interrupted him, and he leant forward to the W/T office speaking tube.

"What is it, Tel'?"

"Message from 96, sir," Harvey said. "They've spotted something."

Anderson glanced across and, sure enough, the distant boat was slowing and might even have stopped.

"Very well, tell him we're on our way," he said. Then, to his captain, "What about Penrose?"

"He may as well go on looking." From Harris' tone it was clear he had little confidence in anything Maddox might have found.

But as the gunboat drew closer it appeared otherwise. Even before they were within two hundred yards of the stationary craft, a message came through on R/T warning them to stay back and was followed by the urgent flickering of an Aldis.

"Seems a mite excitable," Harris grunted. "Ask him what he's caught."

A quick exchange explained everything, and Anderson returned the Aldis to its cradle.

"Not the pilot, I'm afraid," he said. "But Maddox would seem to have stumbled across an unattached sea mine."

"Another loose one, eh?" Harris raised his eyebrows though he was obviously impressed. Such things floated barely level with the surface and were far harder to spot, and a good deal more dangerous, than any downed pilot. Substantial warships were regular victims, and a gunboat would be instantly turned into matchwood. Any error Maddox made that day had been more than made up for.

"Better tell him well done," Harris grunted.

* * *

By the time *194* berthed and was made safe, the nightly patrols had begun and the Pens were alive with active service personnel and craft. Thompson had cleared his weapon early so was one of the first to leave the boat and started on the short walk to *Wasp* alone. As he went, he could hear the distant rumble of engines and an occasional rattle of machine gun and Oerlikon fire as a squadron, already clear of the harbour, set off for any amount of excitement on the other side. The noise was shortly followed by closer pops and minor explosions as several cold Packards fired up. Soon those boats would also be heading off to meet the enemy, and Thompson was uncomfortably aware that, in less than a week, his own craft must join them. Which was a terrible thought, and one barely contemplated when he had been foolish enough to volunteer for Coastal Forces.

Quite what could be done about it was another matter, however. Until he had completed a few decent missions any request for transfer would be looked upon with suspicion and, with no plausible explanation for moving on, probably refused. Although he did have a reason, and one that was about as valid as they came: Thompson was frightened.

It was something he would only admit to himself, yet the prospect of meeting a superior enemy in an over-powered, under-armed, wooden boat was simply too terrible to contemplate.

But equally he had an element of pride and, though perhaps not the brightest button, Thompson was no fool. To back away now, before even hearing a bullet fired in anger, would also make him a laughingstock amongst his mates. Alfie had already gone to join his unit and Morris would soon start basic training with every intention of becoming a paratrooper. When they heard he had walked away from what many considered a soft option, his life would not be worth the living. More to the point, Thompson would be out of a lucrative job for good, and it was this that made the greatest impression.

Even as a child, Thompson had been large for his age; shoulders and chest began developing well before his teens and, by the time he said goodbye to Lime End Elementary, he was already an impressive physical specimen. Not athletic, perhaps, just solid muscle; the type that stood no nonsense; the type old man Granger could use. A little fat might have started appearing in places although he could still act the heavy but, were it to get around there was a shortage in the moral fibre department, it would be the end of everything.

Granger had been paying him a wage far higher than that of an average working man; that stopped with his call-up papers but would return once he was free and became useful again. Yet without his reputation as a fearless hoodlum, someone who gave no quarter and expected none in return, he had nothing. No skills, no qualifications and, when the war ended and Granger refused to take him back, no job.

There was a chance he might earn something close to a living as a labourer, maybe mending roads, rebuilding houses or working on a farm, but that would not bring in the kind of income Thompson was used to.

The uncomfortable thoughts hastened his pace, and Thompson noticed he was overhauling two more walkers. As he drew closer the figures became more recognisable; one was Harvey, the wireless op, the other Nolan, their coxswain.

Thompson felt little either way for Harvey but had already taken a dislike to Nolan and began to slow. Though shorter and lighter than him, the Scouser was clearly not afraid of a ruck, while there was something else about the Liverpudlian's manner that he found especially disconcerting. But Harvey had already heard his footsteps and was looking back.

"That you, Thumper?"

Cursing silently, Thompson speeded up once more. "Aye, making for the dorm, are you?"

"We got a bit of business first," Nolan announced when Thompson caught up.

"Going ashore," Harvey confirmed. "Care to tag along?"

"Into town?" Thompson was surprised.

Joyce had followed him down to Dover and was staying in a nearby Bed and Breakfast while she looked for something more permanent. So far he'd only managed to see her on the one evening they'd been granted liberty, and the temptation to join her now was strong.

"But we ain't got leave," he said.

Nolan raised an eyebrow. "That going to stop you, is it?"

"Easy enough to get past the picket," Harvey assured him. "Long as you're back by ten no one'll take much notice. I been doin' it most nights."

"But what if we're caught?" Thompson flustered. "I mean, if someone on the base notices you're not about?"

"You ever missed me of an evening?" Harvey asked with a grin and Nolan shook his head.

"Must say you don't come over as the nervous type."

"I ain't afraid," Thompson declared. "Just don't want to go ashore right now." Then, when curiosity became too much, he added, "So, where you off to?"

"Told you, bit of business," Nolan said. "But separate, like."

"It just looks better if we pass out together," Harvey added. "Why not string along?"

Thompson's senses were sparked; after the day he'd had, spending a few hours with Joyce would have been nice, yet still he hesitated.

"No," he said at last. "I'll skip it."

"Suit yourself," Harvey shrugged.

"It's your choice, we ain't gonna use force." Nolan was equally blasé. "Though I never had you down for no chicken."

* * *

"We've now had almost two weeks of sea exercise and, I think you'll agree, the flotilla is shaping up nicely."

Harris paused to consider the full ready room. Before him were the captains and first officers of each gunboat under his command and, though he still had a few, unspoken, doubts, generally he was satisfied.

"Certain matters still have to be addressed," he continued. "Hamilton, you have to lean on your telegraphist; he's far too inclined to chatter. And Robson, your docking arrangements can be a mite lax."

The last remark brought a murmur of laughter; that

43

morning Robson's boat had all but rammed the harbour entrance and was currently in the Wellington Dock for minor repairs.

"Inattention on the part of the cox'n, sir." Robson sounded as if he had already repeated the phrase several times that day and there was a further round of laughter.

"Maybe so, but you were in command, and it was your responsibility." Harris' tone was sufficient to bring silence to the room.

"Providing the dock does their stuff we should be up to full strength again in a couple of days, after which we will be considered operational."

He paused and contemplated them all for a moment. "In fact, our first patrol has already been scheduled for Thursday night."

The announcement brought the ripple of comment Harris expected, and he waited for it to fully die out before continuing.

"For some, this will be their first time in action, but everyone, *everyone* must be aware that a mistake is likely to mean the end of their ship, and probably others. We have to rely on each other and know exactly what everyone's doing at any time."

He paused again and looked at them afresh. The more experienced knew what he was talking about and, equally, that such instinct could only be built up over a considerable time. But as for the others – the newbies – though all watched with rapt attention, they didn't really have a clue.

And the worst of these was Maddox. Apart from the slip up early in training, the performance of their MASBs had been acceptable and Harris felt Penrose would turn out to be a competent skipper. But for the first few weeks both would be more liability than asset, and it hardly helped that they had the oldest, and slowest, boats.

"So, the majority of you have only a couple more days of practice before putting it to the test. Don't waste them, learn all you can and don't be afraid to ask if anything proves difficult or doesn't feel right." So far no one had questioned him on any point, although Harris suspected Anderson had been consulted on several occasions. Perhaps he was becoming an aloof commander, someone the others found hard to approach? Well so be it and thank God for Number One.

"A final point," he said. "If anyone else comes across a loose

44

mine, can they keep it to themselves?"

This produced a suitable 'end of briefing' laughter, and Harris was pleased to note the others were treating Maddox well, with several giving the fellow pats on the back as well as the occasional dig. It was just the atmosphere he was hoping for; maybe everything would turn out right after all?

* * *

"I got us a place, Frank."

Thompson pressed the receiver closer. It was their habit for him to call the telephone box at the end of Joyce's road at as close to half-past seven as he could manage; the time both were most certain of being able to make. He invariably used one of the phones outside the NAAFI and, as was also customary, breakfast was still in full swing.

"A place?" he said, one hand resting against his free ear to block out the background noise. "Where?"

"Limekiln Street. It's right near your base; I can almost see the building from the front."

"What is it, a flat?"

"No, an 'ouse." The pride was obvious in her voice. "And quite a big one: three whole floors!"

Thompson had specified a flat, though a house would be so much better, and what the old girl had dug up might well provide the space for one of Mr Granger's enterprises. But houses were not cheap, and it was worrying that Joyce should have gone against his wishes.

"We said a flat," he told her. "Houses are expensive."

"This one ain't." Now a whiff of rebellion was creeping in. "An' it's got a garden."

"Don't need no garden," he said.

"But Frank, it's got everything else we want; bags of space and really private. There's a widow living in the basement; she actually owns the whole buildin' but her kids left years ago an' now only needs a couple of rooms."

"What's it gonna cost?"

"Thirty bob a week."

That was more than he could spare, even with the hard lying allowance from being in Coastal Forces.

45

"We can't afford it," he said.

"Oh, Frank we can." There was now a definite note of insurrection. "Top floor's the old servant's quarters; bedsit with a small kitchen and lav. We could get ten bob a week for that easy, Mrs Donaldson won't mind. An' I've got that money dad left me."

"I'd better check it out," he said.

"Can you come straight away? Only I don't want to lose it."

Straight away? Their first patrol was scheduled for that night, did she think he could just walk off base without a word?

"We ain't got liberty, an' won't have for at least a week."

"But it'll be our home," she said. "Come on, you must be able to do something."

Thompson felt an odd pang of regret; he was letting her down; it was a totally novel sensation.

"It should be easy enough to find somewhere in Dover," he said. "No one lives there no more."

"Don't you believe it; most houses have been bombed or taken over by the military. The old girl only wants a bit of company, so I laid it on thick. Said we were newly married, and you a sailor and she knocked a bit off the rent, though it were already well below anything else I could find. And it's furnished; we can move straight in."

"There ain't much I can do, not with tonight..." Thompson was about to add more when he noticed the petty officer standing nearby. It was unofficial, but everyone knew his job was to keep a check on loose tongues.

"What's 'appening tonight?" Joyce asked.

"Never mind," Thompson said.

"Tomorrow then; she ain't gonna wait forever!"

"Okay, tell the old girl, yes, but I can't get away 'til tomorrow night."

"So, you will be able to get leave?"

He lowered his voice. "Reckon I might." The lie came easily; he could be dead by then. "But don't give over no money, I got to see it first."

"I'm not sure she'll be happy with that."

"Talk her round."

"You'll definitely be there tomorrow?" she checked.

He briefly closed his eyes. "I said I would, didn't I?"

Chapter Five

It would be a simple patrol, at least that was the intention. Brooks had set it up personally and, on one hand, Harris appreciated the gesture. Going a little further into the Channel would be a new experience for some, and knowing there was every chance of meeting the enemy could not harm even the more seasoned. Yet part of him would have preferred something a little more challenging; maybe escorting a British convoy for one leg of their journey north, or even a hit and run on a French port.

As it was, they were being protected in a small way by the weather. The hot summer's day had turned into a clear and balmy night. Even a minimal moon was sufficient to light up the sea as far as the enemy coast and, though it meant action was less likely, neither should there be any surprises. Anderson was standing beside him on the bridge.

"How much further on this leg, Number One?"

"We'll be coming to the edge of our sector in ten minutes, sir."

Harris nodded and looked back at the trailing boats. As this was the flotilla's first time in action, and all were in sound working order, he had detailed his entire force; the time would come for layoffs soon enough. And he was forced to admit that, highlighted as they were in the pale moonlight and under a sky so strewn with stars it gave an equal light, they looked impressive enough.

"Aircraft bearing green ten."

Harris instantly dismissed the frivolous thoughts and raised his glasses, while Anderson acknowledged Daly's sighting. He spotted them almost immediately; several black dots flying high as they headed across the Channel to England. He turned to Anderson, who also had them in sight.

"What do you think?"

"I'd say they were Jerry," Anderson replied after a pause. "Too small for our lot and they don't tend to return from a mission this early and in such tight formation."

"My thought as well, though they usually need more moon." He leant forward to the voice pipe. "Make to Dover

Command, Tel'; 'enemy aircraft in sight and heading their way.'"

"I'll give him our exact position," Anderson announced, turning to go.

"Do that, Number One and get Tel' to copy the others on R/T – some might not be up to monitoring Morse traffic."

Anderson disappeared down the wheelhouse ladder and Harris raised his glasses once more. Yes, German for sure, and possibly of no danger. Such a small force was more likely intending to strike a specific target on the British mainland. However, it might also be a patrol; a group of fighter bombers out to cause trouble any way they could, in which case a flotilla of British gunboats highlighted on a clear, calm sea would be hard to resist.

Anderson returned and took up his own binoculars.

"Coming closer," he said, "and they've deviated slightly; they may also be losing height." He lowered his glasses and turned to his captain. "I'd say they're making for us."

Harris made no reply, though he was inspecting the sighting as well and equally changing his mind.

"And they're definitely fighter bombers." Once more Anderson was voicing Harris' suspicions. "Twin engines; probably 88s, or maybe 110s."

Either would be a nuisance but the Junkers, with their heavier payload and more powerful radial engines, were the greater threat.

"I think you might be right, Number One," Harris finally admitted. "We'd better tell the lads to disperse."

* * *

The first Bridger and Mitchel knew of the impending attack was from *194*'s engines mounted below their position. Until then the Packards had been purring sweetly but, with no warning, the entire boat began to surge forward, accompanied by a steady crescendo of noise. The power continued to build until the deck and every fitting were vibrating with seemingly uncontrolled force while the sea whipped below them in a blur.

Both men were caught by surprise, with Bridger cracking his arm against the gun's mounting, but there was no time for curses or explanations; the acceleration was followed by a clatter from the firing gongs and it was clear they would soon be in action.

"Can't see no enemy," Mitchel bellowed, "but something's sure stirred up the others."

That was definitely the case. What was a neat formation of trailing gunboats had dissolved into utter confusion with each craft adopting a diverse and apparently random course away from the main body.

"Air attack, green fifteen!"

Despite the roar of engines, Anderson's voice came over clear and strong through the nearby speaker and Bridger immediately tightened his leather strap and swung the Oerlikon to starboard.

"Keep an eye for other shipping!" he warned Mitchel. As the leading craft, *194* was accelerating in a straight line, but that didn't mean the other boats could be ignored. Any raid that lasted more than a few seconds would call for violent manoeuvring from every vessel, so danger would not just be from the enemy.

"Fighter-bombers!" Mitchel unconsciously repeated Anderson's words, and there was now no doubt. The enemy aircraft had taken a wide arc and were preparing to dive on the tiny warships. "Looks like we're in for a softening!"

Both men knew the procedure well enough; a high-speed pass with what looked like Junkers firing their forward-facing armament, before turning for a more considered approach, when any vessel winged by the first wave would be centred on.

A series of cracks from slightly forward told how Daly had already opened up on the oncoming force, although it was long range for a half-inch Vickers. Bridger knew he would have more chance with the Oerlikon but was holding his fire. Then, as the leading plane pulled out of its dive and began to skim over the water towards them, he began.

The first shots flew in a line just ahead of their target, yet there was no harm in that; Bridger had known many an enemy pilot turn away on finding themselves flying into an apparent wall of flack. *194* was still travelling fast and beginning to turn into the attack. He soon lost that plane, and quickly reset his sights on another, slightly further away. Each of their attackers was sending out streams of tracer and soon the German shells began to land.

They also came early, cutting a swath in the clear waters just off *194*'s starboard bow. Then the boat herself was hit, a series of punches forward raised splinters and sparks as they punctured her deck. Bridger had the sense to swing round before his gun ran against the guard and was in position in time to fire on the plane as it headed away. His shots appeared to be hitting, indeed they deserved to, but there was no deviation from the aircraft and soon it was lost in the vagaries of the night.

"That was the first," Bridger shouted to Mitchel. "But there'll be others, you can be sure of that!"

* * *

Though far less experienced – this was his first time in action, after all – Thompson, in the port turret, also knew the enemy would be back, yet strangely the knowledge did not faze him. There had been a worrying time before the planes actually struck though, such was the speed in which they arrived, it was nowhere long enough to develop the fear he knew likely. And when Daly began to fire, Thompson did not follow his example. It would have been possible; both turrets had guard rails, so he was unlikely to damage his own ship. Nevertheless, his mind felt uncommonly clear, and he could see it would have been useless. But when the leading plane came properly into his sights it was a different matter. His twin Vickers began to speak without him consciously willing them and, as the enemy passed overhead, he had already spun his turret round and continued to pump at the departing Junkers for the few seconds it remained in range.

Then, when peace returned and he realised almost half his shells had been expended, an odd sense of satisfaction began to take him over. He'd failed; the German plane evaded all his efforts, yet Thompson knew he was not to blame.

All had been correct: all had been right. Any instructor would have given him top marks for what was a splendid effort. And most of all, he'd proved himself equal to the task, with no foolish doubts or attempts to hide. For much of his life, Thompson had relied on his bulk and a certain amount of lip to mask the coward lurking deep within; even the challenge of skipping past sentries for an illegal trip into town was enough to give caution. But all that would change; from now on there'd be no holding him.

* * *

50

"This time it'll be a bombing run." Harris was focusing his glasses on the enemy craft, which had reformed and definitely intended to strike again.

"Which may mean we'll have more chance at hitting back," Anderson replied. He had done his best to keep track of *194*'s air defences and was generally satisfied. Other than firing slightly too early, Daly had handled his weapon with his usual competence, but it was the new men who impressed him most. Bridger and Mitchel were definitely a team, and may well have damaged one plane, while Thompson – a secret concern until then – showed a rare ability to anticipate the enemy's moves. The planes were gathering for their next pass now, and Anderson was quietly confident all aboard *194* would account for themselves well.

"Make to the others, 'wider dispersal.'" Harris had abandoned his inspection of the enemy aircraft and was leaning forward to the W/T office speaking tube. "Let's not make it any easier than we have to," he added, leaning back.

Anderson was in total agreement; the flotilla had already spread over at least half a mile, but the herd instinct remained strong, especially amongst those less experienced.

He took another look at the enemy; they had begun their run and looked to be coming in low, which would make them difficult targets. But a fast moving gunboat was equally elusive, and the likelihood was they would weather the attack. Just as long as everyone kept their heads.

* * *

"Here they come again, Jonnie boy," Bridger announced as he raised the Oerlikon and hitched up his belt. Mitchel had already ditched the part-used magazine, replacing it with a full, and stood ready with another. Then there was little for either of them to do, except wait.

It was the same for Thompson. This time the enemy would be approaching from the port side giving him a first-rate opportunity to aim at oncoming targets and, though they would be low and fast moving, he was determined to put in a good show.

As would Daly in the starboard turret. He might lack

Thompson's grandstand view but, providing *194* made no dramatic turns, could still send up a formidable barrage. Not all would be head on, though; Daly was an experienced gunner who knew the value of engaging a departing target. If his first few shots failed to divert the attack, he would begin to spin the mounting long before the enemy passed overhead and concentrate on their vulnerable tail.

Having the greater range, the Oerlikon was first to speak. Bridger sent a stream of tracer that passed ahead of the leading aircraft and stayed reasonably constant, even when the skipper ordered a further increase in speed followed by a turn to port.

With the usual illusion of a low-flying attacker, the enemy was gone almost as soon as it arrived and, though Bridger did his best to follow round, he could not be quick enough to remain on target. But another appeared almost immediately and, barely conscious of Mitchel's slick change of magazine, he immediately centred on that.

The fresh target was making for another in their flotilla and appeared perfect. It had selected one of the slower gunboats which was drawing things out rather by heading away in a straight line, when savage turns would have been far more beneficial. But Bridger was not one to refuse a sitting duck and cooly focused on the aircraft as it moved in on its speeding prey.

And the circumstances were definitely in his favour; *194*'s recent turn gave him just the right angle, enabling pressure to be maintained and Bridger took grim satisfaction in the sight of his tracer flowing evenly over the enemy aircraft's fuselage. He need only continue a second or two longer, and the German would be history, although the fleeing British gunboat was starting to enter his line of vision, so probably time to hold off.

Mitchel was equally aware of the MASB's proximity. He had been following the exchange just as closely and gave a brief cry of concern when their Oerlikon continued to fire. Not only were Bridger's shells a danger in themselves, but there was every chance the bomber would be wounded enough to crash into the gunboat.

But he did not relent; for several glorious seconds, Bridger continued to target the now doomed aircraft and was gratified by the sudden flash of yellow that filled his gunsight.

"Got the bugger!" he informed Mitchel and was surprised

when the loader did not share his joy. Then, glancing back to where debris still fell on the disturbed water, he realised the British gunboat had exploded as well.

* * *

"That must have been Maddox," Harris shouted. He and Anderson had been following the action as best they could although much of their attention was taken watching other members of the flotilla as they sought to distance themselves from their peers. Two, probably Jarvis and Robson, had come close to colliding, but the latter turned away at the last second and, though the Germans made a concerted effort, the sea had become a positive jumble of speeding craft that must be almost impossible to pin down. Only one, Maddox, maintained a steady course when a Junkers singled him out and so became the sole focus of the two officers' attention.

They watched in growing horror as the MASB accelerated, but did not turn, while its aft gun sent up a derisory barrage at the approaching danger. And they also noticed Bridger, at their own Oerlikon, take more deliberate aim and score hits on the attacking aircraft. Whether the German was able to release his bombs was unclear, however, and neither officer could be sure if their own shelling went on for slightly too long. But the outcome was obvious: either the plane, its bomb load, or fire from *194*'s aft cannon had struck Maddox's vessel, and the massive ball of flame that followed signalled the end for both bomber and gunboat.

* * *

"To my mind, it makes no difference," Anderson said.

194 had made harbour over an hour before and most had departed for *Wasp* and perhaps a bite of supper. Only the engine room staff remained for the essential maintenance Newman preferred to carry out while his Packards were still warm. Only them, and her officers who were currently huddled in their tiny wardroom when they really should be giving the usual debriefing in the base's ready room.

"You mean Maddox and his lot would be just as dead if they were hit by the enemy or their own side?" Harris had not meant to speak quite so harshly, but he was still secretly shocked by the turn

53

of events.

"Something along those lines," Andersons said.

They made a thorough search, but there was no sign of life from either side and the only good thing that could be said was the rest of the German attackers left without bothering them further.

"We don't know if the plane dropped any bombs and cannot be certain Maddox's boat was hit by our gun," Anderson continued, and Harris nodded in response.

"The German's forward cannon would also have been firing," he said. "But you have to agree, Bridger held on too long."

"That is indisputable, though the evidence we have is not enough…" Anderson paused.

"To hang him with?" Harris completed with a wry smile.

"It's not a question of that!"

"Of course not." The captain was quick to agree. "And frankly I can't see anything being served by looking into the matter further. An official inquiry would only come to the same conclusion, with the added bonus of allowing Jerry to make all they could of the possibility that we destroyed one of our own boats."

That was also incontrovertible, yet just as harsh; Anderson was also feeling the strain.

"What say we leave it, for now at least?" he continued. "Hold the usual de-brief and lodge a suitably vague report. The other officers must be wondering where we are. Brooks will have to counter sign your sitrep and, if he senses anything amiss, you can speak with him off the record. But to my mind the sooner this is settled, and forgotten, the better."

"I think you're right, Number One," Harris said. "In fact, I'm sure of it. I just hope all concerned will be able to forget as easily."

* * *

"There's some what say a filter will last two oil changes," Kipling told Newman. "Maybe more."

"An' there's some that should keep their ideas to themselves," Newman replied. As one who naturally avoided any extreme of affection, he did not exactly dislike their new motor mechanic. The lad had a lot of good points and certainly knew his way around a Packard. And he was starting to take instruction a little better, yet there were times when Newman felt it was him who was under constant observation and any fault he made, be it real or imagined, would be instantly jumped on by the youngster.

"We have to preserve supplies," Kipling said.

Newman's personal schedule of engine maintenance laid little emphasis on conservation. After each major run – and that night's definitely counted as such – he would change the oil in one of the three engines. That meant several gallons of the golden liquid being drained off and replaced, which might have been wasteful in the eyes of some. However, a new Packard 4M-2500 cost considerably more than a few cans of oil, while the loss of its 1,350 horsepower could mean the end of an entire gunboat.

"The oil's not wasted," Newman replied. "It gets re-processed."

Even an hour after being shut down, the starboard wing engine was still warm and the rich liquid smoked slightly as it flowed onto the jerrycan's funnel.

"Filter can't be re-processed," Kipling told him.

"Maybe not," Newman replied. It was late, changing the starboard mill's oil was their last duty, and it felt like his naturally stoic nature was being put to the test.

"Plug in?" Kipling asked as the flow began to ebb.

"Leave it," Newman said. "Last drops contain any swarf and filings; it's them we wants to be rid of."

Kipling obediently waited until the sump was dry, then refitted the plug with his oily fingers before finishing with a wrench.

"Not too hard," Newman said, watching. "Don't want to distort the sump or bugger up the thread."

A quick wipe with a rag got rid of the last vestige of old oil, and Kipling reached for a fresh can.

"Hold up, you still have to replace the filter," Newman reminded.

Kipling looked questioningly at his superior, but Newman was having none of it. An oil change meant a filter change and that was that. This must have been communicated to the youngster as he replaced the can and reached instead for the cardboard box that contained a fresh filter.

Newman's left arm still ached on occasions, but then it had

been a nasty break, and not so long ago. It would soon start to feel right, as would being a Chief Motor Mechanic (Temporary Acting). It was a position he never aspired to, nor ever really wanted, yet were he to effectively fail and return to his previous rate, it would be a disappointment. But should that happen, he would rather it was through a lack of technical expertise than the inability to handle the challenging ways of an opinionated junior grease monkey.

"What shall I do with the old filter?" Kipling held up the dripping lump as he waited for an answer and Newman was tempted to give a coarse reply. But rank had responsibilities as well as privileges, and he must not give in to temptation.

"I suggest you re-purpose it," he said.

* * *

"There ain't no good in stewing," Mitchel assured his mate. "You did what you did, nothing'll change it."

Bridger nodded and took another sip of the whiskey that had been smuggled into their dormitory. The others were still in the mess and would also be analysing that night's activities, though none with the same intensity as the Oerlikon's crew.

"You reckon anyone else was watching?" Bridger asked and Mitchel shrugged.

"Can't be sure of nothing in this crazy world," he said. "But the other gunners would have been too intent on their own weapons, as should them at the helms. And, at the end of the day, you're not even certain you hit the launch."

"No, but the plane did," Bridger said. "And I definitely hit that."

Chapter Six

Thompson edged forward in the queue, coming closer to Nolan, *194*'s coxswain, than was strictly necessary. Then bending slightly, he spoke softly into the Liverpudlian's ear. "You still intendin' to go off base?"

Nolan turned and gave such a wicked grin that Thompson almost changed his mind.

"Fancy a run ashore, do ya, Wack?"

"Something like that."

Seeing the other boat destroyed had both shocked Thompson and brought other matters into proportion. He, and all aboard *194*, might have died the previous night; compared with that, a simple matter of skipping into town seemed nothing.

Once the words were out, Thompson felt more vulnerable than ever, but Harvey was nowhere to be seen, leaving Nolan as his only choice. And the place Joyce found did sound ideal; he wasn't going to miss out because of a lack of liberty.

"It's as we told you; just walk out, no one'll think anything."

"But there ain't no leave."

"Not for us, but others have it, and the sentries don't know one from t'other. All you got to do is show a bit of front."

Thompson was still unsure, and Nolan sighed.

"Six thirty," he said. "Meet us at the northern perimeter gate an' we'll take you out. But make sure you're dressed fit for a captain's inspection an' don't say a word more than you have to. If there's trouble, I'll do the talking."

Thompson wouldn't have had it any other way, but there was something else bothering him.

"You won't want me to come with you after?" he checked.

"What, to my business?" Nolan showed his teeth once more. "Na, you go your way, I'll go mine an' Harv'll be no different. Make sure you're at the basin by ten an' we'll see you back in. Any later and you're on your own. Think you can manage that?"

Thompson considered for less than a second. "Reckon so," he said.

"She says, 'I know what you're knocking for,'" Bridger announced, his eyes already creased in anticipation. "'Yes', says the sailor. 'Yes, but you don't know what I'm knocking with!'"

The gunner's slap of the table, followed by his own raucous laugh, was enough to finish the joke and almost made up for his shipmates' mild apathy.

Mitchel watched his partner with concern. Only the day before he had been agonising over whether his actions had finished off one of His Majesty's gunboats, yet here he was laughing and joking like it never happened.

"You don't know what I'm knocking with!" Bridger repeated, and Daly gave a polite smile.

"I don't understand." Kipling scratched at his head. "What *was* he knocking with?"

"Never mind that," Pickering said, "anyone seen Thumper Thompson?"

It was evening and, with no liberty and a limited choice of places to relax, the majority of *194*'s ratings had remained in the NAAFI after their meal.

"Stayed long enough to throw down a plate of hot pot," Daly said. "Then legged it. I thought he were off for a Jimmy, but never came back."

"Nolan's missin' an' all," Mitchel pointed out, "and Harvey."

"Both of 'em are off most evenings," Daly said.

"But we ain't got liberty," Pickering complained.

"Liberty or not, they usually goes." Mitchel again. "Makes you wonder what they gets up to."

"I reckons Harvey's got a girl in town," Bridger said.

"Do you now?" Pickering asked. "And why would that be?"

Bridger shrugged. "Stands to reason, he goes out any night he can, never comes back drunk, but always seems happy."

"You can be happy without booze," Mitchel said. "Though it's not so easy, I'll grant you."

"Well Nolan'll be up to no good – that's if you want my opinion." No one did, but that never bothered Bridger.

"The lad's alreet," Pickering said. "Treats his mates well, always free with the nutty, though Thumper's a different matter."

"Rub you the wrong way, does he, Geordie?" Bridger asked.

"Not exactly. Though there's sommat about the lad I don't like."

"I know what you mean," Mitchel nodded. "As if he's putting on an act."

"Aye." Pickering was quick to agree. "I canna stand that."

"We ain't been knowing the fellow long," Daly said.

"About as long as anyone else," Pickering said. "It's only you an' I that go back further."

"I've had me suspicions from the off," Mitchel admitted. "Though still think we should give him a fair go."

"No doubt about that," Pickering agreed. "Yet I canna help wonderin' what he's up to."

"One thing's still bothering me," Kipling said, and all eyes turned to the boy. "What *was* that sailor knocking with?"

* * *

Harvey glanced at his watch as he walked along Warwick Street. He'd already parted with Thompson and Nolan and was pleased to be alone; had either wanted to accompany him, it would have ruined his entire evening. But Thompson headed straight for another part of the town and Nolan had stayed as tight about his destination as ever and was the first to leave.

There was no raid on, but Dover lay within range of heavy artillery mounted on the French coast and could be shelled with little warning, so he was always eager to reach shelter. And shelter it definitely would be, a sanctuary both physical and mental; somewhere he would be safe and could properly relax. More than that, a place where those of his kind would understand, welcome, and appreciate him.

A turn of a corner and he was there; the department store had been deserted since a German incendiary destroyed the top floor, but its lower levels were intact, and the basement, his particular goal, was completely unaffected.

He opened a plain wooden door and skipped down the stone steps. Already he could hear the music, smell the smoke, feel the atmosphere. Another door, but in front sat Lennie whose bulk, and grin, were obvious, even in the poor light.

"What ho, Sailor!" he said, heaving himself up.

"Evenin' Lennie. Not too late I hope."

"Never too late," the big man told him. "Always pleased to see you, Mr Harvey."

Mr Harvey – he liked that. So different from being on the base or aboard a gunboat when he was liable to be referred to by his position. If it wasn't for the uniform, he might never have been in the Navy.

Lennie opened the door wide, Harvey stepped into the room and paused with a satisfied smile on his face.

The band was playing, and several tables were already full. A few punters turned and gave a wave, but then he was popular – 'an asset to the establishment' as Arnold, the proprietor, often told him.

The lads were coming to the end of their number; soon he would join them and go to work, though Harvey never thought of it as such. To him it was his natural element; something he had known since birth. Something he had worked at while marking time as an apprentice electrician, and was just reaching the stage when it could become his way of life when war broke out.

War, and the call-up that followed, changed everything. He'd stuck with it, of course, and even during basic training there'd been opportunities. Only when he went to sea and spent nine months aboard a cruiser was there reason to pause, even then, any free time was spent researching the theory and he returned the stronger for it.

Returned, then immediately volunteered for Coastal Forces, a branch of the Royal Navy that might allow time off and the opportunity to step ashore on a regular basis.

The band finished as predicted and he exchanged a few more waves and a shouted greeting as he walked towards them. Soon, very soon, the magic would begin again, and Harvey was more than ready.

* * *

Frank Thompson looked around the pleasant living room. It was actually far larger than he'd imagined, as was the entire building; a well-to-do detached house with two storeys plus attic rooms, all of which would soon effectively belong to him. The furniture was also classy; dark wood sideboard, thick carpet; the place was more

60

like a hotel than a rental property. And though there was indeed an old woman living in the basement, it had its own front door so was perfectly private. Joyce had done well: he was impressed.

"What do you think?" she asked, her eyes betraying more than apprehension.

"You can't find something better?" he asked.

"Frank, there's nowhere," she said. "Most places are bomb damaged or without electric; compared to anything else, this is a palace."

That was a fair assessment even without the comparison, but Thompson remained determined not to give anything away.

"An' thirty bob a week, you say?"

It was a bargain, an absolute bargain.

"You wouldn't do no better down Bethnal," she said. "An' thirty bob's all in; electric, gas, rates: the lot!"

Better and better. Joyce wasn't bringing in a penny, of course, but that could change. A place like this had definite possibilities; once Granger got to hear of it, he'd be in like a ferret down a rabbit hole.

"So, what do you think?" Joyce repeated. She was still waiting, still anxious for his reaction, and Thompson felt a thrill of power pass through him.

"It'll do," he said, "for now. Though, you'll have to clean up the attic rooms an all."

"You want to rent them out?" she checked.

"Maybe, though we could also be putting up a few guests."

"Guests?" Now a hint of protest had crept in, and Thompson was not having that.

"You heard," he said. "If you want to live in a place like this, you're going to have to make a few compromises, and one of them will be a spot of entertaining."

"I'm not sure I like that idea." She was starting to sulk. "I thought this would be just for us."

"Well, that's where you're wrong, see?" Thompson recalled Alfie's words. He had to make a stand, and it must be now, from the start, else there'd only be trouble later. Something of this must have shown in his expression as Joyce began to melt.

"If you say so," she said, and he felt a measure of remorse. But only for a moment, the notion soon went leaving him with another.

61

Until then he would never have suspected the mouselike creature could find such a place, let alone negotiate a really decent deal. And it was perfect for one of Mr Granger's businesses. Offering his old boss such a facility could not hurt his position any, while Joyce would also be on hand, he remembered. A bit of fancy talking from him might even see her on the pay roll – better and better.

"Look, I got to be going. Tell the old girl it's fine and I'll be back to sort things out as soon as I'm able." He glanced at his watch; he'd only been there fifteen minutes but there was no point hanging around; the house might be perfect, but Joyce had definitely let him down as far as her personal timings were concerned. Still, there were plenty of pubs between here and the base, and it would be a waste not to try a few.

"Aren't you even going to stay and meet Mrs Donaldson? She'll be very disappointed."

"Told you, I got to be gone," he said, kissed her quickly on the cheek, then made for the front door.

Outside he looked up once more at the house, marvelling at its size and the fact it would soon be his. On marrying Joyce, Thompson hadn't realised quite what a catch he'd landed. Though it would be wrong to tell her so; she might start getting ideas.

* * *

"Evenin' Sister," Nolan said as the massive wooden door opened.

"Mr Nolan, how wonderful! We wondered if you would make it."

"Sorry I'm not on time, like," he said, following the nun into the cold stone entrance hall. "Problems at the base."

"Any time you can spend with us is welcome." She beamed with genuine affection. "I'll tell the Mother Superior; she'll be so pleased."

"Do that, Sister, though I'll get straight down to work if that's alright by you."

"Of course." They walked together to a side room that was partly fitted out as a library. Some shelves were complete, others only partly built and there were planks ready to be used and a mess of sawdust and shavings on the flagstoned floor. "I'll go and get the rest of your tools, we keep them locked up in case the children find

62

them."

"Kind of you," Nolan said as he surveyed his work. It had taken longer than expected but he reckoned this room would be done by the end of the week. After that, there were plenty of other jobs, and he would continue to do them for as long as he was able.

* * *

Harvey sat back from the old piano and drew breath. He'd been working pretty much continually since his arrival, even at the end of the first set, when the rest of the band went off for a break, he'd stayed and played a handful of ragtime numbers to keep the punters happy. Which was fine by him; Jump, Dixie, Trad', even a touch of Dance Band; anything that would swing, he'd play.

And this current band undoubtedly swung, he'd rarely sat in with a hotter crowd. They could never be sure of a full turnout but were used to filling in for each other. Grover, currently draining his trombone, was in a reserved occupation and often called out for Home Guard duty, yet on the nights when he could show, he had lips like leather and the sweetest upper register. And Lee, an American who worked as a caterer on the nearby base, was slightly more reliable and the nearest thing they had to a leader. Lee was a handsome bugger with penetrating blue eyes, fine fair hair, and a reasonable singing voice; just what they needed to front the band, while he could also fire bullets from his cornet with all the finesse of a Beiderbecke.

Playing continually from seven to nine-thirty meant Harvey got the same return as the rest of the lads, yet could leave in time to be back on base by ten. Not that the pay was that great; ten bob between them, if they were lucky and the house had been full, otherwise it could be a handful of loose change. But the cash was immaterial; Harvey would have played for nothing; what he took from one of these evenings was far beyond riches.

"One more number, Harv'?" Lee asked and Harvey glanced at his watch.

"Reckon we might," he replied.

"Any chance you could become a bit more regular?"

For a moment Harvey's mind went back to the previous night and the destruction of that gunboat. "I can't guarantee it," he said. "Fact is I can't guarantee ever being here at all."

63

"No, I guess not." The American, who probably spent much of his days preparing vegetables, nodded as if he understood. "Having a decent rhythm section sure brings us together though. We missed you last night."

"You and the Germans," Harvey agreed with a grin.

Lee turned back to the audience. "Last song with our salty piano player so it's his choice; what's it gonna be, Harv'?"

He'd been expecting this. *"Honeysuckle Rose."*

It was one of his favourites and they played it in F, which pretty much ruled out a duff C sharp on the piano's bass.

"Take it away, Sailor!"

Harvey knew the piece sideways; he'd start them off, before bringing in the rest of the rhythm section followed by Lee and Grover. He rested his hands on the keys, savouring the moment. Then, as if he had no control over it, the music took him over and for the next few minutes *194*'s telegraphist was in heaven.

Chapter Seven

"It's good news and bad, Bob," Commander Brooks told Harris the following morning. "We're replacing Maddox's boat with a new one. And it will be new in every way," the base captain continued. "A MkV, fresh from the builders."

As far as good news went, that was about the best there could be, Harris decided. The British Power Boat Company's new launch was reckoned to be their finest ever and would be a welcome addition to his force.

"She'll have RDF and all the other bells and whistles which include, in case you've forgotten, a forward-facing gun."

Yes, that was one of the features that made it spectacular; having a powerful cannon up front should do much to address the imbalance between British craft and the German E-boats.

"That will be most welcome," Harris said. When called to the base captain's office he had expected a completely different conversation and was intending to express doubts about the way Maddox's craft met her end. Brooks' announcement not only put the kibosh on that, it wiped the entire incident from his mind.

"Wait, I haven't told you the bad news yet: you will be in command."

Harris blinked; that really didn't sound so very terrible. He was fond of *194*, of course, but the old barge had been through much and was bound to start playing up in time.

"I think I can live with that, sir," he said.

"I'm sure you can," Brooks agreed. "But how do you feel about leaving Anderson behind?"

Now that was a different matter, and Harris' excitement palled. "I'm sorry, I don't understand."

"He applied for command some months back," Brooks reminded. "Just after that heavy mission when you were wounded."

"I was aware, sir, but at the time we weren't sure if *194* could even be repaired."

"I seem to recall similar doubts about yourself," Brooks grinned, and Harris was forced to nod in acknowledgement.

"Well, that's just it," the base captain continued. "They sorted her pretty much from the ground up and, even though you knocked her about a bit the other night, she's still a viable boat."

"And?"

"And Anderson has the experience and ability to command her."

"I see," Harris said, and then he did: all too clearly.

"He's a full lieutenant," Brooks continued. "RNVR, of course, but with a man like that such distinctions hardly matter. Fact is, he ticks all the right boxes; it's time you let him go."

Yes, Harris supposed he had been selfish, yet the idea of serving alongside anyone else was simply unthinkable.

"We'll find you someone good." Brooks had clearly been thinking along similar lines. "And a straight striper, if that's what you want. As Flotilla Leader, you may even rate a midshipman as well; how would that be?"

"I'd rather stick with Anderson," Harris said.

"Well, you will, to some extent," Brooks assured him. "He'll still be in the flotilla and, judging by the experience of the rest of your COs, probably the one captain you'll be able to trust."

Brooks tried a smile, but Harris was in no mood for humour.

"This is compulsory, is it, sir?" he asked.

"Compulsory?" Now it was the base captain's turn to be surprised. "Bob, I have any number of commanders screaming for a MkV. Are you really saying you'd turn it down to stay with Anderson?"

Harris pursed his lips and considered this for a moment. "Something along those lines," he said.

* * *

"But you're surely not serious?" Laura had stopped eating and was eyeing him incredulously. It was lunchtime in *The Grand*; one of the few times the couple could be certain of meeting socially yet, as usual, they were talking shop.

Harris shrugged. "I know how it sounds, but our relationship is important to me."

She raised her eyes but did return to her food. "Should I be jealous?"

66

"You know very well what I mean. We've said it before, a gunboat is not your normal run-of-the-mill warship; every department is scaled down; what requires a team aboard a cruiser can often be handled by one man. The captain and his exec. are the only commissioned officers; to work together they have to understand one another, and, with Anderson, that has been possible."

"And only with Anderson?" she asked.

"Oh, I had a few in the past," Harris said. "Believe me, he is the best by far."

She reached for her teacup. "And if you took the new boat, who would act as your number one?"

"There's a new chap coming down; a sub, but a straight striper; regular Navy," Harris continued, his tone still unusually harsh. "I expect I'll get used to him in time."

"You may do even better with a career officer," she said.

"Well, that's what's so strange." Harris had hardly touched his food, yet she had almost finished. "When Anderson joined me, he knew a bit about the sea – but only what was picked up from his time in sweepers. I had to teach him just about everything else, certainly anything to do with Coastal Forces."

"They don't do that sort of thing at *St Christopher*'s?"

"They try, but active service is a different matter."

"But Anderson's RNVR." She sipped at her tea. "A volunteer; I seem to remember your saying how useless they could be."

"Some are," Harris said. "Though not him. Fact is, a chap who wants to learn is a better bet than any straight striper from Dartmouth who already knows it all."

She eyed him over the teacup. "So really the problem is not losing Anderson, but who you might get in his place?"

"You might say that." Harris picked up his knife and cut deep into the rissole.

"And when's the new boat arriving?"

"Next few weeks," he said, after finishing the mouthful. Considering what it must be made from, the lunch was almost acceptable, and Harris supposed he should turn the conversation around to it.

"And your new second in command?"

"Tomorrow." Harris pointed to his plate. "I say, this isn't

too bad."

"Well, that's your answer then." She replaced the teacup and returned to her meal. "Sound the new guy out, maybe take him on a patrol or two."

"With Anderson?" He tried hard not to appear surprised.

"Why not with Anderson? Let him see who he's going to replace. I reckon he'll get a good idea of the rapport you two have built up and, if he thinks he can't match it, you'll soon know."

"I hadn't thought of that," Harris said.

"Of course, Anderson might have had the same idea," she added.

"About meeting my new number one?"

"No, breaking in his exec. The change will be far more dramatic for him; he'll be a captain for the first time, and not used to having a second in command. Has anyone been appointed?"

Harris shook his head. "Not as far as I know."

"I bet he's every bit as worried," Laura said. "And wouldn't be surprised if he wants to try his new man out as well."

"I suppose he might," Harris agreed, before finally smiling. "Looks like it's going to be a crowded bridge."

* * *

Alan Milner was indeed a fellow straight striper, and Harris wondered if Brooks had chosen him for that reason. Smart enough, with short blond hair and serious brown eyes. And definitely younger than Anderson, though only a sub-lieutenant.

"So, you've been in Corvettes for a year and now want to try something smaller?" Harris asked as they sat together in *Wasp*'s officers' mess.

"That's right, sir. To be frank, I'd considered the old Flower Class to be about as small as they came, but we escorted a number of East Coast convoys, and I was impressed at how well MGBs could perform."

"A little faster, I think you'll find." Harris tried a smile, but it seemed to be lost on the youngster.

"Of course, sir." The lad seemed terminally earnest. "Best a Flower can make is sixteen knots."

Harris cleared his throat and reached for the ginger ale

68

before him. "I think you'll find a few more differences," he said, "and not all will have been obvious from your time at *St Christopher's.*"

Milner was clearly waiting for Harris to elaborate.

"For a start, we rarely live aboard, you'll be stationed and probably billeted here and will return to dry land most nights."

"Will that be so very different, sir?" Milner asked.

"Believe me, it is," Harris told him. "Most wars are fought far from home with those involved travelling thousands of miles and spending years away. In Coastal Forces you could be mixing it with Jerry mid-Channel and then, a couple of hours later, be back in relative normality and what comes close to a domestic environment. I think those serving with bomber and fighter command experience something similar and it takes a bit of getting used to. It can be hard fighting a war from your front doorstep."

But Milner was either not listening or simply failed to be impressed. "Most of our trips lasted no longer than a couple of weeks," he said, "and several of the lads took shore accommodation where their wives lived."

"Then it will probably be exactly the same," Harris said, although still he had doubts.

* * *

Ten days later Harris' new command had still to materialise, but Milner was now a regular fixture, both at HMS *Wasp* and aboard *194*. And there was nothing exactly wrong with the young man. His manner, though at times a little serious, and with the tendency to be slightly scholarly, was not uncommon amongst regular junior officers and he certainly knew his stuff. Despite having little experience with Coastal Forces' craft, he was adapting quickly and might already have proved an efficient second in command, were Anderson not present.

Possibly the situation was equally awkward for him. When at sea, Anderson would normally have remained below, in the wheelhouse, where he'd give all his attention to navigation and so allow his captain and the new man to start forging a working relationship. But with *194* soon to become his own command, and

69

knowing Harris would then cease to be his immediate senior, he was loath to waste the last days with a mentor who had also become a close friend.

All of which made Harris' prediction about it becoming a crowded bridge uncomfortably accurate.

But they had already carried out one successful sortie in such a manner as well as several training runs, so when Harris' flotilla was detailed to intercept a northbound enemy convoy carrying ore, they set out with a fair degree of confidence. No replacement was available for Maddox's boat – that would come when the long-awaited MkV was finally delivered, but Penrose was starting to get the best from his aged craft and her raw crew. It was rare for him to be caught out of position and, though lacking in power, the twin Napier engines had responded well to attention from his mechanics.

"Target should be in sight shortly," Anderson reported on his return to the bridge. On hearing this, Milner immediately raised his glasses and began scouring the horizon, giving Anderson the uncomfortable feeling the young man was trying to prove him wrong.

"Won't be long before we'll have a more accurate fix," Harris said, this time making Anderson wonder if he also doubted his figures.

But that was nonsense, and probably a symptom of the current, uneasy situation. In a week or two – possibly less – Harris would have moved on, taking Milner with him, and Anderson could get used to being a captain himself, then training up his own second in command.

And having Milner so on the ball at least gave him more chance to stay in touch with the flotilla. There were only four operational boats that night; Robson's having been stood down due to a leaking cylinder head gasket. Being one short was almost the norm, however, and they had become used to running with reduced numbers.

Two were keeping station off 194's quarters with Penrose running further behind and slightly to starboard of her wake. And though there were clouds in the sky, it was basically clear, with visibility reaching almost as far as the French coast, about four miles ahead. The moon would also be bright but was not due to rise for a little over an hour; Anderson hoped by then they would be making for home with at least one of the convoy's merchants damaged, if not sunk.

Of course, to be truly effective, torpedoes were necessary; most MTB flotillas could boast impressive figures for both warships and merchants sunk. Some would have depended heavily on MGB support, however, which must eventually become a role for their own flotilla once they proved themselves.

"Vessel in sight, Green O-Five!"

It was Daly, in their starboard turret and as Anderson turned forward again, he felt oddly relieved the gunner noticed before Milner.

"That's them alright." Harris was also studying the vague shapes. "And I reckon we're perfectly placed; first-rate positioning, Number One."

Anderson felt a glow of pride; Harris was right, they were making perhaps twenty knots to the enemy's six, so should arrive in time to meet the middle of the convoy. Not having to alter course or speed had an added advantage as a steady approach was less likely to be detected, while this might also be the ideal opportunity to test a tactic he and the captain had been considering for some time.

"Make to the others, 'enemy ahead, maintain formation.'"

That was something best sent by Aldis as any form of wireless transmission was likely to be intercepted. Daly was a skilled signalman, but Harris had addressed those on the bridge and Milner was making no effort to move.

Anderson sighed and collected the Aldis then, turning aft, flashed out the short message.

There was no response, none was expected or required; all three boats should have picked up the flickering blue lamp.

"I have the leading merchant." Milner might have sounded a little smug, but then he had time to look, Anderson told himself.

"I'm more interested in the escorts," Harris snapped. They were growing close now and the tension was rising.

"VP to starboard." Anderson pointed to where the heavy superstructure of an enemy patrol boat could be seen. The converted fishing vessel would be slow, but well-armed, probably mounting several 88mm cannon in concrete-encased emplacements. Normally they would have gone out of their way to avoid such an enemy, but this one was effectively blocking *194*'s entrance into the convoy. Chances were strong a relatively slow and direct approach would not be immediately noticed, although the only way to find out was by putting it to the test.

Milner was twitching with excitement and even Anderson felt the tension grow, but Harris was at his lugubrious best. "Very well," he said. "Keep her as she is."

* * *

"Looks like we're in business," Mitchel muttered as he stood ready with a replacement magazine for the Oerlikon. Then, after looking at his gunner, he added, "You okay, Alec?"

Bridger nodded silently though there was an odd look in his eye.

"Not still thinkin' about that bomber?" the loader checked. The incident had gone unmentioned for some time now with Bridger behaving normally. Apart from a recently acquired habit of telling poor jokes, it was over and forgotten, surely?

"I said, you got nothing to worry over," he continued. "No one's sayin' you hit that gunboat, or the Jerry plane, come to that. Most think it were the MASB's gunners what brought the Junkers down, that or its own bombs exploding directly beneath. We didn't even get credited with a kill."

"I know that, and I'm fine," Bridger snapped, although Mitchel was far from sure.

"Okay, well take it easy," he said. "We're going for a couple of merchants, big fellas by all accounts. Only escort we seen so far's a VP, an' you know what they looks like."

"I know what our gunboats look like an' all, if that's what you're sayin'." Bridger's words were loud enough to draw attention from the turret gunners and Mitchel drew back.

"Course you do, matie, I spoke out of turn. Last time was unfortunate, and it ain't gonna happen again – not that you did anything wrong," he hastened to add. "But it'll be different; you'll be back to your old self, just wait and see."

But his sideways glance at the gunner's pale face and staring eyes was not reassuring, and Mitchel wondered if that could really be true.

Chapter Eight

They would go in with the first three boats travelling line abreast. Harris brought the speed up just as the first escort was coming into range and Jarvis, on their starboard wing, engaged the VP almost immediately. For gunboats to attack in anything other than the classic line ahead formation was unusual although, considering Penrose's lower maximum speed, one he was keen to try. With the throttles fully forward, each of the Packard-powered boats could top forty knots and the former MASB was soon left behind. But that might almost be to the good; while the wing boats concerned themselves with distracting any escorts, *194* could make straight for a merchant, with Penrose following as backup.

The tactic had worked well on every training run and, though his palms were now running with sweat, seemed to be panning out that evening. To port, Hamilton had yet to meet with an enemy but his chance would come. Meanwhile, the VP's gunners were having trouble keeping pace with Jarvis as his boat blasted across the slower vessel's bows.

And ahead was the merchant. Harris watched the bulk carrier's hull grow larger as they approached. A forward-facing gun would be of real use here; were he in the new boat they could have opened fire and softened up the target. As it was, the cargo ship still lay too far off for their Vickers to make any significant impact.

"It'll have to be depth charges," he shouted and, though the comment was not aimed at either of his two lieutenants, he was silently pleased when Anderson took up the challenge.

"I could take Harvey," he said.

It was customary for the telegraphist to carry out such a duty. After confirming the enemy's presence to Dover Command, there should be no further call for wireless communications until the action was over. Harris was about to agree, then wondered if Milner should handle the other charge.

The youngster was performing well enough in a supporting role and it would be interesting to see how he fared when given more autonomy. But no, that was for later, when they had the new boat and Milner was officially his first officer.

"Do that, Number One," he said. "And get back here as soon as you can."

Actually, there had been no reason for that last remark, Harris decided as Anderson left the bridge. Milner was still alongside and a perfectly good second in command. He might remain aft for as long as he wished, though privately Harris would be glad to see him return.

* * *

Anderson had taken station next to the starboard depth charge, with Harvey, bundled under the mass of lifejacket and hastily donned oilskins, to port. It was perfectly possible to fire either charge from the bridge, but the mechanism for doing so was slow and unsuitable for the split-second timing necessary.

This was not what the charges were intended for. Rather than sinking an enemy submarine, he and Harvey would be using the two hundred and ninety pounds of amatol each cylinder contained against a far larger target.

There might be little chance of sinking the vessel; even with both charges perfectly placed most merchants' damage control measures would see them make harbour. But significant injury, especially when caused to the steering gear, would delay the entire convoy while they sought repair. Considering the amount of raw steel their cargo would create, and the subsequent mass of tanks, armour and other materiel that could then be built, even postponing its arrival by a few weeks could be counted as a victory.

194 was still travelling at close to her maximum speed and the constant vibration from the engines mounted below, together with a jolt whenever her hull struck a rogue wave, made simply remaining upright difficult. But Anderson was accustomed to such motion and, glancing across to where the telegraphist was now setting his charge, Harvey appeared equally comfortable. Anderson inserted his key into the fuse housing and turned it a quarter turn clockwise. It was the highest setting: the charge should detonate only a few feet below the surface. By then *194*

74

must be well out of the way. At anything less than twenty feet, a depth charge could penetrate a submarine's pressure hull, and twice that should send it to the surface, meaning the fragile hull of a high-speed launch needed to be further off to avoid significant damage.

Once more he looked across to Harvey and, once more, the rating appeared ready. Behind, Jarvis and Penrose were engaging the German escort, while Hamilton had turned marginally to port in search of further game.

All good, the flotilla was behaving correctly; everything appeared set for a perfect interception. His mind switched back to the job in hand; Harris would bring *194* suitably close to the cargo vessel's stern before passing by and making a quick turn to port. That would be the time of most danger; with the charges exploding behind them, the gunboat listing heavily and a likelihood of meeting with fresh escorts on the other side, he and Harvey would have to be especially careful.

But that would come later; first, he had to make sure the charges were correctly despatched, which must take all his attention.

* * *

It was almost time. Harris' grip on the handrail tightened as the enemy merchant loomed closer. He had lessened their speed slightly and, beside him, Milner was saying something although he had no ear for conversation. Nolan was at the helm and had already proved himself reliable, but Harris would be controlling the forthcoming operation himself. At least with Anderson aft he could rely on the charges being released on time. His job was to see they were positioned correctly.

"Left a touch." In times of stress, even an old salt like Harris was inclined to abandon naval parlance, but Nolan was in tune and eased the wheel closer to the oncoming ship. Heavily laden as she was, her rudder lay well below the surface, but Harris could imagine where the giant fin must be hiding. "And a little more..."

Now it would only be seconds; Harris could see Nolan's

right hand resting on the throttles and felt reassured. Then, almost as if time ceased to exist, they were within touching distance of the grey, rusting hull. A shouted order; *194* fell away and the din from her engines suddenly diminished. No time to check if Anderson was on the ball; the boat's momentum still carried her forward and they were already starting to leave the merchant behind.

"Hard a port and fifteen hundred revs!"

There was no time to repeat the order; even before Harris stopped speaking Nolan had thrust the throttles forward and *194* picked up again, while a firm but brutal turn of the wheel sent her running along the German ship's side. Harris stared out to starboard. The merchant's hull blocked much of the starlight, yet he could still see the outline of an E-boat rushing towards them, a bone of clear white spray lodged firmly in its teeth.

194's Oerlikon immediately opened up, which was exactly the right move although the shots were passing unaccountably high. Even Daly, in the starboard turret, was firing off his Vickers, though little could be expected from half-inch shells at such a range. For as long as they had the merchant to port, Harris knew they were safe and the German must hold its fire, but that protection would soon be gone leaving the faster, better-armed enemy on their tail.

Milner was talking quite animatedly now, though how the fellow expected to be heard above the din of *194*'s engines was a mystery. Then the double explosion of depth charges added to the cacophony.

There was no chance of looking, but the timing had been right; Anderson and Harvey must have done a perfect job. Now Milner was shouting, his face uncharacteristically alive with excitement, though Harris found him easy to ignore. At that moment the only one he wanted alongside was his old second in command.

* * *

Meanwhile, the Oerlikon had run dry; Mitchel whipped out the used magazine and slipped in a new. Bridger immediately took aim once more, sending out a fresh barrage of tracer towards the approaching E-boat. But, just as before, the shots passed high, clearing the enemy craft by several feet. Mitchel collected another magazine and stood ready though he was in no way confident. He, too, knew their shelter would soon be gone, giving free rein to the German gunners and their far more potent weapons. And then they would be for it. With nowhere to hide, he and Bridger were likely to be *194*'s first casualties though, with an E-boat on their tail, the rest would surely follow.

* * *

On the bridge, Harris was less despondent. Anderson was taking a long time to return but, even without his support, he had a solution. *194*'s main defence lay in speed and to reach her maximum meant maintaining as straight a line as possible. A gunboat travelling at forty knots could shake off most pursuers while also making a difficult target for enemy gunners. Yet having stirred up an E-boat changed everything. The German craft was superior in most ways with diesel engines that could outpace his own supercharged Packards. Consequently, a change of plan was called for, as well as some expert seamanship from a hitherto untried helmsman.

"Hard to port and maximum revs, just as soon as you're able!"

Again, there was no time for protocol or further explanation. Nolan had already proved himself no fool and would have judged the situation. As soon as they passed the merchant's bow, he was to throw them into a turn. And it would have to be tight to ensure the E-boat could not follow, although too much rudder might also see the gunboat tip and possibly capsize. The trader's bows were fast approaching; soon they would discover exactly how much the Liverpudlian knew about ship handling.

Though expecting it, the turn was enough to catch both officers out; Harris crashed into Milner before sliding down onto the duckboards while the younger officer was pressed heavily against the side of the bridge, trapping his right arm and hand painfully against the guard rail. But it was done and, despite taking several seconds to fully right herself, *194* was soon heading away from the merchant, and back to where Penrose and Jarvis still argued the toss with the VP.

Harris glanced back; the E-boat was nowhere to be seen and must have been unable to follow *194* into her turn, although the merchant remained in plain sight. And there were definite changes there. Whether it was through his own action with the depth charges, or the German captain's reluctance to continue further, was unclear, but the ship had begun to edge very slightly towards the French coast.

"Reckon that depth charge attack was spot on, sir!" Milner exclaimed and Harris thought he might be right. It would be good to congratulate Anderson, though the fellow was taking an inordinately long time to return.

His eyes fell to *194*'s stern. There was no sign of him or Harvey, only Bridger and Mitchel could be seen aft of the superstructure.

Which meant Anderson must have already made it to the wheelhouse and would be with them shortly. But when no one appeared, and as Harris ordered *194* to join the attack on the VP, a move that finally forced the enemy to turn away, he had decided his second in command, and probably the telegraphist, were missing.

* * *

Neither of the Oerlikon gunners saw them go, although both definitely noticed the savage turn to port that was responsible. Still totally focused on the approaching enemy, Bridger was flung bodily against the bandstand guard, winding himself on the iron top rail while the magazine Mitchel had been holding flew from his grip and the loader crashed into a steel box of ready-use ammunition.

Thompson, being unable to reach the E-boat, had been releasing his energy with ineffective fire on the merchant's iron hull, and also missed the depth charge party's departure. Cosseted, as he was, by the walls of his turret, he rode the turn out well, even managing a few pot shots at the coaster's port bow before it drew out of range.

Meanwhile, secure in his own nest, Daly decided several thousand tons of merchant shipping was an inappropriate target for his ammunition. He also remained unphased by Nolan's manoeuvre and was the only one to notice others not so fortunate.

At the gunboat's stern, both Harvey and Lieutenant Anderson must have been equally ignorant of any intended turn.

78

One moment they were there, the next gone, though there was no mystery as to where. The sea was dark and *194* had travelled a fair distance before the Irishman fully comprehended his shipmates' fate. And when he did, he also realised a sizeable enemy escort force so close by would make any form of search impossible.

Not that Daly cared particularly. Harvey was relatively new and yet to fully integrate himself into *194*'s crew while, though he had known Lieutenant Anderson a fair time and had nothing against the fellow, an officer remained an officer and would always be remote.

But on the bridge Harris was concerned; more than that, the mixture of anger, remorse and outright guilt made him a dangerous man indeed. To turn back would have been senseless, but the temptation remained for some time and, even now, the idea held attraction. Hamilton had taken up his previous station; Penrose and Jarvis would soon be in place while the convoy itself was already several miles astern. The convoy, and probably Anderson, Harris reminded himself as, yet again, he scoured the empty aft deck.

"Lieutenant Hamilton's signalling." Milner's voice broke into his misery.

"Well, what's he saying, damn you?"

"Thinks he might have damaged a Jerry minesweeper, sir." It was not Milner's voice but Daly's, from the starboard turret.

"Very good." Harris' reply was automatic; at that moment nothing in his life could be called so. "Better give us a course for home," he added to Milner.

The man left without a word, leaving only Harris and the helmsman on *194*'s darkened bridge. Yet, even if the small space had been crowded it would have made little difference: without Anderson, Harris would still have felt alone.

Chapter Nine

Anderson was more confused than frightened, although the cold water soon helped his thoughts to focus. His helmet was heavy, he slipped it off and felt it knock against his leg on its way to the seabed; somewhere he would also end up without some quick thinking.

He glanced about; the German merchant ship was in plain sight though now some distance off. He raised his hand and shouted but her darkened decks were deserted, and she appeared to be veering away. There was, however, the sound of approaching engines and he paddled round in time to see the bulletlike hull of an E-boat passing barely fifty feet from him. Her triple screws churned up the water, sending a good amount into his mouth and nose, while the sea itself took some time to settle. And by then he was growing tired of treading water; if only he'd had the sense to wear a lifejacket...

But that was probably more to do with Harris, he decided with something close to a smile. It had taken a serious injury before his captain even considered wearing a steel helmet; had Anderson adopted a lifejacket, he would have felt even more the amateur.

His legs were definitely starting to tire and, as the convoy was now leaving him behind, Anderson knew the sense of loss could easily turn into panic. In desperation he tried to raise himself up in the water while waving a hand and shouting loud enough to burst his raw lungs, but the effort only left him breathless and struggling to stay afloat. There was no sign of *194*, or any of the flotilla – not even the magical rumble of distant Packards, a sound he always welcomed and enjoyed. Then, as the last of the enemy ships slipped slowly into the night, he felt truly on his own.

* * *

"You'll have to see her secured then made ready for fuelling," Harris told Milner as he prepared to leave the boat. It had been an uneventful passage back, the only excitement being Harris' Aldis signal to Jarvis ordering him to contact Dover Command. Without Harvey, *194* effectively lacked wireless communication and they needed to be aware of the situation. And this was not just for the loss of his second in command, he quickly assured himself. Harvey was also missing, while there was a wounded German freighter that should be of interest to others from *Wasp* or even the flyboys. However, privately there was only one thought on his mind. Anderson was unlikely to be wounded; chances were strong he remained alive, conscious, and probably alone in the depths of the Channel. And knowing his own order for that savage turn must have been to blame was simply too hard to bear.

Brooks stood waiting to meet him on the pontoon as Harris expected, but there was no time for pleasantries.

"We have to start a full search straight away," he said, jumping down from the boat.

"All in good time, Bob," the base captain replied. "Every active unit has been informed, and Johnston intends taking his lot for a look once they finish watching a bunch of MLs lay their eggs."

"Minelayers can look after themselves," Harris snapped. "As soon as my boats are fuelled up, we're going back."

"That you are not," Brooks said, and there was a rare firmness in his voice. "We both know nothing is likely to be spotted before morning, at which point there will be a full air and sea, which you will be welcome to join. Until then, get some sleep. You might not feel better in the morning, but your men certainly will – *and* they'll last out the entire day if need be."

Even in his current state Harris could see the logic, yet to go on shore and rest almost mocked Anderson's predicament.

"I think maybe I should contact his girl," he said.

"And let her know he's in danger?" Brooks demanded. "She'll feel just as helpless as we are, do you think he'd want that?"

Harris opened his mouth but made no reply. Brooks was right, he hadn't thought that one through either. Actually, quite a few of his recent decisions may have been slightly off-key; rest was probably a good idea. But he'd be up at first light – they all would. And if Anderson was still out there, they'd find him.

81

By the time the moon rose, he had been treading water for almost an hour and was truly exhausted. Yet the sight did do something to encourage him, even if the water remained as cold and the outside world appeared every bit as far off. But when the extra light picked out a small patch of black that could easily be another person, Anderson felt a definite surge of excitement.

He still wore his ursula; the extra layer should do something to keep in his bodily warmth but, as he struck out in a clumsy breaststroke, the rubber suit might have been purposefully holding him back. Soon his arms were aching as much as his legs, but the shape was coming closer, if imperceptibly so, and could still be that of a fellow human being. When barely yards away Anderson tried calling, though his voice was weak and cracked. Then, on finally drawing near to the bundle, he reached out, only to find it lifeless, and for a moment the disappointment was immense. And then an equally faint voice spoke in return.

"Who's there?"

"Tel?" Anderson asked. The bundle remained every bit as inert but definitely held life within. "Is that you, Harvey?"

The bundle moved, a white face turned towards him, and it was one Anderson recognised. "Ain't no one else," it said.

"How long have you been here?" Anderson asked.

Now the man gave a slight laugh. "Roughly the same as you, I reckons."

Yes, that made sense, and, despite the circumstances, Anderson knew he must watch what he said more carefully. "But you're afloat?" he asked, instantly breaking the rule.

"I've a lifejacket." Harvey was turning to face him properly now and did seem far higher in the water. "Whoever made it knew what they were about," he continued. "Keeps me up lovely; I was even having a bit of a kip when you showed up."

Anderson nodded as he was struck by the sudden change in values. A few hours before the most important things in his life had been Eve, *194* and seeing that freighter stopped. Now he felt he would trade them all for a ten bob lifejacket like Harvey's.

"Why not grab hold?" The rating must have seen the longing on Anderson's face. "I dare say it'll support us both."

"You're sure?" Mid-Channel at night was not the obvious

82

place for politeness, although sharing a man's life preserver called for a measure of courtesy.

"We can only try," Harvey replied. "But be careful not to knock my left hand; it was cut when I fell."

Anderson reached out and placed both arms around Harvey's neck before resting his weight on his shoulders. Immediately the seaman's body sank significantly, although Anderson felt his own rise up and when a balance was reached both were above the water level.

"Only for a while," he said. "Just give me a chance to rest."

"It's fine," Harvey said. "Hang on there as long as you want and get some sleep if you can."

Anderson knew such a thing would be impossible although his debt was now limitless.

* * *

The following morning everything went wrong for Harris. He was at the boat at four, well before first light, and the only one; Milner didn't arrive for another fifteen minutes, and it took almost an hour for the rest of the crew to assemble and see *194* taken to the oiler. Then there had been an annoying wait while the refuelling team made doubly sure all electrical appliances were shut down before work could begin. It was just his luck *194* was almost dry; most runs used a fraction of her capacity, so only necessary to fuel up one day in five, and this would have to be the fifth. But as such things were the responsibility of his first lieutenant – the man he was hoping to rescue – at least he did not blame himself for that.

Taking on ordnance was faster; he'd detailed the gunners to deliver their requirements directly to the armoury and a truck was waiting when *194* returned. Only two of the other boats also needed fuel, but they still took too long for what was a simple enough operation and it was only when they had waited for a collection of minesweepers to depart – vessels that surely could not have been on such an urgent mission – that *194* was finally able to clear harbour.

Once at sea, Harris felt a measure of easing up, if not relief. Milner had mapped out the area well enough, even allowing for the inevitable tides and currents, and the other commanders were fully aware where they needed to search. Yet as they left the

English coast behind, the Channel – normally considered too narrow a waterway for the traffic it carried – appeared impossibly vast for a handful of small boats to cover. There was some encouragement when a slow-moving biplane appeared and began to sweep the area, while the fishing boats, minesweepers and the squadron of exercising MTBs that put out after them would all have instructions to look for two men in the water.

Two men in the water, with not even a life raft to keep them alive or aid identification. It seemed a hopeless task, yet the anger and remorse Harris felt on learning Anderson was missing had not dulled in any way and, if there was any chance of finding his friend, he would exploit that energy to the full.

* * *

Dawn came and, though the rising sun was slow to give actual warmth, Harvey and Anderson were mildly optimistic. They had survived the night and if the day turned out anything like those preceding it, at least their faces would soon be warm. And there was more, even before the sun was finally free of the French coast, a vessel was spotted.

It was not the rescue they were praying for; no dashing British destroyer with warm towels and hot toddies, or even a passing fisher that might offer shelter and the chance to dry off. This appeared to be a life raft; possibly empty, or maybe filled with others as desperate as themselves, but it did offer hope.

Harvey saw it at the same time and, without a word to the other, the pair set off in the general direction. The journey took more than an hour, due mainly to the slow pace dictated by Harvey's injured hand, but Anderson was in no rush and, considering what the rating had already done for him, nothing would have been too much trouble. When the rubber dinghy became more identifiable, the sun was well clear of land and starting to send a measure of heat. And there may have been figures aboard the tiny vessel, Anderson could not be sure although Harvey was more positive and, when proved correct, they began to call out. So, when their shouts were returned, it was expected. What did surprise them was the reply came in German.

* * *

84

Midmorning aboard *194*, and still no sign. The biplane had disappeared sometime before to be replaced by another, larger, aircraft that began searching to the southwest. Harris supposed the rescue boys knew more about local conditions, though still would have preferred it if they'd stayed closer to the point Anderson was lost. And whereas the biplane had been slow, almost ponderous, and maintained a height that would allow such a small target to be spotted, the new single-wing affair seemed determined to set records for both altitude and speed.

Yet he was in no position to criticise. Despite one of the tightest box-pattern searches he'd ever instigated, Harris' small force discovered nothing other than floating wreckage and the occasional clump of dead fish – a common sight during wartime. Now he was forced to decide between repeating the process, beginning once more where he estimated Anderson and Harvey should be, and gradually working outwards, or mounting a fresh search in a different location.

Exactly where was the primary question. Should he follow the rescue plane's example and spread more to the west, or would that area already be fully covered? The Channel's fickle ways were legendary; a freak current might have landed the pair on either beach, or the missing men could have been swept up and into the North Sea, or deeper into the Channel proper and, eventually, the Atlantic.

It was not knowing that fed his anxiety. A simple case of looking in a set area could have been done and done well. But having to decide where, having to risk everything on the chance of being right, was something else entirely and Harris felt totally unequal to the challenge.

* * *

"English," Anderson announced as he reached up for the side rope. "English Navy."

That much should have been obvious from their speech and clothing, yet still the dinghy's occupants stared at them as if they came from another planet.

"We were tipped off our launch," he continued, forcing a smile. "It was late last night; we've been in the water ever since. Are we okay to come aboard?"

85

The pair in the dinghy looked to each other, yet seemed no clearer as to the course they should take. There was an exchange of German that meant nothing to those in the water before one finally stretched out to pull them on board.

Harvey was the first and, when a cry alerted them to his injured hand, they treated him with care. Anderson was able to heave himself in at least some of the way and soon both were safely on board.

At which point there was an impasse; the life raft's original crew made for one end where they viewed the newcomers with obvious mistrust, while the British collected awkwardly at the other.

"Thank you," Anderson began. "*Danke!*"

The taller German gave a serious nod in reply, although the other, who was also far heavier, simply glared.

"Do you know any more?" Harvey whispered. "German, I mean."

Anderson shook his head. "That's about it I'm afraid. Let's check out their English."

"We are most grateful." He spoke slowly, and with great clarity, but their host's faces remained blank.

"Just our luck," Harvey supposed.

"Never mind, we're not beaten yet." Anderson held out a gloved hand. "Ian Anderson, I'm very pleased to meet you."

Once more the taller responded, and even leant forward, but was pulled back by his stockier companion.

"Maybe we try another tack?" Anderson said. "My friend here is wounded." He indicated Harvey's left hand. Being hauled from the water had started the bleeding once more and the glove was clearly soaked.

This prompted discussion amongst the Germans and at one point the larger seemed close to losing his temper. But eventually a small green pack was produced. The taller then delved inside and brought out a field dressing which he offered to the English.

Anderson took it and deftly removed Harvey's glove. The wound ran from the telegraphist's wrist to the base of his forefinger and was bleeding steadily. The field dressing opened in much the same way as British packs, and soon was in place. Anderson fastened the blue tags on Harvey's palm then, after

86

rinsing the glove in the sea, squeezed it back into place.

"How does that feel?" he asked.

"Better," Harvey replied. Then, to the Germans. "Thank you – *Danke*. I'm very much obliged."

This time the taller man smiled while his friend looked slightly less fierce.

"*Wasser*?" It was the stouter man who spoke, which took both Englishmen by surprise.

The time spent in the sea had made their throats extremely dry and Anderson nodded keenly. "Thank you: *Danke*."

A flask was handed across and, by the feel, it was less than half full.

"Better just take a sip," Anderson advised. "Don't want to presume."

Harvey nodded and took a short drink, then handed it back to Anderson. The water was warm and slightly brackish, probably emergency rations stored for some while. But the feel on his throat was close to heaven and it took all his willpower to stop at a single swallow.

The larger German took the flask back and gave it an obvious shake. Then, on discovering there was still a considerable amount inside, his face softened.

"*Danke*," Anderson repeated.

"*Bitte*," the man replied, and now there was a definite smile.

* * *

Harris had come to a decision. With the plane still zooming about over the area off Folkstone, he was now leading his small force to the northeast. Whether such a course met with Milner's approval was a mystery, although Harris had the uncomfortable feeling that an order to return to base, or mount an invasion on the nearby French coast, would have met with similar acceptance. Yet he remained resigned to his choice and, when a trio of minesweepers returned from their morning duties and took up the search to the south, he was in no way dismayed. The Channel was indeed an enigma and, however expert the Air Sea boys might claim to be, few knew all its ways. The minesweepers may be about to cover waters he had already checked but could still find what they had

87

missed. And though he would be heading for the impossibly wide margins of the North Sea, if what was no more than an impulse were ignored, he would regret it for the rest of his life.

* * *

"It's a shame we can't make more conversation," Harvey said, and Anderson nodded. The atmosphere was definitely lifting and, as the day wore on and the sun's warmth started to become painful, both groups were growing more comfortable in the other's company.

"Maybe we could try a song?" Anderson suggested. "What popular tunes do you know?"

"Quite a few," Harvey smiled shyly, "it was going to be my job in peacetime."

"Really?" Anderson was surprised. "I had you down for an electrician."

"That was more a placeholder," Harvey admitted. "I play piano and do a bit of arranging."

Anderson shook his head. "I'd never have guessed; the things you learn about folk in a life raft..."

"I mainly play jazz," Harvey said, "though that might not go down too well with our friends."

Anderson nodded. "Better play it safe."

Harvey cleared his throat and began to sing.

"Underneath the lamplight, by the barrack gate..."

Both Germans showed surprise and the larger one might have been growing angry once more.

"Darling, I remember the way you used to wait."

Anderson smiled encouragingly but there was definitely some discontent at the other end of the float.

Harvey stopped. "I'm not sure they're the right words," he said.

"But if they don't know any English..." Anderson began, before noticing a new look that was now on both Germans' faces. Harvey pursed his lips.

"Cripes, I think I might have upset them."

The larger man leant forward and took a deep breath. And then, in a passable baritone, he also began to sing.

88

"Vor der Kaserne, Vor dem großen Tor.
Stand eine Laterne, Und steht sie noch davor."

Anderson and Harvey immediately joined in and, though the words were as different as the key, the song eventually came to an end with smiles from all.

"I think that might have worked," Anderson said as the larger German, clearly something of an enthusiast, began another song. This was strange to both Englishmen, but the man sang it well and finished to a generous round of applause.

"Guess it's your turn again." Anderson was looking to Harvey but before the telegraphist could reply, another sound made itself known.

And this time it was not from the dinghy itself, but further off. In the far distance, the sound of engines could be heard. They were getting closer and must be from some form of aircraft.

"Can't see a thing," Anderson sighed, as all four began to search the clear blue sky.

"Nor me," Harvey agreed.

And then, at a cry from one of the Germans, their potential rescuer was spotted.

"Coming over the French coast." Anderson was following his host's excited pointing. "But very definitely heading this way; I guess we've been seen."

"Can you tell what it is?" Harvey asked.

"I can," Anderson said after a pause. "And it looks like one of theirs..."

* * *

194 was traveling at speed and the feeling of anticipation mingled with relief was almost too much for Harris to bear. Not so very long before, Penrose had reported a potential sighting at the very edge of his sector. The area was more than three miles from where Harris had been searching yet he immediately set off in that direction.

It was probably nothing; Penrose had yet to qualify his initial signal and, though proving to be a solid enough chap, was still relatively new. Yet the hopes continued to rise and, as the gunboat thundered over the grey waters, Harris began to fidget like a child. A whistle, barely noticeable above the noise of racing

Packards, came from the W/T office speaking tube and Harris easily beat Milner in answering.

"What is it, Tel'?"

"More from *98*, sir." It was yet another voice; their current telegraphist was a temporary man pulled from the reserve pool though he seemed to know his job well enough. "Seems the sighting is a dinghy, but it does have men aboard."

Not so good; Harris felt his spirits drop as he replaced the voice pipe's cover.

"They may have met with others," Milner shouted and, though a possibility, Harris thought it unlikely. However, it looked like someone needed picking up and, even if it wasn't Anderson, he supposed it would not be a total waste of time.

"There's a plane, sir!"

This time it was Thompson, in the port turret. The man was pointing slightly off their port bow and roughly in the direction Penrose's craft was heading.

That put a different light on matters; an enemy plane in the area would make any rescue more complicated, though not impossible, and probably meant *194* must stand off to provide cover while Penrose did the deed.

Harris collected the Tannoy handset and clicked it on. "Stand to, all gunners; suspect plane in sight." They really had no choice – it was a necessary diversion, yet still he had to ignore an inner feeling that, by abandoning their own sector, they may be heading away from Anderson. "Wait for positive identification but prepare to fire."

Milner drew alongside and clearly wished to speak, although Harris ignored him. *194* was doing what she did best. At her current rate she would soon be there and, if a wild goose chase, it wouldn't take that much longer to see them back on their correct station. But until then he needed nothing else to fill his mind, and certainly not conversation.

* * *

"That's probably an Arado," Anderson announced. Both men had been watching the image change from a simple grey dot to something with real form and colour. The latter was a dark, solid green rarely seen in British aircraft and the fact that it had come from the enemy coast was equally significant. But the two long floats running under the fuselage were the final clincher.

"Do you think they'll pick us up?" Harvey asked.

The Germans were talking excitedly and had no eyes for them, so Anderson felt able to discuss the situation.

"I doubt it, there probably wouldn't be room. But they'll be calling up help. You can expect an E-boat or something similar presently."

Anderson's tone was level, although inwardly the disappointment was starting to grow. To have survived so long in the water after falling from a speeding boat was remarkable enough – had it happened in winter both would have been dead within minutes. And then to chance upon other survivors in a dinghy large enough to take them had been a definite stroke of good fortune. But now it seemed their luck was at an end; soon they would be collected like so many other prisoners of war, only to see Blighty again if Britain were able to win this stupid fight.

The taller German began to wave at the oncoming plane while his friend collected the water bottle and treated himself to a hefty swig. Then, on noticing the British, he gave a smile and tossed the flask across. Anderson caught it in one hand and removed the cork before passing it to Harvey.

"Maybe it won't be so bad," he said.

"Maybe not," Anderson agreed. "And it looks like we've already made a couple of friends."

* * *

"Four men in a dinghy," Milner reported. "Though it ain't a Q-type – too short and far more rounded."

Harris had already come to a similar conclusion and felt no need to comment. The colour and shape pretty much ruled out any English being aboard. It would be a German bomber crew, probably heading back after causing no end of carnage on the mainland, and he had interrupted his search for Anderson to save them.

But what of the aircraft? Harris raised his glasses to the dot now approaching the French coast. The German seaplane made off as soon as the two British launches appeared, though it would doubtless have reported their presence, and probably summoned

91

either naval or air support to disrupt their search further. Perfect.

"Penrose is picking the survivors up now." The young man paused for a moment, and when he spoke again it was with much more care. "And his lot seem mighty pleased about something..."

Harris could see that as well and, for once, was in complete agreement with Milner. *98* had closed with the dinghy and one of its occupants was already on board. And rather than being treated with the caution expected when collecting prisoners of war, Penrose's seamen seemed to be greeting him like an old friend.

It was all very confusing.

Chapter Ten

Anderson could hear Harvey singing softly to himself as he opened *194*'s wheelhouse door. As the gunboat's first lieutenant, and due shortly to become her commanding officer, he had much to do, but it would be worth spending a few minutes with the telegraphist, considering what they had been through together so recently.

The song stopped abruptly as Anderson looked in at the W/T office, and Harvey stood up at his desk.

"Good morning, sir – sorry about that, I didn't think there was anyone about."

"Not at all, and please sit." Anderson crouched down to be on the same level. "How's your hand?"

Harvey glanced at the light bandage.

"Mending fine, sir. It was a shallow cut, and the seawater cleaned it out nicely. They reckon I can make do with a plaster before long."

"And the piano; are you still able to play?"

"Even with the bandage," Harvey grinned. "Luckily it's the left – bass is less demanding."

"I suppose so. I remember you liking jazz, are you in a band?"

"There's one in town. I sit in when I can – when leave allows that is," he added quickly.

"I was always an Ellington man, though some of Miller's recent stuff is good."

"Too sweet for me," Harvey said. "And way too orchestrated. I'm more into small bands and a slightly freer sound. If I could, I'd like to run my own outfit, though at the moment..."

"War changes everything," Anderson agreed. "But that's where you're heading, when this lot is over, I mean?"

"I'd like to, sir."

"Well, I wish you luck, and wanted to thank you; there are few I'd have preferred to share a dinghy with."

"It was quite an experience," Harvey agreed.

"Oh, I meant to say," Anderson was standing now and had been about to go when the thought occurred, "I found out a little

93

more about those Jerrys."

"The one's in the raft?"

"That's right. Bomber crew, it seems. Their plane was damaged over England and forced to ditch; they were the only two that survived."

Harvey nodded, apparently satisfied. "Explains the larger float," he said.

"I must say I didn't think they could be navy," Anderson added. "They weren't dressed like it."

"I suppose not, sir. But then sailors wear all sorts of strange stuff." He looked pointedly at Anderson, currently wrapped in an Army greatcoat, and grinned.

"They do indeed," Anderson agreed, then paused for a moment. "But would it have made any difference if they'd been seamen?" he asked.

"I don't see why it should. We didn't get to speak much, but they treated us well, considering we're supposed to be enemies."

"Maybe," Anderson said. "But then they were returning from a bombing run; a few hours before they'd have been knocking the hell out of some part of town, destroying buildings, homes, even people."

"Do you think they intended to kill people?" Harvey asked.

"Probably not," Anderson said. "I expect it was just what they'd been detailed to do, in the same way we're ordered to attack a convoy."

"And when that happens, is it the crew you're trying to kill?"

"No." Anderson shook his head. "No of course not; it's the ship, always the ship."

Harvey sat back in his seat. "It's strange, we understand what we're fighting for, but very few know exactly who we're fighting against: what the average German is really like."

"But it's not them we're fighting," Anderson said, "it's their leaders and the politics they support."

"Absolutely," Harvey agreed, "and yet it's the average German that always seems to get killed."

Anderson grinned. "I'm learning more about you all the time," he said.

"I'm just a radio op, sir. I don't have to fire a gun, but I do get to listen in to enemy wireless transmissions. Not much makes sense as I don't understand German, but they do sound kind of normal – almost like us."

"I'm sure most will be, and probably about as keen to fight."

"So really the only difference between a friend and an enemy is the circumstances?"

"And possibly their leaders?" Anderson chanced.

Harvey gave a sudden grin. "And for all we know, some might even like Glenn Miller," he said.

* * *

"Frank, you have to do something."

Joyce's voice sounded so strained he hadn't recognised it at first. And it wasn't just the tone; the NAAFI phone lines had been down for almost a week and, during that time, her manner had altered as well.

"They came a few days ago. I sent you messages by the Welfare but didn't hear nothing so they couldn't have got through."

Thompson still had the yellow slips in his pocket and was about say something in reply, but Joyce was on a roll.

"Ted was with them – you remember him? And Charlie, though they had a couple of others as well; men I didn't know and not the sort I wanted in my home."

That was to be expected; Granger would have got Thompson's letter a week or so back and was not the kind to let grass grow under his feet. Which was one reason why Thompson had been keeping his head down. They'd had regular evening passes while *194* was in dock but he'd remained on base and considered it fortunate indeed there'd been no phone lines. Once more he opened his mouth to speak, but Joyce was still talking.

"An' they moved in," she said. "With me, in my house! I said you wouldn't like it, and they just laughed."

Thompson had expected that as well.

"Two of them took the attic flat, but Ted and Charlie started off in one of the other bedrooms. They moved our bed downstairs to the dining room for me, but I still don't like it, Frank, not one bit!"

No, he hadn't supposed she would, but Joyce would be

reasonably safe with Granger's men – as long as they kept away from the booze.

"Then they started turning up with all sorts of wood and stuff and began working on the upstairs rooms."

Yes, that was also what he expected.

"They've divided them up, made narrow little cubicles in each, with a sort of corridor connecting." She was slowing down now so Thompson thought he might get a word in.

"What about her downstairs?" he asked. "Noticed, has she?"

"Mrs Donaldson? I should say, and she weren't happy," Joyce replied. "Must have heard the noise or seen all their comin's and goin's. Struck up something rotten she did."

Thompson couldn't see Granger's lot being intimidated by an old woman and was soon proved correct.

"Anyways, two of them said they'd sort her out. I called later to see if everything was alright, only she wouldn't open the door."

"So, where are they now? Have they finished?"

"The upstairs, yes, and I'm comfortable enough in the dining room."

"And what exactly have they done?" he asked.

"Just the partitions really, lots of funny little rooms; don't make sense."

It did to Thompson: perfect sense.

"Though then they said they were going to do the whole house! I told 'em you'd have something to say about that, an' they laughed a bit more."

Taking over the entire place was pushing it a bit, though it would secure a greater return for Granger, along with what should be a permanent job for him.

"You can find us somewhere else," he said.

"Somewhere else? But Frank, it's our home; our first home and they're ruining it!"

"Don't sound like it," Frank grunted.

"Well, it's not what I would have chosen, and I don't like having to share with four strange men, thank you very much."

That was going too far; Thompson accepted she was upset, but there was no need to start on him.

"Here, less of your lip," he said. "Charlie and Ted are

mates, and they came down 'cause I told 'em to."

"Told 'em? I don't understand."

"No, well you don't have to, see? It's man's business, keep your nose out."

"You might have told me."

"And I chose not to. Now shut it."

There was a pause and Thompson wondered if she was still on the line.

"Why are they doing it, Frank?"

"Like I say, man's business; don't concern you."

"But I got to feed them, and wash, and tidy up."

"And are they paying?"

"Oh yes, all the money I need though that's not a lot of good when everything's on the coupons."

"Then find yourself a spiv," Thompson snapped. "But make sure you treat them right; believe me, it'll be better for us in the long run."

With London now little more than a shell, Granger had been intending to spread out along the south coast for some time. Thompson's place would probably be his first acquisition and, if it worked out, the old man was likely to be generous. And if the first of many, Thompson would be firmly installed in the driving seat. However, were anything to go wrong, like Joyce putting her spoke in, it could be disastrous for them both.

"I'm not happy, Frank. Not happy at all."

"That's alright," he told her. "You don't have to be."

* * *

To those who did not know him, Bridger was behaving perfectly normally. Some might even say he had settled faster than any of the new intake at *Wasp*. His sense of humour had definitely developed if not improved but, however it was judged, he told a lot more jokes.

Yet Mitchel had known him longer and wasn't so easily fooled. And though their friendship had been forced upon them by the officer who paired them up at Whale Island, he was concerned.

It all started with their first, and to date only, kill in Coastal Forces. Aboard their previous ship, air attack was almost commonplace with he and Bridger responsible for more than their share of downed aircraft. Each event would normally be marked with a riotous night that made up for what it lacked in alcohol with raw enthusiasm. Yet nailing that Junkers had left a very different impression on the gunner.

Obviously, there was doubt about whether or not he should have ceased fire, though nothing had come of that; no official inquiry, not even a private word from one of the officers. And when Bridger appeared to have forgotten, Mitchel honestly considered the matter to be at rest.

But of late he had been less sure, and that last encounter, when Bridger's shots flew wild and the E-boat came close to accounting for them, almost convinced him.

Ostensibly he was the same Alec Bridger. There'd been countless firing drills since and all had gone swimmingly, while only an absolute pedant could complain about a mate telling a few jokes or acting the fool. Still, there remained something odd about the fellow, something Mitchel did not like, yet nothing that could be put into words an officer, or a medic, would understand. And if he were to report his mate, where would that leave them as a team that relied so heavily on trust?

Whatever, until he could think of some way around the dilemma, Bridger would remain in charge of the gunboat's main armament. And, Mitchel had to admit, it frightened him.

* * *

"She's finally here," Harris announced as he caught up with Anderson outside the officers' mess. "Came in this morning with a transit crew and moored in one of the Pen's temporary berths."

"Good to hear," Anderson beamed. "I guess that means I finally get my hands on *194*?"

"All in good time, Number One, all in good time. The new boat still needs snagging and ordnance can't fit her out until the end of the week."

"So, I've got to put up with you as my CO for a while longer?" It was not such a terrible prospect.

"And I shall expect you to treat me with the same respect and deference," Harris grinned in reply. "Care to look her over?"

"Indeed, I've not had the chance to see a MkV close up, but shouldn't Milner?"

"He's already down there and will have his work cut out for the next week or so if I'm any judge. Come on, Number One, let's take a gander."

Anderson grinned. "Right you are, sir, though you'd better stop calling me Number One."

* * *

Thompson might have confined himself to barracks, but Nolan had work to do ashore and was spending every available hour off base. The library was almost finished, just a touch more sanding and he could start on the varnish, though there was plenty more for him to do and he was pleased to be of service. Despite being raised a Catholic, Nolan had long since abandoned the formal world of bells and smells, so it was strange that the work he did for the sisters always left him with a feeling of fulfilment. Were he to remain in Dover there was much more he might achieve, and he was thinking of this when the army officer approached him in the street.

Nolan gave the customary salute as they passed, although it soon became clear the young subaltern wanted something more than simple respect.

"I say, Sailor!"

The Liverpudlian stopped and turned.

"I need change for an important call," the officer told him. "Can you split a half-crown?"

Nolan relaxed and reached into his pocket. "I think I might at that," he said, "give us a mo'."

"Give you a mo'?" Although roughly Nolan's age, the subaltern's bearing and manner were of a totally different generation. "Do you realise who you're speaking to?"

The seaman paused in his search. "Beg pardon?"

"I am an officer of the King; you will address me as sir."

Nolan blinked. "Sir."

"And stand to attention; don't they even teach you nautical types the basics?"

99

Withdrawing his hand, Nolan straightened himself sufficiently although his stance remained decidedly casual.

"Now I need at least six coppers." The officer held up a large silver coin. "So as many as you have, the rest can be in sixpences and shillings."

Nolan shook his head. "Sorry, can't help you there," he said. "Ain't carrying a penny in change." And then he added, "Sir."

* * *

"Let go for'ard, let go stern rope, hold your after spring."

It would be a significant night, and one to remember for the rest of his life. Anderson had known it was coming and thought himself prepared yet, as he saw 194 from her berth for the last time under Harris' command, he still felt oddly emotional.

"Slow astern starboard, stop starboard, slow ahead starboard."

They were to supplement a small convoy's regular protection and 194 would not be alone. Every boat in Harris' flotilla had been deemed operational, while there would also be at least two corvettes as well as a minesweeper from the permanent escort. And their particular sector would not be long – just as far as Ramsgate, where a squadron from HMS *Badger* would take over. But however mundane their duty, the occasion was bound to be memorable.

Of course, it would not be the last time he served with his old captain; 194 would remain under Harris' overall control. As Flotilla Leader, the old man would also be hosting pre-mission briefings along with the inevitable post-mortems that followed. And Anderson would have to be sure 194 performed as well under his command as she had when Harris had charge; however trusting their relationship, he was not one to play favourites.

"Slow ahead port, take her down, Cox'n."

And, with 320, Harris' new command, to lead them, the missions should become more adventurous. The MkV was hardly any larger than the majority of the flotilla, and neither could she beat most for speed. But with a forward-facing two-pounder, twin 20mm Oerlikons, two Lewis 303s, and even a Holman projector, she packed a greater punch. More significantly, she was due to be fitted with the latest RDF set, so no more groping about in bad weather. Harris would lead them straight to the enemy, then just as directly home, while doubtless checking each member of the flotilla maintained their correct station throughout.

"Last time, Number One." Harris repeated Anderson's earlier thoughts as he clambered up the wheelhouse ladder.

"Indeed, sir."

"Been quite a journey, you and me."

"I guess it has."

"Must say, it's been good having you as my second in command, though it looks like Milner will make a fair fist of it."

"I'm sure he will." Those last words were true. Despite his initial awkwardness, the young sub-lieutenant was shaping up nicely and, with some subtle advice from Anderson, had made a good start in fitting out Harris' new command.

"I hope you get someone as good, though Brooks seems to have been a trifle lax on that front."

"There's talk of a new man though some problem with his transfer I gather," Anderson said. "Another RNVR, currently in minesweepers."

"Which seems as good a start as any," Harris commented. "And if he turns out half as good as you did, there'll be no problems at all."

Anderson went to reply, but somehow a simple 'thank you' seemed inadequate, and he remained silent.

* * *

"Alright, Alec?" Mitchel checked and received a cheeky grin in return.

"Aye, reckon so."

"Think we'll meet any action?"

"Maybe." The gunner slapped their Oerlikon affectionately. "Though if we do, we'll be ready for it."

"That's good," Mitchel said, though he remained uncertain.

"Here, Mitch." Bridger jumped suddenly as if stuck with a pin. "Did you hear the one about the monks and the barrel?"

* * *

It may have been a simple enough detail, but the weather was definitely turning against them. Almost as soon as the convoy was sighted off Beachy Head, and Harris' force relieved a training flotilla from HMS *Hornet*, the cloud that had been darkening the sky for some time began to send sheets of solid rain down on the unhappy cluster of shipping.

"In a week or so's time, this won't mean a thing." Harris was having to shout, though *194*'s engines barely gave a rumble at so plodding a pace. The rain created far more of a racket and even made odd popping sounds as it struck their heavy rubber ursulas. "With RDF we'll be able to keep track of everyone *and* watch for Jerries hiding in our path."

In the current circumstances that sounded good indeed, Anderson decided. Since falling from *194*'s stern he had taken to wearing a lifejacket at all times, even on the least adventurous coastal exercises but, though Harris must have noticed this and shown restraint enough not to comment, the old salt continued to shun such things.

"It's no good, Number One, I can't stand this pace," Harris continued. "What say we check out the head of the convoy?"

Anderson made no comment. Experience had taught him this was not so much a question, more a statement of intent. But he, too, was getting tired of the constant wallowing of a gunboat off the plane and when Nolan eased forward on the throttles, and they rose up to relative stability, it was indeed a relief.

They passed the line of coasters close by, provoking an eclectic mixture of waves and shaken fists that barely caught their attention, eventually drawing level with the leading corvette.

"Queer looking barge," Harris shouted. "Can't make more'n sixteen knots, yet they send them across the Atlantic."

Anderson also considered the vessel. With similar lines to a deep-sea whaler, the little ships were rumoured to be built in under five months and, though lacking in substantial weaponry, had already proved deadly to the more warlike U-boats.

"I can see why Milner opted for Coastal Forces," Anderson said.

"And he seems to be settling," Harris replied.

"Indeed, he does."

Anderson was privately pleased the young sub-lieutenant had remained ashore to see to the new boat. It felt good to end his long association with Harris as it had started, with just the two of them.

There was a whistle from the W/T office speaking tube and Anderson answered.

"Tel's patching through an R/T from the escort leader," he said, with a nod towards the warship. Instantly the bridge repeater came alive with the scratchy buzz of a low-powered transmission.

"Is there a problem, *194*?"

Harris picked up the handset. "Not as such, sir, we just felt the need to stretch our legs."

"Very good." It was an elderly voice, doubtless yet another RNR officer called back for the duration; there would be little he had not seen, and probably done. "Well, if you've so much energy you might want to check out a suspicious contact."

Harris swapped a grim smile with Anderson. "Happy to, sir; can you give me a direction?"

"Our RDF showed it to the northeast, but only for a second. My number one's having nightmares about a bunch of E's hiding behind Dungeness, but then he always was the excitable type."

"It's the nature of the job, sir," Harris agreed with a wink at his second in command.

"If you truly want to burn some of that precious fuel you may as well put his mind at rest."

"We'll certainly take a look."

"Very good, *194*, but not too close, eh? If E-boats really are sheltering, I'd rather not learn about it from a gunboat brewing up."

"We'll do our best to see you don't," Harris said.

"Shall I plot a course to see us around Dungeness?" Anderson asked as Harris replaced the handset.

"Do that, but what our friend said makes sense: not too close."

Anderson turned to go but Harris called him back.

"One more thing, Number One."

Anderson waited.

"Better take your lifejacket off when going below."

"Really, sir?"

Harris nodded wisely. "Otherwise, you won't feel the benefit when you come back."

103

Chapter Eleven

They were less than two miles off, yet, such was the visibility, only the vaguest outline of the Dungeness promontory could be made out.

"I could do with it easing just a bit," Harris said and, once more, it was the rain that forced him to shout; *194*'s engines were barely ticking over.

Anderson agreed, though it was strange to hear his captain complain about something they had no control over: usually he was more phlegmatic.

"Do we go in closer?" he asked, but Harris shook his head.

"Not from this direction; let's gain a bit more sea room and have a proper look at St Mary's Bay. Take us to starboard, 'Swain, half speed."

Nolan obediently brought the boat back up onto the plane, then eased her steadily over until Dungeness, and more significantly the dark patch of water it protected, was being left in their wake. Both Anderson and Harris continued to look, but nothing of note was revealed.

"If Jerrys are hiding, they're making a darn good job of it," Anderson said.

"Alright, that'll do." Harris had turned to Nolan. "Bring her round again and we'll lie cut for a while."

The boat came to rest with her bows pointing directly at the shore, though the current soon began to sweep her about.

"What do you think?" Harris asked and Anderson inspected the suspect area once more. *194* must have been a good three miles offshore, though the atrocious weather made it seem further and, with the blackout strictly enforced, the nearby land might have been deserted.

"Nothing, I'm afraid, though that doesn't mean they aren't there."

Harris nodded: he was in total agreement. The gentle bay stretched from Dungeness to Folkestone and was known to be shallow. Even light craft like E-boats could find themselves in trouble if they closed to less than a mile off, yet that still left plenty of room to hide several of the deadly vessels.

The British merchants would shortly be rounding Dungeness; perfect prey for a pack of enemy torpedo boats, yet all those aboard *194* could do was wallow in the swell and watch.

"It's no good," Harris said at last. "We'll have to move in and give it a thorough survey."

Again, Anderson could only agree, yet the prospect of playing blind man's buff with what was bound to be a vastly superior force did not appeal.

"Fire her up, 'Swain," Harris added, "and eyes peeled everyone!"

* * *

Stationed aft, as they were, little was required of Mitchel and Bridger. And with Thompson and Daly in their turrets, both officers on the bridge and Nolan at the helm, there was really no call for additional lookouts forward. Besides, leaving their posts while at action stations was a serious offence, and a watch must always be maintained aft in case an enemy decided to attack from the sea.

But Bridger was not watching, instead he had launched into yet another tirade of jokes that seemed every bit as pointless, humourless, and unnecessarily crude as when Mitchel heard them the first time. The loader sighed.

"Can it, Alec!"

His mate paused on the approach to a punch line. "What's that?"

"Shut up, you're giving me grief!"

"What do ya mean?"

"I mean I'm sick to death of your constant prattle." Mitchel was staring at the sodden deck, although he could feel the gunner's eyes on him. "It's cold, wet and we're a long way from home, can't you give it a moment's rest?"

"I were only trying to be cheerful, Mitch."

"Is that right?" He looked up, fixing his mate with his eyes. "So why now?"

"What do you mean?"

"Why suddenly become the comic?"

Bridger shrugged. "We got nothing else to do, an..."

"I'm not just talking about this very second, it's all the time; in the dorm, at the NAAFI, when we're in the bog – you never bleedin' stop!"

"It helps," Bridger said.

"Helps what?"

"Helps me get a grip on things." Bridger was speaking softly, and the rain hammered down all around, yet Mitchel caught every word. "I never needed to before," he continued, "but on the old *Makua* it were different."

"I don't see how."

"She were bigger, there were more of us."

"More?"

"More guns... more men, I guess. She didn't seem so exposed. So flippin' weak."

"You've had plenty of time to get used to it." This was not the right occasion, and Mitchel was beginning to regret even starting the conversation, although he did recognise its importance.

"I never have," Bridger confessed. "It were a bad start."

"You mean shooting down that bomber?"

"That's just it, I don't know I did; I think I may have hit the other boat an' all. Honestly, Mitch, I'm not sure of anything no more."

Even in the poor light, Mitchel could see nothing but desperation on the gunner's face and a wave of understanding washed over him.

"You didn't do nothing wrong. The worst that can be said is it were an accident."

"Accidents come from people making mistakes."

"Maybe so, but we're doing a bloody hard job. Everyone makes mistakes, from the captain downwards. Why should you be any different?"

Bridger shrugged but said nothing.

"They've stuck us back here, given us a bloody great gun and sent us out in the worst possible conditions: we're gonna get it wrong occasionally. What do you think you are, some sort of hero?"

"I'm no hero," Bridger said. "I'm cold, tired, and I'm frightened. Frightened of the Hun, frightened of the boat brewing up, frightened of falling overboard like Harv' an' the Jimmy.

106

Frightened of making another mistake..." There might have been a sob, in such a downpour Mitchel could not be sure. "It's gone on too long, Mitch, I can't take it no more."

"Then it'll have to end," his loader told him. "Navy got procedures for everything; you won't be the first."

"You think I can really get out?"

"I'm sure of it, and I'll see you through if that's what you want."

"They won't ask about that bomber?"

"I don't think so," he said, "but even if they do, I'll sort that out an' all. I were there as well, remember?"

"I'd like that, Mitch, you're a mate."

"Maybe," Mitchel said. "Let's just get through tonight. And no more jokes, okay?"

* * *

194 was easing gently towards the shore, a solid line that was Dungeness to port and the invisible town of Folkestone further off to starboard. All three engines were running but at minimal revs and her hull, cumbersome and barely manoeuvrable at such low power, dipped and swayed horribly. Yet the attention of those on her bridge and in the turrets was set entirely on the approaching land.

"I don't want to bring her any closer," Harris told Anderson. Then, to Nolan, "Take us to starboard, 'Swain, we'll follow the shore for a while.

The turn was slow and vague. Even as she straightened, Nolan had to struggle to keep the gunboat on an even course, yet still the darkened bay was keeping her secrets.

Anderson turned back and looked at the headland they were slowly leaving behind. If his estimates were correct, the convoy should be in sight in less than fifteen minutes; they had that long to check the area was indeed clear.

And then suddenly it wasn't.

With a roar of diesels, a trio of E-boats burst through the deadly haze; light hulls cutting through the black waters as they made straight for the lone gunboat still stolidly heading in their direction. Without waiting for orders, Nolan spun the wheel to starboard while bearing down on the throttles; within seconds

194's hull had risen, and she was scurrying for safety.

Harris and Anderson watched in stunned silence. The coxswain's quick reactions had saved them; even now, lines of green tracer were playing about the waters *194* had so recently inhabited, and there was nothing further they could say to Nolan, or any of the gunners when it came to it. Even sounding the firing gongs would have been redundant; Bridger and Mitchel had been right on the ball and waves of red tracer were already sweeping back towards the oncoming enemy. Harris pulled himself forward and flipped open the W/T office speaking tube.

"Make to convoy, repeat Dover Command: 'have encountered E-boats off Dungeness.' Continue sending that until I tell you to stop."

He flipped the cover closed and glanced at Anderson; already they were drawing level with the tip of Dungeness and soon would be in clearer waters when it might be possible to shake off the trailing Germans. Yet tracer was starting to fly past; the E-boats were nibbling at their heels.

"Starboard five!"

Nolan obeyed without verbal response and the boat tipped slightly as she altered course.

"Midships – and five to port!"

Those at the Oerlikon would curse and every subsequent change must confuse them more. But a 20cm round could do little against the armoured prows of three more powerful launches; it was far more important that *194* avoided their heavier shells.

"Starboard five – hold it." He waited several seconds. "And back to port!"

Harris finally glanced back and was horrified by how close the danger had come. All three were continuing to fire and, so far, they had been lucky. But the E-boats were well within range and closing all the time; even with *194* running at maximum revs, the enemy had several knots in hand.

Ahead, and to the west, the convoy was due to round Dungeness, but there could be no immediate help, or distraction, from that quarter. Yet he had Anderson beside him; as Harris glanced in his direction the fellow gave a reassuring nod. They had been in difficult scrapes before; maybe this would become yet one more amusing anecdote, to be recited and repeated countless times in front of a late-night wardroom fire. He certainly hoped so.

* * *

Mitchel had no time to consider the reason, but Bridger was like a new man. Their 20mm shells were unlikely to worry an E-boat's armour, but red flashes were playing about the leading boat's bridge as if drawn to it.

The magazine needed changing. He whipped out the old and heard it clatter to the deck as he slipped in a new, with Bridger picking up the pace as soon as the lugs engaged. There was no way of telling what effect their shells were having, but no one could have done better, Mitchel was sure of that.

* * *

However, the German gunners were proving equally accurate. Anderson felt a series of jolts as more shells struck *194*'s topsides, although there was no reduction in the gunboat's speed and those at her Oerlikon were continuing to fire. Soon, when the lighter Vickers came properly into range, they would be joined by Thompson and Daly, though what use that would be against three seemingly impregnable E-boats was in doubt.

He looked forward again and to starboard where the convoy could finally be seen. Several smaller vessels had taken the lead and were making for them at maximum speed. It would be the rest of Harris' flotilla, Anderson decided. They must have been released to assist and a handful of gunboats would be of far more use than any stately old corvette.

Beside him, Harris had also noticed and immediately directed Nolan to steer for the oncoming boats. Both officers knew it to be a futile gesture, however; the enemy's aim was improving all the time; it could only be minutes – seconds probably – before *194* received a truly serious blow.

Yet when it came, Anderson barely noticed. The E-boats' secondary armament had also come into range and a spray of heavy machine gun fire raked *194*'s bridge, tearing the klaxon from its mount and reducing their screen to a shower of glass. But Anderson was not hit, Nolan remained untouched and the boat herself appeared otherwise undamaged. So when he looked to his left, it came as a shock to see Harris had collapsed and was lying in an untidy heap on the duckboards.

Anderson dropped to his knees. It was dark; little detail could be seen, yet the captain was clearly bleeding profusely.

The boat turned suddenly, then righted – Nolan must be continuing to dodge, or perhaps there was another reason, though Anderson hardly cared.

He slapped the weathered face, desperate for some form of response, but the eyes, though open, might have been made of glass and Harris' body was quite limp.

Several shattering blows struck *194* in quick succession. One of the engines started to race at impossibly high revs, while the boat herself began to lose way and flopped down from the plane. Someone close by was swearing and he could hear muffled screams from below, but Harris lay mute and lifeless, and Anderson knew it was finally over.

Chapter Twelve

Thompson opened his eyes and reached for the bedside travel clock. Just gone eight – late by service standards though incredibly early for someone at leisure, as he currently was. He looked across; Joyce had left but the bed was still warm. She would be making his morning tea, as had become the norm, and he rested back moderately satisfied.

That last, terrible, mission was now over two weeks in the past and Thompson, along with the rest of *194*'s lot, had been on leave pretty much ever since. Such a thing was customary, or so he understood. *194* made it back to Dover, courtesy of a tow by another gunboat, but was quickly judged unsalvageable and would probably be little more than a pile of partly used spares by now.

Which didn't bother Thompson unduly, he had never felt anything for the boat, or its captain, if it came to it. Despite his action station being barely eight feet from Lieutenant Commander Harris, the man always appeared remote. And, though it was probably a shame for anyone to die in such a way, Thompson could only feel grateful the E-boat's gunner had not strayed further and found him as well.

The rest of that night remained a blur; all Thompson could remember was a feeling of relief when the other gunboats joined them, which increased dramatically once the E-boats turned tail and ran. And he had learned much, the first lesson being the Navy was definitely not the place for him; the sooner he got out the better.

Exactly how remained a problem, though one he was confident of solving. Seeing that first gunboat blow had been a sobering enough experience but having his own almost shot from under him, as well as watching someone – however detached – meet his maker, proved the clincher. Then there was a more private revelation; something else he had learned in action that was probably just as life changing.

To that point, Thompson had never felt the need for a gun. He might have carried the odd blade, but firearms always remained a step too far; if a problem couldn't be solved by eighteen stone of British beef it probably wasn't worth the bother. His gunnery training, and what came afterwards, changed all that and properly introduced him to the wonders of modern weaponry.

The recent course at Whale Island included everything from pistols to fifteen-inch battleship ordnance though Thompson was mainly attracted to the lighter weapons, the kind he might find useful in civilian life. And his brief exposure to active service simply added icing to the cake.

His twin Vickers would never have a civilian role, yet the potent little beasts had taught him much. Principally, Thompson now knew himself capable of using such a thing, and not just in theory or on exercise: during the heat of battle and against flesh and blood opponents. He'd come close to downing that bomber on his first shout; even Jimmy the One said so. And though those E-boats had dealt his own craft a devastating blow, he'd not been backwards in returning the compliment. Even now he remembered the sensation of playing the lines of tracer over an enemy's prow. Whether he'd caused serious damage or injury would never be known, but the act was deeply satisfying. And knowing such a simple weapon could elevate him – an East End lad – to the level where he could wound something as complex as an aircraft or even a minor warship, had been an epiphany in itself.

From the kitchen came the sound of a rising whistle that fell away abruptly. Joyce would be in with his tea soon, and he rolled onto his back, ready to receive. As he did, Thompson noticed his arms, still impressive for a man of his age, although the belly before him showed proud above the level of his ribs. This, and other changes, had been noticed in the past and he knew the time when weight took over from muscle could not be far away. At which point his position as one of Mr Granger's heavies would take on a truer meaning.

He'd known others, former boxers or sportsmen, who outlived their strength and were forced to rely on bulk and reputation to carry out their duties. Well, he wouldn't be joining them, not since discovering something far more permanent. A decent gun in his pocket would make him invincible.

"Tea, love?"

Joyce had entered and was carrying two cups and saucers.

"Stick it down," he said, nodding towards the bedside cabinet.

To do so she had to walk past the end of their bed, where Thompson's feet extended proud of the mattress, but she managed without him having to move and soon returned to her own side.

"Nearly the last time," she told him through a smile. "You'll be back at your base tomorrow."

"Don't remind me."

"It's been nice having you here," she said. "And nice having the place to ourselves at last."

By the time Thompson was given leave, all of Granger's crowd had gone. But they'd done a neat job, and he and Joyce were comfortable enough sleeping in the dining room.

"You do like it here?" she checked. "Even after what Charlie and the others did to the upstairs?"

"I like it fine," he reached for his drink.

"Maybe so, but it weren't what I wanted," she said, before taking a sip from her own cup.

"Think yourself lucky you got a place at all," Thompson told her. On picking up his tea he had spilt some into the saucer which was now almost full.

"But I did find it," Joyce said. "An' I've been paying the rent."

"Just as it should be." On trying to tip the tea back into his cup, Thompson sent a good deal onto the bed linen. "Else you won't get me coming back when I'm on leave."

"Careful what you're doing, Frank, I got to wash them sheets."

Thompson glared in her direction. "That's how it should be an' all," he said.

* * *

"It's going to take a while." Brooks spoke with apparent knowledge though Anderson barely heard. "You were right to use all your survivor leave; did you go far?"

"My parents," he replied. It had been a terrible time and their trying to empathise only made matters worse, while Eve, the one person he wanted to confide in, had remained annoyingly out of contact throughout.

The day was hot enough to allow the base captain's office window to be open, yet Anderson gave a sudden shiver; he had not felt properly warm for some time.

"I did come back for the funeral," he reminded.

"Of course, I remember," Brooks said.

Anderson nodded, as did he.

The old country church had also been cold and many of the other mourners were unknown to him. Most civilians turned out to be friends of Harris' parents but several of the officers were also strangers, including one superannuated Rear Admiral who fell asleep during the sermon. Laura was there, of course, looking composed and almost severe. They had shaken hands, but she remained reserved and appeared to regard Anderson as if he were in some way responsible for Harris' death. And there had been others from the flotilla; mainly officers although Pickering and Daly showed up as well.

Little of the old boy came through in their various eulogies, yet the ceremony did serve a personal purpose for Anderson. As he walked away from the churchyard – not for him awkward conversations in a country pub over egg sandwiches and carrot cake – he was finally able to get one thing straight. Harris was gone. The mentor relied upon throughout his time in Coastal Forces would never return; from that moment it was up to him.

"Things will get better," Brooks told him. "But don't expect to forget, because you never will."

Anderson considered the face. Until then the base captain had been a remote figure; someone who only spoke with senior men, yet here he was, a real person and interested in him.

He remembered his old boarding school headmaster behaving in much the same way when a favoured uncle died. After breaking the news, someone Anderson respected and secretly feared accepted a nine year old's tears without censure, then went on to give comfort, and chocolate cake, with a parent's understanding.

"What's going to happen now, sir?"

Anderson knew it a foolish, and possibly unanswerable, question though Brooks seemed to take it in his stride.

"Well *194* is no more," he said, "though Lieutenant Commander Harris was her only serious casualty. The rest aren't due back until tonight but will probably want to stay together as a unit – it's normal in such cases. And I would equally expect them to accept you as their new commanding officer."

Although unable to fully appreciate the compliment, Anderson did feel a measure of warmth return.

"Whether you wish to continue with them is very much up to you, of course, but do bear in mind it was always going to be *194*'s last trip under Bob's captaincy," Brooks reminded. "You were to take them over and I still think you're ready for command."

It was not an opinion Anderson shared although he made no comment. Being back in familiar surroundings and mixing with those who knew Harris did feel surprisingly good. But to move on to a new boat and a new position would not be easy, and he wondered if being with men who had served aboard *194* would make it any more so.

"I'll be honest with you, Ian, I'm no stranger to grief myself," the base captain continued. "I'd suggest you have two options..."

The unexpected use of his first name surprised Anderson and he listened all the harder.

"You can remain in the past, reliving old times and wallowing in memories, or move on. At the moment the former may feel right, but I would urge you otherwise."

Anderson supposed he had a point, though exactly how to forget remained a mystery.

"So," Brooks said after a moment. "Why not hear about the vessel I have in mind?"

"Of course, sir; yes."

"I propose giving you MGB*320*."

"Harris' MkV?"

"It was to have been; she can be yours now."

Anderson shook his head. "But what about the flotilla? I heard someone else has taken it over."

"Indeed, Robson's in charge, though you won't be returning to it. Instead, I'd like to send you straight to HMS *Bee*."

"*Bee*?" The name was not familiar.

"It's the new Coastal Forces training establishment at Weymouth." The base captain's voice was decidedly matter of fact now. "It's being run by a Commander Swinley; an experienced chap though something of a stickler, or so I understand. Expect to remain there for at least five weeks and be prepared to jump about a bit."

It had been very much the same at *St Christopher*'s, although then Anderson had been new to Coastal Forces.

"Whether or not you decide to include *194*'s old guard, there'll still be a measure of recruiting as a MkV requires more men."

That also seemed reasonable although Anderson's doubts remained. A new boat – more than that, a new *type* of boat – was bound to take some getting used to. And he would be in command: a captain. He'd been ready enough to take on a known quantity in *194* when Harris was around, how would he cope without the older man's dry wit and inexhaustible knowledge? In his current state, Anderson felt simply returning to active service would be enough, yet he must integrate fresh men into the crew, and then go through what sounded like intensive training.

And there was still more.

"Of course, Milner'll be able to assist with the new men, and a few other things I've no doubt."

"Milner?" Now Anderson was really struggling.

"Alan Milner was to be Harris' first officer," Brooks reminded. "The fellow's been standing by *320* since she arrived and is willing to come along if you'll take him. That's something else you'll need to get used to: having a second in command."

Anderson had hardly thought of the young sub-lieutenant since the loss of *194* and didn't remember seeing him at Harris' funeral. And Milner was a straight striper – despite what Brooks might have been told, how would a regular man react to serving under a reserve officer?

"What I said still holds." Brooks might have been reading his mind. "You can choose pretty much whoever is willing, but he seems genuinely keen and has already taken the new boat out on a number of occasions."

"I understand." The man's experience of *320* would be invaluable, at least at first, and he really should not disparage the knowledge a Dartmouth graduate could bring to his new command. Yet however supportive Milner might turn out, Anderson knew he would find it hard not to suspect him of watching his every move, and maybe silently criticising.

"And after *Bee*?" he asked.

"Back here," Brooks replied. "If things turn out as we're hoping, you'll be assigned to a flotilla and can continue as before, though you'll be in the driving seat, of course. But first, you'll have to prove yourself."

Now Brooks' expression became more intense.

"And that does not just mean how you handle *320*. You'll be expected to leave *Bee* as a competent ship's master and a true leader of men. It was something Bob thought you capable of and I'm happy to back his opinion."

Put like that Anderson felt he had little choice, though the responsibility would be enormous.

"Can I think on it?" Anderson asked.

"Of course." And this time he noticed a twinkle in the base captain's eye while something of his old manner also returned. "But remember what I said about that choice; stay in the past or move on: only you can decide which."

"I understand, sir," Anderson said.

"And one more thing." Now Brooks was definitely smiling. "Commander Swinley is expecting you at *Bee* by the end of next week."

* * *

"Frank, there're some men to see you!"

Thompson looked up from the half-filled duffel bag that lay on their bed. Joyce had ironed his spare uniform, polished his boots and Blancoed the webbing. He only needed to pack everything away, yet whoever was interrupting him would get the sharp edge of his tongue.

"Who's that then?" he asked, returning to the front room. Then, on seeing Mr Granger, his expression softened considerably.

"Hello, Frank. Me and Charlie thought we'd drop by and see what the boys have made of the place."

"Of course, sir, make yourself at home."

But Granger already had; after a brief look around the Thompsons' front room, both visitors headed for the stairs that led to the upper floor.

Left alone, Joyce mouthed, "Why didn't you tell me?" before tossing the raincoat she had taken from Granger onto the settee.

117

"I didn't know myself," he shrugged. "An' less of your lip!"

"All very satisfactory." Granger's pot belly flopped over his belt as he trotted back down the stairs. "Boys have done a grand job. We should be in business in no time."

"And what sort of business might that be?" Joyce demanded, while Thompson took a sharp intake of breath. Granger considered her.

"That's none of your concern, Mrs Thompson," he said. "Keep your eyes closed and mouth shut and all will be fine."

"I was wonderin' if Joyce here might get involved?" Thompson chanced.

"Involved?" she seemed horrified, but Granger regarded the woman more closely.

"I'm not so sure about that," he said. "My clients are looking for a bit more in the glitz department."

"Glitz?" she exclaimed. "What sort of business you got in mind?"

Granger pulled himself up to his full height. "If you can't guess it's best you don't know." He was still assessing her and clearly yet to be impressed. "I suppose you might make yourself useful as a cleaner, or maybe some sort of cook, but frankly I don't like your attitude." He turned to his companion. "What do you think, Charlie? Shall we give her a chance, or the old heave-ho?"

"But this is my house! Tell 'em, Frank!"

"I'm sure we can sort this out, Mr Granger," Thompson said. "Maybe if we all have some tea; see to that will you, love?"

"I'm not makin' tea for no one," Joyce declared, "an' certainly not actin' as no cleaner. It were me what found this place, an' me what pays the rent. I never asked for all that stuff upstairs to be done an' as far as I'm concerned it can go. As can you!"

Granger smiled at Charlie. "I think we're being asked to leave!"

Thompson went to intervene, but Joyce was not to be placated.

"Damn right you are, and don't come back!"

"Alright, I've heard enough," Granger held up a hand, "and didn't come all this way to be messed about by no woman." He fixed Thompson with his eyes. "You'd better take your missis in hand. The pair of you have a day to clear out an' I don't want to see either of you here afterwards."

118

Joyce made for Granger but instead met the solid bulk of Charlie.

"Hang on," she said. "I'm the one who's got the arrangement with Mrs Donaldson..."

"Then we'll just have to make another," Granger told her.

She spun round to her husband. "Are you going to put up with him speakin' to me like that?"

Thompson's mouth opened, then closed.

"Frank knows what's good for him," Granger announced with a smile. "And so should you. Now we already have keys; if either of you are here when my lads come back it'll be the worst for you. Come on Charlie, there must be a decent restaurant in this godforsaken place."

"Well," Joyce said, hands on hips, when both men had gone. "I must say you were a proper let down!"

"Me?" With the immediate danger over, Thompson felt more in control. "Sounding off like that – what in heaven's name were you thinkin' of?"

"I was thinking of our home, Frank Thompson, which is more than you were!"

Her words hit a tender spot, though he was in no way placated.

"An' what good did it do us?" he demanded. "Now we got no place, and you'll have to start lookin' all over again!"

"Well, I won't do it," she declared. "I'm not usin' another penny of Dad's money to pay rent for your fat friends. You sort it out, I'll be on the first train back to Mum."

His self-respect now firmly back in place, Thompson grabbed her by the wrist.

"You'll do as I say!" Despite the anger, he could see a pleasing look of fear in her eyes.

"It's all right for you," she said. "You got somewhere to sleep tonight – and will be long gone when them goons come back!"

"Then you'd better find us a different billet first thing," he said. "And make sure it's every bit as good as this one!"

"Maybe I don't want to," she said. "Maybe I'd be better off back in London and a long way from you."

"Now look here," he said. "No one messes me about, least of all a woman!"

119

"No?" She laughed and he felt the rage grow. He raised his hand, expecting a return of that look but this time, rather than fear, he saw something else; something very different.

"Don't you dare, Frank Thompson," she told him. "Don't you bloody dare!"

* * *

It was their first morning together following fourteen days' survivors' leave and, after being brought up to date by one of Brooks' deputies in the ready room, most of *194*'s former crew had headed straight for the NAAFI. But though they were generally pleased at remaining together, the prospect of further training was not popular.

"Weymouth!" Bridger exclaimed. "That's miles away!"

"Can't fault the lad for geography," Nolan muttered.

"It's a training depot," Harvey explained. "We're gettin' a new boat, an' they're going to show us how to use it."

"Sure, but it won't make any difference to me," Daly said. "Gun's a gun wherever they stick it."

"You could say the same about most of us," the telegraphist agreed.

"But there's the new skipper," Bridger said. "We'll have to get used to him an' all."

"He's our old Jimmy," Mitchel replied.

He had been watching Bridger intently. The pair spent their leave separately and he hadn't been sure his mate would even return. Yet the gunner seemed quite at home amongst the other ratings.

"Might be the same person, but it's a whole different position," Bridger added.

"Anderson'll be straight, so he will." Daly spoke with an element of authority. He had served aboard *194* longer than any present and was the only one to have been at St Nazaire.

"Aye, he's all right," Harvey agreed. After sharing a German dinghy with the officer, he knew him almost as well.

"Have to go a long way to better the old skipper," Nolan said. "Knew where you were with him. Always respectful, like."

"You'll know where you are with Anderson," Daly insisted. "And he's Wavy – a volunteer, like us."

"Yeah, but the new Jimmy ain't." Nolan again. "Straight striper and likely Dartmouth trained; everything'll be by the book an' I reckon we'll soon spot the difference."

"I've not had much to do with him," Bridger said.

"He came on a couple of earlier runs," Harvey said. "When we thought everyone were staying with the old boat once the skip moved on. Seemed reasonable enough, though I never reckoned our two were that fond of him."

"What, Harris and Anderson?" Mitchel asked.

"That's right," Harvey agreed. "There's no knowing how a college boy will like taking orders from a Wavy like Anderson."

"Officers arguing don't make for a happy ship," Bridger said.

Thompson had been watching, listening, but saying nothing. Granger's appearance the previous day, followed by that confrontation with Joyce, affected him more than he would have expected. Until then he'd let the men's conversation pass over him but when arguments were mentioned, it touched a nerve.

"An' what would you be knowing about officers' quarrelling?" Daly demanded.

"Bridger's an expert when it comes to arguments," Harvey said. "He starts them all the time."

The telegraphist's quip proved popular although Thompson was finding it hard to laugh.

"What's the matter, Thumps?" Harvey must have noticed this. "Look like you lost sixpence and found a penny."

"An' what would you have been doing to your paw?" Daly added.

Thompson flexed his fingers experimentally as his mind went back to the previous day.

"Bashed it on a door," he said.

The hand was only swollen; it should soon go down, then everything would be forgotten. Fortunately, the others soon lost interest allowing him to return to his shell.

"New boat'll mean a few adjustments for some of us," Bridger said. "You 'specially, Scouse."

"Not me, I can steer anythin' with a wheel."

"Well, Newman's lot'll have their work cut out," Harvey said.

"It's why they ain't here," Daly replied. "Sent them straight down to the new tub to get acquainted, so they did."

"Suppose that's important." Harvey again. "They got to get us to Weymouth after all."

"When we going?" Bridger asked.

"From what Smudger told us, pretty much straight away," Mitchel replied. "And should expect to be gone several weeks."

"Is it anywhere near Falmouth?" Daly asked. "Only I knows of a fine billet thereabouts."

"You're joking!" Harvey told him. "Weymouth and Falmouth aren't even in the same county."

"They just rhyme," Nolan added.

* * *

The MkV had been a fixture at the Pens for some time; Anderson even toured her several weeks before in company with Harris when he was to take her over. But now she would be his, and his alone, with no crusty old salt horse to remark or advise, he inspected the gunboat with far greater care.

Of roughly the same size as *194* and similarly driven, though, rather than being an American build, *320* would have come from a yard further down the south coast. That said, she lacked the prominent 'whaleback' common in British Power Boat vessels, though her hull had similar, graceful, lines. However, what immediately drew his attention was her main armament.

It was a Vickers quick-firing two-pounder; heavier than the Oerlikon *194* mounted and with a greater range. Yet the weapon's major advantage lay in its position. Until then the only forward-facing weapons Anderson was used to were half-inch machine guns; now he could approach a target properly armed. A two-pound shell was hardly heavy ordnance, though it should still do notable damage to surface craft and even be effective against shore targets.

His gaze moved back, noting the lack of turrets for machine guns, instead a twin Oerlikon had been mounted aft of the bridge. To either side of the wheelhouse lay a single depth charge, while two Lewis machine guns stood in their place at the stern, with a Holman projector between.

320 would still be outgunned by an E-boat, yet it remained a reasonable armament for the size of craft. Much depended on how she handled, and that was something he was keen to find out.

But before then he must become properly acquainted with his first officer. Anderson could see Milner from where he stood; the man was apparently waiting for him on the bridge and, even from such a distance, appeared every bit the archetypical Royal Navy career officer. He pursed his lips; there was so much to discover, and not all could be learned from a book. Anderson wondered for a moment if his old captain were ever this apprehensive and decided not. Harris was a professional seaman destined for command; his main concern would have been having a former geography teacher as his first officer. And now the situation was reversed that same ex-teacher would be playing the part of captain, with a Dartmouth-trained professional as his deputy. He sighed; at that moment Anderson could think of more appealing prospects.

Chapter Thirteen

"And that's about it, sir," Milner concluded.

He had finished his tour in the officers' wardroom, a tiny space set to port and immediately below the wheelhouse.

"I could rustle up some tea if you wish?"

"No, thank you, but let's sit awhile and you can tell me a little more about the boat."

Milner made himself comfortable at the other end of the small settee while Anderson leafed through 320's signing off papers and builders' observations. And he was undeniably impressed. Even as he found her, with RDF still to be fitted and lacking a full crew, 320 was a remarkable craft, yet one he felt he could handle, given the chance. But his second in command was proving almost as outstanding. They had met before, of course, when Milner was nothing more than an annoying know-it-all who would be taking Harris from him. Now Anderson could look through different eyes he was ready to change his opinion.

Though young, the lad had been at sea for almost a year and seen a fair amount of action. This might be his first posting in Coastal Forces, yet the time spent waiting for 320 to be commissioned was not wasted. He had clearly made a complete study of the marque and could speak eloquently about any aspect.

"Tell me about the engine tests," Anderson said, looking up from his reading.

"There have only been the rudimentary ones, sir," Milner replied. "I was waiting for a full crew to be appointed before taking her too far out. But new Packards are now tuned before installation and the CMM seems happy with them."

Anderson nodded knowingly as he returned to the papers. "And what model are they?"

"4M-2500." The answer came without hesitation, then Milner added, "Fed from five tanks mounted amidships, total capacity 2,600 gallons."

"Which gives us a range of..."

"Maximum six hundred nautical miles at fifteen knots, sir."

"That's very impressive," Anderson said, finally looking up. "I understand you were in corvettes before this," he added.

"Indeed, sir. I was third officer in a Flower Class."

"And did you like it?"

For a moment Milner's expression clouded. "That's not the word I would have chosen," he said. "We were on the east coast and, though not as bad as the Atlantic, saw a fair amount of action; you could say I learned quite a bit."

"From the other officers?"

"Mainly from the other officers." Now he was starting to relax. "They teach a lot at Dartmouth, but nothing prepares you for the real thing. And nothing is better than having someone more experienced alongside."

Anderson could only agree with that and was definitely warming to the new man.

"Flower Class, that would have meant two other officers?"

"Commissioned, yes, sir," Milner agreed. "Though we had a CPO who everyone reckoned must have sailed with Jellico."

"And he would have stood watch?"

"Yes, sir. There were three watchkeepers, and the captain joined whenever he was needed."

That was also customary, but Anderson was learning far more about the new man than when inspecting the boat.

"So, the CPO was regular Navy," he supposed. "What about your captain?"

"Naval Reserve," Milner replied. "He'd commanded a liner before the war. Number one was RNVR."

The fact that he volunteered that last piece of information without expression or emphasis told Anderson much.

"And did you get on, as a command group, I am meaning?"

"Oh yes, sir. I was only a midshipman for the first few months, but I crammed in quite a bit from them all. I only asked for a transfer because *Dalia* was due for an extended refit."

That was all proving very satisfactory, and Anderson was starting to wonder why he had been concerned. But Milner had more surprises to offer.

"I suppose you may have expected problems, what with me being a straight striper, sir?"

Anderson grinned; had he really been that obvious? "I thought you might want to do things by the book," he admitted.

"I come from a naval family," Milner said. "Dad served as a lieutenant aboard a dreadnought and his father skippered a tall ship, so I was always going to sea. But I'm the first regular."

"So your father was...?"

"RNVR, like yourself, sir. And, I have to say, he didn't always do things by the book."

"Indeed?"

"This is probably the right time to admit it's not just the boat I've been researching." Milner gave an awkward smile. "I've also done a fair bit of checking up on you as well."

That did come as a surprise. "And?" Anderson prompted.

"Well, I already knew you were at St Nazaire, and one of the few to have made it back."

Anderson nodded.

"But I wasn't aware *194* had been successful in other ways, along with the boat you had before."

"Both of which were captained by Lieutenant Commander Harris."

"Of course, sir," Milner agreed. "And, if you'll forgive me, he was not the type to suffer fools. If you were his first officer, I'll be proud to serve under you – book or no book."

* * *

"I found a place," Joyce informed Thompson the next morning. He'd called the phone box at the usual time, but it had taken three attempts spaced over several minutes before his wife answered and, even then, she sounded decidedly off key.

"What, like we had before?" he asked.

"Not even close," she said. "A bedsitter that'll work out almost as pricy."

"Never mind, it'll do till you can find something better."

"I got something better in London," she told him flatly. "My old room, and probably my old job."

"Now we discussed that," Thompson's voice rose slightly, and he added, "an' everything was sorted," more softly.

"You might think so, Frank Thompson, I ain't so sure."

"What do you mean by that?" He asked the question

without thinking and really didn't want to hear the answer.

"I ain't sure I want to be married to a man who won't stand up for his home, or his wife. An' I ain't got no time for bullies of any description."

"You don't know what you're talking about."

"It's the other way round if you asks me. Watchin' you kowtowing to that fat slob, then trying to take it out on me after; I tell you now, I'm not havin' it!"

"What do you mean? I didn't hit you," he protested.

"Only 'cause I ducked," she said. "So, you thumped the door instead and left a nasty mark – have you thought what you might have done if that'd been me?"

He had, but this was not the time to say.

"You don't understand," he said. "Granger's important."

"An' I ain't?"

It was something Thompson had only recently considered. "Of course," he said. "You're my wife."

"Maybe for now."

"Look, it's going to be different, Joycie, just wait and see." He cupped a hand around the receiver and, with his eyes firmly fixed on the customary petty officer, continued in a softer tone. "Navy's not for me; I'm gettin' out, soon as I can swing it."

"Oh yeah? Going to be that easy is it?"

"I'll find a way," he said. "But first I'm being posted."

"Posted? Where?"

"Can't say," he said, still watching the petty officer. "But it ain't far and I'll be back before long. Anyway, better give me your new address."

"Why would you be wanting that?"

"So I can write."

Thompson had a pencil and paper ready but there was a pause and then the pips began to sound.

"Come on, Joycie," he said. "I ain't got no more coppers."

"I'm not sure, Frank. Maybe you should send anything to my mother, she'll see it reaches me."

He went to reply but the pips continued and then came the dialling tone. For a moment he stared blankly at the wall before finally replacing the receiver and turning away. And there, right behind him, was the petty officer.

Thompson felt a moment of panic; exactly how much had

127

the PO heard and what would he make of it? But the man gave a knowing smile.

"Trouble at home?"

"Wives!" Thompson said, shaking his head in apparent disbelief.

"Tell me about it." The petty officer nodded in sympathy. "You only learn how marriage changes 'em after it happens."

* * *

"So, are you sticking with the Andrew?" It was the first time Mitchel was able to corner Bridger alone, although he'd already guessed the answer.

"I suppose so," the gunner replied. "After what you said, and then having two weeks to think further, I reckon it's worth another go."

"When them Es came for us, it were pretty hairy," Mitchel said, "but you did well."

"Maybe, but knowing I couldn't be blamed for that bomber, and there was a way out, made all the difference."

"You were being too hard on yourself."

"Aye, probably, but then we're doing a hard job," Bridger said.

"If ever you change your mind, I'll always listen."

"I appreciate that." Bridger smiled.

"Then we can go back to normal?" Mitchel chanced.

"I reckon so. Hey, did you hear the one about the nuns on the vegetable patch?"

* * *

Transferring the men to *320* was far easier than Anderson expected. After speaking with Milner, he returned to *Wasp* and summoned *194*'s former crew to the ready room where he met most for the first time since the night Harris died. A few – Pickering, Newman and Daly – Anderson had known for some time, the rest joined relatively recently but all appeared ready to follow him into the new boat. The only exception was Thompson, a man Anderson had yet to get to know, or like. Of them all, he asked the most questions and, on discovering they would remain

128

in Weymouth for over a month, showed any sign of disapproval.

The rest took it in good heart and might have been pleased at the prospect of a change of base. Daly especially asked about their accommodation, which drew a deal of amusement and Anderson guessed it to be a private joke.

Harvey completed a short course in RDF during his telegraphist training but was keen to know more and happy to take over those duties in addition to his wireless work. So, when Anderson reported to Brooks in the base captain's office, he was relatively optimistic.

"And you are happy with Milner?"

"Very, sir," Anderson confirmed. "It's early days yet, but I think we'll get along fine."

Brooks nodded approvingly. "I must say I'm relieved," he said. "It appears being a captain agrees with you." He referred to a sheet of paper in front of him. "Now you are still awaiting gunners for the Vickers two-pounder, other than that you can start working up."

"Will that be at Weymouth?"

"I should say not!" Brooks gave a light smile. "A lot has changed since you and Harris commissioned *194* and I'd like to think we're doing things a little more professionally now. There'll be enough to learn at *Bee* besides how to drive the boat. Get to sea as soon as you can and make any minor adjustments before seeing her down to Weymouth. If you start tomorrow, you'll have three days of sea time before you have to leave. With luck, your new gunners will have arrived by then, if not they can meet you at *Bee*. But don't waste a second; the forecast's good for tomorrow at least, after that we expect storms, which should give you some heavy weather experience. Try everything out in daylight to begin with but most of your work will be done at night, so make good use of that as well." Brooks considered him. "Think you can do that?"

"I'm sure I can, sir."

* * *

After speaking with their new captain, the men headed for the Camber to inspect *320*. Then, following a cursory glance all around, made for their own particular areas of expertise.

For Harvey, it was the W/T Office, and he was pleased to

see a slightly larger area was allocated and the two wireless sets already installed. He looked about approvingly; there was room for a decent-sized chair as well as shelf space, though much would be taken up by the RDF equipment due to be fitted when they reached HMS *Bee*. The prospect of running this, as well as keeping track of communications, was not exactly daunting; his brief exposure to what many now called radar had been encouraging and he was keen to learn more about the new technology.

Newman, Pickering, and Kipling were similarly impressed. All three of the gleaming Packards were indeed tuned although they had already made some minor adjustments. They too, would have more toys to play with; having an RDF set to power, as well as fifteen hundred pounds of forward-facing cannon, meant larger generators and a more complex hydraulic system, all of which still had to be fully investigated. And there was an additional engine; a ten horsepower Ford that could carry the gunboat at up to six knots in near silence.

Having to house this in a space hardly larger than they were used to would be inconvenient, but none of them were exactly heavyweights. Besides, the fresh asbestos covering the exhaust system and other hot surfaces had not even begun to flake, so it would be less dusty.

Nolan, too, was content. It was a larger bridge, slightly offset to allow for the port side passageway, and the gunboat had an over-sized spray rail that should keep much of the weather out. It was also good to note a full set of instruments mirroring those in the lower steering position; so no more peering down to the wheelhouse.

However, Thompson, and to some extent, Daly, were less impressed. Gone were their turrets that, though unlikely to stop anything larger than an airgun pellet, did at least protect them from a rising sea. Gone also were their powered mounts, along with the matched pair of half-inch machine guns they had both valued so much. Even their former positioning, aft of the bridge and high enough to give a commanding view of the action, had changed. Instead, they would be expected to stand, unprotected, at the very stern of the boat where a couple of ancient Lewis 303s awaited them.

"Last time I saw anythin' close they was in a museum," Thompson commented as he inspected the weapons.

"Aye, nothing like the range or power of the old Vickers," Daly agreed. "An' look where we's supposed to stand!" he continued.

Thompson didn't have to; even in harbour, their current perch felt vulnerable with barely a foot of deck and minimal freeboard between them and the oily water below. How it would be with the boat travelling at speed was too terrifying to imagine.

"Don't feel safe to me," he said.

"Sure, an' didn't we lose the Jimmy an' Tel' in just such a spot?" the Irishman agreed. "An' we got this old flinger to play with."

Thompson had failed to notice the contraption sitting between their two gun positions.

"I never seen the like," he said.

"An' why don't that surprise me?" Daly snorted. "It's a Holman Projector, and rubbish by any other name; blessed things should have been scrapped years back."

Thompson was examining the device more carefully. It appeared something between a mortar and a radio receiver with no magazine or obvious firing mechanism, while a pneumatic pipe ran from the breach to the deck below.

"May be a sight more modern than what we trained on," Daly supposed, "though I still say it'll turn out as useful as a chocolate teapot."

"How does it work?" Thompson asked.

"Compressed air." Daly kicked at the rubber pipe. "Fires grenades or anything you care to load it with."

"At what?"

Daly shrugged. "Attackin' aircraft; that's the general notion."

Thompson nodded.

"Mind, the barrel's no more'n a pipe and as loose as they come, so there's no telling where the bomb'll end up."

"Does it work?"

Daly shrugged. "Some say, though I've never known it bring anything down. Best use is for lobbing spuds at y'r mates, though I heard some poor sailor was knocked for six so s'pose it can do damage. Ask me, the space would've been better spent on a single decent Vickers," he added. "Then there'd be no chance of either of us hitting the other."

131

That was something Thompson had not considered. He looked back at what would be his Lewis. It had a manual mount that moved easily enough, but yes, Daly was right; no guard – nothing prevented it from bearing on the other gun, or the rest of the boat if it came to it.

Which felt like the last straw. They were asking him to take over a weaker weapon in a more exposed position along with the added responsibility of something that flung vegetables at attacking aircraft. And if he wasn't washed over the side, there was every chance of being gunned down by his oppo. He had to get out. The only questions were when? And how?

* * *

Seaman Gunner Mark Hickman clambered from the train and dumped his duffel bag on the platform.

"So, this is Dover." He glanced about at the grey, dusty buildings, the canopy with several sections missing and a pile of rubble dumped, for no apparent reason, next to the gentleman's toilet. "Can't say I'm over impressed."

"Seems like any other station," Adam Peters replied as he also exited the train. The couple were paired up many weeks before at gunnery school, Hickman's steady and reliable loading being a perfect balance to Peters who was an especially solid gunner. Together they came close to receiving top marks in most aspects of what had been alien work at first – Peters having been a groundsman, while Hickman made his living in the butchery trade. And due to spending so much time in the other's company, a friendship had developed, although not one either expected or especially looked for.

"They say the base is nearby." Hickman collected his bag and slung it over his shoulder. "Do you want to take a look around the town or make straight there?"

"We'll go to the base," Peters said, and it was clearly not a subject for discussion.

"Something I wanted to mention," Hickman began, after showing his travel warrant to the ticket collector. "When we gets to HMS *Wasp*..."

Peters waited.

"You won't mention anything about gumboots."

132

"Gumboots?" He might have been feigning ignorance.

"Yes, you know," Hickman continued. "When they were looking for Coastal Forces volunteers…"

"And you misheard?"

"That's right, I misheard," the loader agreed. "We'd just had two hours live practice an' I were a bit Mutt and Jeff."

"I remember." Peters gave a wicked smile.

"Well, you won't say anything, will you?" Hickman asked.

"I don't see it's worth mentioning," Peters said. "An easy mistake: anyone could have made it. After all, 'Who wants to serve in gunboats?' sounds very much like 'Who wants to serve in gumboots?'"

"Exactly!" Hickman exclaimed, though there was still a look in the other's eye he did not like.

"Can't see any of the new crowd thinking it funny," Peters continued, his tone completely flat. "Besides there's nothing to be ashamed of; my brother flies in Wellingtons after all."

"Can it!" Hickman snapped, though the laughter continued a while longer.

"Alright, I won't say a word," the gunner finally assured. "Even if someone asks."

"I'm serious!" There was now an edge to Hickman's voice which Peters was quick to pick up on. He might be partial to a scrap himself, but Hickman was bigger and by far the better fighter.

"Not a word," he repeated, this time with a totally straight face.

"See that you don't." Hickman considered his partner for a moment longer, and though there was more he'd like to say, the subject appeared to be closed.

* * *

The new gunners were in time for their first proper sea trials so, when *320* singled down to her stern wire, she had a complete crew – in theory at least.

Then there was the short trip to the oiler, shutting down all electrical devices and taking on two thousand gallons of 100 octane petrol. The familiar and strangely attractive odour of what was effectively high explosive – a teacup of the stuff was rumoured to have the same power as five sticks of dynamite – stayed with them for some while and it was with diffidence that Anderson finally gave the order for their engines to fire up. But at least the Pens were relatively quiet when *320* nosed her way past the south jetty and towards the harbour entrance. A few idlers were standing on the eastern arm of the harbour wall but, were there a major problem, he could have tackled it in relative privacy.

And then, almost before most fully realised it, they were at sea. It was a bright morning with little cloud and only a gentle wind, though the Channel chop was still evident. He glanced at Milner standing nearby; *320* was running at under six hundred revs, so had yet to rise on the plane.

"Bit on the bumpy side," he said, and the younger man grinned in reply.

Most on board would not have been to sea for several weeks and some might find the motion uncomfortable. But Anderson had more to do than discover who had lost their sea legs.

"Very well, 'Swain, bring her up to fifteen hundred."

"Fifteen hundred it is, sir."

A gloved hand bore down on the throttles and *320* surged forwards; within seconds the bows had taken to the air. Anderson glanced about; a solitary minesweeper was heading back but too far off to be of concern, and there were a pair of fishers several miles to port. Apart from that the grey-blue waters of the Narrow Seas were theirs.

"Eighteen hundred."

Newman had reported the engines up to temperature; if there was to be a problem Anderson would prefer it revealed now, before land was so very far behind.

"And two thousand!"

He needed to shout the last order and totally missed Nolan's response, though the coxswain heard and several more knots were added to their speed.

And that was it, as fast as she was permitted to travel, at least during exercise. The two officers exchanged grins once more as the boat continued to scud over the waves with far more stability than at lower speeds.

"According to the book, we should be making thirty-five knots!" Milner shouted, and Anderson nodded in reply. That would be roughly forty miles an hour – fast enough on land but with all the associated vulnerability of a wooden boat at sea, truly spectacular.

"And at least another four hundred revs in reserve!" he bellowed back.

Ahead, the French coast was picked out in clear relief by the late morning sun, making it look anything but the enemy territory it represented, and as the warm air rushed by it was hard to believe they were even at war.

Hickman and Peters, the new men, were in position at their forward two-pounder and, though the gun had yet to be properly sighted in, seemed happy in the current conditions. Anderson glanced back – as were Bridger and Mitchel at the Oerlikon. Of Thompson and Daly he could see nothing, though *320* was travelling at speed, and their stations were so close to the rushing water, he could forgive them for taking shelter when possible.

All he'd done was crank up the speed and sail in a straight line but there was no doubting the boat worked, and now they had three days and as many evenings to make her a proper going concern. Anderson grinned once more at Milner as suddenly, and probably for the first time, he truly believed it would be possible.

Chapter Fourteen

320 had moored at Weymouth's Old Customs House Quay an hour before and, after checking in with the port authorities and harbour master, then officially recording their arrival at the port captain's office, Anderson and Milner were finally able to leave her and make their way to the training base.

Which was initially disappointing. Despite the heavily sandbagged entrance and a formidable band of armed sentries, it was quite obvious that, until very recently, it had been The Pavilion Theatre.

"Two for the upper circle," Milner told the warrant officer who asked for their papers.

"Very droll, gentlemen," the WO told them, scrutinising carefully. "Though my guess is you won't find much to laugh about for the next few weeks."

The officers exchanged dubious glances and then were directed towards a pair of heavily taped glass doors.

Inside, it was still very evidently a theatre foyer. The mottled red and black carpet led to a dark, panelled box office which was set between two brass-railed staircases that swept elegantly to an upper level.

"That looks encouraging at least," Milner said, nodding towards a closed door boldly labelled 'Green Room Bar'.

"HM Gunboat *320*?" a voice demanded. It belonged to a slim, middle-aged man with short grey hair. He was dressed in civilian clothing, though the stance and attitude were distinctly military.

"Name's Hansen, I look after the new entrants; this is Collins, my secretary."

The Third Officer Wren was far younger and very pretty though no less professional; she shook hands every bit as firmly as her boss.

"I report directly to Commander Swinley," Hansen continued. "You'll be meeting him shortly, though Collins and I will give you the general run of the place first."

So saying, he led Anderson and Milner away from the bar

entrance.

"You'll be billeted in the hotel next door, though your ratings'll be accommodated separately. All meals are served in a communal NAAFI, that is until we can arrange something more civilised for commissioned ranks." Hansen stopped and seemed about to confide. "We've only been operational a couple of weeks," he said. "Still getting the place sorted so you may have to put up with a few inconveniences."

Neither officer looked likely to lodge an objection, so Hansen felt able to move on.

"Auditorium itself is used for gunnery training," he continued. "In it, we have examples of the most common light naval ordnance, while the gallery has been partitioned off into classroom space. There are also separate working rigs that can be practised upon, though obviously much of the practical work will be done at sea. And you'll have noticed the bar, I have no doubt?"

Both men nodded and Collins gave a knowing chuckle.

"Well don't go getting any ideas, that's been made over to the telegraphy department; you'll find Morse tappers where the bar pulls used to be. There's something similar for the RDF boys and we'll have joint exercises when both can practice directing you gentlemen in various combat situations."

Again, Hansen stopped and, if anything, became even more matter of fact. "Daytimes you'll mainly be involved with theory, at night we put it all into practice and, towards the end of your time, there'll be something a little more challenging – providing the enemy proves cooperative, that is.

"We'll speak more later but for now I'm going to leave you in the capable hands of Miss Collins; she'll see to your berths, then look after your men. Evening meal will be served in under an hour; there's only ever one sitting at *Bee*, so don't be late. Breakfast is at seven and we start at oh-eight hundred sharp. I'd get as much sleep as you can; it may be your last full night for quite a while."

And with that Hansen strutted off, leaving them with the Wren officer.

"You'll find he mellows in time," she told them more gently. "All our trainers are highly experienced with many just back from active service."

"I was active myself until very recently," Anderson said.

"Indeed, sir, and I gather present at St Nazaire, which must have been quite a show. But please don't think anyone will try and teach you to suck eggs. The ethos at *Bee* is very much on anything new; think of it as a training masterclass. Have you worked with RDF before?"

"Only indirectly," Anderson admitted, while Milner merely shook his head.

"That, and other innovations – such as incorporating sign language for engine room personnel and fresh tactics when dealing with the new class of E-boat – is what we are about. And though it won't be a holiday, there'll be the chance to try a few things out for yourself, as well as making the occasional mistake in relative safety; quite a few of our gentlemen find that a break in itself."

"I can see that," Anderson agreed.

"So, let me take you to your berths. It may be better to wait until after dinner to bring in your luggage; Lieutenant Commander Hansen wasn't joking when he said meals here are pretty punctual."

* * *

After being billeted in what appeared to be a former storeroom in the pavilion complex, *320*'s ratings had been directed to a NAAFI set up in the restaurant of a requisitioned hotel next door. There they had eaten cottage pie identical to that served at their old base, followed by a bread and butter pudding that tasted strongly of margarine. And now, with the food going down and nothing more required of them, it was time to treat the newcomers to their customary interrogation.

"So, come on, spill the beans," Nolan urged.

"I think our northern friend would like to know more about you," Harvey explained.

"Not much to say, I reckon," Peters, replied. "We're both down from Whale. Paired us up there and looks like we're stuck with each other."

"So, not seen active service?" Nolan checked.

"Not like you guys." Hickman was the shorter of the two though more heavily built; he had close-cropped red hair and

138

mildly pockmarked skin. "Done a few exercises, and on one occasion the TO pointed out a distant German destroyer."

"Only it were going the wrong way," Peters added.

"What's the story with *320*?" Hickman asked.

"New boat," Pickering replied. "We don't know much more about her than you."

"S'right," Mitchel agreed. "Trip down here were the longest we done, though she seems straight enough."

"Have to go a long way to match *194*," Daly sighed. "Now, she were a lucky ship."

"And you all came from her?" Peters checked. He was lighter than his mate with a lantern jaw and freckles.

"I were with her from the start," Pickering said.

"Me an' all," Daly added. "Along with Newman the CMM. Our current skipper were Jimmy the One."

"What happened to her?" Hickman asked.

"One hell of a scrape," Nolan said. "Skipper bought it."

"Her captain was killed?" Peters was incredulous.

"Aye, and the boat were a mess," Daly continued. "'Tis a wonder she made it back in one piece."

"Several pieces," Nolan corrected.

"And that's a lucky ship?" Peters pulled a face, but Pickering shook his head.

"There was a sight more to it than that," he said.

"Well, this is a rum show." Bridger was glancing about the crowded NAAFI. "We may as well be back at *Wasp*, place don't look no different."

"Next door is," Harvey, the telegraphist said.

"Aye, not your average training base," Pickering agreed.

"I don't know so much," Mitchel said. "Aren't they using holiday camps now?"

"Pavilion Weymouth was a prime night spot in the past," Harvey said. "I saw Lew Stone's lot there a few years back – cracking band."

"Dancin', was there?" Nolan asked.

"Aye, dancing," Harvey agreed.

"Don't think there'll be much of that over the next few weeks," Mitchel said.

"Right, sounds like we're going to be put through the mangle," Pickering agreed.

"I spy scrambled egg." Nolan pointed, and all turned to where a group of senior officers were taking their meals at the far end of the room.

"No queuing at the counter for them," Pickering said.

"Right, they got stewards," Bridger agreed.

"And tablecloths," Mitchel added with a hint of suspicion. "Though the food looks the same."

"The commissioned lovely what took us to our room said we'd be sharing our NAAFI while they sort out their own mess," Harvey said.

"Officers should always sort out their own mess." Bridger's pompous accent raised a few smiles though the atmosphere remained cautious.

"Last time we were sent to the West Country they billeted us in a pub," Pickering said.

"Get away." Bridger was clearly voicing the opinion of several others.

"True as I'm sitting here," Pickering confirmed. "It were before some of you joined. Tell 'em, Paddy."

Daly nodded seriously. "What your man says is correct."

"Canny number it were," the Geordie continued. "Old woman called Mona ran it, though there were nee beer."

"Pub with no beer?" Peters again. "You chaps do have all the luck."

"Maybe so, but there ain't many of us left, not from the original crowd," Pickering sighed.

"Sure, didn't Smith an' Godliman buy it shortly after?" Daly remembered. "And Mr Carter."

"He were a warrant officer, not at *The Rose*," Pickering interrupted.

"No, but he died," Daly said. "Then there was Jelly. And Gibson, they were both there."

"They croak an' all did they?" Hickman asked.

"Jelly got shell shock and Gibson was arrested for murder," Pickering replied, adding, "Of course, that were under the old skipper."

"The one what got killed when his boat were shot to pieces?" Peters asked.

"Aye, that's the lad," Nolan agreed.

There was a pause while they all digested this. Then

Hickman cleared his throat.

"And this new boat, *320*," he said. "Reckon she'll be lucky an' all, do ya?"

"No doubt about it," Daly said.

"And do you tell this to all the new blokes?" Peters asked.

"Or somethin' similar," Nolan grinned. "It encourages them."

* * *

This wasn't the first time Thompson had attempted to contact Joyce. There was only one open line at the Weymouth NAAFI and usually a long queue. Yet he'd tried each morning and, four weeks after they arrived at HMS *Bee*, she finally answered. But even then he had the distinct impression it was chance, and Joyce had been intending to make a call and not receive one.

"Weymouth?" she asked. "Where the hell is Weymouth?"

Thompson pressed the receiver closer to his ear, though this time there was no petty officer to overhear.

"Further along the south coast," he said. "Past Portsmouth."

"Never heard of it," Joyce snapped.

"Didn't you get my letters?" he asked.

"Got one," she said. "You were still in Dover then."

"But I sent loads."

"Then I dare say mum'll send 'em on eventually."

"Well, I been here a month but won't be much longer," Thompson continued. "With luck no more'n a week."

"Is that right?"

Her tone said it all; not only had Joyce not missed him, she didn't seem to care whether he came back or not, and Thompson was aware of a dreadful feeling of loss.

"Providin' all goes well we can meet up then," he said. "Maybe see the new place and find out how you've been."

"Concerned, are you?"

"Now don't be like that, Joycie, it were just a bad day. You know about Granger and how important he is."

"I do now," she said. "An' I've found out a bit more since."

"Oh, yes?"

"Ran into your mates Charlie and Ted a few weeks back." They said there were trouble at the old place."

Thompson didn't like the sound of that.

"Apparently Granger thinks you grassed him up."

"I ain't told nothing to nobody," Thompson protested.

"That's as maybe, but the Old Bill got wind of what were being planned. Rozzers came round and took a look; next thing you know he an' the rest of 'em were being told to clear out sharpish. Ted said they were lucky nothing more came of it but then Granger hadn't even got going. Anyway, he's legged it for now, but Ted an' Charlie are still about."

"An' are they lookin' for me?"

"Why would they?" Joyce asked. "You ain't important."

Thompson went to speak but the words would not come.

"Seems they're still set on Dover and lookin' for somethin' similar," Joyce continued. "Asked if I knew of anywhere as good as the last, an' I told 'em where to go."

Thompson winced; Granger and his lot weren't ones to take lip lightly. "I'm lookin' forward to seeing your new place," he said.

"Well, you can forget that an' all." Her tone was depressingly matter of fact. "If you think I'm letting you anywhere close, you got another think comin'."

"Come on, Joycie; I'll never raise my hand to you again. It were just the one time."

"First, last, and only if you asks me, Frank Thompson." She paused and may have been considering. "P'raps, when you next get leave, we might meet somewhere public."

"That shouldn't be long," Thompson told her eagerly. "They say we're due a few days once we're back at Dover."

"Well alright then, though I thought you said you was gettin' out of the Navy."

"That's still on the cards," he said. "Only I been proper busy, what with training an' all."

"Not much point training if you're gonna be gone."

"Suppose not." Thompson had never felt so useless.

"I got to be going," she said.

"Joyce, I'm sorry." There, he'd said it, and afterwards bit his lip.

"That's as may be," she said and, again, there was a pause. "But it's been too long in coming. Got to go, things to do."

The line went dead, but Thompson went on listening for some time before he finally replaced the receiver.

* * *

"Nice kickers, kidda," Nolan told Hickman. "New, are they?"

The gunner finished lacing up his standard pair of deck boots. It was early morning in their improvised dormitory, and they were late for breakfast; there wasn't time to discuss footwear.

"No," he said. "Had 'em about six months."

"Smart," Harvey said. "Though you want to make sure you keep 'em clean."

"Right," Pickering agreed. "Don't go through no mud or nuthin'."

"Need specialist boots for that," Nolan added.

"Gumboots." Harvey nodded. "Nothing like gumboots for keeping your feet dry."

"Lot of fellas spend all their time in gumboots," Pickering announced.

"Aye," Nolan agreed. "Some even volunteers to."

Hickman eyed his new mates warily. "Alright," he said at last. "What's so bloody funny?"

* * *

Hansen had been right on the mark, Anderson decided as he returned to his room. It was the end of a particularly harrowing day, but at least his time at *Bee* would soon be over. And, as predicted, it had been no holiday.

From the first day, a meticulously drawn-up schedule carried him from one classroom to the next while he brushed up on everything from different attack formations to maintaining crew morale. Other activities did not demand his direct participation but, as Commanding Officer, he needed to be aware, so was also expected to sit in on lectures covering everything from navigating by RDF to efficient engine management.

Then there were the practical demonstrations; he could not count the number of times *320* had put to sea, either alone or in company, but on each there was always one training officer on the bridge and at least another somewhere else, both watching intensely while they practised a particular manoeuvre or procedure. And, though these drills often extended well into the early hours, there was no change in the regime, and he had to report – dressed, shaven and ready for work – first thing each morning.

But on that particular evening there would be some relief. At the beginning of the week, Lieutenant Commander Hansen announced the opening of a dedicated officers' mess in a nearby terrace of houses. Consequently, that night's exercises were to be replaced by dinner in new surroundings, while his remaining meals would be taken with slightly more decorum than had been possible in the NAAFI.

Anderson was not greatly troubled by having to dine with ratings, and neither did he care much for steward service, or late night port. The prospect of a meal that did not follow the usual NAAFI menu did appeal, however, along with an early night. If the new facilities provided that, then he was all in favour.

And there was better to look forward to. For most of his time at *Bee* it had been raining cats and dogs; something initially greeted by the base's more masochistic trainers. But it was finally accepted there'd been enough heavy weather work and, for as long as the rain continued, practical exercises were suspended. Several of *320*'s specialist ratings were facing assessments the following day, which he was not expected to attend and, as the only item on his agenda was a two-hour seminar on petrol fires – their causes and prevention – he was looking forward to a bit of rest.

In reality, only one major obstacle remained, and that would come at the very end of his time at *Bee*. The scheduled active service practical experience could take many forms; *320* might join an escort group for an eastbound convoy or stage a hit and run attack on the enemy coast. He had experienced both in the past and on several occasions, though never while in command or with a team of pedantic experts watching his every move. Passing such a test would determine whether they were allowed back to *Wasp*, or retained a further week when the exercise – or one similar – would be repeated, and Anderson had no wish to linger further.

He slipped off his shoes and unbuttoned his tunic, then slumped back on the bed. Anderson had been fortunate in being allocated a single room; during his short time at *Bee,* there was a dramatic increase in attending officers and most now had to share accommodation. He closed his eyes and was just drifting off when a knock at the door made him start.

Instantly the eyes opened and, so used was he to reacting to immediate problems, Anderson was gripped by momentary panic. Why were they seeking him out? What had he missed, misinterpreted, or in any way left undone? But by the time the knock was repeated, he had composed himself. The day's work was over, he had every right to be there, every right to relax and whoever had the nerve to disturb him would get short shrift.

Yet, as he heaved himself off the bed and padded to the door, there was still a modicum of doubt. This could hardly be good news, not when the immediate future seemed so bright and, as he slipped the catch and pulled the door back, he braced himself mentally.

"Ian?"

The raincoat was saturated, as was the hat covering her long, auburn hair. But there was no mistaking that face or the expression of pleased anticipation.

"Eve?" he said, his voice cracking in disbelief.

And just when he'd promised himself a quiet evening.

Chapter Fifteen

"Officers is gone, we finally got the place to ourselves," Bridger announced when *320*'s ratings filed into the NAAFI.

"Let's go see what we been missin'," Nolan suggested and, as a man, they made for the far area so recently out of bounds. But they were not the only ones. The improvised NAAFI could hold up to a hundred souls and, with the fixed service times, most were present. Most also had the same idea so what had been the officers' preserve – now bereft of tablecloths and other refinements – was already crammed with the curious.

"Least there's a bit more room down this end," Mitchel said when they had retreated to their old table. "And we needn't stay long."

"Damn right," Bridger agreed. "First leave for an age, and I'm ready for a pint of best."

"I hope Weymouth pubs are up to *The Lion*," Pickering said.

Harvey shook his head. "Might be in for a let down there."

"Why's that?" Peters asked.

"Dover's got a concession with booze," the telegraphist replied. "It's still being allocated for a full population, yet most of the civilians legged it long since.

"He's right," Mitchel confirmed. "Alf rarely runs out of beer, but it ain't the same elsewhere."

"An' just when I could murder a jug of brown," Pickering sighed.

"Or a drop of the black stuff," Daly added dreamily.

"I don't care what they serves, long as it's wet and brewed." Bridger this time.

"I'd just like to get clear of this place," Harvey said. "See a few different faces, breathe a bit of fresh air, maybe find some decent music."

"Music?" Mitchel questioned.

"Aye, music," Harvey insisted.

"An' maybe dancin'!" Nolan added hopefully.

"Well, we won't find much of anything sitting here."

Hickman, was eyeing his food – a toad in the hole that seemed singularly lacking in sausages. "What say we get this lot down and see what Weymouth has to offer?"

* * *

"Sounds more like boot camp than officer training," Eve said.

Her sudden appearance had made Anderson conscious of the room's untidiness. It was the standard hotel offering; single bed, small washbasin, bedside cabinet, desk, chair, and a wardrobe, but they no longer offered a turn-down service.

"It's not just for officers," he said, collecting a wad of unread newspapers. "My entire crew's been through the mill." A pile of unwashed underwear was pressed beneath the desk with his foot. "And the new boat's in Weymouth harbour."

"*Your* boat," Eve reminded with a smile. She had seated herself sideways on the bed – *his* bed – and, with legs crossed and showing a fair amount of nylon, was leaning back against the headboard; an act Anderson found both sensual and mildly provocative. "You've done so well to get a command."

"Not performed too shabbily yourself," he smiled, settling himself more genteelly on the chair opposite. "How's training going, or can't you say?"

"Oh, I can tell you masses face to face," she said, "it's just phone calls and letters they get touchy about."

"I'm sure there's good reason."

She nodded. "We live in a bubble of security; one word out of place and everyone suffers."

"So how are things?"

"Good, I guess," she shrugged, "though it's hard to be sure. SOE is such a new organisation there's no real benchmark and no formal training; at least nothing like the sort of thing you've been going through."

"And your position...?"

"I'm going to be what they call an escorting officer."

"Escorting?" he stiffened slightly. "Would that be agents?"

"Yes, but I won't follow them to the drop, usually not as far as the plane, in fact. My job is simply to make sure they don't rattle or shine."

He raised an eyebrow.

147

"That they'll blend in and aren't carrying anything to give them away," she explained. "Gillette razor blades, Sandre bras – that sort of thing."

"So, there are female agents as well?"

"The vast majority are," she said. "I'm in the French section where they blend in more easily. For a start a woman won't be expected to have a job, and neither will she attract the attention a man of military age might."

"You mean it won't be assumed a woman is part of the resistance?"

"Exactly. The Gestapo has a reputation for being ruthless, but believe me, Ian, they ain't that bright."

"I guess not," he said, and she smiled.

"It's funny, speaking to you in this way," she placed her hands behind her head and rested back further, "saying all the things I cannot mention to anyone else. We haven't seen each other for ages, yet it just seems to come naturally."

Anderson stood, then took a step towards her, before settling himself on the side of the bed. "It feels natural to me, too," he said.

"So..." she was eyeing him speculatively, "what about this evening?"

"There's a brand new officers' mess," he said. "Inaugural dinner tonight. I dare say I could get you in; you're an officer, after all."

"It's a lovely offer," she smiled, "but I'm not that hungry. What about you?"

He grinned and slumped down next to her. "Me?" he asked. "I couldn't eat a thing."

* * *

"If that's all you got, nine pints of mild," Nolan conceded. "But what about some neckers?"

"Neckers?" The publican eyed them warily. A group of sailors might mean good business, but they could also spell trouble, and he appeared to have decided where this current lot were heading.

"Yeah, you know, a tot of spirits to make the beer go down."

"You mean chasers."

148

Nolan shrugged. "If you like."

"No spirits. Best I can do is a drop of sweet sherry; sixpence a nip."

"A tanner, for sherry!"

"There's a war on," the publican told him.

"Not in Spain," Nolan replied. "Go on, then, you robber."

"Hey, Scouse, they got proper beer at that table."

He turned to look, and Mitchel was right. A group of Army privates were downing pints of stout.

"What's that all about then?" he demanded of the publican, now well into pulling their round.

"Them's forces, from the local barracks," he said.

"And what do you think we are?" Nolan pulled himself up to his full five foot six.

"He's right, we're Navy – can't you tell from the uniform?" Mitchel added. "Our base is round the corner."

"Army drinks here most nights," the publican maintained. "Or at least some of them do. Don't see any of your lot from one week to the next."

"Well three bezzies for them. Most of our nights are spent at sea keepin' you lot safe!" Nolan was starting to get angry now and, if his mates weren't aware, the publican certainly was.

"You want beer, I'll serve you," he said. "But only with mild; that way I keeps my licence *and* my regulars."

"Come on, Scouce, this won't be the only pub."

"Damn right," Nolan turned to go.

"Hey, wait up," the barman called after them. "What about your beer?" He pointed to the line of pints already pulled. "What am I supposed to do with this little lot?"

Nolan told him.

* * *

"I thought we'd agreed not to talk shop," Third Officer Collins said.

"It's rather hard not to in a place like this," Milner grinned.

The surroundings definitely made such a thing difficult. On its first night in operation, *Bee*'s officers' mess positively abounded with the uniforms and gold lace of those far above his meagre rank. Milner had made for the end of the furthest table from the president and was delighted when the Wren they met on the first day seated herself opposite. And even more so when their immediate neighbours left before dessert, allowing them a modicum of privacy.

"Besides, I don't think it's shop, as such," he continued. "I wasn't talking about my time here, or how well you lot do things."

"I'm rather glad." She had a lovely smile. "Especially about that last bit. The past few weeks have been a learning experience for us as much as you."

"It hasn't been obvious." Milner had seen Caroline, as he discovered her name to be, on numerous occasions since that first meeting, but there was never the time, or space, to speak to her. That was being made up for now, though, and rather than make the mistake of most young men by talking about himself, they settled on a very different subject.

"Does it bother you," she asked, "working for a reservist, I mean?"

"Not as such." Milner looked around the room. "You can't spend much time in Coastal Forces without realising the RNVR virtually runs the show."

"And there are more coming all the time," she agreed. "But it's different for me. My boss is Royal Navy Reserve; spent several years as a regular until the Geddes Axe fell, and after that he was mainly captaining tankers."

"So, he still behaves like a regular RN?"

"Pretty much."

Milner began to play with his empty wine glass. "The first Coastal Forces captain I met was different," he said.

"The one who died?"

He nodded. "We were lucky in the old *Dalia*. Never lost a man all the time I was with her."

"So it must have been hard," she said. "When it happened, I mean."

"Oh, I was safely ashore," he said. "But it was the reaction of his number one that surprised me. He was standing alongside, and it affected him for a long time after."

"I can't say I'm surprised."

"No, it was more than just losing his skipper." Again, a pause. "There was genuine affection there I think."

"Really?"

"Not like that!" he added quickly. "More mutual respect, at

150

least from Lieutenant Anderson's side." Once more he considered this. "And now he'll be my captain, and me his number one."

"And the prospect bothers you?" She was looking deeply into his eyes, although Milner appeared not to notice.

"It'll just be different, I suppose. If things had gone as intended, Lieutenant Commander Harris would have been my captain. With both of us regular officers, I'd have known how to behave; the kind of chap he'd want as his second in command."

"And with Anderson, you don't?"

He grinned. "With Anderson, I'm still very much at the learning stage."

"It sounds like Harris and Anderson were a team," she said. "Despite coming from different backgrounds."

"Oh, indeed."

"And how is Anderson, as an officer, I mean?"

"Not so stiff," Milner said. "And far more pally with the men, though that's no bad thing in my book."

"So why do you find it hard to serve under him?"

"Oh, I don't," he assured her. "My last ship was pretty much run by RNR and RNVR officers and I've nothing but respect for them. But it was different being Number Three. As Second in Command I'll really need to understand my CO. And the one thing you can say about RNVRs is they tend to be individuals. At least with a Dartmouth grad. you get a measure of conformity."

"You mean they stamp them out like peas in a pod?" she asked.

"Something like that," he grinned again, "myself included."

"And you would prefer it if Anderson were the standard naval product?"

"Not really. As I say, I do prefer the more casual approach, though it does take a bit of getting used to. And I can't help thinking if I ever support a regular officer in the future, I might be too relaxed myself."

She had reached out and was gently stroking her dessert spoon, her hand temptingly close. "I didn't train at Dartmouth, though doubt Greenwich Royal Naval College is terribly different." She looked up and gave a wicked grin. "How do you feel about being alongside me?"

"Oh, very relaxed," he smiled. "Very relaxed indeed."

* * *

"Dead-and-alive hole, that's what this place is," Nolan pronounced as they made their way along the Esplanade. "Pubs everywhere, but most of them shut and those that ain't have no decent beer."

"Or not for British sailors," Mitchel corrected.

"So, what do we do?" Harvey asked. "Try another, or head back to the NAAFI for a bite of supper?"

"Bite of supper?" Nolan repeated scornfully. "And what d'you think you'll get from that tight lot; a slice of Wet Nelly or perhaps some Welsh Rarebit? Did you see that toad they served up tonight?"

"We've spent so long there, I ain't in no hurry to go back," Mitchel said.

"Nor me." It was the first time Kipling had been out with the ratings and, though some were only a couple of years older than him, he felt very much the baby.

"Right, then let's try down the next road," Nolan suggested. Maybe getting away from the sea front'll do us more good."

"Lookin' for something, lads?"

They'd been so busy talking no one noticed the nondescript man in a trilby and long brown overcoat until he was almost upon them.

"Decent night out would be nice," Bridger said.

"Might be able to help you there," he told them. "Fancy a fish supper, do you? I've two chip shops in town." He raised the hat. "Name's Frères; mention that an' they'll see you're all right."

"Weren't food so much," Mitchel began.

"Entertainment then, is it?" Frères leered. "Somethin' to brighten the lives of a bunch of sailor boys? Got a nice little place by the front an' all; good clean girls an' only five bob a dance."

"Five shillin'!" Peters was incensed.

"An' a modest entrance fee," Frères added.

"We were really lookin' for a decent wet," Mitchel said.

"Aye, a drop of the brown stuff," Pickering agreed.

"And dancin'." Nolan this time. "But nothing so pricy."

"Then I can still be of service." Frères treated them to a brief display of yellowed teeth. "There's another place that might suit you better."

"Has it got beer?" Bridger again.

152

"Along with a few spirits," Frères assured. "An' some local cider."

"I'll stick with the beer," Bridger said. "London brew, is it?"

"I gets what I can, but there's plenty of scrumpy."

"Cider's a girl's drink," Kipling snorted.

"And you'll be knowin' all about that," Daly told the boy.

"This ain't," they were assured. "It'll knock your socks off. There's a band as well if you've a mind. Place is no more than five minutes away; you interested?"

Harvey brightened visibly. "Band, you say?"

"That's right, with a girl singer. All the latest from America."

"An' dancin'?" Nolan added.

Again that wry look. "If you've a mind," Frères said. "Cost you a quid on the door, but it's better than walkin' the streets."

"One whole pound?"

"Alright, it's a quiet night, we'll make it ten bob."

The ratings immediately fell into a huddle.

"Sounds a bit rich." Mitchel shook his head.

"I'm not so sure," Nolan said. "If there's dancin'..."

"I ain't spent a farthing in the last few weeks," Pickering announced, "none of us have. If ten shillin'll buy me a decent wet, I'm up for it."

"Tell you what, I'll make it five bob apiece," they were told. "And you can dance till morning if that's what you want."

"Due back at the base by ten," Mitchel reminded.

"Then we'd better get a move on," Nolan said. "Come on, grandad, show us the way."

* * *

"So, what happens – after *Bee*, I mean?"

Looking up at a cracked ceiling was somehow easier than into each other's eyes – at least Anderson found it so.

"Back to *Wasp*, I suppose," he said. "Though there are a few more hoops to jump through before that can happen."

"The active service exercise you mean?"

"That, and a few more drills. I'm surprised we weren't detailed tonight; weather would have been perfect, though I must say I'm glad they didn't."

153

"And at *Wasp*, will it be the same?" she asked.

"Probably," he said. "Though obviously without Harris. And I'll have my own boat; in time there'll probably be the chance of advancement."

"And would you like that?"

"To be a flotilla leader?" he considered. "That's a difficult one. I never intended joining the Navy and will be glad to get back to teaching. Yet part of me wants to do the job as well as I can, for as long as I can."

"Which will mean regular patrols from *Wasp*?"

"I guess so; convoy and minesweeper escort, enemy convoy and coastal attack, sea rescue; all things I've spent the last month or so boning up on. I suppose that might change if we ever mount an invasion, though it will probably only mean transferring to another base in the Med or maybe the Pacific. And then it won't be any different," he continued, "except the water should be warmer."

"And do you want that?"

"I don't see there's much choice," he said. "It's what Coastal Forces do and are starting to do well. And they need RNVR bods like me to do it."

"You wouldn't feel as useful doing anything else?"

There was something in her questions and tone that told him this was not just idle conversation.

"As I've said, it's what we're there for. Why do you ask?"

She shrugged. "No reason, or at least not one I can give at the moment."

"You never used to be quite so secretive."

"I never used to work for SOE," she smiled. "Now come on, where are you taking me for supper?"

* * *

"'*Les Frères*'," Bridger read the makeshift sign with an element of doubt. "Rum name for a bar."

It stood over what must have once been a shop and, though they could see nothing through the boarded-up windows, the place looked singularly uninviting. Had they not been led there, none of them would have given it a second look.

"It's French," Harvey informed them. "Means brothers. Guess it must be some sort of family enterprise."

154

"Are you 'avin' a laugh?" Their guide was obviously appalled.

"Well, what then?" Harvey asked.

"I told you, it's me name: I'm Les Frères."

"But you ain't French," Mitchel told him.

"I ain't but me muvver was. Father? 'Avent got a clue. Now, do you want a drink or not?"

Inside, the club seemed even less inspiring. Their initial impression was spot on; the place had been some form of showroom. Blast damage must have shattered the plate glass windows, now made safe with a patchwork of assorted panels though some wicked shards remained and caught the candlelight from a dozen empty tables.

These stood in a circle as if in anticipation of what might happen in their centre. A four-piece band, wedged into the far corner, struck up and a pimply youth appeared, as if summoned, behind a makeshift bar; apart from them, and *320*'s ratings, the place was empty.

"Must have been expectin' us," Pickering grunted.

"That'll be five bob each." Frères held out a grimy hand.

"A whole bleedin' crown?" Nolan exclaimed. "For this?"

* * *

They hadn't planned a walk as such, but the officers' mess had grown thick with cigar smoke and Collins expressed a craving for fresh air. The moon, though far from full, was rising in a crystal clear sky. A perfect night for a raid, in fact, yet the town was still and, though universally dark, it might have been peacetime.

Which was very much on their mind as, arm in arm, and with thoughts equally attuned, they made slow and steady progress.

"We can't ever go back," Milner said. "To what it was like before the war, I mean."

"Of course not," Caroline replied. "It'll never be the same, and we'll probably be broke."

"I always have been," he said.

"No, I meant countries. We're already in hock to the Americans and what everyone's spending on arms and munitions doesn't bear thinking about."

155

"You're naturally assuming we'll win," he told her.

"Of course, I always have," she gave a small chuckle, "though probably with more reason now."

"The mood is certainly changing," he agreed. "In which case Germany will be broke as well – probably more so."

They paused, as if to a secret signal, and turned to stare out over the placid ocean.

"It really does seem a shame," she said. "In normal times we would be coming to the end of the holiday season. Today that beach would have been filled with families sunbathing, taking donkey rides and building sandcastles. Instead, it's covered with sea defences and the occasional land mine."

"We didn't ask for this war," he reminded her.

"Of course not, though we did allow it to happen."

"I suppose you can always say that," he sighed. "Things are so easy to judge in retrospect."

"But surely there's nothing wrong in learning from the past?" she insisted. "If we could only remember how this nonsense came about, future generations might not make the same mistake."

"That's the problem," he said. "Everyone wants to make their own mistakes. Until that changes, nothing else will."

"That doesn't seem very optimistic."

"It's not," he said. "Right now all I'm able to think about is the immediate future; everything else seems just too far away."

"Then don't think too far ahead," she said. "Let's just concentrate on right now. And right now, there is no raid, no fighting and neither of us are at work. Right now, there might not even be a war."

"It's a wonderful thought," he agreed. "If only 'right now' would last."

* * *

No one knew who had summoned them but, by the time the shore patrol arrived, they were definitely needed.

Nolan had drunk the most and, urged on by his shipmates, tried the threatened cider. Which was pleasant enough although he only began to fully appreciate its strength after sinking his fifth pint. By which time the fact that they were the only customers, and the one woman present was singing with the band, hardly

156

mattered. And neither did it stop him from dancing with each of his shipmates in turn.

Once the other ratings were equally oiled, most showed willing. Hickman, one of the new men, proved himself proficient in the jitterbug while Kipling was sick and passed out before finishing his second cider.

And Harvey was happy enough, despite drinking less than anyone. It was a halfway decent band; trumpet and saxophone playing over drums and bass while the singer could certainly carry a tune. He soon noticed the redundant piano that seemed to be beckoning. A quick introduction led to a cautious invitation for him to sit in and he would have happily played to the end of the evening had the fight not broken out.

Which actually took most of *320*'s ratings by surprise. Having an improvised club to themselves proved less of a novelty with each successive pint, so when an influx of commandos from the local barracks turned up, they were welcomed.

Unfortunately, the new men expected more in the form of company than a bunch of semi-drunk sailors, and Nolan's invitation to dance was misinterpreted. Fists began to fly and were quickly joined by chairs, tables and the occasional musical instrument. A starched naval detail was soon on the scene but, rather than bring order, their ear-piercing whistles only provoked further violence.

Recognising the shore patrol was from their own service, and guessing they'd be up on a charge, the seamen immediately set upon them, while the soldiers, who had been trained to fight after all, joined in. Order was finally restored after a detachment of MPs was summoned and when those from both forces were finally separated it was at the cost of most of the club's fittings.

And so, bruised, battered, but defiant, the ratings were returned to *Bee*, to await future sentencing. But at least it had been the break from routine they had all been hoping for.

* * *

The time had come for *320* to finally prove her worth. Anderson read through the schedule for a second time, then looked up at Commander Bristow, who had issued it.

"It says here three boats," he said. "With us in the lead."

"That's correct," Bristow replied. The training officers at *Bee* fell into two categories; some were on short-term rotation, effectively taking a break from active service, while others had been superannuated, in some cases for several years, but called back to use their time and experience grooming the next generation. Bristow fell into the second camp having captained CMBs in an earlier war. He gave a wry grin. "You'll be acting as Flotilla Leader," he said. "On a temporary basis, of course."

Anderson looked for a third time. "No pressure then."

"It's well within your capabilities, otherwise we wouldn't have considered you. And you won't be alone."

No, that was definitely the case, Anderson remembered. There would be another, more senior, officer beside him throughout. One who had seen it all and probably made the same mistakes he might make. And, if Anderson was fortunate, it could be a young TO, who could rescue the situation should it be necessary.

"It's a simple hit and run," Bristow gave a knowing chuckle, "supposing such a thing exists, of course. Drop down to the tip of France and blow up a minor signal station we've had our eye on for a while. You'll be precious close to Cherbourg, so there could be some interference from Es, and expect a modicum of coastal defences, though only light stuff. Nothing a MkV can't take – not if she's handled properly."

"And the other two boats?"

"They'll be MkVs as well," the commander assured. "And it's Jennings' second trip. He was detailed to attack a Jerry convoy which turned out more heavily escorted than we expected. No slight on him, of course, but we do like our chaps to leave with at least one success under their belts."

Anderson had run into Jennings a couple of times during exercises. A sub-lieutenant and straight striper – like Milner. But unlike Milner, something of a prima donna; it would be interesting to see how the man took to being under his command.

"What about the third?" he asked, and Bristow took a breath.

"That's a little more difficult," he said. "Cooke's another sub, and a Wavy like yourself. Before he came here, he'd done remarkably well as first officer in two MLs and had all the signs of making an excellent gunboat CO. But somehow he hasn't taken to the training environment."

"So, he's also done a practical before?"

"Several, I'm afraid. And, though not exactly messed up, neither has he shown the ability to follow orders. As you may have gathered, acting on initiative is fine and almost encouraged if on independent assignment, but no good when part of a team. You may have to mother him somewhat."

Anderson had not come across Cooke, though with the number of officers, and boats, currently at *Bee* that was hardly surprising. He sighed. Until called for the briefing he was relatively confident. The practical assessment would be his last obstacle; if all went well, he could expect to be back at *Wasp* within a few days. And the time away had not been wasted; he'd learned much and felt himself a better captain, while seeing Eve had bolstered him in quite a different way. But to be told his test mission would involve a full Channel crossing, leading two other boats whose commanders did not appear to be the easiest, seemed to change everything.

"You needn't worry," Bristow assured him. "There'll be training officers aboard the other boats as well. They'll see none of you get into trouble. Though from what I've just been hearing, your men and trouble seem to go together..."

Chapter Sixteen

The engines had fired up some time before and continued to turn over while Anderson waited for the rest of his small force to be ready. The two other boats lay in consecutive berths behind *320* and it was his intention they should leave harbour in that order. But Jennings reported one engine failing to start, then Cooke began to single up, clearly intending to leave first and forcing Anderson to order him to remain. This aroused a fatuous response from the young officer who claimed he was simply making the correct preparations.

Of course, all was witnessed by Lieutenant Commander Crehan, a veteran whose solid and mainly mute body took up a sizeable amount of *320*'s bridge. Anderson was aware he would be judged not only by his own actions, but how he reacted to those of others, and showing any sign of temper while still moored to the Customs House Quay would definitely have counted against him. Yet feeling unable even to comment to Milner was frustrating and when Jennings eventually announced himself ready, and they could finally leave, Anderson already felt jaded.

It was a still night with minimal cloud and only a quarter moon due. Once all three boats had carried out their radio and weapon checks, then accelerated onto the plane, and *320* took up position at their head, he was feeling a little more optimistic.

Allowing for the Channel's currents, it would be just over eighty nautical miles to the headland that was their objective. At a moderate cruising speed, they should make the journey out in well under four hours and have more than enough fuel to delay a while, before making the trip back. Nevertheless, the little adventure would still burn several thousand gallons of high-octane petrol, to say nothing of the ammunition they would expend, and together with the risk of losing at least one vessel, Anderson could not help wondering if it were truly worthwhile.

But then one of the things learned at *Bee* was how much the Royal Navy now valued training. It had not always been so; on volunteering for minesweepers, both officers and men were forced to learn much of their craft at sea and often in action. Even later, after transferring to Coastal Forces, the induction course at *St Christopher*'s merely covered the basics, relying on those at the coal face to complete his training. The night might turn out to be nothing more than several hours of frustration that wasted fuel and munitions while also placing the lives of thirty or so young men, and a handful of experienced officers, at risk. But if, as was hoped, they came back stronger, it would have been worthwhile.

"Make to Jennings, 'resume proper station.'"

The gunboat was creeping up on *320*'s quarter. Anderson had not wished for unnecessary signals but, unless something was done, it would soon be alongside. The straight striper was obviously set on challenging him at every opportunity, but Anderson was equally determined to nip such acts in the bud, and this was one occasion when having training officers on board might actually be an advantage. Unless Jennings wanted to repeat the exercise, he would be wise to take his leader's instructions a little more seriously.

"*348* acknowledges, sir," Milner reported, replacing the Aldis.

"Very good," Anderson replied before peeling back the sleeve of his ursula and peering at his watch. They had been travelling for less than an hour, it was going to be a long night.

* * *

Robbed of the comfort their turrets provided aboard *194*, Thompson and Daly had taken to moving forward when not in action and sharing the dubious shelter of the Oerlikon's bandstand. The splinter mattresses might not be effective against anything larger than a pistol bullet, but at least they kept out much of the wind and sea.

"Could do with a mug of kye," Bridger said. "Someone should see to it." He was the Oerlikon's gunner, Mitchel being merely a loader, while Thompson and the Irishman were just visitors, so he felt entitled to make pronouncements.

"Well don't be lookin' at me," Daly exclaimed.

Even at cruising speed, the triple Packards made a sizeable racket, yet it was a regular sound and, in time, barely noticed.

"I weren't suggesting no one," Bridger said. "Least no one hereabouts. It wouldn't hurt them two up front to shake a leg occasionally."

The rivalry between those at the Oerlikon who, having been present aboard *194*, considered themselves senior, was now ingrained and hardly helped by a similar attitude from Peters and Hickman who manned the more powerful gun.

"Don't know about kye, I could use a smoko," Thompson said.

"You're kiddin' me," Daly told him, though there was doubt in the Irishman's voice. "Light up back here and you'll be off the boat in seconds!"

Thompson showed brief interest. "That right, is it Paddy?"

"Sure as hell is." Bridger was keen to assert his position. "No naked flame aft of the bridge – you should know that."

"An' we're goin' into action," Daly added.

"So what exactly would happen?" Thompson asked.

"A charge is the least you could expect." Bridger was unusually serious. "But it ain't a rule made for the fun of it; we're sitting on several ton of petrol. When Paddy says you'll leave, that's exactly what'll happen, with a jet of flame up your arse and us lot close alongside."

"He's right, Thumper," Mitchel confirmed more gently. "Forget it."

Thompson accepted this in silence. He hadn't really wanted a fag; it was more something to say. But with the way he had been feeling of late, Daly's prediction didn't seem all that terrible.

* * *

Just on two o'clock: they'd been at sea for a little over three hours and the coast of France loomed ominously in the starlight.

"Moonrise expected in just over an hour." This was Milner, who must have noticed Anderson glancing at his watch. Their target lay to the east, just beyond the headland, and so far they'd been fortunate, the only Germans spotted being two flights of bombers heading north. If their luck held, they would be in, out, and heading back to Blighty before the light increased. Anderson leant forward to the W/T voice pipe.

"How's the RDF plot, Tel'?"

"Land is crisp and clear though our objective lies in a

shadow."

That was to be expected. "Alright, I'll take us to port, and we'll make our approach from there."

Closing the voice pipe, he turned to Milner while trying not to notice the training officer making a note on his pad.

"You heard that, Number One; better get below and keep watch over Harvey's shoulder. First sight of shipping of any description, let me know."

"Very good, sir."

"Okay, 'Swain, take us ten degrees to port."

"Port ten, sir."

There was slightly more space with Milner gone, yet Anderson already missed his presence and found himself wondering if Harris had noticed when he left the bridge in the past.

"Watch your tail, captain."

The training officer's remark immediately brought Anderson back to reality. On such a clear night it surely hadn't been necessary to alert the trailing boats to his turn: all should have expected such a move. But though Jennings, to port, followed perfectly, Cooke was maintaining his previous course and steadily pulling away to starboard.

Cursing softly, Anderson reached for the Aldis; it had a blue lens and would be directed away from shore, but any light shown so close to enemy territory was best avoided. Fortunately, either someone on the bridge reported his mistake, or Cooke himself came to his senses as the gunboat turned to port and was soon making for her correct station.

Anderson replaced the unused Aldis without a word, and Lieutenant Commander Crehan, the training officer, was equally silent as he made another note in that damned book.

* * *

The trio of gunboats were creeping beyond the headland now and, avoiding the bulk of Crehan standing resolutely to his right, Anderson began to inspect the nearby coast through his binoculars. The turn had been made several minutes before and, though he could not pick out individual buildings or any traffic on the roads, the enemy coast did not appear threatening. Actually, so clear was the night they would probably have survived well enough without the magical powers of RDF.

Yet incorporating the modern wonder was part of the exercise and, after flipping open the W/T voice pipe cover, Anderson felt a measure of relief when it was Milner who answered.

"I'm about to start our starboard turn and will be making towards Port Racine." This was the medieval village that lay deep in the bay and just to the west of their objective. "Keep me posted on what you see." Then, to Nolan at the helm, "Okay, 'Swain, be ready to take us in on my word."

320 was still several miles from the shore, though that could be covered in no time at the gunboats' maximum speed, and Anderson wanted to be sure the rest of his small force would follow. His standing orders were for a line ahead to be formed, with Jennings immediately behind and Cooke at the rear. The nearest significant enemy gun emplacement was several miles to the west, where it swept the channel between the French coast and Alderney, while another, mounted on the eastern headland, was not much further off. Neither could reach deep into the bay that lay directly ahead, although there was bound to be lighter, mobile ordnance waiting to meet them there. With hulls made from little more than strips of mahogany, the gunboats' security mainly lay in speed and manoeuvrability. After surviving considerably heavier defences at St Nazaire, Anderson felt he could keep his own command safe; only time would tell if Jennings and Cooke would do as well.

"The rest of your squadron are on station." It was an unexpected remark; the more so as it came from the training officer. Anderson smiled to himself; though pretty much mute until this point, it seemed Lieutenant Commander Crehan was starting to take more of an interest in the mission.

And he was correct, a quick glance confirmed Anderson now led an impressive attack force, with each boat maintaining the correct distance and positioning.

"To starboard, 'Swain," he directed. "Make for the small harbour ahead."

It might not have been the most technical of helm orders, yet Nolan knew what he meant, and *320* began to head deeper into the bay.

The chart had shown adequate depth within fifty yards of the shore, though Anderson had no wish to creep that near. Closing to a hundred would be more than adequate and allow them to skim the land at a speed that should confuse any batteries sited there.

But as they drew nearer, and the structure of the medieval harbour grew in detail, there was no sign of opposition from the shore.

"Ready to turn to port," he warned, and noticed Nolan tensing at the wheel. There would be no time to watch the others, if they missed 320's manoeuvre, choosing instead to run hell for leather onto the harbour wall, it would be their concern.

"Now, hard over!"

320 turned on the proverbial sixpence then, following a further order from Anderson, surged ahead as Nolan pressed all three throttles forward. Then, directly before them, lay their objective.

Even lit by nothing more than starlight, the sharp outline of the signal station stood out boldly. It probably would have been built to withstand a heavier bombardment than they were about to inflict, though the small tower mounted on its roof should prove vulnerable and any attack on an enemy installation was worth a fortune in propaganda.

This one would not be simple, however; even as 320 closed, two separate streams of green tracer began to flow in their direction. Anderson reached for the firing gongs but before he could give formal permission, Peters and Hickman opened up with the forward-mounted Vickers.

The initial shots fell low and, as Anderson was obliged to weave slightly to avoid a thorough pounding, the next flew wide. Peters was on the ball, though, and needed no more than two seconds of relative stability to nail one of the batteries before moving on to the second. But there would be no time for that, their objective was the signal station and, though destroying further ground defences might have benefitted the following boats, Anderson was determined to land a few shells there himself.

And Peters had clearly listened at the briefing. As the stark building rushed up on their starboard bow, the two-pounder began a savage assault on its concrete walls. Chips must have been flying, although Anderson wanted something more substantial;

something to put the station out of action and cause problems for his unseen enemy. Then, just as they were almost level, Peters raised his aim and sent the mast tumbling backwards.

That would be all from the forward cannon, though Bridger, at the Oerlikon had taken over and was dusting the wreckage with red tracer. But Anderson's attention was needed elsewhere; the bay was coming to a close, he must take *320* back out to sea or risk running aground.

"Port fifteen, 'Swain," he ordered.

Glancing back, he saw Jennings' boat engaging the signal station, her forward gun causing further damage before the aft Oerlikon apparently knocked out the second shore battery leaving the coast clear for the following craft.

With no significant defence, Cooke had the sense to slow slightly and treat the battered structure to a more intense bombardment that wreaked true havoc; Anderson even thought he saw one of the walls and part of the roof collapse.

But there was no time for further inspection, another helm order sent *320* heading directly for the open sea and, eventually, safety.

A head appeared at the wheelhouse ladder.

"Not much on the set," Milner shouted. "Thought I'd be more use up top."

"I'm afraid you missed most of the excitement."

Milner glanced back. "Looks like you did a thorough job."

A whistle from the W/T office speaking tube broke into their conversation. Milner flipped the lip open to answer, but Harvey's frantic voice cut through before he could.

"Vessel clearing the eastern headland and heading our way!"

Instantly the two officers raised their binoculars.

"And she's moving fast." Harvey continued, "I'd say it were an E, or something similar!"

Nothing was visible by the dark line of land or on the horizon beyond. And then something slightly further to the east did catch Anderson's attention.

"E-boat, starboard bow!" It was Nolan, at the helm; even without glasses, the coxswain had noticed the vague oncoming shape.

Though a good two miles off, and now well beyond the

headland, the German's bow wave – so much smaller than that created by a planing hull – could soon be made out. And, as Anderson was painfully aware, it might not be alone. His presence must be well known by now, and more E-boats would be following, either immediately, or in time.

He also knew there were effectively only two choices; turn to port and make a run for it or head towards the threat at maximum revs with all guns firing. And, in less than a second, Anderson had made up his mind.

* * *

It was a warm night and, even before engaging the shore guns, then pounding that signal station into what they hoped would be dust, both Peters and Hickman had been sweating profusely. But as *320* headed out of the bay, they began to cool somewhat. And when they heard Nolan's shout, and saw the hated craft off the starboard bow, they were both suddenly, and deathly, cold.

"That'll be an E," Peters said.

"Aye, more'n likely." Hickman ran a dry tongue around his lips. "Reckon we can take it?"

Peters said nothing for a moment, then shrugged and seemed to relax as he settled himself in the firing position. "There's only one way to find out," he said.

* * *

"Just the one," Milner remarked, although that in no way diminished the threat. Even ignoring torpedoes that could sink a vessel far larger than any of the British launches, the E-boat was superior in almost every way. The one advantage Anderson held was in numbers; used effectively, his small squadron might run rings around the oncoming vessel though only if Jennings and Cooke chose to cooperate.

For he would be totally dependent on the other commanders' efficiency and, so far, both had failed to impress. Admittedly they'd not placed the rest of Anderson's force in any

167

actual danger but this time it would be different. Unless they obeyed the next order – along with those that followed – to the letter, it could spell disaster.

"Make to the others," Anderson told Milner. "'Close up and form line abreast.'"

It was sufficient for an Aldis signal; Jennings and Cooke were some distance behind and might not know of the E-boat's existence though that would soon change. And if it really needed the threat of an enemy close by to make them come to heel, it was better he found out now.

"Both are manoeuvring," Milner said, replacing the signal lamp.

"Very good. Bring her down to eighteen hundred." Anderson looked back. Sure enough, the trailing gunboats were already pulling out of line and accelerating. Within thirty seconds they had taken station on either side of 320.

"Okay, 'Swain, up to twenty hundred and make for the E."

Again, it was hardly a conventional order, but Nolan understood and the intake of breath from Lieutenant Commander Crehan, be it real or imagined, probably had more to do with the equally unusual tactics.

Yet Anderson felt comfortable with his decision. Though a powerful craft, the MkV was slower than a triple-diesel-driven E-boat. To run would only encourage pursuit, and a return to the ill-matched contest of an aft-mounted and exposed Oerlikon firing against heavier weaponry in an armoured housing. Their forward-mounted Vickers would be far more effective, while having Jennings and Cooke to either side adding to the barrage might just be enough to see off the solitary German.

Which was in plain sight now, and still obviously heading for them at speed.

"What do you think, Number One?" Anderson bellowed. "Any further sign of company?"

Milner was already sweeping the horizon and lowered his glasses after a final check.

"None that I can see, sir," he shouted in reply. "And there's been nothing from the RDF."

"Very well, open her up fully, 'Swain!"

The enemy craft was growing visibly closer with every second, her displacement hull cutting through the water with the speed and portent of a torpedo. Soon it would be down to him and how he handled both *320* and the other boats. So, he supposed, it wasn't so very strange that, even after so much had happened, Anderson found himself missing Harris more than ever.

* * *

Peters and Hickman were unaware of the last point; until he demonstrated otherwise, the skipper would have their entire confidence. And neither were they worried by the prospect of further E-boats appearing; so fixated were they on the oncoming German, the fact it might have company had not occurred. Even the clatter of firing gongs failed to fully register; it was merely permission to open fire, not an order to do so. The final judgement as to when they might reach the approaching craft would be down to them.

   With both vessels closing at a combined speed of close to ninety miles an hour, the time soon came and, without a word to the other, *320*'s forward Vickers quickly settled into the distinctive pom-pom rhythm and sent streaks of red tracer snaking towards the speeding enemy.

   Soon it was joined by further lines as all three gunboats unleashed their main weaponry. *320*'s shots appeared to be falling slightly in advance of the E-boat, which was how it should be: how Peters liked it. Tracer was only an indication and likely to fall short of the actual shells, while to effectively be steering into a wall of fire was known to disconcert an enemy.

   But the German was no less eager, and soon flashes of green were heading for *320*, apparently accelerating as they drew near until it seemed impossible they would fail to find a home. But miss they did, and the skipper's confidence that they would, and in keeping the boat on a steady course, was appreciated by both gunners.

   And then the British shots were apparently flying wild rather than dusting the waters ahead of their quarry; the German must have slowed. Peters who had been steadily altering the elevation, increased until the wheel was little more than a blur, yet still it was not enough. And then it became apparent that, rather than stopping, the enemy was turning – and sharply – to starboard.

169

"On the run!" Hickman's comment went unheard as Peters fought to train the Vickers around fast enough. Their starboard gunboat was making better practice and already landing shots on the E-boat's tail, while the German began sending back a positive barrage from her heavier aft ordnance. But their own skipper was holding his nerve, and did not alter course, and soon all three British cannon had centred on the retreating enemy.

Within seconds the lines of green were shut down, which only encouraged the British gunners further. And then they were reaching the limit of their elevation. For some time the shots had been wandering and now fell increasingly short as the German edged deeper into the night.

The firing gongs rattled once more although Peters had already ceased to fire. Stepping back and wiping the sweat from his forehead, he drew breath.

"That's a sight and no questioning," Hickman said as the pair watched the image fade further. In the time they had been engaging, *320* had all but left the coast behind, while a tender moon was just lifting over the horizon and starting to shed further light on the dark waters. Then came a change in engine pitch. For too long their Packards had been pressed to the limit and, now as a more acceptable level was reached, the entire boat seemed to be relaxing with them.

Three gunboats coming at speed and with forward cannon blazing," Peters said. "I think I'd 'ave legged it an' all."

* * *

"Well, I can't pretend your tactics were conventional, captain," Lieutenant Commander Crehan announced as they approached the same berth *320* had left the previous evening. Since then they had engaged two enemy gun emplacements, a signal station and, latterly, that E-boat. And, despite not taking any rest or even leaving the bridge, the journey back seemed to have been over in an instant although Anderson equally felt all might have happened the previous week. "And I think you can count yourself lucky that German was alone. Were there more than one S-Craft it could have been a very different story."

"Indeed, sir."

Anderson's reluctance to explain further was not totally

170

down to exhaustion. He accepted the training officer was experienced and had commanded CMBs both in the previous war and during the twenties. But Crehan had never faced an E-boat and, like so many of the older trainers, regularly referred to them by their German designation. And perhaps even someone as seasoned as him might be just a little intimidated by their specifications.

As Anderson had been, along with so many of his contemporaries, when they were first encountered. But experience taught him E-boats were primarily used to protect their own merchants, along with the occasional, and usually deadly, attack on British cargo vessels. Rarely were they risked in an all-out fight with Coastal Forces launches. Anderson had figured – gambled almost – a concerted effort would drive the solitary enemy away, and so it proved.

And Crehan was wrong on a further point; Anderson had been equally confident it was a single opponent. RDF might be in its infancy and swept a relatively shallow field, yet no further craft were detected, granting him the rare luxury of knowing his enemy's strength.

"Still, I have to concede, it was a well-planned action and competently carried out."

"Thank you, sir." Anderson's reply was automatic. Despite the importance of the lieutenant commander's words, his mind had been elsewhere.

"I shall say as much in my report. Now, I'll bid you good night," a rare smile, "or should it be morning – and wish you luck in future actions."

"It might have been worse," Milner said, once the training officer left the bridge and could be seen marching stiffly down the quay.

"I guess so," Anderson replied, though inwardly he was more than pleased with the night's progress.

"No, sir," Milner insisted. "I really mean it might have been worse."

Despite his tiredness, there was a look in his second in command's eye that made Anderson stop and even sounded an inner alarm bell. Nolan had completed the shutdown procedure and was squeezing down the ladder to the wheelhouse.

"We lost RDF," Milner said.

"Indeed?" This was important. "When?"

"Just before the attack on that E," Milner replied. "I only discovered on going below after the action. Harvey's adamant he tried to report it, though I'm blowed if I heard anything."

"Nor me," Anderson confessed.

"Nor Lieutenant Commander Crehan, or so it would appear."

Anderson's mind began to race; in the heat of action, at maximum revs, and with a two-pound pom-pom sounding off forward, a voice pipe whistle may well have been missed. The fact that it was a single E-boat had been pivotal to his actions; even the chance of it being joined by others would have altered matters considerably.

"But the others," he said. "Jennings' and Cooke's boats – they're equipped with RDF and would have reported if reinforcements were sighted."

"Why should they?" Milner replied. "Neither had any idea our set was down."

Anderson supposed that was correct and wondered for a moment what he would have done had he known.

"When exactly did you discover?" he asked.

"Shortly after the action. I went below to plot our course home and ran into Harvey. It wasn't a major problem and is fixed now; he sorted it almost immediately, in fact, so I decided we should keep it from the TO."

"Absolutely," Anderson agreed. If Crehan knew they had effectively taken on an E-boat blind, his assessment might have been very different. "You did the right thing."

"Thank you, sir." Milner grinned. "It felt so at the time. And it was a good exercise."

"It was," Anderson agreed. "I think we all learned quite a bit."

Chapter Seventeen

"It seems you impressed Commander Swinley's lot." The base captain was leafing through several typewritten sheets on the desk before him. "Though not always for the right reasons."

"No, sir." Anderson was well aware of the problems his crew had caused ashore, though found it hard to condemn them for it. After several weeks of intense instruction, the need to release a little energy should be expected. And if their frustration came as a surprise to those managing the new training establishment, perhaps it was something they might learn from. He had no wish to command a gunboat crewed by saints.

As it was, he had done his best to see the punishments were as lenient as possible and, on discovering his men faced a month confined to barracks, successfully argued the time had already been spent during their training period.

"So, you're back at *Wasp*, for the time being at least," Brooks continued, and Anderson raised an eyebrow. This sounded less than permanent.

"I'm not assigning you to a flotilla, instead you'll act as our spare, standing in for any with major mechanical problems, and maybe carrying out the odd solo mission."

"That's not what I expected, sir," Anderson said.

"Nor me." The base captain looked up. "Frankly, Ian, I'm at a loss, though have been told specifically to hold *320* back. It could be they're planning something special – as I said, your report from *Bee* was basically very good."

"So, I'm just supposed to hang fire and wait? That doesn't make sense."

"What does in this crazy war?" The base captain gave a tired smile. "But take my advice and don't make any long-term plans for remaining in Dover."

* * *

"I'm back in Dover, permanent," Thompson told Joyce.

"Nice for you." There was a distinct lack of enthusiasm, but he persisted.

"So, I'd like to look you up."

There was a pause; it was almost as if he could hear her thinking.

"If that's what you want," she said at last. "Though you're not coming to my place."

"Fair enough," he said. "Maybe we could meet in the town?"

"Alright; Market Square."

He smiled to himself; it was about the most public part of Dover; the old girl wasn't taking any chances.

"Fine, we've got twenty-four hours liberty."

"Then one o'clock this afternoon, I'll be outside the *Crown and Anchor*. But we ain't going inside," she added hurriedly, "and I warn you, Frank Thompson, I'm not standing for no more of your nonsense."

* * *

320 was back in her old berth at the Camber and, as Anderson approached, there was obvious activity on board. Bridger and Mitchel were aft of the bridge working on the Oerlikon and Newman must be doing something messy in the engine room as periodic clouds of black smoke were being expelled from the exhausts. He stepped from the pontoon and up onto the gunboat's deck, then opened the wheelhouse door and entered.

"Good morning, sir!" Milner stood up from a stool by the chart table. "Just in time, there's fresh tea brewing."

"That would be welcome." Anderson took off his cap and hung it next to the oilskins. "I've just come from the base captain's office," he began, before realising Milner had already set off down to the galley.

"Is it good news?" the officer asked, returning with two full tin mugs.

"Good and bad; we've been designated 'spare boat'." Anderson took one of the mugs then placed it down quickly as the enamelled surface was too hot to hold for very long.

"So, no flotilla?" Milner resumed his seat at the chart table

174

as Anderson collected another stool and retrieved his drink.

"No, but from what I gather it's not permanent."

"You think we might be transferred?"

"Who can tell? Commander Brooks was none the wiser."

"Well, we're up to date on board." Milner picked up a small notepad. "I've booked fuelling for first thing tomorrow morning. Those on liberty today will be back then and there'll be more than enough to cope. Ammunition for the Lewis guns is being delivered later, along with some spares for the Vickers Bridger requested and further Mills bombs for the Holman."

Practice with the Holman Projector had taken an entire day at *Bee* and not been impressive. Despite using up the best part of two boxes of explosives, the beast remained unpredictable in terms of range and direction.

"Oil will be taken on board at the same time as fuel and I've put in for seven pounds of dried soup."

"Soup?" Anderson questioned.

"We're heading for Autumn; it's going to be colder at night. I've also put in for a safari jar, though that might take a little longer."

"Very good."

"And frankly sir, I'm not too happy about our stove."

"Stove? Is it not the standard issue?"

"No, I think the builders pulled a fast one. All the MkVs I've come across have electrical units, whereas ours is fitted with an oil. It works well enough though there is additional risk from further inflammable liquid below deck as well as naked flames in the accommodation."

That was something Anderson had not considered, although a couple of gallons of heating oil was nothing to the vast quantities of far more volatile liquid the gunboat regularly carried. "I see," he said, "and what do you propose to do about it?"

"I've already sent a fizzer to the builders and copied it to Vice Admiral Talbot."

"Talbot?" Anderson shook his head. "Who he?"

Milner looked mildly apologetic. "Fourth Sea Lord, sir: Director of Dockyards. His younger son and I were at prep school together."

"And you don't think such an approach was a little out of proportion?"

175

"I think it might have some effect," Milner grinned, "certainly if the builders want any more government contracts."

Anderson smiled briefly, it was not a tactic he would have chosen, though that should not rule it out.

"The Oerlikon's being serviced as we speak," Milner continued, "and Thompson and Daly are up to date with their weapons. Peters and Hickman are on leave today but will be servicing their weapon after helping with the refuelling. And I've ordered the following supplies."

Anderson scanned the proffered list. Some were essential, such as replacements for the medical tin, others, such as tea and kye, could probably have waited. But as *320* only put in the previous afternoon, Milner had achieved much.

"Very good, Number One," he said, handing the paper back. And it was strange how automatic that title was becoming. "I have to say you're turning out a far more efficient first officer than I ever was."

Milner's face betrayed a moment of doubt then, on realising his captain's words were sincere, blushed slightly. "Good of you to say so, sir."

"Our time at *Bee* wasn't exactly easy but would have been far worse without your help."

Milner was very obviously trying to think of a suitable response, but Anderson thought it better to move on.

"So how do you feel about us being the spare?" he asked, before taking a sip from his mug.

"It'll be strange not being part of a flotilla, though I'm more interested in where we might be sent."

"I'm with you there," Anderson agreed, replacing the tea, which was still too hot. "And what exactly we'll be doing."

* * *

"Hello Frank." Her tone was flat but there was a glimmer of affability – or was it resignation?

"Joyce," he replied, and she allowed him to kiss her formally on the cheek. "You're looking well."

The days were definitely starting to chill, and it was windy outside the pub, but Thompson knew better than to suggest they

176

went inside. "There're some seats, under the trees," he said, pointing to the far side of the square. "Why don't we sit awhile?"

Though not a market day, Dover felt unusually busy and, once they were settled, both preferred watching the hurrying figures to conversation. It was Thompson who finally broke the silence.

"I *am* sorry," he said. "You got to believe me. I never went to hit a woman before, and don't want to, not ever again."

"I don't want you to neither." Joyce's voice was slightly lighter.

"Well, I won't and that's it," he said.

"You've lost weight," she told him.

"Have I?" He was wearing his number three square rig and, until then, had wished he'd added a coat. "We been training," he added. "Lots of runnin' about."

"Must have done you good."

"How's the new place?"

She shrugged. "Not as nice as that house – before your mates started messin' with it, that is."

"I'd like to see it," he said.

"Maybe, Frank. In time."

"Well look who it ain't!" The voice came from behind and made them both jump.

Thompson was the first to turn around and looked up in surprise. "Hello, Ted."

"Hello yourself. Got a bleedin' cheek, haven't you?"

"Cheek?"

"Showin' yourself like this, after what you done."

"I ain't done nothing." As Thompson stood and turned, he noticed Ted was not alone.

"That's not what Mr Granger thinks," Charlie said. "Told us to give you a message if we ran into you."

"Must be your lucky day!" Ted added.

"Look, I don't know what you think," Thompson began, but Ted pushed him firmly in the chest, and he fell back onto the grass.

"Leave him alone, he ain't done nuthin'!" Joyce shouted.

"An' you can shut it an' all," Charlie told her as the men passed either side of the bench and approached the still recumbent Thompson.

"Lads, you got it all wrong!" One hand was raised, and he

177

went to rise, but nothing stopped the boot from landing squarely in Thompson's belly.

"Stop it!" It was more of a scream than a shout but neither man took notice of Joyce and continued to pummel Thompson with kicks as he rolled, gasping, on the grass.

"Leave him!" She had taken off her shoe and began hitting the nearest – Charlie – who looked at her in surprise and mild disgust. A quick and not so gentle shove sent her away, leaving the men to focus fully on Thompson – so much so they missed the arrival of two further seamen.

"Alright, Thumper, we got this!"

It was Hickman, the loader for *320*'s forward-facing Vickers. He grabbed Ted's arm, pulling him backwards and sideways while Peters, who had accompanied his mate for a spot of shopping, found greater stimulation in laying into Charlie with his right fist.

It was over relatively quickly. From Thompson being surprised, to Granger's men beating an ignominious retreat took less than ninety seconds, yet a lot had happened. And Thompson was in a bad way, with wheezing lungs, bleeding nose, and a cut forehead. His shipmates helped him back to the bench where Joyce tried to stop the blood with her handkerchief.

"Friends of yours?" Peters asked.

"I know 'em," Thompson spluttered.

"And it weren't right," Joyce added. "He never deserved that."

"Reckon no one deserves a beating," Hickman agreed.

"We'd better get him back to *Wasp*," Peters said, but Joyce shook her head.

"My place is only round the corner; I'll look after him there."

"Want us to stick around?" Hickman asked. "In case them monkeys come back?"

"No, it'll be alright," she said. "Thanks for helping, but I can manage him from now on."

* * *

It was minelayer protection. Anderson handed the brief to Milner who read it without a word. *320* was to shepherd a launch to the west of the Ruytingen sandbanks, about a mile off the coast of France.

"Should be an in and out job," he said when his second in command had finished. "No more than forty miles to the lay; we ought to be back in under six hours, even if they take their time about it."

"Just the one minelayer," Milner said, after reading through for a second time. "I've not done this sort of thing before but aren't there usually six or seven layers and a decent-sized escort?"

"That's normally the case," Anderson agreed.

They were alone aboard the gunboat, Newman and his men having left half an hour before and, though now fuelled, stored, and ready for action, *320* was yet to be assigned for active service. But this would be an unofficial trip, one Commander Brooks had been asked to organise, and Anderson was unsure exactly how much he should tell his second in command.

"I gather it's a little hush-hush," he said. "They'll be laying a new type of mine in an existing field. Don't ask me the exact details but I gather it incorporates a novel form of snag line which the boffins are keen to try out."

"Hence the secrecy."

"I guess so, it's still at the experimental stage. This is the first practical test, and they don't want Jerry getting wind until we're sure it works properly."

"So just two boats?"

"That's the general idea, less chance of being detected and, if we are, more of getting away."

"A lot will depend on the type of minelayer they use," Milner mused. "Many can't make twenty knots."

"That we have yet to discover," Anderson replied. "But whatever they choose, we have to protect it."

"And will we be entering the field?"

"Absolutely not. Our nursemaid duties end on reaching the danger area."

"I suppose it's a compliment, of sorts."

Anderson looked up from the weather forecast that had also been issued. "In what way?"

"We're a relatively new boat. Untried," Milner raised his eyebrows, "rather like the mine."

"And rather like the mine, expendable," Anderson replied. "Remember, we're not attached to any flotilla so are also pretty much superfluous."

"All the same..." Milner began reading for the third time, "do you think this is connected with any future plans?"

Anderson pulled a face. "You mean, are we to become full-time minelayer support?"

"Or something along those lines. It wouldn't be out of the question."

"You may be right," Anderson finally agreed. "Though not an idea I'd warm to."

* * *

"Lookin' a bit better now," Peters told Thompson as he pressed a fresh piece of sticking plaster on the gunner's face. "Reckon you'll pass muster."

"No one said anything when I turned up for duty yesterday," Thompson said. "All they needed were hands to see the boat to the oiler; couldn't give tuppence about what any of us 'ad been up to."

"I think you were lucky," Hickman said. "If an officer noticed your phiz he might have had a few questions."

Thompson was lying on his bed in the dormitory; a position he had held for much of the time since returning from Joyce's flat. And though the cut on his forehead wasn't the only part that hurt, he did not feel as bad as he might.

For a start, he and Joyce were on better terms. He wasn't exactly sure why, but watching him taking a beating seemed to have built a few bridges in their relationship. Thompson would never have inflicted anything like the seeing-to on her, but he was as powerless to stop Granger's boys as she would have been with him.

"Word is we're on a shout tomorrow night," Harvey announced from his own bed on the opposite side of the room. "Think you'll be up for it?"

"Oh, I'll be there." Thompson still spoke through a slightly swollen nose, but Peters was right, he was showing considerable improvement.

And that was another thing that had gone his way. Having Peters and Hickman come to his rescue was unexpected, especially as they were recent additions to *320*'s crew. But his shipmates' help had gone beyond two of them laying into Granger's louts and seeing them on their way. On his return to *Wasp*, all in the dorm showed genuine concern. It was Thompson's first experience of such compassion, and he was affected far more than he cared to admit.

"Still think you should be on to the Rozzers," Pickering said. "Can't have servicemen attacked in broad daylight for nee reason."

"Not as if Thumper did anything wrong," Mitchel agreed.

"I didn't want to make a fuss." Thompson had quickly learned making light of the situation was appreciated by his mates.

"Maybe, but you can be too agreeable," Harvey said, and Thompson had to hold back a chuckle. It was not a description he was used to.

"Right," Mitchel agreed. "Scum like that shouldn't be allowed to get away with it."

"String 'em up, that's what I say," Nolan added with a wry grin.

"Talkin' of which, I hear Gibson's for the drop." Daly was reading a newspaper and his lack of compassion for a former shipmate stood out in contrast.

"Weren't he the bloke I took over from?" Thompson asked.

"Aye, you were firin' his guns until recently." Pickering was equally dispassionate.

"An' Scouse still sleeps in his bed," Daly added.

"What's that?" Nolan exclaimed.

"Sure, but they changed the sheets," the Irishman assured.

"Murder, weren't it?" Bridger asked.

"Amongst other things." Daly turned the page. "Can't say I ever liked the fellow and, even if I did, there are some things you don't forgive."

"What else did he do?" Kipling asked.

Pickering considered the youngster for a moment. "Interfered with a young girl," he said.

"An' tried it on with another, so he did," Daly added.

181

"That's the one thing I can't stomach," Peters said.

"Any man who so much as touches a woman deserves stringing up," Hickman agreed.

Thompson swallowed.

"You feelin' alright, Thumper?" Harvey asked.

"I'm fine. Just a bit wobbly."

"Probably still shaken," Bridger agreed. "Get an early night."

"I think I might," Thompson said.

* * *

320 had fired up and was resting on her final wires when the minelayer came into view.

"It's a Fairmile B all right." Milner's disappointment was plain. "There go our chances of a quick passage."

"There were a load at St Nazaire," Anderson said. "And not many made it back."

Milner turned to him. "I was forgetting, sir, you must be familiar with the type."

"They catch fire horribly easily," Anderson agreed. "And when you've seen so many destroyed..."

The launch was passing them now and they already had permission to proceed. Milner shifted his weight uncertainly, and then Anderson appeared to snap out of his trance.

"Never mind, we won't be facing the same odds tonight," he said. "And Tommy Washburn's in command. I've known him a while; there are few more capable. Cast off all and let's get it over with."

320 took up position behind the minelayer and soon they had cleared harbour and were in the Channel chops.

"Weather's due to remain clear for the next hour or so." They were running at no more than twenty knots; close to the Fairmile's maximum speed but half of *320*'s potential and dawdling so would soon start to frustrate. "Then we can expect rain followed by a waxing moon."

"Fine for us," Anderson replied. "We just have to stooge about and keep the elephants away. Washburn will need to find

182

the minefield, then lay his eggs."

"Not a job I'd like," Milner agreed. "Makes you wonder why they put in for it."

"Makes you wonder why any of us did," Anderson agreed.

* * *

It was just under three hours later when the flicker of blue from the Fairmile's Aldis warned them they were reaching the designated area. To that point it had been a trouble-free run, with only the sight of outgoing British bombers to break the monotony. But as Nolan brought their speed down, before cutting the engines completely, all knew they were in for a wait.

320 soon lost momentum and began to reel and lurch horribly, although all eyes remained on the minelayer as she entered the danger area. In theory, it would be safe; providing the mines were properly laid, the Fairmile's shallow draught should allow her to pass over without problems while her wooden hull would have no effect on those of the magnetic variety. But even the stoutest securing wires could stretch or fail, while a faulty sensor might be set off by the metal contained in a pair of marine engines.

And the rain came exactly as predicted. Even before the small craft was a mile away, she began to fade and in no time was totally lost from sight.

"Washburn told me he was carrying two navigators," Anderson said, remembering the young, smiling man he had met at that evening's briefing – could that really have been only a few hours before?

"And he'll probably need them." Milner's voice sounded unusually loud in the near silence.

Anderson nodded. Even with the extra manpower, and a system of wires that he had never properly understood, laying mines still seemed an unusually dangerous occupation.

"Strange," he continued to gaze in the general direction of the now invisible launch. "One small boat and no more than twenty men, yet he'll be carrying enough explosives to sink an entire fleet."

"But to those chaps it's just another night's work," Milner

183

said. "This might be slightly different; new type and all that. But I bet it won't be the first time they've needed to enter a live field."

"I suppose not," Anderson agreed. "Let's hope it isn't the last."

* * *

Despite their goon suits, both Thompson and Daly were soaked to the skin. And with *320* lying cut, and in an extremely vulnerable position, they had little choice other than to stay at their action stations next to the Lewis guns, and not seek the limited shelter of the Oerlikon's bandstand. But Thompson, at least, was not downhearted. His relationship with Joyce was repaired to some extent and the recent support of his shipmates had been more than encouraging. He might still be in Coastal Forces, and the Navy in general, although no longer did he feel any need to leave. Nonetheless, he would still have preferred it to stop raining and, with the boat rising and falling so, was starting to doubt the strength of his stomach.

"How long do you think they'll be?" he shouted across to Daly, at the opposite gun.

"Now how would any of us be knowing that?" The Irishman replied and Thompson's attention returned to where they'd lost sight of the minelayer. If anything, the rain was growing worse. The French coast must surely be close, yet was totally invisible; indeed, he could see little beyond *320*'s prow.

"Bit of sweet?"

Daly had left his post and was standing next to him with a paper bag in hand. Thompson removed a glove and helped himself to a barley sugar.

"Don't reckon there'll be much for us to do," he said as his mouth came alive with the flavour.

"Sure, but think of the time we'll get off from purgatory." Daly's tone was totally neutral.

"I'd rather this than arguing the toss with an E-boat," Thompson added. The barley sugar had taken away some of his nausea, leaving him simply cold and wet.

"An' better than dealing with mines, like them poor buggers." Daly gave a nod into the distance. "Can't be much fun."

"Fun?" Thompson questioned.

"Carrying all that explosive on deck."

"They probably feel the same about us," Thompson said. "Stuck out here with nothing to do."

"Sure, I bet they're thinking of nothing else," Daly agreed.

* * *

"Shouldn't be much longer," Milner said. The wind increased with the storm, forcing them to start their auxiliary engine just to maintain station, and the faint humming was becoming soporific.

"At the briefing, Tommy Washburn reckoned it could be done in half an hour," Anderson replied. "Though he's had almost twice that."

"Ought to be a little faster on the way home," Milner supposed. "Less to carry and all that."

"Must say, I could do with a warm."

"Shall I send down for more kye?"

Anderson shook his head. They'd already had a mug of the hot, thick cocoa, and he really did expect to see the minelayer's prow emerging from the mist at any moment.

"Too close for RDF," Milner said, "and we can't call him up on R/T."

"This near to the shore would be an open invitation to the enemy," Anderson agreed.

"Might draw them onto the minefield." The younger man grinned, and he was about to say more when the darkness dissolved in a welter of intense light.

A mushroom of flame rose up, defying the rain and ruining the night vision of all topside. And then came the bolt of sound, far sharper than thunder and several times as loud.

"What the..." Milner began but Anderson was calling for all engines and as *320* began to ease forward, the shockwave hit, forcing her bow to starboard and making the entire craft tip alarmingly.

"Can you see anything?" Anderson shouted.

"Not a sausage," Milner replied. The eruption had died as quickly as it came, leaving only a stain on their eyes, but *320* was rising onto the plane and at least a degree of stability had returned.

"Wait," Nolan shouted from the helm. "There's a light!"

Both officers followed the coxswain's pointed finger where

flames could definitely be made out.

"Too far to port," Milner said.

There was no doubting that, even with *320* having lain cut for so long, Anderson was reasonably sure of their position. If that patch of fire represented what was left of the minelayer, she must have strayed considerably.

"Throttle back," he ordered. The burning debris was still some way off, yet the outer edges of the minefield must be close, and the remains of Washburn's boat lay within. He turned to Milner.

"What do you think, Number One?"

Milner wiped the rain from his face. "I'd say the night's about to get a lot more interesting."

* * *

They were back to just the auxiliary engine and barely making steerage way, while the foredeck was crowded with men peering into the darkness. Milner was with them and the yellowed beam of his large rubber torch swept the area immediately ahead. Even such a feeble light would be visible for some way but the alternative, to blunder blind into what might be the same fate as the Fairmile, was unthinkable.

"We should be immune to anything below; it's just what might be on the surface that has to be avoided." This was not the first time Milner had made the statement, but it could bear repetition. Ahead, and now less than fifty yards off, the remaining glimmers of flame told them they would soon be looking for something other than sea mines.

Quite what had caused the explosion was a mystery and probably destined to remain so. If, as seemed likely, it was down to one of the new mines, the securing wires of existing charges could have been shattered, making the area lethal to vessels of every shape and design.

But drifting mines weren't Milner's only concern. *320* was being exposed to such a danger in the hope of rescuing survivors, however unlikely such a thing might be. And not just for the saving of life, with an experimental weapon, any clues as to what caused the failure would be invaluable.

The first body was spotted shortly afterwards though

186

Milner made no comment when Bridger pointed it out. Despite being a seaman and, by the goon suit and lifejacket, from Coastal Forces, there was no possibility of life, and to delay would only place all aboard *320* at greater risk. Yet even such a grisly find did give encouragement of sorts, and shortly afterwards they began to encounter further detritus from the minelayer.

The vast majority was of the material variety, though almost as poignant. A vacant life preserver, several lengths of line and what looked like part of a cupboard, or perhaps a drawer. Milner raised a hand, and the single motor spluttered and then died. Such a mass of wreckage made further progress impossible; all they could do now was wait and listen.

It appeared the captain had other ideas, however, and a beam of bright white light reached out from the bridge and began to cut through the rain, illuminating the surrounding water while presumably making the gunboat visible for many miles around.

Few were thinking of their own vulnerability, however; the majority simply watched in stunned silence as further sad reminders of a boat so recently alive were picked out amid the floating chunks of decking and frame. Articles of clothing and further lifejackets – all sadly empty. A cushion, probably from the mess deck, that gave momentary hope, an ammunition locker – presumably empty – an upturned seaman's hat and several empty oil cans. And there were other fragments that may once have gone to make up men, but Milner did not investigate those too closely.

There was no sound other than the water lapping against *320*'s hull, nothing to see apart from the little that remained of their recent companion, and with the dark waters hiding a danger capable of creating exactly the same mess from their own precious craft, little reason to remain. After several desperate, dangerous minutes, the searchlight died and there was a collective sigh from all on deck.

"I'm taking her about," Anderson called from the bridge as the Ford V8 rumbled into life once more. Then, after a tortuously slow turn that was stopped once by Milner, when a piece of wreckage came suspiciously close to their prow, the gunboat straightened and began a slow and careful retreat. It was some time before Anderson decided they were truly out of danger. Then the Packards fired up, *320* turned for Dover and made a faster passage back than anyone expected. Or wanted.

Chapter Eighteen

"It looks like you're returning to Weymouth." Brooks made the announcement with a totally straight face. It was the morning after Washburn's boat was destroyed, Anderson had just finished relating his part in the incident and neither felt like smiling.

"Weymouth?" he questioned. "Was there some problem with our training?"

"The very reverse, as far as I can tell," the base captain replied. "Frankly, Ian, they're saying very little, even to me. But it's not to *Bee* – officially, that is – though you'll be based there and will berth at Custom House Quay as before."

Anderson waited; Brooks was not one for enigmas, there would be an explanation of sorts, he was sure.

"I gather they're forming a brand new flotilla, though not of the conventional type. In fact, convention has been rather thrown out the window," the base captain continued. "As far as anyone is concerned, you and all other personnel will be listed as 'trainers'."

"Okay..." Anderson remained doubtful.

"You'll have heard of 15 Flotilla?"

"Of course. Relatively new, based at Dartmouth and used for anything hush-hush."

Brooks gave an ironic smile. "Yes, despite all the cover stories, it does seem to be common knowledge," he said. "A mistake they don't wish to repeat, or so it seems."

There was still more to come, Anderson was certain.

"15 Flotilla was indeed formed to carry out clandestine operations; collecting agents and escaping POWs, delivering arms and anything that cannot be dropped by parachute. They mainly serve the Brittany coast and are doing so rather well, from what I gather."

This was starting to become clearer, though Anderson was still uncertain.

"The plan is for a similar operation but one that can work further to the east covering the Channel Islands, Normandy, and all points as far as Dieppe. And this time they intend keeping it

188

firmly under their hat."

That made sense, and the training base would be an excellent cover.

"And I'm being considered?" Anderson asked.

"Not considered, you're in," Brooks told him. "There'll be three boats in all – as I said, hardly a conventional flotilla though 15's not much different. Fellow called Livingston's heading your lot. A commander and a straight striper, though not one I've come across."

"Forgive me, sir, but a MkV is hardly suited to clandestine work."

"Maybe not, she hasn't the size for a start, though your auxiliary Ford might come in handy."

"Then why..."

"They want you to ride shotgun," Brooks replied. "A task you're quite familiar with, and I'm not just thinking about last night."

"You mean St Nazaire?"

"Amongst others," Brooks agreed. "Apart from *320*, Livingston has Fairmile Cs; you'll be familiar with the type, I'm sure."

"Hundred and ten foot, triple Hall Scott engines and well armed," Anderson said. "Commander Ryder used one at St Nazaire."

"That was on loan from 15 Flotilla," Brooks said.

"I wasn't aware of that," Anderson said. "It's a shame he wasn't able to return it."

"But you'll know they are extremely strong workhorses," Brooks continued, "though lacking in power. They top out at not much more than twenty-five knots, whereas your MkV..."

"Nearer forty, sir."

"Exactly. 15 Flotilla are using Cs pretty much exclusively, though their catchment area is not so near the centre of things. The general feeling is something faster will be needed; something that'll see off an E-boat should the situation occur."

Anderson closed his eyes; *194* had been brought in to join Operation Chariot for very much the same reason. And, though his new command might be better armed, she was still inferior to the larger and eminently more powerful German vessels.

"If I may, sir, you know as well as I do, *320* is no match for an E."

"On paper, maybe," Brooks agreed. "But then neither was *194*, and she managed rather well, as I recall."

"What about one of the Grey class?" Anderson asked. "Steam gunboats have decent armament and a stable firing platform, yet they can still outpace a Fairmile C by a good ten knots."

Brooks picked up a pencil which he began to examine in minute detail. "Fact is, Ian, we can't spare anything larger," he said. "And, even if we could, a vessel of that size would hardly maintain the secrecy essential in such missions."

Anderson was still considering this as the base captain continued. "And you'll be getting another officer."

"Indeed?"

"An additional one," Brooks clarified. "Fellow named Morgan, from Guernsey by all accounts. Knows the waters well and even speaks a little French. They've rated him midshipman though he's older than you and Milner put together."

"And he'll be our navigator?"

"More a pilot I gather." Brooks replaced the pencil with a clatter and gave Anderson his full attention. "The streams and currents in that area are notorious; you'll need all the help you can get, and there's little to beat local knowledge."

Having an older man as a junior officer would add yet another ingredient to his current cocktail of command.

"That's about it, you'll know more at Weymouth. Tell Milner, of course, but probably best if you say nothing to the men. They'll discover in time but as far as anyone round here is concerned, *320* is being transferred for training duties."

"How long will this last?"

"Your deployment?" Brooks looked quizzical. "Open-ended, as far as I know. Really, they've told me very little."

"Then you don't know why I've been selected?"

"Not a clue – apart from your past record of escort work, of course. I did wonder if something was up when you returned," Brooks continued. "Not being allocated to a flotilla was a big indication, and I gather you impressed the trainers at *Bee*."

Anderson pursed his lips. "We weren't exactly successful last night."

"Maybe not, but that was hardly your fault; no one could

have done any better."

"It still sounds like a post best suited to someone a little more experienced."

"I wouldn't be so sure. A lot of the old school are too set in their ways; too used to the usual Coastal Forces' fare of convoy protection with the occasional skirmish thrown in for good measure. Where you'll be going will need a different sort of mind. Clandestine work, and there'll be a measure of diplomacy needed, something that I have to say your old captain rather lacked. You'll remain part of the Royal Navy, of course, but Commander Slocum's lot at Dartmouth is run by the SIS."

"The Secret Intelligence Service?"

"That's them," Brooks agreed. "The chaps some still blame for the invasion of Holland."

"And I'll be working for them?"

"Actually, no. You might be aware SIS and SOE don't get along."

"SOE?"

Yes, Special Operations Executive – the 'Set Europe Ablaze' mob. You've heard of them?"

Anderson smiled. "I have indeed."

"SIS and SOE are pretty much at loggerheads, which is understandable to some extent. As the name suggests, SIS prefer the cloak-and-dagger approach; stuff the enemy is often unaware of, whereas SOE seem determined to make as much noise as possible. In the past SOE tried setting up their own outstation on the Helford River in Cornwall, but that was too far off and simply duplicated the effort. Now they're thinking again, and want something further to the east, which is why we're talking."

"So, I'll still be with Coastal Forces but working for SOE?" Now things were definitely falling into place.

"Intrinsically, yes, as well as MI9 – they look after escape routes and the collection of downed airmen."

"I think I see now, sir," Anderson said, smiling at last.

"I'm glad someone does," Brooks grunted. "Far as I'm concerned, I'll be losing a MkV and one of my best commanders on what might be another wasted enterprise." He fixed Anderson with a penetrating stare. "A lot of important people will be depending on you to see it isn't."

"But we've only just got back," Bridger said as they filed out of the ready room. *320*'s ratings had been given news of the move, though not full details of their next deployment, or even that they would be joining a new flotilla. With the boat refuelled and no further duties for the rest of that day they had been granted twenty-four hours' liberty. Only Nolan, Harvey and Thompson showed any intention of going ashore, however. The rest, as if drawn by a common need, made straight for the NAAFI. But it wasn't for the standard tea and a wad; the communal space was good for other uses, and they had some serious discussing to do.

"Can't say the place appealed," Pickering said when they had found a table away from the servery. "Now if we were going back to Falmouth, it would be a different matter."

"To be sure, a spell with Mona at *The Rose*," Daly agreed. "Wouldn't that be a fine billet?"

"I don't know, Weymouth had its possibilities," Mitchel said. "Not that we were allowed to explore them much."

"Only one place gave us any sort of a welcome," Bridger mused, "and we wrecked it."

"Well maybe they'll have made it nice again by now," Hickman said.

"In which case they'll not be too pleased to see us turn up," Peters added. "Though I still don't see why we're going back."

"To be trainers?" Bridger suggested.

"You think?" Peters shook his head. "Only a couple of weeks ago they were telling *us* what to do."

"Can't see it miself," Pickering agreed." Not as if we've got to grips with the new boat."

"There's got to be something more," Peters added. "Something they haven't told us."

No one spoke while this was digested, and it was Hickman who finally broke the silence.

"Maybe they want to use the old barge for something else," he said.

"Like what?" Daly asked, and the loader shrugged.

"Blowed if I knows, though if they had something else in mind, something they wanted to keep quiet, I can't think of a better cover."

"You mean we might not be training as such?" Mitchel this time.

"I mean it's a possibility," Hickman said.

"But why?" Bridger asked.

"Like Hickers said, 'cause they're planning sommat and didnae want to let on about it." Pickering was definitely picking up Hickman's thread. "Flotilla base locations are common knowledge, an' everyone knows what goes on. Yet they use our sort of boats for other stuff as well."

"There's one what makes regular trips to Sweden picking up ball bearings," Mitchel added.

"So I hears," Pickering agreed. "They sails from somewhere up north, and you can be reet certain she ain't part o' no flotilla."

Daly seemed disappointed. "Can't see us getting ball bearings from the French, and don't see what else they might have."

"Snails and frogs legs?" Bridger's joke failed to get a response; his shipmates were far too absorbed.

"Something *they* have that *we'd* want..." Mitchel pondered.

"Or *we* have that *they'd* want," Peters added.

Hickman clicked his fingers. "It'll be smuggling," he said. "We been at it with France for centuries, why stop now?"

"What, booze and fags?" Pickering asked.

"I can think of worse cargos," Peters said.

"Not that sort of smuggling," Hickman continued. "This'll be agents and the like. And guns, explosives – you must have heard of the French Resistance."

"There's an outfit further west what keeps that lot supplied," Mitchel said.

"So maybe we'll be doing the same, only nearer to home," Hickman again.

"It's a thought I suppose," Bridger said. "Though why try and keep it to themselves?"

"Probably so the Germans don't get wind." Mitchel's sarcasm raised a laugh from some but was lost on Hickman.

"Well, if that's their idea of a secret, I ain't impressed," he said. "We soon sussed it."

* * *

"I didn't ask for you as such," Eve told him over a crackling telephone line. "But meeting up, as we did, gave me a good chance to look around."

Anderson went to speak, but she had more to say.

"There's an existing taxi service, and relatively new, though it's already stretched and frankly we don't get on with the owners."

"I've heard as much."

"My people decided we need our own company and one that can take us a little further – to more distant places where we can do more or less what we like," she added, and he could almost hear her smile.

"And I'll be a driver?"

"One of them," she said, "I hope..."

"And what about you?" he asked. "Will you be involved?

"Oh yes."

"And moving – to the area I mean?"

"Well, that's the funny thing." Hearing Eve's familiar chuckle made him miss her all the more. "I already have; we'll be near neighbours."

"Wonderful!"

"Just what I thought," she said. "Not exactly on your doorstep, though close enough for us to pay the other an occasional visit."

"Eve, I couldn't wish for anything better," he said. But even as he spoke Anderson realised the cardinal sin he had committed, and the line went dead.

* * *

"Weymouth?" Joyce looked surprised. "I thought you'd come back from there."

"Only just left," Thompson agreed. "Only just finished training, in fact, yet now we're gonna do the teaching."

Joyce put the teacup down on the small table next to his chair, then took a seat on the sofa opposite.

"Way of the world, it seems," she said. "Everything's movin' so quickly."

"That's what I wanted to talk to you about," Thompson

194

said. "Movin'."

"Movin'?" She looked astonished. "What me? You don't mean to Weymouth?"

"Why not?" he asked. "I'm gonna be there a while, an' it'll be nice having you close."

"I'm not sure, Frank." The doubt in her eyes was almost painful. He leant forward in his chair.

"Think about it, Joycie. Weymouth's not such a bad place, from what we saw of it. But I should have more regular hours and maybe a bit of leave.

"It didn't work out too well last time," she said.

"It will from now on," he insisted. "I'm sorry about before – mixing up with Granger's lot, and then frightening you like that. But I'm different now: changed. I can look after you properly."

"Couldn't look after yourself the other day," she said.

"There were two of 'em, and I weren't expecting it," he said. "Besides, me mates showed up and sorted things. And that's just it, Joycie, I got mates now, and not like in the past; these are proper pals."

"Joining the Navy sure has changed you," she said. "Are you still set on getting out?"

He collected his teacup and leant back. "Tell you the truth, I'm no longer sure. But you're not wrong; I've learned a lot in a short time, and not just about weapons and fightin' either."

"You weren't much different when you finished basic training." She was eyeing him suspiciously again, though this time he didn't mind. And he didn't mind talking to her in such a way; honestly, and without trying, or needing, to score points – something else that was relatively new.

"Basic training was the start of it, I reckon," he said. "Havin' to get on with others; I never needed to before, an' never lived with anyone but my family, or myself. But the blokes you meet in the Navy are different, nothing like those I used to know."

"Charlie and Ted?" she suggested.

"Time was I thought they were friends," he said. "And Granger's line of work, along with the rest of his lot, seemed to be my world," Thompson agreed. "But now I know better; I've met better people."

"There's certainly been a difference," she said. "And I can't say it's a bad one."

195

"So will you follow me?" he asked. "Come down to Weymouth and find a place. Nothing fancy, just somewhere I can call on when we gets leave. Go on Joycie, give it a go."

* * *

It was a daylight passage and, though the late summer sun treated them well, one they'd completed relatively recently so there was little novelty in it. But since what many considered to be *320*'s maiden voyage, there'd been many changes, both in the gunboat and her crew.

For some only recently introduced to their duties, that initial trip west had been their first long passage aboard a high-speed launch; the first time they endured the discomfort and noise for more than a couple of hours. And even those more seasoned were still coming to grips with the new boat while secretly missing the old. The weeks of intensive training that followed, together with a major encounter with the enemy, then having to watch helplessly as one of their own was destroyed, had altered the human angle, while adjustments, additions and more than a touch of general wear had modified the boat herself.

Milner's 'fizzer' had done its work and a new electric stove, together with a safari jar provided with the compliments and apologies of *320*'s builders, was now in place, while extra brackets and several lengths of four-by-two timber had stopped an annoying rattle in the deckhead above the officer's mess. An additional table lamp in the W/T office allowed Harvey to shut down the brighter bulkhead light and read the RDF screen more clearly, while short squares of canvas rigged at the stern were giving a measure of protection to Thompson and Daly when at their action stations. Doors and lockers that proved hard to open or close had been eased and a replacement catch fitted to the portside wheelhouse door.

The changes to the men were more subtle and not so easily achieved. After several more confrontations with Kipling, Newman felt he was finally bringing the youngster to heel, and the engine room team were settling into a good working relationship while Harvey was now used to dividing his time between his wireless sets and the RDF. But, though it may have been missed by those in charge, the greatest transformation was in Thompson.

Despite the additional shelter, both he and Daly avoided their new, exposed, positions whenever possible, but there was less general bleating from the Londoner. The arrival of an improved stove had been helpful here, Thomson quickly adopted it as his own and soon became *320*'s unofficial mess caterer, cheerfully ignoring his shipmate's ribbing that this was merely an excuse to shelter in the galley. It was while doing so that he discovered the dried stores ordered by Milner, which led to an almost constant flow of soup throughout the journey.

However, by the time Weymouth's north pier was sighted, the afternoon had turned into evening and most were hoping for something more substantial. Anderson was on the bridge, a position he held for the entire passage, and beside him Milner, who had only deserted to check their progress in the wheelhouse below.

"Harvey's raised the harbour on R/T," he announced, stepping away from the voice pipe.

"Very good," Anderson replied. They would have to make their number physically before entering but that time was still some way off. He had also learned quite a bit since their last passage and had no intention of rushing. To signal now, when still a good distance off, could cause confusion; better to wait and do the job properly.

"Hopefully *Bee* won't be buzzing quite so loudly this time." Even as he made the remark Anderson knew he was deviating strongly from his old captain's manner of command. Towards the end Harris could be jovial on occasions, though he rarely descended into word play and some of his prepared jokes were hard work.

"Absolutely, sir," Milner grinned. "Have you worked with Fairmile Cs before?"

Anderson gave a wry grin. "At the risk of repetition, there was one alongside us at St Nazaire," he said. "But they're sound vessels, and a goodly size."

"Though lacking in power."

"Which is why we're here," Anderson agreed.

They had yet to share the news of *320*'s posting, so Nolan, at the helm, must have wondered slightly but both were content to ignore his presence for now.

"I wonder when we'll start operations," Milner again.

"The two Cs are already on station, we just have to take on our new midshipman, then I'd say we were ready."

"From Jersey, I hear," Milner said.

"Guernsey actually. He'll be responsible for navigation, so will take some of the pressure from you."

"Glad to hear it. And there's nothing like having a kid about," Milner, who was barely in his twenties, continued. "He'll keep us all young."

Anderson went to say more, before deciding that was another matter that could wait until later.

* * *

"Happy to see you, gentlemen," the elderly man told them as they stepped from the freshly moored gunboat onto Weymouth's quayside. "I expect you'll be ready for your tea."

He wore no cap, although Anderson noticed the shabby greatcoat covered what might have been a naval uniform.

"And you are?" Milner demanded.

"Name's Morgan, Peter Morgan." Then, as an afterthought, he raised a grimy paw to his forehead. "I were sent to meet you and'll be piloting your boat."

"Then you're our navigation officer," Anderson corrected, returning the salute. On looking more closely he could see the telltail white flashes of a midshipman on the old man's lapels, yet the fellow must have been fifty if he was a day. Anderson sighed; relaxed command or not, there had to be certain limits. "It's customary to wear a cap when you salute," he said, "and you really should call me sir."

"Of course, sir, I was forgetting." Morgan went to salute again, then apparently changed his mind, but did appear genuinely contrite.

"Never mind, it's probably been a long day for us all." The new man had the unmistakable air of a seaman and was old enough to be his father; for him to pay deference to an amateur, however senior in rank, felt awkward in the extreme. "You mentioned food," Anderson prompted.

"There's a regular NAAFI not too far off and an officers'

mess," Morgan said. "But they're connected with the training school an' keep set hours; I've lived in Weymouth a while and know a place what will serve you now."

"Then perhaps you could show us?"

"I'd be glad to, sir."

Morgan clumped off determinedly and it seemed completely natural for the younger men to follow.

Chapter Nineteen

"The first thing we have to get straight is this will be a Royal Navy outstation," Commander Livingston announced. "Much of what we do might be at the instigation of SOE, and occasionally MI9, but that's of no consequence. We are King's officers, and it is to the RN we owe allegiance."

Of the nine men who sat facing Livingston, eight nodded in agreement. Only Morgan, sitting slightly apart from 320's other officers, remained wrapped in his greatcoat and appeared decidedly out of place.

They were in what had been referred to as the drill hall, though the title was slightly optimistic; to Anderson the draughty building appeared more suited to school assemblies. High windows covered with a crosshatching of paper tape let in streams of light that picked out a vast amount of floating dust and, apart from their chairs and the table set to one end, behind which Livingston and his second in command sat, there was no furniture.

"This will be our centre of operations." The officer indicated vaguely with the stem of his pipe. "I'm hoping to get some partitions installed but until then it will be ready room and office space combined. And we only have the three boats," he continued, "but that does not mean it won't be a professional set up. Is that clear?"

It appeared so, and Livingston, a well-built man of middling years with hair just turning grey, appeared satisfied.

"We've had a brief discussion with the bods at SOE and Matthews here can give you an outline of what will be expected." He turned to the younger lieutenant who collected a page of notes before standing to address his small audience.

"First of all, I should say this will not be an exact copy of what Commander Slocum's doing at Dartmouth," he said. "15 Flotilla primarily serves SIS, the Secret Intelligence Service, which, as the name suggests, are far more clandestine in their approach than the SOE. We do not intend making a noise, as such, but are quite prepared to if needs must. And as much of our covert work will be close to busier ports and the narrower waters of the

Channel, we are more likely to run in with enemy craft. Consequently, rather than avoiding offensive action – which 15 Flotilla are encouraged to – there will be times when we actively seek it out.

"Our main craft will be Fairmile Cs, of which we currently have two." He nodded towards the group of officers to Anderson's right. "They may not be the best combat vessels though we will have one of the latest British Power Boat MGBs with us as well." Now Matthews' eyes moved to where *320*'s officers sat, and Anderson wriggled uncomfortably in his seat. "As most of you will know, the MkVs are well armed and extremely fast while they also come equipped with RDF, though that cannot be used on every mission."

That certainly came as a shock; after finally landing such a wonder of technology it seemed they would have to give it up.

"Sadly, the signal such things give out is all too easily detected by enemy shipping or monitoring stations," Matthews continued. "However, the RAF are making inroads into a form of navigation by radio waves and will include us, and Commander Slocum's unit, when it becomes available."

Anderson pursed his lips. That might come about, and it might not, but losing radar was bad news indeed.

"*320* will accompany us on all missions and might also find herself operating independently on occasions. And most covert operations will take place during the darker phases of the moon, although none of us are going to be idle. The clandestine work will include deliveries to – and collections from – the French coast. We should expect to be carrying everything from supplies not so suited to parachute drops – I'm thinking wireless equipment, medical stores, provisions, along with arms and ammunition; lardering trips, as I believe they are known. And, of course, we will be delivering, and collecting, human cargo...

"Most will be British agents though there should also be a regular number of escaping POWs." Matthews paused and briefly looked apologetic. "I'm hoping the latter will only be collected."

The joke raised polite laughter from most present although Livingston appeared vaguely irritated and Morgan remained detached.

"Thank you, Matthews." Livingston had lit his pipe while his deputy was speaking and now sent out clouds of sweet-smelling smoke. "Are there any questions?"

Castle, who captained one of the Fairmile Cs, raised his hand. Anderson was briefly introduced to the RNVR lieutenant before the meeting and liked what he saw, though it was early to form a proper impression.

"How will our craft be maintained and supplied?"

"We'll be borrowing *Bee*'s staff and facilities." Livingston unconsciously nodded to his right; the training station was less than five hundred yards along the sea front. "And for as long as it can be managed, be regarded as part of that establishment. I trust you find your accommodation acceptable?"

This received a series of nods; Anderson was not sure how Livingston arranged it, but both he and Milner had been allocated rooms in his previous hotel without having to share.

"Excellent, thank you, sir," Castle said.

"Better thank Matthews," Livingston snorted.

"I made the point that we would be acting independently to HMS *Bee*," the lieutenant explained, "so won't keep the same regime as far as timings are concerned. They were worried our comings and goings might disturb their candidates, so the top two floors have been made over for our use."

Anderson had the impression Matthews was an efficient second in command; such a thing might be valuable in the coming months.

"I think that about sums it up," Livingston said. "Despite the location, this is not going to be a holiday and we will have to make do in many areas. There are no spare boats or crews; if a craft cannot go out, the rest will just have to manage. But Matthews and I will be doing all we can to make your lives easier and, in time, I hope to add to our force. Now, if there's nothing more, I suggest we disperse. Next meeting will be at ten tomorrow and I expect to signal our flotilla active immediately afterwards."

Anderson stood and stretched; Livingston and Matthews were talking to Castle while Milner had fallen into conversation with Barrows, who commanded the other Fairmile C. But Morgan, still wrapped in that awful greatcoat, sat alone and he decided to make a closer acquaintance.

"This all must seem very strange to you," Anderson said.

"Aye, sir, not my world at all."

"You don't feel like talking to the other navigators?"

At this the old man smiled. "Beggin' your pardon, they're hardly dry."

Anderson glanced across and could see what he meant, neither of the junior officers looked older than eighteen.

"I don't doubt they'll know all the book side of things," Morgan continued, "but I'm more your traditional seaman if you get my meaning."

"Then you know the waters well?"

"Very well, sir. Started out aboard my father's fisher when I were nine and have been sailing thereabouts ever since. Mind, I ain't so sharp elsewhere," Morgan admitted. "Put me on the Pacific, or even the German Sea and I'll lead you on a proper rainbow chase."

"I'll bear that in mind. I assume you volunteered?"

"That's right, too old for the draft but they reckoned I might still have something to offer. Though when I look at some of these youngsters... To be honest, sir, I can't see an' old dog like me fitting in."

"Nothing beats experience," Anderson told him. "Besides, they'll have duties other than navigating. From what I gather, ours will be the lead boat and, given the choice, I'd rather have an experienced man give me a course I can depend upon. If I promise to keep clear of the Pacific, do you think you can manage that?"

The older man gave another smile. "Reckon so, sir. And don't get me wrong, I can read a chart, take bearings an' shoot the sun, though maybe not in the way you're used to. But I'll never get us lost, you can count on that."

"Thank you," Anderson said. "You can take it I will be."

* * *

Orchard Court was on the Baker Street side of Portman Square, a fashionable part of London. Eve found it easily enough and lugged the leather suitcase up to a gleaming black front door adorned with a chromium-plated number six. A pale man of middle age and unassuming manner answered her knock and, such was his presence, when he reached for the suitcase she had been guarding all morning, Eve gave it up without a word.

"You must be Miss Newman," he said, leading her along a freshly decorated hall. "My name is Park, but do call me Arthur," he added, pausing by a white panelled door. "Miss Atkins has only just arrived."

Park knocked once before opening the door without waiting for a reply, then stood aside for Eve to enter.

The room was equally well appointed with good quality furniture that included a highly polished oak dining table and chairs. But closer, seated on a leather Chesterfield and looking every bit as elegant, was Vera Atkins.

Eve had met F Section's assistant head several times, but this was the first occasion they would be working together, and she was apprehensive. Though still in her early thirties, the woman had a maturity that made her appear older although, if the rumours were true, her earlier life had been quite eventful. Most claimed her agents were handled with a rare sensitivity, yet her manner could also be abrupt, and she was definitely not one to cross. However, there was little sign of this as the woman rose, smiled, and extended a hand.

"Eve, how nice to see you; I hope the journey was bearable." There was the slightest trace of an accent that gave away her Romanian origins, yet the smart suit and cotton blouse were decidedly English.

"It was fine, Miss Atkins," Eve replied, "And I hope I'm not late."

"Punctual to the minute, and it's Vera, please. Is that the clothing?" she added, glancing at the suitcase Park still held.

"Amongst other things," Eve agreed.

"Pop it on the dining table, Arthur, and then maybe we can all have some tea?"

Once alone, the older woman indicated one of the red leather club chairs. "Do take a seat – have you met Arthur before?"

"I haven't," Eve admitted.

"Acts as our gatekeeper, a sort of amiable Cerberus, and one of nature's gentlemen. Until recently Arthur worked at the Westminster Bank's Paris branch; his wife still lives in France."

"I see, would you like to go through the suitcase?"

"All in good time, let's get to know each other a little better first. You're Sarah Jenkins' replacement?"

"I am," Eve admitted. "It was all rather sudden, I gather."

"I should say! Pregnancy's a wonderful thing though does have a timescale; why she couldn't have alerted us sooner is a mystery. But never mind, I understand this is your first time as an escorting officer."

"It is."

"And you've met your current charge, Drummer?"

"Not yet, though I've read his notes."

"Then you will know his name – at least his assumed one," Vera added with a smile. "What you may not know is his history."

"Only from when he returned to England after his last mission. I understand it did not go well."

"No, bad show all round, I'm afraid. Only there a matter of days before being picked up by the Abwehr and delivered straight to the Gestapo. We're still not entirely sure if he was betrayed though obviously that network was quickly closed down. Fortunately, there was little to incriminate him and, you may as well know, he's one of the toughest agents on our books. Gestapo finally gave him up as he feigned tuberculosis and he was able to make his way back to England, though it cannot have been easy."

"No, of course not," Eve replied. "But how did he fake TB?"

"Oh, it's a simple enough matter." The tone was dismissive. "Bit his tongue and pretended to be coughing up blood."

Eve swallowed dryly.

"Yes, a man with such determination is not to be wasted; we can only hope his next mission proves more successful. Ah, here's the tea, will you join us, Arthur?"

"Thank you, madam, but I have things to do in preparation for our next visitor."

The tray was of polished mahogany and Park placed it on a marble side table before leaving the room as quietly as he had arrived.

"Let me pour." Eve stood and picked up the bone china teapot. "Do you take milk?"

"I don't, thank you, or sugar."

The cup and saucer was wafer thin and Eve felt something might crack with the hot water, but she passed both across safely, then poured tea, with plenty of milk, for herself.

"I'd better just go through the procedure," the older woman continued when Eve was seated again. "Drummer's due in under half an hour, and I'll interview him here. It'll be a general check to see everything's been remembered – birthday, places of work, that sort of thing. Considering the time factor, there's little chance of putting anything right, but we owe it to those placing themselves in danger to be as sure as we can."

She took a deep sip of tea which must have been close to boiling before continuing.

"Drummer was born in France and lived there before the war. He's been in England since, and not much would have been picked up on his last visit. It's amazing how fast one acclimatises to a different country; even something as simple as looking the wrong way when crossing a road can be enough to attract suspicion."

"Of course."

"While I'm doing that, perhaps you'd like to take the suitcase into the bedroom. Lay everything out and double-check." A brief smile. "Don't want any rogue labels giving the game away. Then we can get him dressed and await Mr Buckmaster."

Eve was aware the head of section F made a habit of seeing all agents off, yet knowing he was coming added further gravity to the occasion. Until that point, she had only mixed with those still under training or recently returned. Working with the two most important people in SOE's F Section, together with a man who, in a few short hours, would be on enemy territory and in risk of his life, definitely upped the stakes.

There was a stout knock at the front door and Vera Atkins glanced at her watch.

"Early," she said, though it was impossible to tell if she approved. Eve waited while the visitor and Park had a brief conversation, then a more genteel knock and the lounge door opened.

"Mr Drummer, ladies," Park announced, and another figure entered.

There had been no expectations on Eve's part; merely curiosity as to what a person prepared to risk unpleasant death in the cause of his country would look like. Yet still she was surprised. Drummer was listed as being twenty-five, though the face and bearing was of an older man. But there was definitely fire in those bright blue eyes, and the blond hair – cut, unsurprisingly, in the French fashion – was also striking. He wore an undistinguished British suit, yet the tone of his skin and something about the smile was unmistakenly continental.

"Ah, Drummer, welcome." Vera shook hands with the man,

206

then turned to Eve. "Allow me to present Eve Newman, she's taken over from Miss Jenkins and will be your new escorting officer."

"Miss Newman," the man said, extending a hand and she caught a whiff of cologne. "I shall be delighted to have you escort me."

Eve found the handshake surprisingly warm, and that smile was definitely infectious. Though perhaps the look in his eye was rather too forward for the occasion.

* * *

"Place hasn't changed that much," Mitchel commented as he glanced about the partially deserted NAAFI. They had just been told of their true purpose at Weymouth, although the news came as no surprise and had not affected them greatly. With the indifference common in their type, 320's ratings had other matters on their mind.

"Hardly suprisin'," Peters told him. "We only been gone a couple of weeks."

"Still ain't servin' grub out of hours," Pickering grumbled.

"What you bleatin' about, Geordie, got your wad, didn't ya?" Daly said.

Pickering regarded the fairy cake with a look of distain. "That ain't enough to feed a workin' man," he said.

"It were free," Mitchel pointed out. "Donation from the WVS; be grateful."

"Only allowin' one each, so they are," Daly added.

"Aye, an' none of you wanted one!"

"What's your point, Pickers?" Peters asked.

"Wouldn't have hurt anyone to help themselves."

"Maybe we ain't that hungry," Hickman said.

"Or greedy," Bridger added.

"You could 'ave given it to me." Pickering sounded mildly hurt.

"Well, we'll have real food in an hour or so," Harvey soothed. "Soon as them in training get out of classes."

"An' then there'll be a proper crowd," Pickering said, raising the cake to his lips, before thinking better of it.

"Can't see how they can go on keeping school hours," Harvey said. "Not if what Jimmy the One told us is right."

"Aye," Daly agreed. "If we're gonna be on active service, we'll need hot food and tea after a shout."

"An' decent cake at other times," Pickering added.

"There're only three boats," Peters said. "That's less than fifty men."

"Still worth stayin' open for." Bridger this time. "An' we won't be wantin' breakfast first thing, neither."

"S'right; need our kip, so we will," Daly agreed.

"I can't see us going far on what Pickers has," Harvey said, and all eyes returned to the Geordie, still holding his cake in one grimy hand.

"If you ain't going to eat that, why not pass it on."

For a moment Pickering's eyes flashed concern. Then, in one swift movement he slipped the cake into his mouth and began to chew.

"It's like watchin' an elephant feed," Bridger marvelled.

"Don't think it even touched the sides," Mitchel added, and Daly scratched at his chin.

"Well, at least he won't be wantin' any dinner."

* * *

Vera Atkins kept the Frenchman – Eve found it hard to think of him by a codeword – for longer than she expected, although it did give her the chance to sort his clothing and associated items. The bedroom was furnished to the same high standard as the rest of the flat except it was clear the bed – a double, with an art deco style mahogany headboard – had not been slept in for some while: possibly never. It did, however, provide the ideal platform to lay out the agent's clothing, while a dressing table, thankfully bare of the usual trappings, served for the other items. She looked again at the small piles that could protect or expose a man. Many had been chosen and sourced by Sarah, her predecessor, but some were down to her, and the responsibility felt great.

She turned as the door opened and he was standing before her once more, that same damned smile on his lips.

"You are ready to discuss your wardrobe, Drummer?" Her tone was as neutral as she could make it, yet still the man seemed amused.

"If you wish," he said. "Though I would prefer not to be called so."

"I believe it is customary," she said.

"Maybe for you, but in a few hours I will be Andre Dubois. I have just spent some time talking about my proposed identity with Mademoiselle Atkins, maybe if I start to think of myself so it will be easier?"

It was a good point even if, and for a number of reasons, Eve would have preferred to treat the man dispassionately. "Very well, it will be Dubois," she said, though now he looked slightly sad.

"And not Andre?"

"Dubois will do fine." Her tone was harsh though she also felt herself blush.

"You have been very busy," he told her, looking at the piles of clothing.

"Most of this was assembled by Miss Jenkins," Eve said. "I'd like to run through it, if I may."

"Of course."

She collected the jacket of a light-grey suit. "This will be for general use and was made and purchased in the area where you will be active."

Dubois reached out and examined the cloth.

"It is second hand, no?"

"Definitely," Eve agreed. "Belonged to an escaping refugee, or so I believe. He's been provided with better, but this will allow you to blend in, and everything has been cleaned."

"Of course, I had something similar the last time."

The last time: Eve remembered the trick Dubois had pulled to secure his release and found her defences weakening.

"And this will be for smarter wear." She had turned to another jacket. Though of a similar shade of grey, it was obviously better quality.

"That is more to my liking," Dubois nodded approvingly.

"It was made in England but by a French tailor in Great Titchfield Street."

Dubois took the jacket from her to examine more closely, and it was probably just chance that their hands briefly touched.

"It is very important to get every detail right," she

continued. "Even the way a button is sewed, or the style of a lapel, can give you away."

"I can see it is a very good job," he said. "Though still not new?"

"It was made to your measurements and has been worn by a volunteer of the same size to make it look more..." she struggled for the word.

"Used?" he asked with a smile.

"Something like that."

"And this." He waved to the bed's contents. "All have been assembled in the same way?"

"They come from our clothing depot at Queen's Gate," she told him. "It's run by former buyers from the film industry, and everything is either made in France or a precise copy."

"Then I will be like the film star, no?"

It was hard not to return his grin and Eve knew she would soon have to stop trying.

"Over here we have more personal items." She turned to the dressing table. "Things a man such as yourself would be expected to carry and all authentic."

Dubois picked up a used leather wallet and checked inside.

"That is just a small amount of money," Eve said. "Further funds will be supplied separately, and you will have access to more should they be needed."

"Of course. And this tin?"

"It is for the ends of cigarettes," she said.

"Ah, what you are calling dog-ends?" he asked.

"Yes, I understand in your country it has become customary to roll them again." She picked up a small leather case. "These spectacles were made in England, though by a French manufacturer who used the correct hinges."

"But I do not wear glasses."

No, he would not; those blue eyes looked perfect.

"They have clear lenses," she said. "In case you wish to change your identity slightly."

"Miss Newman, you have been most thoughtful," he said. "And now I must change?"

"There is probably a bathroom, would you like me to check?"

"No, thank you, I shall find it."

210

"I would suggest starting with the cheaper suit and, if you wouldn't mind wearing the sweater, everything else should fit in this." She held up a canvas duffel bag.

He collected a selection of clothing then paused before leaving the room. "I repeat, you have been most kind."

There was a knock at the front door; it would be Maurice Buckmaster. The section head made a point of seeing every agent off and usually passed on a small gift; something anonymous, such as a lighter or pen. And then Dubois would be on his way to France and who could tell what future.

"I hope you will be here to meet me when I return," he added.

"I hope so too," Eve replied, and was conscious of meaning every word.

* * *

"Alan, you're back with us!"

"Caroline!" Milner blinked.

He remembered Third Officer Collins from their last visit. Indeed, he'd thought of her often and considered chancing a letter more than once, while the main attraction of returning to *Bee* was the possibility of them meeting once more. But now they had, and in this unexpected way on a quiet Weymouth street, he was taken aback.

"I am," he admitted, and went to say more, before wondering how much he should actually divulge.

"But I thought you had returned to your station – and with flying colours. Top marks all round, as I recall." She grinned.

"Yes." He shifted uneasily. It was early evening, and he had been heading for his room at the end of a busy day. And Caroline was clearly in no rush, though the problem remained of how much he could tell her.

"So, are you joining us as a trainer?" she asked.

"No," he said.

"But you are stationed here, for a while I mean?"

"Yes." Now Milner could feel a blush forming.

"Is that it?" she smiled. "Yes, and no?"

"Yes," he said, then, "No. No, there's more."

211

She waited.

"It's g-good to see you," he stammered.

"It's good to see you too." She slipped her hand under his arm and led him away. "Come on, lemon, let's take a walk and you can tell me all about it."

* * *

Though it was a fact best kept to himself, Dubois hated flying. And he especially hated small, slow, and cramped aircraft like this one. Though it had taken off steeply, the rumbling radial engine appeared determinedly stuck in the lowest of revs making every inch of progress excruciating while it felt as if their precarious hold on the sky might break at any moment. But at least there should be no need to leave by parachute – another thing Dubois disliked intensely. If all went according to plan, it would be the briefest of touch-and-go put downs, a clumsy and undignified procedure but so much safer than trusting his life to a few pounds of silk.

He moved awkwardly on the Lysander's rearward-facing bench seat and treated the conducting officer facing him to a wry smile. The man was an experienced agent. Due to a duodenal ulcer, he had only recently retired, so could probably guess Dubois' current state of mind.

They had been in the air for almost two hours and, from the start, Dubois was supremely uncomfortable. This was mainly due to the heat. In addition to vest, shirt, jumper, and jacket, he wore a coarse canvas overall, padded in places, that made him feel like a baked potato. Even when they crossed the Channel, at all times keeping less than five hundred feet above the waves to avoid detection, it had been unpleasant. And later, when the threat of anti-aircraft fire forced them higher, he still sweated profusely. But now, with his final destination almost in sight, Dubois had no mind for personal comfort. The plane was descending to less than a thousand feet; the dropping zone would be in sight soon and he must be ready.

Not that it would be a drop as such, Dubois reminded himself. And with nothing to collect and little personal baggage, the pilot would have been well within his rights to insist on him using that parachute after all; a far safer procedure for the plane and her two-man crew. But no one volunteers for special services for their personal wellbeing and a touchdown, however brief, was a better bet for Dubois' safe arrival. Yet even that was not without risk; in the next few minutes he might well be dead; that, or wishing he was.

This would be his second trip home, the second time he risked everything to walk the streets he once knew so well; streets that now held nothing but danger. The second time he would have to hide his face from childhood friends who might turn him in for a good meal, or some equally wretched reward. Six weeks was the average time an agent could expect to remain safe; Dubois managed less than six days before, so he had much to make up for. Consequently it was strange that other matters filled his mind as the departure point drew closer.

The three months he spent in England had been peaceful enough, though few could feel at home in a country so bereft of provisions and culture. And despite meeting many women during the time abroad, none came close to the one who appeared during his last few hours on English soil.

Which probably added to the attraction, he accepted that totally. They had barely spoken; a second meeting might have turned out very different with one disappointing the other. And there was another aspect; knowing he would soon be making this trip, returning to his home and into danger, must surely have distorted things. Yet Dubois was man enough to know when the chemistry was right and recognise Eve Newman would be equally aware.

The conducting officer leant forward and bellowed into Dubois' ear. "We're getting close."

He nodded and pressed his face against the aircraft's window. Below, and barely highlighted by the moon, he could see areas of grey divided by hedgerows with only the occasional road – or perhaps lane would be a better description – passing between. One of those patches would be the landing field and he was glad not to have to decide which. But the pilot appeared more confident as he began a slow, low bank. And then, even as Dubois looked, a flickering light appeared further away.

The plane levelled and started to head for what must be a beacon, while the pilot began to tap a small control, presumably sending a reply. Then, as they were passing overhead, a more permanent lamp lit up, followed by another, and another after that, in an L shaped formation.

Dubois collected his bag as the Lysander described another circuit; it could not be long now.

"Remember to leave by the port side," the conducting officer told him, and he nodded. Anyone approaching the plane from the right was liable to be an enemy and shot. And that was no idle threat; his companion had already collected a Sten gun which he was resting against an open window on the right side of the plane.

The engine note lowered, and Dubois knew this would be it. Collecting his bag, he moved towards the large door, resting one hand on the catch while peering at the dark landscape outside. Then, before he fully expected it, the plane began to buck and lurch as its wheels touched ground.

A light flashed by as the engine note dropped further still and, as Dubois opened the flimsy door, he was caught by a blast of cold air that all but took his breath away. Below, the earth was moving too fast, but he knew this to be an illusion and, at a shout from the other man, he threw himself out.

The right way to fall was in a ball, rolling with the momentum until friction brought him to a halt. And Dubois almost made it but, whether by fault or chance, his left foot caught a rut in the ploughed earth, sending searing pain up the entire leg, leaving him breathless and in agony, as he finally came to rest.

For a moment he could hear nothing other than the departing aircraft accelerating for home and safety. He thought back to that cramped space with longing. Then there was the sound of running feet and finally he winced as light from an electric torch found him.

"Are you Drummer?" a voice enquired.

"I am," he replied, squinting still. There would now be passwords though such things appeared foolish considering the method of his arrival and current predicament. Seconds before he had been aboard a plane that would soon be back in England; now his position was far more vulnerable, and it might be weeks – months – before he were truly safe again.

"We must be moving." Whoever it was had the same regard to passwords. "You'd better get up."

"I cannot," Dubois replied through gritted teeth. "My leg: it is broken."

Chapter Twenty

"I think I may have gathered you here under false pretences." There was a gleam of humour in Commander Livingston's eyes which made Anderson wonder how much of his previously gruff manner could be put down to caution. "I've had the chance to read through your reports and there are areas for improvement in every vessel. I was proposing to address these this morning, but events have conspired to overtake us. Instead, I'm considering this outstation ready, and have already signalled the same to Southern Command."

That was excellent news, the last thing any of the assembled officers wanted was a public dressing down.

"Which brings me back to the false pretences..." This time there was a definite smile; Livingston was really pushing the boat out and had yet to light his pipe, which was another positive sign. "And the reason for such a quick shift to active service; we have our first proper job, and it will be tonight."

So far it had been a particularly quiet morning. Anderson and Milner enjoyed an early breakfast in the officers' mess, followed by a brief visit to *320*. An advanced echo sounder was available and this, along with some subtle changes Harvey wished to make to the W/T office, was discussed before they collected Morgan and made for the drill hall and Livingston's briefing. When they left her, the gunboat was fully fuelled, armed, and apparently ready for anything although hearing she might be in action that very night stirred the doubts in both her senior officers.

"A missive came through from MI9 this morning." Livingston held up a piece of paper though not for long enough for anyone to read. "One of their escape routes has been particularly busy; they intend transferring seven airmen to an island close to the communes of Jobourg and Herqueville. To the uninitiated, these are on the western coast of Normandy."

The news brought a murmur of interest from Livingston's audience that ceased as soon as he began to speak once more.

"We need to pick them up and sharpish; losing any who have already made efforts to be free would be bad enough, but recaptured POWs are prone to reveal details of our escape channels, which must be avoided at all costs."

There were general nods of agreement.

"Normally the collection of such a number would only require a single Fairmile and a couple of trips in a surf boat, but we will be using both, if only for the practice. And *320* will be leading, so I'd like all navigating officers to remain behind for a separate briefing. We will meet again at fourteen hundred hours by which time confirmation of the mission should have arrived."

Any concerns about what the commander could have found fault with aboard *320* were now forgotten; the day's excitement was increasing by the minute.

"Sadly, the elements are not in our favour," Livingston continued. Met. boys say to expect a fine and clear night, which is the last thing any of us wants – any of us, other than our navigators, that is," he added with a wry smile. "Astronomical sunset is at nineteen hundred hours but the moon, though in its last quarter, will rise two hours later. You'll have that time, and that time only, to locate the pinpoint, collect and embark our guests, and be free of the area."

Two hours was surely cutting it fine, even sending boats ashore for the simplest of pickups was bound to take more than sixty minutes.

"Passage time will be roughly three and a half hours, so you should be ready to depart by fifteen hundred hours at the latest. Now are there any observations before I speak to the navigators?"

Again, three and a half hours would be tight, yet Anderson could see no concrete reason to object. Others were not of the same opinion, however, and it was with surprise that he noticed Morgan had broken free of his greatcoat and was raising a hand.

"What is it, Mid?" Livingston had much to attend to and appeared irritated by the old man's interruption.

"Beggin' your pardon, sir, but three an' a half hours ain't long enough."

"Indeed?" The commander barely feigned interest.

"Might be for such a distance when you sees it on a chart, but that which is sailed will differ."

"We are allowing for stream and currents, if that's what you mean," Livingston replied. "And this is surely a navigational problem, so better addressed when the ships' officers have been allowed to depart."

"It's autumn, sir," Morgan maintained.

Now there was a definite sigh. "I am aware of that."

"Then you've not allowed enough." Morgan was uncharacteristically emphatic. "The flow around The Race and Fosse de la Hague is higher than most written pilots reckon, and especially so this time of year. You ought to allow considerably more if we're to negotiate them an' the shoals off Les Bréquets."

"I repeat, this were better discussed at the navigators' briefing," Livingston insisted.

"Yes, sir. But if we put out at three like you're suggestin' we'll be too late an' won't have time to collect anyone. An' if we leave earlier, like we should, the skippers have to know about it now."

Livingston scratched his head and Anderson could see the commander's dilemma. To change what had obviously been carefully drawn-up plans on the hoof must go against the grain, especially on the word of an old man doomed never to rise above midshipman.

"Then what time do you think we should depart?" he demanded.

"At least an hour earlier." Morgan was keeping his composure remarkably well, but then Anderson sensed he knew right was on his side. "That's the only way to see us off Santagno at sunset."

"Who said anything about Santagno?" Now Livingston seemed more surprised than annoyed.

"It would have to be, sir," Morgan maintained. "Santagno's the only suitable island in that area. Rest is just rocks; no one could survive long, and there'd be no cover."

Livingston considered this for several seconds then reached into his pocket and produced the pipe. After tapping it a couple of times, then blowing through, he finally came to a decision.

"Very well. Acting on Mr Morgan's information I'll bring departure time forward by one hour. We will meet here again at thirteen hundred hours and, if it means putting out before confirmation comes, it can be sent by wireless; you will be recalled, or not, as the situation demands."

At this, most present seemed to breathe a sigh of relief,

while Morgan was content to sink back into his coat.

"Navigators stay behind, everyone else can repair to their vessels and call up the crews."

Anderson leant across to Morgan.

"You did well there," he said.

"Do you think so, sir?" The old man seemed unsure. "I tends to speak first and think later. Wife used to say it don't do to make waves an', as a seaman, I ought to know better."

* * *

"An operation? But we only just got here!"

Nolan had a point, 320's ratings had barely unpacked. Their billet was part of a military barracks a quarter of a mile from the gunboat's mooring. An outbuilding was set aside for Naval use though they would have to use the NAAFI at HMS *Bee*, which was further away, and the lack of facilities was already a talking point.

"That's what it says." Harvey looked at the yellow sheet once more. "Assemble at thirteen hundred hours for a two o'clock departure."

"I hate it when they mix up the timings like that," Bridger grumbled. "Means you have to work things out."

"Means we'll only have an hour to get the engines warm," Kipling said.

"Aye," Pickering agreed. "P'raps we should get there a touch early?"

"An' go without our dinner?" The younger mechanic was appalled.

"Lad's right," Mitchel said. "NAAFI at *Bee* don't start servin' till twelve, an' there's usually a rush when all them training get let out at once. We'll be lucky to make it to the boat by one."

"I ain't missin' out on me grub," Bridger said.

"In which case they might be missing out on you." Harvey tossed the sheet aside. There was no doubt their recent posting was not going well. It was bad enough when they were stationed at *Bee* for training, but the base's set hours and strict routine definitely didn't work for an active service unit.

"Don't know why we can't just eat with the soldiers," Mitchel said.

Bridger snorted. "You got a short memory."

"Sailors and military don't mix," Harvey said. "Too much inter-service rivalry."

"I wouldn't be knowing about that," Daly said. "They just don't think the same as us."

"They just don't think," Bridger added with a grin.

"That's what I mean," Harvey again.

"So, do we try to find somewhere off base?" This was Peters, the Vickers gunner.

"Tried that before," Hickman said. "If the pubs won't serve us decent beer, they won't give no food without coupons."

"That place we ended up last time might be worth a look," Bridger said.

"The one what we wrecked?" Pickering exclaimed. "Can't see us being welcome there any time soon."

"It were a simple misunderstanding," Bridger maintained.

"An' probably why we've been banned from sharing the soldier's grub."

"Well, they got to do somethin' about the eatin' arrangements," Bridger said. "Else this war ain't going to be worth the botherin' over."

* * *

It was broad daylight, and would remain so for some while, yet *320* had already left harbour and was leading a small vic of gunboats across the Channel. One advantage of an early afternoon departure was the training station's activities allowed them to leave unnoticed; of the disadvantages they were less certain.

One would be the risk of a premature arrival at the scheduled collection point. This was several miles south of the Cap de la Hague; well inside enemy waters and definitely not a place to be in broad daylight. *320* and her crew had made a similar crossing at the end of their training, but that had been to the eastern side of the peninsula where the currents and streams had a very different effect. And there was a far more fundamental matter; whether the mission proved successful or not would rest on the word of an unassuming, and elderly, midshipman.

But Anderson was not unduly worried. His brief time in the Navy had been pockmarked with incidents that depended on less and, even though yet to be properly tested, Morgan was steadily

219

gaining his confidence.

"You've yet to tell me about the navigation briefing," he reminded the older man. So much had happened since that morning's meeting it was understandable, although Anderson suspected Morgan was keeping quiet for another reason.

"Not much to say, sir," the midshipman replied. *320* was setting a manageable pace of seventeen knots over calm waters so conversation was not difficult.

"The youngsters were a bit chary, an' I might have put your boss' back up."

"I think you'll find he's your boss as well," Anderson told him.

"That's as maybe," Morgan replied, "though a man can only serve one captain. I came into this navy voluntarily an' if I don't like what I sees, will go."

The point was debatable, though Anderson had no intention of discussing matters further.

"But we agreed on waypoints and the like," the older man continued.

Apart from speaking out that morning, Morgan had always been reclusive, yet being afloat made him far more loquacious, and he might even have grown a few inches.

"Very good. I guess we'll just have to see how things pan out. Is this your first mission?" Anderson added.

"For the Navy, yes," Morgan replied. "Though I've made this crossin' often enough and knows all about where we're bound."

"Would that be trading?" Anderson noticed Morgan give a slight start.

"Yes, sir," he said. "Though not in the conventional sense."

Milner clambered up from the wheelhouse and joined them on the bridge. Anderson turned to him.

"How's the RDF, Number One?"

"All clear, sir. There are a few of what look like fishers about five miles off our port bow but heading east, probably for Cherbourg. Apart from that, nothing."

"And how far off is the enemy coast?"

"Still a good forty miles, an' that's not accounting for our present course."

Which was southwest-by-west, and marginally more

220

severe than that recommended to counter the Channel current. Morgan had been adamant, however, and Anderson agreed without hesitation; so much was depending on their unusual midshipman it would have been foolish to do otherwise.

"Harvey's shut the set down now," Milner continued. "And confirmation that the POWs are in place came through while I was below, though I believe you are aware."

"Tel' did say," Anderson agreed. "So," he added, conscious that, for now at least, there was little to occupy any of them, "all we can do is wait."

"Soon as we raise the French coast, Alderney'll come into sight," Morgan said. "It'll take a fair old time to get through the Bréquets, but I still reckons we'll be at your pinpoint spot on."

Both Anderson and Milner regarded the elderly mariner with obvious respect and, feeling their eyes upon them, Morgan shrugged and added, "Or within an hour or so either way..."

* * *

"Reckon the old boy got it about right," Peters said from his position at the forward two-pounder.

"Aye," Hickman agreed. "Though he's a strange one for an officer."

They were speaking in relatively hushed tones as their action stations were not that far from the bridge, while *320*'s engines had been running at low revs for some while. But the French coast was in sight for all that time and, just as the failing sun finally dipped below the western horizon, it picked out the mound of a small island with the last of its rays.

The two men watched in silence as the Fairmiles eased past at a speed barely in excess of their own and faded into the increasing gloom.

"Word is they're picking up men," Peters said.

"Aye, downed aircrew or escaping POWs," Hickman agreed. "Either way, they'll be glad to see that little lot."

"Still got to make the collection," Peters said. "And I wouldn't like to be tied to the shore while they do."

"Been quiet enough so far."

Quiet, but hardly uneventful. *320* had led the small force over the nearby shoals confidently enough and, though there was always a plentiful supply of water beneath their hulls, the constant and variable currents made the slow-moving craft hard to control.

"That could soon change," Peters replied. "This may not be Hellfire Corner, but its busy enough all the same. We're a darn sight further from home than when based at Dover and could be bounced by pretty much anything at any moment."

"Then let's just hope we're not," Hickman said.

"Aye," Peters agreed. "Let's just hope."

* * *

"The surf boats are in the water," Milner announced.

As darkness fell, *320* had followed her charges in and now waited close to the pinpoint. Using both Fairmiles would speed up the evacuation; each carried a fourteen-foot pram dinghy that held up to five passengers so it should only mean one journey from both. But all on the bridge were equally aware of the anchored gunboats' vulnerable position, and that *320* offered their only protection.

So, while Milner kept what watch he could on the Fairmile's activities, Anderson swept the general area with his own glasses, while Bridger and Mitchel, at the Oerlikon's slightly raised position aft, checked the horizon.

And, so far, there was nothing to report though their task was made easier as each new star appeared, and eventually the moon would rise to make everything clearer still. But for the time being, and hopefully throughout the rescue, *320* would remain in relative darkness and lying cut about a mile off.

"Morgan still below?" Anderson asked as he continued to search.

"On the foredeck," Milner replied.

Anderson lowered his glasses and glanced forward. Sure enough, the elderly midshipman was apparently taking the air on *320*'s prow.

"Odd bod," he said, before returning to his vigil. "But no complaints; he got us here perfectly."

"And we should be heading home before long," Milner added. "First surf boat's just beached, the other's right behind."

"Any sign of the POWs?"

Milner shook his head. "Impossible to see in this light," he said.

"Can you gents hear that?" It was Nolan at the redundant helm, and for several seconds all three listened intently.

"What was it, 'Swain?"

"Gone now, sir," Nolan replied. "Though it sounded mechanical-like."

Both officers knew what the coxswain meant. Silence at sea is a rare commodity and, having to distinguish between the sound of surf, wind, and occasional birdlife could be next to impossible. But there was something different about a manmade noise; something that set it apart from all others.

"Hear anything, Bridger?" Anderson called back to those at the Oerlikon.

"Nothing, sir – no, wait, I think..."

"It's engines, sir," Daly interrupted, the Irishman having joined his shipmates on the bandstand. "And coming from the south, or so I thinks."

"I'd say more east." Bridger again.

Both officers turned and swept what was a small area, the horizon being not more than a few miles off.

"I've lost it completely now," Nolan half-whispered and once more Anderson, who had heard nothing to begin with, understood.

"This is where we could use the RDF," Milner muttered. Knowing equipment that would tell them so much more lay cold and unattended in the W/T office only added to their frustration. And then, suddenly, there was no doubt.

Whether carried on a fortunate wind, or abrupt acceleration raised both pitch and volume, could only be guessed, but the sound of a diesel-powered vessel suddenly rang clear, and it was heading in their direction.

"That's no merchant," Anderson snapped as, once more, he scoured the gloom for the source of the noise.

"Dinghy putting out from the shore," Milner reported. "Can't tell how loaded but she's making heavy weather."

"Off the starboard quarter!" This was Daly, and Anderson switched his attention further to the south but could see nothing.

"What is it?"

"Was, sir, I lost it now. Looked to have a bow wave, but I might have been mistaken."

223

It would take several minutes for the surf boat to meet with its mother ship. Then whoever was inside must be transferred; Anderson only hoped the officer in charge would have the sense to ditch the dinghy.

"Second boat's pulling away," Milner again. "First is under halfway there."

This was impossible, Anderson lowered his glasses and swore once before common sense took hold. Lying cut was all very well, but if an enemy truly was bearing down, *320* must move, and her engines were growing colder by the second. "Alright, fire her up!"

Milner bent forward to the engine room voice pipe and Nolan took a grip of the wheel. The brief rumble that followed was enough to block out most distant sounds and when the first Packard burst into life, all were relying on eyes alone.

"To starboard!"

Nolan's shout was enough to send everyone spinning to where a pair of German R-boats sailing line abreast were making straight for them.

"Now where did they come from?"

There was no time to answer Milner's question. *Räumbootes* were roughly equivalent to a Fairmile C in terms of size and speed, though usually carried a heavier armament. Were they allowed near the anchored British shipping it would be carnage. Anderson could hardly tell if the Fairmiles had been spotted, but whatever the case, it was his duty to create as much of a distraction as possible.

"Full speed, 'Swain," he ordered, "and hard to port."

320's screws bit deep, sending a tower of water into the still air while the roar of unrestricted engines must have been audible on the distant mainland. But Anderson had not just been seeking speed, his job was to protect the collection party which he would do in any way he could.

The British gunboat lurched forward across the dark water and was up on the plane in a few brief seconds.

"Meet her, midships and down to eighteen hundred!"

Now they were heading directly away from any attempts to rescue the airmen and in the general direction of Alderney. However, Anderson's main concern was whether the Germans would follow, and an arrogant display of speed might put them off.

320 slowed as a worried face appeared at the wheelhouse ladder. Anderson had forgotten about Morgan and was relieved the old man had not been knocked from his perch. But there was no time for further concern, he turned and looked astern, trying desperately to see through the wall of water thrown behind as the gunboat continued into the night.

"Any sign there?"

Bridger clearly failed to hear the question and was concentrating solely on rigging his 20mm cannon while Thompson and Daly were making their way aft to take position at the Lewis guns. The sight gave Anderson the germ of an idea but first he had to be sure the Germans were in pursuit.

"Half to port and down to sixteen hundred."

320 heeled very slightly and the lessening speed became noticeable as she began to broach the steady stream of waves. But all aboard the gunboat guessed what their captain was about and stared out to port.

"I have them!" Bridger's shout had to compete with the engines but those on the bridge heard it clearly enough and followed his pointing finger. And there, a good three miles off their port quarter, was the unmistakeable sight of an R-boat, her hull punching through the dark water like an oversized torpedo.

"The other's alongside," Milner shouted and, sure enough, the faint image of an accompanying launch could be seen about fifty yards further off.

"They're turning!" Milner again, and again he was right.

Though lacking the agility and, Anderson would say, grace, of a planing hull, the enemy craft were excellent sea boats that could turn well enough. Just as these were doing, and in *320*'s direction. The enemy was taking up the chase and he could forget about them interfering with what was going on at Santagno Island. There would be other matters to think about.

* * *

"Looks like it'll be our show," Bridger shouted to Mitchel as he took grip on the light cannon. A stern chase was certainly their domain, yet having two targets would divide his attention, while R-boats were known to carry far heavier SK C/30s mounted forward. The enemy cannon fired a shell almost twice the size of their Oerlikon and Bridger could not help remembering his shipmates' tales of previous teams who had manned the aft gun.

"Just keep a steady eye," Mitchel warned, and Bridger knew his loader was thinking along similar lines. Even without friendly craft in sight, and despite the near constant practice at HMS *Bee*, he was still inclined to aim high and to do so now would mean disaster.

The enemy still lay a good way off and the skipper was maintaining their lead. They might be held back, with neither side firing a shot, or could have spotted the anchored gunboats and decide to turn back for easier prey. In which case *320* must follow and there would be an all-out firefight. Either way, Bridger had plenty of time to prepare himself.

* * *

"The Holman!" Anderson shouted and, whether it was from the many hours of training, or simple intuition, Milner instantly picked up his captain's train of thought and headed for the wheelhouse ladder.

"Wait on my word," Anderson shouted after him and, shortly afterwards, saw the young officer making his way aft. *320* must have been heading away from the pinpoint area for several minutes, which would be a considerable distance at such a speed and room enough for what he had in mind. No one knew what summoned the two enemy launches, but they could lose interest in the chase at any moment. It was up to him to see that did not happen.

He collected the Tannoy's handset. "Shortly turning to port, prepare for star shells." Then, to Nolan, "Be ready for a swift one, 'Swain."

Nolan gave a nod in reply and Anderson looked aft once more. Milner was at the Holman; the weapon looked about as menacing as a drainage system; was he really pinning his hopes on such a contraption? Then, on his wave, the beast was fired.

There was no sign of the projectile in the dark sky; not even a flash of discharge, the whole thing might have been some glorious ruse while the pursuing boats were definitely slowing and might turn back at any moment.

And then vindication; a light, brighter than any star, burst

226

overhead and roughly mid-distance between the German craft and *320*, illuminating the entire area and blinding any unprepared.

"Hard a port!"

The gunboat heeled dramatically as the helm was thrown across and she was round in a matter of seconds.

"Meet her, midships. Now, maximum revs!"

A quick slap on the firing gongs; they were out of range but that would soon change; *320* was eating up the distance. Anderson leant forward, pointing at the nearest R-boat.

"Pass her to starboard," he shouted to Nolan. "Close as you like."

That was important, the nearer *320* could come to one enemy, the less likely she would receive fire from the other, and hopefully her sudden, and close, proximity would add further to the confusion.

Peters, at the forward Vickers, was the first to fire and, though the opening shots fell short, he was soon peppering the larger craft with a well-placed barrage. Bridger, his Oerlikon trained forward to the full extent, soon joined and as *320* swept past, continued for longer. Yet despite the suddenness, the German boat responded, sending flashes of green to dance about *320* as she sped into the night.

"Starboard – hard about – but bring her down to twelve hundred!"

With a well-trained crew that was all the order necessary. Nolan eased back on the throttles before throwing the gunboat into the tightest of turns that could so easily have tipped her completely. But she righted quickly enough and, despite the reduction in speed, was soon returning for a second pass.

However, this time the Germans were prepared and *320* steered into a barrage of green tracer. But it was one soon penetrated by a brutal onslaught from her forward-mounted Vickers and, before she was fully abreast of her nearest enemy, the R-boat's fire had dwindled to nothing. Flames were also appearing on the enemy vessel's superstructure, while her sudden veer to starboard was either due to damage to the steering or a vain attempt to avoid her tormentor.

The second R-boat remained unharmed, however. It began chancing shots over her wounded colleague that mercifully also passed above *320* but Anderson knew he would have to deal with her next.

"Starboard," he told Nolan. "Clear her as close as you can!"

Once more *320* swept by the stricken launch and both main guns soon switched to the new target. But the element of surprise was missing, and enemy shots began to rain down, puncturing her foredeck.

The damage did little to affect her speed however and went unnoticed, even by Peters and Hickman barely feet away. Both they, and those at the Oerlikon, maintained a steady flow of red tracer on the enemy, as did Thompson and Daly at the aft Lewis machine guns. And the fire remained constant even when Anderson ordered maximum revs once more. The manoeuvre was enough to throw the German gunners however, and as *320* was pulling out of range, it seemed they'd done enough.

There had been no sign of flame or even significant damage to the second launch when the night was suddenly torn apart by a brilliant yellow flash that quickly turned to red, and just as swiftly died.

Anderson paused in the act of sending them about once more, and instead ordered a reduction in speed.

"Gone," he said, staring back.

"I'd say," Milner agreed. The parachute flare had long since extinguished itself in the dark waters, but light from the still-burning *räumboote* was sufficient. One of the enemy launches had simply ceased to exist and all aboard *320* knew their work was complete.

Chapter Twenty-One

"And your damage, is it significant?" Commander Livingston asked.

With the perils of the previous night still raw in Anderson's mind, the drill hall seemed surprisingly civilised. Work had even started in dividing the space into separate rooms; a stack of rudimentary partitions lay to one side and two were already in place, though the workers must have been dismissed before he was summoned to this meeting.

"The local yard think they can handle it, sir," he replied. "At the time, Morgan carried out a thorough check and reported all was well."

"Morgan – your elderly midshipman?" Livingston raised his eyebrows.

"I was aware we were taking hits though other matters demanded my attention," Anderson continued. "Mr Morgan went below on his own initiative; I understand he also extinguished a small fire."

"I suppose it's within the old boy's brief, though I never expected..."

"I'd also considered his duties limited to pilotage," Anderson agreed. "He told me he was being paid to be a naval officer and intended behaving like one."

"Can't argue with that." Livingston chewed at the stem of his pipe. "Strange though, damned strange." He looked back to Anderson. "But his navigation, I assume it was up to the mark?"

"Spot on, sir. We arrived as planned and were out of the area before moonrise."

"With two R-boats destroyed." Livingston was starting to fill the pipe.

"One definitely," Anderson corrected. "We could have finished the other one off but..."

"No, you did right; your task was very much to protect the Fairmiles. And we got six men back to England, which is fewer than we were told, though a victory nonetheless."

The commander paused as if considering. "When taking on

this bag, I thought it would be the sort to expect, yet on our first mission you take out two *räumbootes*."

"I can't promise to do that every time," Anderson's tone was cautious, "and an R is very different to an E."

"Oh, certainly, certainly."

The strike of Livingston's match brought back memories of that exploding enemy, and Anderson swallowed.

"But it bodes well," the commander continued through puffs of blue smoke. "If we can show ourselves to be an efficient unit, one that can strike as well as defend, they might give us more craft."

"I guess so, sir."

"And men." Livingston was slowly being hidden behind a cloud of smoke. "Maybe some proper navigators," he added.

"If it's all the same to you, sir, I'll be happy to stick with Morgan."

* * *

Though slight, repairing the damage would take several days, so *320*'s ratings were delighted when their skipper arranged for seventy-two hours' liberty. And the time was being well spent, with the first day dedicated to learning more about the new town, although, when evening came, they were hardly enthused. Despite lacking the inconvenience of their old base's frequent nighttime air raids, or unannounced shelling that could make their lives a misery at any hour of the day, Weymouth was proving a disappointment.

For a start, it was crowded. A large proportion of Dover's civilian population left in the first few months of the war and, though there were service personnel stationed at HMS *Wasp* and HMS *Lynx*, as well as a military presence at the castle, it lacked the feel of a garrison town. But it was a term that could easily describe Weymouth, where soldiers were a common sight. And when the Army's needs were combined with a lower alcohol allocation, the seamen found themselves missing their old stamping ground.

"What say we try that club?" Harvey suggested the

following morning. The strict service times at HMS *Bee*'s NAAFI meant there was no lying in bed even when at liberty and the idea of walking the same streets, with the same lack of affable pubs, was depressing them all.

"The one what we wrecked?" Bridger asked. "I don't think so."

"It weren't just us what wrecked it," Nolan said.

"Sure, didn't those brown jobs do their share?" Daly agreed. "And there'd have been no trouble at all if they hadn't shown."

"I doubt the owner'll see it that way," Mitchel said.

"Perhaps if we explain?" Harvey suggested. Despite the trouble that came later, he'd enjoyed playing with a band again, and that singer had definite potential.

"Try if you wants," Bridger shrugged. "Can't lose, an' it might break up the day."

"Can't break up my day," Thompson spoke with a strange certainty.

"To be sure," Daly said, remembering. "Your missis is comin' down, so she is."

"Got a place lined up for her, have you?" Mitchel asked.

Thompson appeared awkward. "Not exactly. Actually, not at all; I was hoping to find somewhere yesterday, though nothing came of it."

"What's she after?" Peters asked and Thompson shrugged.

"Dunno, a flat, maybe a small house. From what I saw there weren't many of either, least not to rent, an' there'll only be my wages till she finds work."

"Didn't notice you lookin' that carefully," Peters said.

"I shall today," Thomson said. "She's not coming till later this afternoon; plenty of time."

"You reckon?" Harvey was not so sure.

"An' if not, we'll find a bed and breakfast and she can sort something out for herself, like before," Thompson said. "The one thing you can say about my Joycie is, she gets things done."

* * *

"That's quite close," Anderson said.

"Less than a mile," Eve agreed, "as the crow flies. It used to belong to a rich family who only used it for a few weeks in the summer. Splendid view of the sea and really quite palatial. We call it The Ranch."

"I take it you're living there as well?"

"While there's space, but my firm seems to be on a recruiting drive; more are turning up every week so there's talk of finding us billets elsewhere."

"Any chance of a visit?"

She smiled. "I think that could be arranged; as long as you came in uniform and promised not to take too many photographs."

They'd spotted the tearoom before the walk along the harbour wall and were glad to see it still open on their return. And though mildly chintzy, with lace tablecloths, knitted tea cosies and painted china vases, it suited them perfectly. Despite twelve tables being laid up ready, they were the only customers, which also fell in with their plans.

The middle-aged owner must have seen it all before. After serving the tea and cutting two generous slices of a bright-yellow Madeira cake, she returned to the kitchen and probably her cats, shutting the door, and leaving them in glorious privacy.

He shook his head. "It's really strange, us ending up so close. Almost as if someone had a hand in it."

"You can wipe that idea from your mind." Eve looked away as she spoke. "I'm very much the new girl on station."

"Maybe," he allowed. "But this will mean us working together."

"It might," she agreed. "Though I think we should be slightly cautious." Eve was in mufti; a tight tweed skirt, white blouse, and knitted cardigan but her attitude remained distinctly military, and Anderson wondered slightly at the change.

"You mean there could be a conflict of interests?"

"I mean, I have to look after my... people." Anderson sensed she had been about to use a different word. "They rely on me; it's the least I can do."

"I don't see how that alters anything."

"Perhaps not." She smiled, and he sensed the old Eve returning. "How are you settling in Weymouth?"

232

"Oh fine. It's a lot better than being stationed at *Bee* – more chance for time off for a start. They've given commissioned and warrant officers the top floor of a hotel, so your brother's there as well."

In the early days of their relationship, Anderson had been concerned that serving aboard the same boat as Bill Newman – Eve's brother – might cause problems, though none had materialised.

"I'm hoping to see Billy tomorrow."

"I think you might find a conflict of interests there," Anderson said. "His rating as Chief Motor Mechanic's been confirmed, and it's made him keener than ever. The boat's currently having her foredeck rebuilt, but that hasn't stopped his team from servicing one of the Packard's and I think they might have their eye on another."

"Billy always was a one for engines."

"It hasn't done him any harm, or us for that matter," Anderson said. "There've been times when a dodgy motor would have messed things up, but he's always been solid."

He took a sip of tea, which was strong and remarkably good.

"So, tell me about your work," he said, "what you can, of course."

"An outline, maybe, though it's not what I expected."

"In what way?"

She shrugged. "There was a lot of training before I became active, and somehow that hid the more personal side."

"Personal?"

"Yes, I didn't fully realise how wrapped up I could become in the people."

"You mean the ones going into danger?"

"The ones I'm *sending* into danger," she corrected. "At least that's how it feels."

"I thought you were only involved as far as their departure?"

"That's officially where my responsibilities end," she agreed. "Though the whole department remains informed throughout a mission, and we all take an interest. I suppose 'interest' isn't right either – we're committed; does that sound odd?"

"I guess not." He started playing with a teaspoon. "You have an investment after all."

"Yes, I suppose that's it. We feel connected to each of our people and, when things go wrong – when we hear someone's in danger, or worse – I have to say, it hurts."

"It must," he agreed. Despite their apparent solitude, he lowered his voice. "We collected a bunch of fliers only the other day."

"I heard, mainly Americans, weren't they?"

"That's right and some had been on the run for a while so were pretty pleased to be back on English soil. I ran into a group of them in *Bee*'s officers' mess last night; it was an unofficial 'Welcome Back to Blighty party'; you can guess the sort of thing."

Eve nodded.

"We'd all expected them to lay into the booze and have a good time, but it didn't work out like that." He paused, remembering. "The very reverse, in fact; I've had more fun at a wake."

She waited while he gathered his thoughts.

"Some had spent several months in one safe house or another. A pilot told me a regular hiding place was a hollowed-out haystack. Such constant strain must be hard to bear, and it's definitely affected them."

"I'm sure," Eve said. "We find it usually takes longer than anyone expects before they're fully over it."

"So, to go voluntarily," he raised his eyes to look at her, "to willingly place yourself in harm's way; that must take a certain type of courage."

"Especially when you know what they might face if captured." She leant forward slightly. "There's one at the moment, we've lost contact but know them to be in trouble."

"Can you say what kind of trouble?" he asked.

"Damaged on arrival." She pulled a glum face. "Only a minor injury; we were hoping all would be well and are considering asking you chaps to help out."

"Extractions are what we do."

"But since then, everything's gone horribly quiet, and you wouldn't believe the atmosphere at The Ranch."

"Do you know them well?"

"I met him once, and then only briefly, but that makes no

difference; as I said, there's a collective responsibility for all our people."

"Him? I thought you mainly worked with women."

"On the whole, yes, though this was definitely a man."

"Well, I hope things turn out alright."

"Thanks. We're rather holding our breath."

* * *

"Sure, I remember you," Frères told them. "An' I remember the damage you did." He gave a snort. "You only have to look for yourselves."

"That weren't just us," Nolan was quick to point out. "Military was involved an' all."

Apart from appearing much smaller in daylight, the former showroom looked little different, with the same ramshackle selection of furniture, much of which now lay broken while the bar was little more than splinters.

"There'd be those who'd say it was them what caused it," Daly added as he glanced about.

"That don't make much difference to me. It'll take an age to get the place back to normal again, and I'll have to shell out for a new bar. What with the chip shops and my place on the front I can't spare the time – got other fish to fry." He gave a short laugh.

"So, you just going to walk away?" Harvey asked.

"Oh, I'll hang on," Frères said. "I own the freehold and it should be worth a pretty penny – once you lot've won the war, that is."

"That's quite an incentive," Harvey muttered.

"It were only ever supposed to be a sideline," Frères continued.

"But you are going to reopen?" Bridger checked.

"Not sure I'll bother," Frères said. "Army's been banned, so what's the point?"

"What about the Navy?" Harvey asked.

"Oh, you fellers are still allowed," the man agreed. "Though we don't get many. I know some are staying at the Old Pavilion, but they never seem to let 'em out."

"That might be changing," Harvey said. "How about if we arrange for a good number of well-behaved matelots on a regular

235

basis?"

"Why would you do that?"

Daly reared up. "Because there's nowhere else in..."

"Because we liked the place," Nolan interrupted.

"And I liked the band," Harvey added.

"I heard you played the piano," Frères acknowledged. "An' weren't that bad."

"So, are we in?" Nolan again. "You open up and we'll provide the business while Harv' here tinkles the ivories?"

Frères shook his head. "I dunno. Like I said, there's more to running a place than serving booze. What staff I had 've gone elsewhere an' bar supplies are like hen's teeth. I'd be better off lookin' after the main club and me chippies."

"What you need is a manager," Nolan said.

"Aye, someone to take responsibility," Harvey agreed.

Frères sighed. "I can't believe I'm even listening to this."

"Come on, we've the ideal person." Harvey again. "Thumper's wife!"

"Now hang on there," Thompson began, but Harvey was ahead of him.

"She's just the ticket," he insisted. "Used to run a chain of Lyons Corner Houses."

Once more Thompson went to speak but Daly cut in this time.

"London joints, packed them in, so she did," he said.

"And won't stand no nonsense," Bridger added.

"Keeps Thumps in check, that's for sure," Daly said.

"I'm not sure about having a woman..."

"Hey up, we got ourselves another dinosaur!" Peters announced.

Harvey placed an arm round the old man's shoulder. "You do realise what women are doing to win this war?"

"A mighty sight more'n some," Daly said.

"And they don't attract trouble." Mitchel this time.

"Does she live nearby?" Frères asked.

"She could do," Thompson said.

"Currently looking for suitable accommodation." Harvey again. "Relocating from Dover due to a change in personal circumstances."

"I thought you said she came from London."

"Dover were on the way," Bridger explained.

"If she's as good as you say, she could have the rooms upstairs," Frères supposed, "but I'd have to see her first: give her a trial."

"Fine, we'll bring her along later." Once more Harvey spoke a split second before Thompson.

"An' in the meantime we could start fixing the place up," Bridger added.

"Fixing up?" Now Frères looked decidedly doubtful.

"Why not?" Bridger demanded. "Never underestimate the skills of your average British tar."

"Turn our hands to anything, so we can," Daly assured.

"Aye," Peters added. "Plenty can be done with a few screws an' a spot of sticky."

"If you're serious, there's more furniture out back," the old man said. "But I'll not be messed about. Get this place in order and I'll think about opening up again." He glanced at Thompson. "And if your old lady fits the bill, she can manage it."

"And live upstairs?" the seaman checked.

"Instead of wages," Frères agreed.

"Any chance we could take a look?"

"At the accommodation?" the old man snorted. "You guys don't hang about."

"Can't afford to in our business," Peters told him.

"Alright, get this place sorted by noon tomorrow and we'll give it a go." He looked at Thompson. "And you may as well come with me now."

Harvey watched as the unlikely pair made their way to the staircase, then turned back to his mates.

"We'll have this place shipshape in no time," he said.

"Sure, it'll be up and running by tomorrow night," Daly agreed, but Hickman pulled a face.

"Just in time for the end of our leave."

"Yes, but it'll still be here for next time," Bridger grinned. "Reckon we found ourselves an 'ome!"

* * *

237

"That is the best I can do," the doctor told Dubois as he stood up from his bedside. "It really needs an operation, which might be arranged. But there would be anaesthesia and..."

"No." Dubois was adamant. His face was coated in sweat from the examination, and nothing could persuade him to undergo more without some form of analgesia. Yet he knew the side effects such things produced; as dilemmas went, this was about the worst he could imagine.

The doctor shrugged. "We have sympathisers at the local hospital," he said. "There's a chance everything can be kept quiet."

"It is not worth the risk."

That was undoubtedly the case; he might be safe enough now, in a shepherd's hut set away from the main farmhouse. But in a hospital environment it would only need one word out of place from him to bring suspicion on the farmer along with his family. And should he be identified, it would not just mean one arrest, one internment, one death; the entire network must be in jeopardy. And though he might tell himself otherwise, Dubois knew enough of the Gestapo's methods to accept there were some few could withstand.

"Then we will have to get you back to England."

This was Marcel, the farmer whose family had looked after him since his recovery from the landing field.

Dubois closed his eyes. Never had a mission gone so terribly wrong; rather than reinforce the network he was bringing it deeper into danger. Since his fateful arrival two members had been arrested and, though that may have little to do with him, his presence was bound to be resented. And it made matters worse that one turned out to be the radio operator he was sent to replace. The fellow should be safely across the Channel by now rather than in enemy hands; really it was a miracle he was being cared for at all.

"We will have to request assistance from London," Marcel said. "But without a radio operator..."

"You have one: me," Dubois said.

"But you should not be moved," the doctor insisted.

"If I am going back to England, it will involve some degree of movement."

It was a fair point.

"Jaques' wireless equipment is safe," Marcel said. "If we

could get you to it – or it to you – we might send a signal."

"It will have to be the latter," the doctor said. "There really should be as little movement as possible."

"But power?" the farmer questioned.

"It will be fitted with accumulators," Dubois said. "They should be sufficient for several hours' use."

Marcel nodded. "Then I will collect it."

"It should not be brought here," Dubois said. "Methods for detecting signals are improving all the time; if we are caught your family will be at risk."

"Not so much at risk," the doctor corrected. "They will be arrested and transportation to Germany is the best that can be expected."

Marcel turned to the doctor. "Will his leg not heal; with rest, I am meaning?"

The man shrugged. "It is likely an infection will set in and then he will need more than treatment from the local hospital. In a larger establishment we will have no control over the staff, or his recovery."

"Then I do not think we have a choice," Marcel said. "If I bring the set here, will you be able to use it?"

"Of course," Dubois said, "though you are aware of the risk?"

"I am," the farmer sighed. "And I will talk to Paul and Simone, the sooner it is done the better."

* * *

It had actually taken less time than they expected. Even before Joyce was collected from the station and all but carried to the club to be introduced to Frères and her new accommodation, most of the furniture had been glued and clamped. Nolan, at the head of a scavenging party, had also chanced upon several crates far stronger than those which made up the original bar. When covered with a suitable cloth the effect was good enough for what they had in mind. The following morning a sweeping party cleared much of the dust and debris from the main room while Kipling and Pickering – persuaded away from their precious engines to perform radical surgery on the plumbing – had set the cloakrooms to rights. So, when the noon deadline came, the old man was reasonably satisfied; not only was his club ready to open, the seamen appeared quite respectable in their number ones. After leaving them his keys, he stumbled off to attend to his other interests.

Harvey had been unable to get all the piano's sticking notes working, but he could alter keys accordingly and was running through a few solo numbers, while everyone else seemed ready to enjoy themselves, when Joyce Thompson made a sudden appearance at the foot of the stairs.

"That's a reasonable start, I suppose," she said, after her own brief, but thorough, inspection. "Though we're going to need a few changes."

The men, who had considered their work for the day over, stared back, bemused.

"For a start we'll need someone behind the bar," she said.

"We was rather thinkin' we could help ourselves," Bridger told her.

"Help yourselves?" Joyce repeated aghast. "Can't run a catering business on that basis. Drink's got to be paid for and what about the other customers – they going to take dibs as well, are they?"

"No one knows we're going to be open." There was more than a little pride in Mitchel's statement. The lack of advertising was something they had kept from Frères, having the place to themselves being a far better option.

"Never heard of passing trade?" she enquired. "Besides, how long do you think this is going to last with just a handful of sailors for customers?"

"So, what do you want doing?" Bridger asked.

"For a start, we need glasses."

"All boxed up in the kitchen," Harvey said.

"Then they need to be taken out and washed," she said. "And they're no use stuck out the back, put one of them tables behind the bar and line 'em up on it."

Harvey dutifully loped off, and Joyce turned her attention to the remaining ratings.

"You can serve," she said, pointing at Bridger. "And you can clear tables," she added to Mitchel. "Both make a start by helping your mate at the wash up first."

Bridger and Mitchel exchanged glances before also making

240

their way to the kitchen.

"And what will we be serving?" she asked.

"Cider mainly," Pickering replied. "Got that on draught. No barrelled beer but there're a few bottles."

"Might do for now," she supposed, "that is, until we can get some proper supplies. Any spirits?"

Peters shook his head.

"What about tea?"

"Two boxes of builders' out the back, an' some sugar," Pickering said. "Cups an' saucers, an' all, though they'll need a wash."

"And we ain't got no milk," Peters added.

"Then you'd better get down to it," Joyce told him. "If they want milk, they'll have to bring their own; most are used to that."

She sighed, and looked about, although there was a fire in her eyes that disconcerted the remaining seamen.

"We'll have to get some permanent staff," she said, "and register as a British Restaurant. Then find regular suppliers, though we can probably keep going for now, 'specially if we cadge a bit from the neighbours."

Judging from their reception when they first ventured into Weymouth, the possibility seemed small though Thompson, who was keeping a low profile, had no intention of telling her so. Consequently, when his wife's eyes lighted on him, he took a step back.

"That chap Frères, didn't he say something about having another place in town?"

"Chip shops," he agreed.

"Nothing else?"

"There's another club," Peters replied. "Up-market joint near the front."

"Fine, we can borrow from there," she said.

"Not sure he'll be too willing."

"We'll see about that. Frank, you're coming with me," she told him. "And fetch some empty boxes – you can use them from the glasses. We're going to get ourselves some proper supplies."

Chapter Twenty-Two

It was a filthy night; the rain fell like proverbial stair rods and there was no moon, nor would there be, while a strong westerly was predicted to rise in the early hours of morning. By which time they would still be off the enemy coast, Anderson reminded himself as he pulled his oilskins closer.

In the five weeks *320* had been on station she had completed fewer official missions than most active Coastal Forces' craft. However, considering the distances involved, as well as the nature of her official work, Anderson felt she was pulling her weight. Besides, there had been other jobs unconnected with SOE and MI9. Mostly these concerned the activities at HMS *Bee* and took place between the first and third quarters of the moon – a time when clandestine operations were rarely carried out. On these occasions, *320* put to sea to assist with training and, hopefully, cement the fiction of her involvement with the station, while she had also joined other local craft in searches for downed airmen. But the covert missions remained her raison d'être and put the most strain on the gunboat and her crew.

And that night was a good example. *320* was in company with a single Fairmile C, captained by Lieutenant Derek Castle; a fellow Anderson had dined with on several occasions and was starting to like. But as he looked across to where the larger boat was battling through the cold dark night, the warmth and camaraderie of *Bee*'s officers' mess seemed a long way off.

The mission was a simple one; rendezvous with members of the resistance on the Normandy peninsula and deliver a shipment of goods. This could include anything from mail, radio equipment, medical supplies, or straightforward cash, though Anderson had not been told exactly what, and neither did he care. His only wish was to be anywhere but mid-Channel on such a godforsaken night.

Though not back at *Wasp* – that was for certain. *Bee* was still a new posting and not officially their base, yet he was far happier there than Dover. Even accepting the operations were longer; previously they could have reached the enemy coast in under an hour, and might be in action far sooner: now it took closer to four when tied to the lumbering pace of a Fairmile C. But for him *Bee*, and the Weymouth location, had one major advantage, and that was Eve.

She'd called at his hotel once, though they'd run into her brother in the corridor, which had been mildly embarrassing. But her SOE base was a different matter and The Ranch turned out to be a fine house built in the Empire style. Eve's room had a veranda looking out onto the sea and was the perfect place to meet.

The house was impressive in other ways. Heavily, though discreetly, guarded, there were many places he could not go, and his first visit was spent answering questions about his past employment. But once accepted by their security, Anderson was given a relatively free run and the differences between a secret service establishment and the standard military offering became obvious.

For a start there was an apparent casualness. What uniforms there were always seemed incomplete in some way; a Woolly Pully worn with flannels and a hacking jacket or an army battledress blouse above a Wren's skirt, though Anderson was quick to realise this in no way reflected the ethos towards work. All were professionals doing a dangerous job and, despite appearing relaxed and affable, a mettle ran through them that was easy to sense.

Even Eve displayed this. Ostensibly she remained the same warm and tender person, yet something had definitely been added. Once, when they were drinking tea on her veranda, a message was delivered. She read it immediately and, though dismissed as unimportant – and, he was quick to notice, carefully saved – it clearly affected her. She remained detached for the rest of the evening while at other times she could be remote.

Which was understandable, as he quickly assured himself. Though lacking the physical danger of his, her job was probably equally taxing and, when working closely with those going into danger, strong bonds were bound to form. Besides, now they lived so close, there was less of a novelty in his own visits, and she had never tried to cancel or curtail any without good reason.

War made a dramatic impression on all manner of relationships and this, he supposed, was just one more. Once the agony ended, or altered to some extent, they would return to their former intimacy, and he was quite prepared to wait.

"Kye, sir?"

Morgan clambered up from the wheelhouse, two mugs clamped tightly in his left hand. Anderson took both and placed one in front of Nolan, who nodded his thanks.

"Is Mr Milner still in W/T?" he asked the older man.

"Believe so, sir; I warned them we were getting close."

Twenty miles from land was an arbitrary limit for their RDF; no one could be sure how far the Germans could detect its use, or even how precise the enemy's own radar would be.

"Providing the coast is clear, I'd like to change course as soon as he shuts down."

"I'm allowing for that, sir."

By then they should have travelled roughly seventy miles on a sou'-southeasterly course and would be ready for the final run in.

"A turn to west-sou'-west should bring us past Barfleur," Morgan continued. "I'm hoping to get a sight of the Gatteville Lighthouse. Won't be lit, of course, but should provide a bearing, even in this." He nodded to port, from where the rain continued to drive at them with demonic force.

Anderson wasn't sure if he wished to come that close to enemy territory, especially as there was at least one permanent heavy battery on the eastern side of the Normandy peninsula and probably several lighter.

"From there it should be an easy run into the pinpoint," Morgan added.

Once more that sounded wildly optimistic. The chart was grey with shoals in that area and though both gunboats had extremely shallow draughts, they were not immune to running aground, while the savage currents low water encouraged would affect them far more. But Morgan was equally aware of the risks, and Anderson now trusted the old seaman implicitly.

He sipped at his drink, still welcomingly hot and strong. And it was in a china mug – the enamel ones issued with the boat must have been replaced. Though obviously vulnerable, china was far more pleasant to drink from and didn't burn the lips. Milner must have organised the switch and done so without bothering him; he truly was turning into an excellent executive officer.

The drink itself would have been made by Thompson, who

244

now treated *320*'s tiny galley and all it contained as his personal property. Harvey was proving a first-rate telegraphist, and Nolan had a natural talent at the helm. In fact, the entire boat was coming together nicely, while he himself felt increasingly more comfortable as her captain. With Eve living less than a mile down the road, Anderson was starting to think things were truly going his way. He just wished the darn rain would stop.

* * *

Thompson was no less optimistic than his captain and a good deal warmer. The galley duty had almost been delivered on a plate and suited him fine. Not only could he shelter from the weather, he found genuine pleasure in boiling up pans of soup or kye. This was reaching the stage where he was considering providing snacks; maybe some form of bun or teacake. With most of *320*'s missions lasting eight hours or more, solid sustenance was definitely called for and, after discovering friendships firmer than any known before, Thompson was especially keen to provide for his shipmates.

He'd also found something more in Joyce than expected. It was hard to believe the naïve, young thing he'd married was the same person that now regularly bossed him and his mates about, and did so to such good effect.

Within a week the club was attracting enough passing trade to keep old man Frères quiet. And since then she'd built the business up to the extent there were now two fulltime members of staff, a good range of local beer, and enough regular punters to make it worth offering food.

Registering as a British Restaurant was not the success she'd hoped for, as recent legislation was capping the cost of a main meal to five shillings. However, Joyce soon found a way round that by adding a supplement for cabaret entertainment – a wide interpretation she was prepared to defend. Frères had also fallen under her spell and called upon his network to provide much of their requirements. Whether the venture survived or failed was still in the hands of the gods but, if the latter, it would not have been for lack of trying.

Consequently, Thompson was also happier at the Weymouth outstation than *Wasp*. For a start there was far greater trust and, though no long-term leave would be granted for some while, they were given evening passes more often and only carried out clandestine operations for two weeks in the month. They were also allowed off base most mornings, so he could call on Joyce on a regular basis. This meant an early start clearing up after the night before, or perhaps a few minor repairs, and usually ended with them sharing a cup of tea and a snack.

On the evenings when *320*'s crew were not on call, they had to be back by ten, yet Thompson remained serving behind the bar, or clearing glasses to the last minute. And his efforts were not going unnoticed. Of late there'd been a definite thawing in her resolve; he might still be kept at arm's length, but progress was being made.

Besides, Thompson was prepared to wait. Joyce was not the only one to have changed; he'd noticed a similar transformation in himself and, when he remembered the arrogant bully who almost tricked her into marriage, it was with a mixture of disgust and mild wonder.

He sensed he need only continue a little longer; maintain the friendly contact along with practical support, and some degree of intimacy might be regained. It would require persistence, of course – something he might have lacked in the past, though was rapidly acquiring now. Yet however great the effort, it would be worthwhile and, as Thompson was uncomfortably aware, he had a lot to make up for.

In the W/T office, Harvey was equally content. It might be cold and wet up top, but he was dry and, with the best part of a mug of kye in his belly, tolerably warm. He also had hopes and expectations, and these similarly revolved around the makeshift bar on the edge of town.

He'd played piano on that first night and, despite the low B flat and some of the trebles continuing to stick, thoroughly enjoyed himself. It began as a solo gig, then the grapevine that kept itinerant musicians in work all over England proved as effective in Weymouth. The next time he visited, the drummer from the club's old band showed up and, within a week, they'd also acquired a bass player and were starting to swing.

Musically, Harvey put this down to the newest member. Though considered by many to be the least important, a decent driving, bottom line could lift any group. The drummer, a

246

youngster whose lung condition excused him from military service, was another major asset. Though as mad as most of his type, he had a remarkable technique that, with a modicum of effort, would have placed him in one of the country's top bands.

He'd also heard from Lee, the Yank trumpet player from the old Dover group. His unit was moving to nearby Swanage, which should make him available for some nights, while a reed man occasionally sat in on clarinet and C Melody sax who showed real promise. But the main reason Harvey also spent so much time at the club, was Nichole, their singer.

At twenty-eight, she was five years older than him and considerably more experienced. Tall, slender, with prominent cheek bones and jet-black hair that was usually allowed to fly free, Nichole had the air about her that suggested little was out of bounds and there were few efforts she would not make for her personal pleasure. Though married, her husband was training pilots in Rhodesia and not expected to return – to her at least. Until then, Harvey had been content to remain single, devoting any spare time and passion to his music. Encountering such an uninhibited spirit almost frightened him, especially on realising the attraction was shared. Even when he became more comfortable in her presence, Nichole's bohemian manner could still disconcert and, rather than any inability for him to stay late, was the main reason it took so long for their relationship to fully develop.

But with their collective cherry now soundly popped, Harvey was finding life fine indeed. Not only did he have the comfort of a willing, and inventive, lover, the pair were discovering true synergy in their music. Nichole would have fronted any band well but with the addition of some truly fine players and – he would like to think – his own thrusting rhythm, the group was taking on new energy. Staid charts began to swing, solos grew in style and complexity, while Harvey's skills as an arranger were also returning.

And not just for the music; the sets themselves were being planned. It soon became customary for the couple to duet together at the beginning of the second; Nichole's sultry tones melding perfectly with the slightly trashy sound of Harvey's worn-out piano. Together they would fumble their way through a couple of downbeat blues or jazz numbers that usually left the audience entranced, though oddly excluded.

Obviously, this might not last. Her husband could still return, or Harvey find himself posted elsewhere. But three years of warfare and the insecurity it created had already altered so many standards, the young telegraphist was inclined to take whatever was offered, whenever he could. In some ways the very fragility of their relationship made it that much stronger, that much more exciting. Even if they'd played their last number together, she'd already taught him much, while the prospect of any sort of future with such a partner, and in such a band, was enough to keep him warm on the coldest, wettest, nights.

* * *

Not much more than an hour later they were less than a mile from the enemy coast, yet the gloom of land off their starboard bow was barely visible through the rain, and there was no sign of a reassuring lighthouse, unlit or otherwise.

"It could be like this in peace time," Morgan muttered. "Darn thing were dark more often than alight."

With *320* running on her auxiliary engine alone, all that stopped them maintaining a normal conversation was the drumming of rain on the gunboat's topsides though, so constant was the noise, even that could be discounted. Milner had joined them on the bridge, and all were straining to see while Castle, in the Fairmile, stood off and awaited instruction.

"Pardon me, gents, but that appears to be it."

All looked in the direction of Nolan's gloved hand pointing further forward, and Milner focussed his glasses.

"Impossible to be sure," he said, lowering the binoculars and shaking water from their lenses.

"Very well, take us closer," Anderson ordered.

Nolan brought the separate throttle forward and the gunboat began to churn through the dark waters while the rain, now hitting at a more acute angle, magnified their misery. Though uncertain of their exact location, they knew themselves far enough from land to be safe from any risk of grounding, but there could be no such immunity from enemy attack. In such conditions a blacked-out gunboat must surely be invisible but, were the Germans able to track them on their own radar, it would be a different story and one that did not end well.

"I have it!" Morgan was also looking through binoculars; proof indeed of his concern as the old mariner rarely used such crude instruments. "Port ten – if you please, sir."

"Port ten and increase auxiliary to maximum revs," Anderson ordered, pleased to be pulling away from the shore, even by such a small margin. Castle, in the Fairmile, would have them in sight and was bound to follow. On gaining sea room they could start at least one of the main engines, then pass the dormant lighthouse and turn to the south. With luck they should be off the pinpoint within twenty minutes and, within an hour or so, heading home to Weymouth, *Bee* and, in Anderson's case, Eve.

And that was when it happened.

The first warning came from the gunboat's firing gongs. Suddenly, and without input from the bridge, each of the electronic buzzers placed by *320*'s main armament snarled into life, the crisp sound cutting through that of driving rain and causing confusion throughout. Thompson, who had been in the process of preparing three pints of oxtail soup, came rushing from the galley, while those already at their posts searched in vain for a non-existent enemy.

The klaxon came next, and any nearby vessel not previously aware of their existence must surely have become so as the raucous, rasping, din reverberated through the storm. Then came the lights; though rarely used, *320* had a full set for navigational purposes, while a variety of coloured lamps were mounted on her short mast for signalling or recognition. After the briefest of flickers, all burst into brilliant life, making the covert warship as obvious as any peacetime liner.

"Fuses!" Anderson shouted; he was pounding on each of the controls although both sound and light were set to stay. Milner made for the wheelhouse ladder and, blinded by the sudden brightness, crashed painfully into the narrow doorway before rolling back onto the duckboards. But it was no time for humour; there would be gun emplacements ashore, and *320* was well within range. Morgan heaved the younger man up and he continued his journey while Anderson carried on working the switches to no avail.

"All engines start. Port fifteen and full speed!" He needed to bellow over the klaxon's din, but Nolan was on the ball and reacted instantly.

Or apparently before; the rumble from their centre Packard came slightly in advance of Anderson's order, Newman having anticipated the command. Port and starboard wing engines soon followed and, with every attempt at secrecy now blown, *320* began to gather way.

There was no chance of completing their mission now, they must beat as far offshore as they could, and fast. Anderson glanced round; Castle, in the Fairmile, had reached the same conclusion, and was steering away from the veritable Christmas tree *320* had become as if fearing the condition infectious.

Ashore, all seemed quiet, although with so much glare reflecting on the driving rain, it was impossible to be certain. And then one distant searchlight flickered into life, followed by another and soon the entire coast was reaching out to make them more visible still.

This added danger was too far for *320*'s guns to reach, all Anderson could do was order Nolan to weave and, as the first enemy shells began to fall, everyone held their breath.

The gunfire came from three points, and none were the heavy weaponry that could be expected in such an area. Yet even portable ordnance – Anderson suspected 88mm – was enough to sink *320* with a single shot, and the nearest position would keep them in reach for a good while.

Anderson continued to hit the redundant buttons while a trio of enemy shells landed off their bow after presumably passing close overhead. Then, whether by his own actions, or those of Milner below, the klaxon finally stopped, and a little order was restored. But the firing gongs continued, and every lamp still shone as bright.

320 was reaching her maximum speed now and, despite her apparent willingness to be hit, must prove a difficult target. Nevertheless, the German gunners were making good practice as two more fountains erupted no more than fifteen yards from their hull.

And then, as suddenly as the nightmare began, it was over. The firing gongs were the next to close down, followed by *320*'s navigation lamps and then the tower of lights that had been dazzling them all was finally extinguished. For several seconds the shelling continued though, robbed of such prime markers, fell wide and soon ceased completely.

"Newman pulled the fuses," Milner announced from the top of the wheelhouse ladder.

"Very good, Number One," Anderson shouted. Then, to Nolan, "Bring her down to fifteen hundred."

The engines steadily decelerated until something approaching normal conversation was again possible.

"We've lost the wireless and all internal lights," Milner continued. "How's it with you, 'Swain?"

Nolan was directing a black rubber torch at the gunboat's instrument panel while the other hand rested on the wheel. "Sound, sir. I can manage," he said.

"Where's Castle?" Anderson asked, but the recent run must have covered several miles and there was no longer any sign of the Fairmile, or the enemy coast.

"We might raise him with the Aldis?" Milner suggested but Anderson shook his head.

"He can make it back to Weymouth on his own," he said. "The mission's blown and frankly I've had enough of lights for one evening."

* * *

Dubois had lost weight. He had no way of telling exactly how much, and his carers were providing him with the same amount of food as they themselves ate. But when he ran his fingers over his chest, or felt arms or elbows, it was all bone, while his face was loose and flabby.

And his leg hurt. Despite trying a variety of bandages and straps, there was no sign of healing while the constant nagging pain could only be dulled with the use of rare and valued painkillers. That he must return to England had been decided long since, though exactly how, and when, remained in doubt.

But there had at least been progress. In the weeks since he said thanks and farewell to Marcel there were a succession of journeys in open carts and the occasional farm vehicle. Against his instincts, but on the insistence of his guides, they travelled by day and on the busiest of roads, wherever possible timing each leg to coincide with a local market or farm sale. And throughout, Dubois' total contribution had been to suppress his moans while providing

251

regular, and unpleasant, duties for those caring for him.

However, of late even this last indignity bothered him less while, such was the nightmare world the drugs induced, even keeping his mouth shut was becoming more difficult. Strange and frightening images appeared to torture his brain, steadily becoming more real than any actual danger. Then, after one sudden and ill-timed scream that surprised him as much as his carers, Dubois accepted the lump of cotton pressed into his mouth with something close to relief.

His gag gave comfort of sorts, though the ability to relax, even to such a small extent, only brought the nightmares closer. And then, as if willed by a gracious god, another vision emerged to combat the demons.

Again, this must have been heightened by the drugs, though it had all the qualities of an angel. They had only met the once, and Dubois knew no more than her name, but the image of Eve Newman came to him, together with a backstory filled with caring, love and understanding. With a little practice he learned to summon her at will; whenever the pain became too much or if the evil ones threatened to take him over, her ghostly presence would appear and make everything right. Before long he began to expect this, and even call when there was little need. And then, as a constant presence, she became his friend, his advocate, his protector and, finally, his lover.

Chapter Twenty-Three

"Water ingress," Anderson announced. The partitioning had been completed some weeks before although Livingston's new office still lacked any form of ceiling and was about as secret as a Covent Garden market stall.

"From the earlier damage?" the commander enquired.

"I guess so," Anderson shrugged. "Though to be fair to our yard, we'd never been in a storm like it before."

"Must have been a hell of a sight," Livingston puffed at his pipe, "*320* lit up like that; Jerries must have thought all their Christmases had come at once!"

Anderson felt the old fool was taking the incident far too lightly; for him, it was still anything but amusing.

"Well, I suppose we should learn from it," the commander continued. "No point in investing in S-pipes and the like if we're going to give the game away quite so easily."

"I'd like to commend my chief motor mechanic," Anderson said, and Livingston looked his surprise.

"Indeed?"

"It was mainly due to his quick thinking that we were able to get away at all," Anderson continued. "He fired up our central engine well before I'd given the command and then had the sense to pull the fuses."

"The latter I can understand; I hope anyone in such a position would do the same," Livingston considered. "But yes, I see your point. Fellow would have needed to disconnect your auxiliary in advance – a bold move in itself – whereas starting the Packards when you were running silent showed a bit of spirit." He sat back in his chair and puffed some more. "Frankly it will do no harm to honour an engineer. Bods like him are passed over too often though they take as much risk as anyone."

"Thank you, sir."

"Of course, I can't make any promises," Livingston continued. "Best he might get is a 'mention', though that would still be one up on his captain, what?"

Anderson nodded in agreement. Newman definitely

253

deserved the recognition, and he wasn't blind to the fact that Eve would also be delighted.

"Now the fault's been discovered, I trust repairs will be relatively quick," Livingston said.

"It's mainly a case of making everything fully weathertight," Anderson said. "Then replacing the relevant electrics."

"Good, because I need you to be active again, probably by the end of the week."

The older man was speaking more softly now; Anderson had to lean forward to hear properly.

"It'll only need one Fairmile, but I'd rather they didn't go unescorted. And a return to Santagno," Livingston continued.

That would be fine; they had already used the pinpoint for several successful operations. Its offshore location and reasonable cover made the island ideal for both men and equipment to be stored for several days if need be. In time it must be discovered, this next mission might even be the one to blow the gaff, but they may as well make good use of it while they could.

"It'll be Friday for sure, though they are hoping to get there sooner, in which case we'll be bringing it forward."

Now that was unusual; such operations were normally planned with great accuracy, there being no room for vagaries.

"And it's a collection." Livingston was now barely whispering. "The agent concerned is in a bad way: needs medical attention tout suite."

"I understand. Yard says Wednesday, so we should be ready for then."

"Very well; that's two days. After last night's show I'd say your chaps could do with some liberty. With no boat to bother with, why don't we give them forty-eight hours?"

"I'm sure that would be appreciated."

"No more than they deserve," Livingston said, his voice, and humour, now restored. "Considering last night's excitement, it'll give them the chance to do some laundry."

* * *

By eight that evening the club was almost full, a succession of plates was going to and from the tables while Harvey and the band, currently filled out with both trumpet and saxophone, were well into their second set. Paid staff now relieved 320's ratings of their duties allowing them to set their minds to enjoying themselves and with a steady flow of reasonable beer, cracking music, and even a few female faces to lust over, they were satisfied.

So satisfied, in fact, that most missed the two well-built but otherwise nondescript men who entered and made straight for the bar. But Thompson noticed and knew exactly who they were.

Apart from Harvey, he was the only one who still worked at the club, serving drinks at every opportunity. And he happened to be on his own when the men approached.

"Frank, me old China!" Ted had to raise his voice above the band. "Fancy seein' you here – what are the chances?"

Though patently no coincidence, Thompson decided to play along. "Long time no see. What can I get you?"

"Well, ain't that a question?" Ted beamed. "Charlie an' me were lookin' for a nice quiet pint, though it seems a bit on the noisy side." The smile vanished. "Tell 'em to shut it."

Thompson glanced at the band who had just started a number and weren't due a break for some time. Nolan, Bridger, and the rest were also close by and would be at his side if he needed help.

"If you don't like it, you can go," he told them.

"Now, that ain't so very chummy," Charlie said. "What with us being mates an' all. Why, we even came to your weddin'."

That was true, Thompson hadn't forgotten.

"Stayed with your old lady afterwards an' all," Ted reminded. "Lovely she were, and so kind, so generous."

Thompson's ire was starting to rise, but that could be controlled; he'd learned how.

"Still, can't deny, it's a busy little place," Ted continued.

"Mr Granger's got similar, mind," Charlie said. "All along the south coast they are, far as Swanage. Reckon Weymouth'll be the next."

"Maybe this one?" Ted suggested, as if the thought had just occurred. "Then Frank would be working for us once more."

"It ain't my place," Thompson said. "Belongs to a fellow called Frères, an' his lot don't stand no nonsense."

"Now there's a thing," Charlie remarked. "I know a Les Frères, but it can't be the same bloke."

"Can't be," Ted agreed. "He ain't got that sort of muscle."

"Not used to dealing with Londoners." Charlie nodded wisely. "Do you think he'd mind if Mr Granger put in an offer?"

The music stopped at just the wrong time; Thompson was lost for words, and it showed.

"What are you two doing here?" It was Joyce, she must have noticed and come in from the kitchen.

"Why, Joyce, how nice to see you," Ted told her. "We was just saying to Frank here how we got on so well at your Dover gaff – it's quite like old times!"

"Get out, and get out now," Joyce said.

"You heard," Thompson added. "There's nothing for you here. Bugger off."

"Well, ain't that nice?" Ted beamed. "Husband supportin' his wife like that."

"Though it weren't always so in the past." Charlie appeared to be remembering. "I can remember a time when he more or less dropped her in it."

"And it were up to his missis to say something then," Ted agreed. "Reckon we know who wears the trousers!"

"I'm tellin' you, go!" Thompson's shout coincided with a loud chord at the start of the next number so lacked impact, although the two men did take notice.

"That really ain't friendly at all, Frank," Charlie said. "Treat all your customers like that, do you?"

"You ain't a customer," Joyce said.

"Supposin' we wanted something; refuse to serve us would you?" Charlie looked to his friend. "What you say, Ted; maybe a meal, bottle of wine?" He turned back to Thompson. "Serve wine do you, Frank, only Ted an' me is partial to a drop of the old vino."

"Is that it?" Thompson asked and Ted shrugged.

"To be going on with. And maybe something after?" Charlie considered. "Like a couple of quid from the till?"

* * *

256

It was quiet by the fireside; quiet and extremely peaceable: it always had been. Sometimes, when at sea, Morgan would think of this small house in Weymouth and the fire burning while he walked a rain-soaked deck. And Marjorie; she would have been there as well and probably missing him.

Of course, Marjorie was gone now. In effect he had taken her place by the fire, and it was hard not to think of all those wasted evenings.

But at least there was a distraction. On the small table, once so highly polished, lay a stack of books that Morgan was steadily working through. Some told him what he already knew, but in a different way; a way those who might not have grown up with the sea could understand. And several contained mistakes; small errors only a true seaman would notice: when he did, Morgan made a pencil mark in the margin. These were the easy ones; others, the technical or those that concerned his place in the Royal Navy, were more difficult.

Difficult because they might have been speaking another language. And it was that of order, discipline, rank, and status; things that confused his natural mind even if much could be condensed down to who to salute and when. And though they said a great deal there was one major omission; none of them told him exactly how to behave; how to acquire that air of relaxed competence that was the hallmark of so many Royal Navy officers.

Still Morgan continued to read, and continued to make notes, though the latter were of a very different nature, and mainly questions.

They needed answers, however. In over forty years at sea, Morgan had only ever regarded the Royal Navy as an unnecessary nuisance and, when his activities stretched beyond the strict line of law, the enemy. But with Marjorie gone, and his old way of life now denied him, he felt differently. Now he wanted nothing more than to be accepted and become part of an organisation he always, secretly, respected.

It was something Marjorie would have liked. Though Morgan never explained in so many words, she was no fool and knew little of their income came from the fishing. But income it was, and steady. In a time when many foundered, he always provided enough for this house, this fire, and the life they thought they wanted. Perhaps if he had joined the Navy then, at the start, it would have been different; he might be master of his own vessel by now and may even know how to behave.

Whatever, he was making up for lost time. By luck, and a little negotiation, Morgan had found his way beyond the age limitations and, due to his specialist knowledge and Weymouth base, even secured a position well in excess of his true worth. The rank of midshipman attracted far more respect than the petty officer post initially offered yet was usually associated with aspirant lads. But then, in a world where regulations and procedure frequently replaced old-fashioned seamanship, Morgan was very much a child.

One determined to grow, however, though he had no wish to leave his present ship or be anywhere other than her current location. If he could learn enough to be accepted as a regular officer aboard *320*, it would be enough. And then, when the time came to totally turn away from the sea, Morgan could do so with an easy heart and a modicum of respectability; albeit alone.

* * *

The club was quiet, eerily so. Like an empty theatre or an abandoned railway station, for somewhere normally so teaming with people to be bereft of life put a chill in the air. Thompson was wiping down the bar – now a far better affair with a proper lino counter – when Joyce entered, and the pair exchanged a rare smile.

Rare because, despite their growing closer and the success of the business, their relationship had effectively stalled; there was still too much between them to allow anything other than a commercial partnership. But that might be about to change and, as his wife took a seat at the bar opposite, Thompson felt a warmth from her that was greater than any known for some time.

"I still don't like the idea of you staying here on your tod," he said, and she drew a deep sigh.

"Frank, we've been through this. Granger's boys are exactly that – kids. They might talk big and maybe heave a bit of weight, but that's all. And when it comes down to actual fighting, they ain't all that clever – your mates showed them that."

"Peters and Hickman won't be around," Thompson said. "So, I should be."

"There's a decent lock on the door, and even the windows is boarded up; I'll be as safe as 'ouses. My worry is what happens next."

"You mean what they intend?"

"Right. Is this going to be a problem, or have we already done enough?"

There was a pause while Thompson considered this.

"Well come on," Joyce prompted. "You've worked with them; how do they usually behave?"

"They didn't *get* nothing," Thompson said. "Not even a drink on the house. And they didn't *do* nothing. If Granger was looking for protection money, he'd have caused us a bit of damage, thrown over a few tables, that sort of thing, for show."

"Couldn't see them getting away with that, not with a club full of sailors."

It was a fair point, and only emphasised Thompson's reluctance to leave Joyce on her own, but he knew enough to say nothing more on that front.

"I suppose we could talk to Frères," she continued. "He's got a few businesses in the area and might pack some muscle."

Thompson shook his head. "London's different to round here," he said. "Much harder, much tougher. Whatever you think of Ted and Charlie, they ain't pussy and there are bound to be more where they came from. If Granger felt like it, he could take over all Weymouth's night spots in a couple of days."

"How does he do it? I mean, why aren't all his men in the forces?"

"Reserved occupations," Thompson grunted. "Not for real, of course, but most of his top blokes are registered in trades that can't be conscripted: railway and dockworkers, farmers, teachers, even shop stewards."

"How come that never happened to you?" she asked.

"I wondered at the time," Thompson admitted. "Now I reckon old man Granger were cleverer than I thought; he must have known I never really fitted in."

"In that case I think we should go to the police," she said.

"Can if you like. Won't do much good. Force is all but run by Specials – most of the good coppers are too wrapped up in major crime to give this a second look."

"But it's intimidation," she insisted.

"They won't see it like that; Ted and Charlie simply made a business offer and when we told them to go, they did."

"And do you think they're going to leave it?" she asked.

"I'm not sure," he said. "Depends on how badly Granger wants a piece of Weymouth. Don't see it myself, but with the rest of the south coast tied up, I suppose he might; especially if he intends spreading further west."

"You'd better go." Joyce spoke as if suddenly coming to a decision, and one she didn't want to take.

"I'm on leave," Thompson said. "Don't have to be back at any time."

"I know." Still that air of determination. "But I think you should be gone."

He sighed, put down the towel, then made his way to the front. "Be sure to bolt the door behind me," he said. "I already checked the back: that's sound."

"I will," she said following. "And don't worry, I shall be fine."

He opened the door and stepped out into the night, only turning at the last moment.

"I'll be back here first thing," he said.

And then the door closed, the bolt was thrown across, and Joyce was left alone.

* * *

Having Caroline on site, as it were, was a dream come true for Milner. Of course, she had to work during the day and her boss, Lieutenant Commander Hansen, kept her late some evenings. But that night she had been free, and that night had been fantastic.

They were hand in hand as they left the cinema. It was a double feature, with one of the films barely a year old, though Milner would have preferred to have spent more of the precious time doing something other than staring at flickering images. But the walk back really made the evening and, when they said goodnight under a darkened awning, and her body closed with his for the first time, he felt a satisfaction that had been denied for too long. Something of this must have been communicated – that or she simply felt the same – for there was an answering look in her eyes.

And then finally, reluctantly, they parted. He set off for his own, solitary, room and everything seemed normal once more. There was a meeting with Lieutenant Anderson in the morning; together they would inspect the progress to *320*'s repairs, and then he'd go through the additions and corrections necessary to their charts with Morgan. Yet all this still seemed so rudimentary, so mundane. That night he discovered something special, something so truly earth shattering even a war could not diminish it. Milner had little idea what it might be but the feeling it left behind was simply wonderful.

* * *

Despite what he told Joyce, Thompson might have a problem getting into the base. It was gone ten after all – long gone – and would soon be midnight, when everything became that much harder. In the past this could have phased him, but he had overcome so many obstacles of late it felt like just one more. Besides, their dormitory was in an outbuilding of a military barracks and the security detail paid less attention to anyone in bell-bottoms.

And anyway, *320*'s true reason for being at Weymouth was steadily becoming more widely known. Not that any details of their missions were being released, but enough boats had returned damaged and carrying wounded to show they regularly met with the enemy. Thompson, and his shipmates, had also become a familiar sight in the town and was even attracting a measure of respect.

For someone whose only impact on his fellow beings had been to inflict injury or fear, this came as a pleasant change and, when combined with the fellowship and support experienced from his first true friends, made Thompson a very happy man indeed. And he certainly wasn't giving up on Joyce; with a little persistence they must surely return to being man and wife. It was just a shame that now, with everything falling nicely into place, his past had caught up in the form of Granger's boys.

There was rain earlier and the streets were still damp, though the lack of a decent moon meant Weymouth had been spared air raids for several nights. Cracks of light even showed at some of the curtained windows giving the impression war may not be permanent after all. He crossed the street, boots ringing in the dark as his thoughts continued.

Once there was true peace he would have a lot of thinking to do, and many more changes to make. For a start, there was no way he could return to his old line of business, yet the prospect of finding something else was not so terrible. A year ago he could never imagine wanting Joyce the way he did now, and neither could he have seen himself serving behind a bar or providing refreshments aboard a warship. There was the vague thought this might even be his true calling, though that still lay very much in the future. First, he must address a more immediate problem.

Of course, they only had Ted and Charlie's word Granger was moving in. For all he knew it was a ruse; the pair could have been chucked from the organisation and be trying to set up on their own; it was just their sort of ploy. And even if not, Granger's mob could hardly have grown that much since he left. Having commitments in most of the major coastal towns would eat into his manpower; if he wasn't already stretched, he soon would be.

And Thompson was not without resources. Peters and Hickman had already laid in on his side; if the rest of his shipmates knew what was about, and their newfound watering hole was in jeopardy, they'd back him, of that he was certain.

Maybe he should have created a greater fuss that evening? Sending Charlie and Ted away with more than a flea in their ear might have made a greater impact. But then a fight at the club would hardly have gone down well with Joyce, and Thompson was more concerned than ever she should not be upset.

He glanced at his watch – still ten minutes to midnight, he ought to make it in time. And there was that cut-through Pickering recently found – a snicket he'd called it. Though dark and narrow, it led straight to the barracks and knocked several minutes from the journey; Thompson would take that.

Perhaps he might still enlist the help of his shipmates; arrange a reception party for when Ted and Charlie came back? But then most of *320*'s ratings spent their evenings in the club as it was, all he really need do was alert them to the problem. He remained concerned about leaving Joyce but, as she had said, the place was secure and, besides, no one would know she was alone.

Yes, that was the answer, talk to the lads and enlist their help. A couple might even come up with a better idea – that was the benefit of having friends, they often turned out smarter.

But one thing still worried him; Thompson hadn't been totally square with Joyce and knew more of Granger's methods than he'd admitted. Once his boys made contact they clung on and allowed no time for thinking. Charlie, Ted and probably a few others would return; it could be tomorrow, or the next day, but certainly by the end of the week. With only one day's leave remaining, that might put him in a difficult position. If it came to it, Thompson would go AWOL, though he couldn't expect the same from his shipmates. And one man would not be enough to stand up to Granger's goons.

Someone turned down the alley and was heading towards him. They were too far off to be a danger, but Thompson was already regretting taking the short cut. The figure stopped and appeared to be blocking his path. Thompson slowed but continued to walk. Then, when about ten feet away, he spoke.

"Who is it?"

There was no response, though Thompson was now reasonably sure it would be Charlie or Ted.

"You're not getting' nothing from me," he said. "An' if you cause trouble, it'll only come back on you. I got friends now, see. Friends in the forces, and you really don't want to go messin' with them."

Still nothing and Thompson balled both hands into fists. If they wanted trouble, they'd get it; he wasn't too old to fight and, for the first time in his life, he had something worth fighting for.

Closer still, details of the face were becoming clearer; yes, that was Ted for sure – so where was Charlie? Then, as the kick landed in the small of his back, he found out.

* * *

"Because on Thursdays it'll be your turn in the barrel!"

Bridger waited for the anticipated laughter and, when none came, added some of his own. The joke had served a purpose though; it was well past lights-out, yet all were wide awake and, although the fact was yet to be openly acknowledged, knew they would remain so until Thompson returned. Bridger's joke broke a silence and opened the way for more general conversation.

"I suppose he might have been picked up by a shore

patrol," Harvey said.

"That or stayed over with his missis," Daly added.

"They're not that close." Peters spoke with rare certainty. "She's keeping him at arm's length."

"In which case there must be another reason," Hickman said.

Tell the truth, I never cared for him much," Nolan said, "least not at first. Seemed to be all front and no middle, if you follow."

"Reckon he was with a bad crowd – in the past," Harvey said.

"And not much better now," Bridger added.

"But he's worked hard on the club," Harvey said. "Wouldn't be in the state it's in without him."

"And he's taking more of a part aboard ship," Pickering agreed.

"Good kye," Kipling added with feeling.

"There was trouble earlier," Nolan said. "Anyone else notice?"

"What sort?"

"Couple of fellers came in and were talking at the bar."

"Don't sound much like trouble," Bridger said.

"No, but that's it; all they were doing was talking, though Thumper weren't looking too happy."

"So maybe he did stay over?" Mitchel spoke as a far-off door clattered, and there was the sound of hesitant footsteps approaching. "Or maybe that's him now..."

The door opened and, unusually, the room's lights were switched on; an act that normally brought forth a chorus of protests from those in bed. But this time no one objected, they were far too concerned by the state of their shipmate.

Chapter Twenty-Four

"A man down?" Anderson repeated. "How come?"

"It's Thompson." Milner was joining his captain at the breakfast table. "One of the Lewis gunners. He was attacked in town last night."

"I see; bar fight, was it?"

"Slightly worse than that." Milner shook out his napkin and reached for a piece of toast. "Happened in the street; they think it might have been an attempted robbery, though that hardly makes sense as nothing was stolen."

"How does he look?"

Milner shrugged as he searched for the margarine. "I only saw him briefly on the way here. Bit of a mess, though I think he'll live. PMO's patched him up for now but reckons it's mainly superficial."

"Then we'll have to wait and see."

"He's hardly essential." Milner had been up since six, the toast was cold, one of the men had gone down and the boat would have to be collected, inspected, and put through a rudimentary sea trial before their next job. Yet his feelings of a few hours before remained and, as he should be seeing Caroline again that evening, he could not be downhearted. "We're not due out until Friday and there's still one day of leave before then."

"And if he isn't fit, we could borrow a trainee gunner from *Bee*," Anderson supposed. "But it's a terrible thing to have happened."

He meant every word. Though not a particular favourite, Thompson was prepared to risk his life at sea for the sake of his country. For him to be attacked by what was probably no more than a common criminal – one unlikely to come closer to a true enemy than the cinema newsreel – felt like a personal affront.

"Thought I might find you here, gentlemen."

Both officers glanced up to see Lieutenant Matthews, Livingston's second in command, looking down on them. "I understand your boat's ready."

Milner paused with his knife half in the margarine. "Due to

be signed off later this morning," he said.

"Good, then I'm afraid I have bad news. Commander Livingston would like to see you in the ready room at oh-nine hundred," he said.

"Really?" Anderson exclaimed. "Why?"

Matthews grew confidential. "Friday's job's been brought forward; something of an emergency it seems." The young lieutenant looked about the crowded room; all were officers, though the majority would be on training courses, and not attuned to the pressures of active service. "I gather your parcel will be ready for collection slightly earlier than expected," he continued, enigmatically. "And if we leave it lying around, someone else might pick it up first."

"Most of the electrics have been replaced," Anderson this time, "but we'll need to shake down."

"That'll have to wait, I'm afraid," Matthews said. "And all leave is cancelled with immediate effect. Commander Livingston'll give you the details at nine. At least the weather looks fair, and it should be a doddle."

* * *

"Cancelled?" Bridger exclaimed.

"I'm afraid so," Sub-Lieutenant Milner confirmed. "Where are the rest?"

"Probably still in the dorm," Mitchel replied. The pair had just come back from breakfast at the NAAFI. "We was going into town."

"Well, you can forget about that," Milner said. "Boat's due for release at one, we'll be putting out at six and before then she'll have to be fuelled, stored and ammunitioned."

"Thumper's gone already," Bridger said.

"Thompson? Isn't he laid off sick?"

Mitchel shrugged. "He were on leave, so reckoned it don't count," he said.

Milner sighed. "Okay, one of you go and fetch Thompson, the other tells the rest; just make sure everyone's in the ready room by noon at the latest."

* * *

266

There was the usual amount of cleaning and re-stocking at the club, though that morning it seemed more. But then Thompson was not used to sweeping floors or washing down the bar with a black eye, a burst lip and bandages about his chest. Joyce had been sympathetic, which was pleasant enough, yet her work needed to be done as well, and their regular staff didn't come in until much later. And, for all her assurances, Thompson could tell she was just as worried as him.

At least the lads would be there shortly; that thought alone perked them both up, yet the morning was moving on with still no sign. No sign of Granger's men either and Thompson was starting to wonder who would appear first.

And then they did have a visitor. Even on normal mornings, Joyce kept the front door bolted so delivery drivers were inclined to knock. But when the entire building began to vibrate to a colossal banging, both knew who had won that particular race.

"Come on, open up!" It was Ted's voice.

"We'd better," Thompson told his wife, "otherwise they'll only bash the door down."

"So where are your mates?" she demanded. "They said they'd come."

"They did," he was every bit as disappointed. "But don't worry, I'm still here."

"You?" One look was enough, although Thompson was in full agreement. Bandaged as he was, he would be about as useful as an Egyptian mummy.

"Oh Frank, I'm sorry." She reached out to him for the first time since Dover. "I know you done your best, and I'm grateful, really. But it looks like it's come to an end; we'd better let 'em in."

* * *

"Bit of a shiner you got there, Frank old boy," Charlie told him. "Walk into a door, did you?"

Thompson said nothing, even if it hadn't been for last night's hiding, he was outnumbered. And not just by Ted and Charlie; two others stood behind, both equally well-built.

"Don't take on so," Ted said. "It's only a bit of business. You'd have done the same in our place."

"That's right," Charlie agreed. "And you know what they say; if you can't kick a man when he's down, when can you kick him?"

"But you've nothing to worry about, Mrs Thompson," Ted said, turning to her. "We don't intend harming a hair on your pretty little head."

"And neither will we touch your place," Charlie added. "We've had a word with Mr Frères, and he's more than happy to let us take it over – lock, stock, and barrel. All you got to do is move out."

"Hang on, I got money invested," she said. "More'n twenty pound – it's what paid for the stock, and some of the fittin's."

"Is that right?" Ted seemed surprised and oddly pleased. "I'm sure Mr Granger will be grateful for your little donation. And come back, both of you, any time. You'll always be welcome customers."

Thompson shifted uneasily. Knowing all their efforts had come to nothing felt bad enough, although being let down by his shipmates was probably worse.

"So, you going then?" Ted asked. "Bennie here'll give you a hand with your luggage."

"I got to pack first," Joyce said.

"That's alright, Bennie'll help with that an' all. Particularly fond of women's clothin' is our Ben."

The man, a balding monster who must have been eighteen stone of solid muscle, pulled a face, but when Joyce made her reluctant way to the stairs, he followed.

Watching, Thompson had never felt so useless in his life yet, even in his fitter days, he could have done little.

"Cheer up, Frank old lad," Ted told him. "Ain't the end of the world – you can always start another place." He grinned. "Only make sure you tells us where."

Thompson opened his mouth to reply when something behind Ted caught his attention. They'd left the door unlocked, and it might just have been blowing in the breeze, or the brewery's drey could be early. Thompson looked away to hide the hope that was growing inside. Or his mates might have turned up at last.

* * *

It was probably something to do with the drug either wearing off or taking effect, but there were moments when Dubois felt almost normal. His foot still ached, of course, only now it was the entire leg, and the pain was worse than ever. It was pain he could deal with, though, or at least anticipate. In some ways he wished he might stay that way forever, with just a physical hurt. But, depending on whether his medication's effects were waxing or waning, the ache would increase until he screamed for more, or was sucked back into that nightmare world where demons did battle with his one solitary angel.

The times of relative sanity were precious, they enabled him to assess his situation and, occasionally, come to a conclusion that could be remembered later. And some things he knew as if by instinct, the most important being he would soon be making the final part of his journey back to England.

The thought occupied what was left of his mind so much it was hard to think beyond it. In England he would receive proper medical attention and must certainly lose the leg – that much was decided, and accepted, long ago. But what then; how exactly could a one-legged agent be effective in carrying on the fight to free his country?

There was precedent here of course; one of SOE's agents was an American reporter who'd lost her leg in a hunting accident before the war. As far as Dubois knew, she was still active, so he had every reason to follow her example.

Except Dubois knew it was not just his leg that was failing him. At first, his carers were cautious with his treatment, as they had every right to be; drugs were rare and could be dangerous. However, for several weeks he had been given a succession of stronger painkillers until the point was reached where his mind must surely be broken.

His injuries, both physical and mental, would force him into some other form of employment and it was there his thoughts came to an end. And right that they should, he still had to be taken to the pickup point, still had to be seen onto whatever boat was sent to meet him.

And he still had to get back across La Manche – what the English insisted on referring to as 'their' Channel. Another name, The Narrow Seas, was equally misleading, as he would have to cross many miles of treacherous waters before facing a potentially deadly operation.

Yet whenever he possibly could, Dubois continued to think of the future with the determination of one whose remaining strength lay in hope. Somehow, he would get through this; he had to, if only to make the risks so many had run for him worthwhile. They would find him a post in England; he would insist on it. This, and the previous mission might have ended in failure, but he had learned much. There must be some way of utilising that experience, some work he might do to support other agents. And soon he would meet up with his own personal angel once more, of that he was equally certain.

Eve Newman had been part of his nightmare for so long it was hard to remember the real girl. But imagined or not, she helped him as much as any of the French; as much as the drugs he hated – and loved – so much. And though Dubois knew their relationship was purely ethereal, there was the strangest feeling the real woman must be aware of it, and what had gone on between them in his distorted mind.

"You are awake?"

He tried to focus on the face, though clear eyesight had been one of the drug's first victims. It was a man's voice, and one Dubois thought he recognised, although there had been so many he could not be certain.

"I am."

"Good, we shall be taking you on a short journey by boat."

"Short?"

There might have been a laugh. "It won't be back to England, my friend, just to a small island. Tonight, the English will come and by this time tomorrow you should be safe and getting proper medical attention."

That sounded good, although time was yet another casualty of his present condition.

"I will give you a further dose now," the voice continued. "You will then sleep and think about nothing for some time."

Dubois braced himself for the glorious pain of the injection. Think about nothing for some time – ah, if only that were truly the case...

* * *

270

They were expected in the ready room in less than fifteen minutes, yet *320*'s ratings were finding it impossible to run. Which was strange; after what they'd all been through, their blood was definitely up. And some was actually visible; Peters' nosebleed had finally stopped though his tunic was soaked, while a cut over Bridger's eye had also encouraged the crimson. Yet in no way were they downhearted – the very reverse. As they ambled along the street, each felt linked by a spirit of shared excitement and comradeship.

"Never took you for a scrapper." Mitchel gave Harvey's slight figure a friendly shove, nearly knocking him sideways. "But you was dishing it out like a good 'un."

"I chose my targets wisely," the telegraphist confessed. "Only went for the wounded."

"An' there was no lack of them at the end," Hickman added.

"Aye, I'd reckon they've seen better days," Pickering agreed.

Actually, the fight had been brief. Granger's men were no fools; when an overwhelming group of trained seamen blasted in, their main concern was how to get out without being hurt. The ratings were against any hurried departure, however, and inflicted what damage they could on their fleeing prey. And some had fought back, which explained their injuries, although those inflicted in return were worse and all but guaranteed no immediate rematch.

"Think we'll see 'em again?" Peters' mind was running on similar lines.

"Never," Thompson was unusually positive.

"They don't know we're headin' out to sea tonight," Mitchel said.

"Won't make no difference, I know them of old. We've bested them once and can do so again. They're gone for good."

Thompson believed this implicitly, while several other things had also become as clear. For a start, he was back with Joyce; he'd suspected as much that morning, but her farewell kiss just now must surely have confirmed it. And the club would continue; the only repairs necessary could be carried out with a mop. But the support received from men he'd barely known a few months before literally changed his life. Not as significant as the saving of his marriage, perhaps, although it had done that as well.

"Jimmy'll do his nut when he sees the state we're in." Bridger's announcement came with a total lack of concern or remorse.

"Won't be happy if we gets their late, neither," Mitchel added and, though there was general agreement with both remarks, no one thought to increase their pace.

"Sure, but aren't they lucky to have us?" Daly asked. "Shortly we'll be fighting for our country, least they can do is give us time to do the same for a shipmate."

* * *

As it happened, Milner was only too pleased to see them. Leave had been cancelled with the briefest of notice and, even after despatching Bridger and Mitchel, he assumed the men might not form up as quickly as usual. But when it was ten minutes past muster time, with no sign of any of them either in the ready room, *Bee*'s NAAFI or, when he sent messengers to check, the barracks, he began to grow anxious. *320* was due for release and would need a good deal of attention before she put out. That, and the fact her repairs could not be properly tested, was bad enough but faded to nothing if she lacked a crew.

"I'm not even going to ask what kept you," he announced when the first rating finally appeared at the drill hall door. "And neither am I particularly interested." He considered Bridger's eye and Peters' bloodstained tunic for a moment. "For now... But the boat will need a thorough hog out before we take on fuel, stores, and ammunition."

The men nodded with something like appreciation as they settled.

"Our mission tonight should be simple enough." Milner collected a long wooden pointer and turned to the map behind him. "In company with *369* we'll be making a pickup from Santagno Island." After tapping the map with his pointer, he turned to consider the motley bunch before him. "You've been there often enough; who knows, some of you may even remember..."

Harvey laughed, most nodded in acknowledgement and a

272

couple appeared mildly baffled.

"There'll be the usual concerns of course; we're aware of a convoy putting out tonight, in which case they could be in our area at the same time. And though far from full, the moon will be brighter than we would normally like. Apart from that, there are the usual warnings about interfering E-boats and anything else the Kriegsmarine choose to throw at us. But a bit of a brawl shouldn't be a problem, and some of you would appear to have started early."

This time a murmur of polite laughter circulated about the room, although a couple still looked confused.

"Right then, mechanics and special sea duty men repair to the yard, the rest can await *320*'s arrival at the quay. Oil and dry stores are already on the hard." He glanced at his watch. "You'll have a little over five hours – any longer and there'll be charges for your late arrival. Now scoot!"

The room emptied faster than it had filled, and Milner was replacing the pointer when his captain came in.

"All straight, Number One?" Anderson asked.

"I think so, sir. A little late mustering but they'll catch up."

"From what I saw several have been in action already."

"Indeed, sir; in the circumstances I thought it best not to investigate too closely."

"That was very wise," Anderson said, "though hardly by the book."

"Sometimes the book has to be ignored," Milner grinned.

"Sometimes it does," Anderson agreed. "Now I guess we'd both better scoot."

* * *

At 18.00 hours on the evening of 3rd November 1942, MGB*320* left Weymouth in company with *369*, a Fairmile C gunboat. Ahead of them lay a four-hour trip across one of the wider stretches of the English Channel and a major German convoy route. After that they must locate a pinpoint and collect a wounded intelligence agent. The latter would entail the use of an unpowered and barely manoeuvrable dinghy landing on a shallow beach. Ideally this should be done on a rising tide, to remove any evidence in the sand. Once completed, they must then return, at all times avoiding contact with the enemy.

320 carried three officers, only one of whom had been trained specifically for his post, a single warrant officer and a handful of ratings of differing backgrounds and experience. If everything went well, they would be back on British soil in under ten hours, otherwise some, or all, might never be seen again. And so, once more, they went to war.

Chapter Twenty-Five

The night was dark and, although clear when they put out, the Met. Office got it completely wrong and heavy cloud soon blanked out the stars while rain was definitely on the way. Which would be the best test for their recent weatherproofing, Anderson grimly decided. Indeed, it would have to be the only one; other than the shiny new junction box and a strong smell of bitumen, the repairs might never have been carried out. After two hours running at eighteen knots, they were a little under halfway to the pinpoint and it would soon be time to shut down the RDF. Castle's Fairmile was keeping station off their port quarter; apart from her, and several distant jigs on the screen that Harvey was certain would be fishers, 320 was alone. Certainly, as Anderson stood on the bridge and stared out over the dark waters, there was little to distract him.

"Do we know anything about the pickup?" Milner, beside him, asked.

"Do we ever?" Anderson replied. "Though Livingston did let slip it was just the one agent."

"Must be important," the younger man said.

"I believe they are injured."

Milner nodded. "That explains it."

Then, feeling conversation would do neither of them any harm, Anderson added, "Did you have anything fixed for this evening?"

"Oh yes," Milner grinned, though this time there was a trace of regret in his voice. "Prettiest girl on the base."

"On the base, I'll allow." Anderson smiled in return.

"Your girl's nearby, isn't she, sir?"

It was strange how the honorific should creep in when a personal matter was touched upon.

"A few miles off," he said. "She's stationed at Cloverly Grange."

"The SOE base?"

Anderson nodded.

"I understand they call it The Ranch," the younger man said, and Anderson turned to him.

275

"However did you know that?"

Milner shrugged. "Common knowledge," he said. "At least I thought it was."

Anderson scratched at his chin. The fact that Milner should be aware of something so trivial was no big deal; they were in the same business after all. But it did serve as a good example of how information was bound to leak, however good the security. He was reasonably sure the trainers at *Bee* knew all about their small outstation, and that the work *320* and the Fairmiles did was not confined to standard gunboat duties. And though none would speak about it openly, a few hints might inadvertently drop to their students. In which case it was likely most of Coastal Forces would know before long, just as all were aware what Slocum's lot were up to at Dartmouth. So much for security.

Morgan appeared at the head of the wheelhouse ladder just as Anderson came to this conclusion.

"Set's still clear, though Mr Harvey will need to shut down presently."

"No sign of any enemy convoy?"

"Nothing, sir, though it'll be an hour before we're in that area and the RDF's only got a limited field."

"How far off is the coast?" Anderson knew of Morgan's dislike for estimating distances on a chart, yet he could do so with amazing accuracy by sight.

"Just under forty mile, sir."

320 was actually heading several points from her objective to allow for the regular current while the stream that carried them closer to France was steadily decreasing. There would be a brief hiatus – probably just as they were approaching the pinpoint – before it returned in the opposite direction, and all must be accounted for. Not for the first time, Anderson was pleased to have relinquished navigational duties.

"Reckon this weather's for the turn."

Anderson was as ready to listen to Morgan's meteorological observations as he was his piloting.

"Really?" Milner questioned. "Met boys said there may even be air raids."

"Not tonight." Morgan was positive. "Heavy rain long before midnight and a fair old wind, if I'm any judge," he added. "Reckon we're in for a good old fashioned thunder-plump."

"Let's hope the dockyard's repairs hold out," Milner added with an unusual lack of tact.

Anderson closed his eyes; their recent experience with the faulty klaxon and lamps was still very much on his mind. At the time he put it down to bad luck, only when considering the matter more carefully did he realise the part good fortune played. German artillerymen had an excellent reputation and those on the northern coast of France were rumoured to be the best. *320* would have made a prime target and to have survived such a predicament was almost miraculous.

He heard a mild patter; the first heavy drops were starting to fall, and he hoped there would be no repetition.

* * *

Thompson's thoughts were not on what might go wrong for the rest of that day, instead they remained set on what had already gone right. Only an idiot would regard Granger's men coming to Weymouth as anything other than a disaster; no one enjoys taking a beating after all. Yet it seemed their appearance, or rather how he dealt with it, was enough to nudge Joyce back to her proper place – or what he considered it to be a few months ago. But a lot had happened since; not only had he learned much, Thompson knew himself to be a better man for having done so.

Although it was not all his doing; without his mates' intervention nothing could have been sorted, the club would be under Granger's control, and he'd probably still be suffering from a proper mauling way back in that Dover market square. Not only did they come to his aid, but it was without question or conditions. Thompson had never encountered such loyalty before and wondered if he ever would again. Not in civvy street, that was for certain though, if he remained in the Navy, it might be a different matter. Whatever, it was an experience he would never forget, while he was equally conscious of the bond that now linked him with the other members of *320*'s crew; one he would be careful never to break.

Harvey, in the silent W/T office, was also pleased at the outcome. Finding a place to play had been important but totally eclipsed by encountering Nichole, and what was becoming his hottest band ever.

If their regular gig at the club had been lost, they probably wouldn't have found another; certainly not one that allowed the same musical freedom. His relationship with Nichole was solid, but the other musicians would simply have drifted away; he'd seen that happen many times when a venue closed. In which case Harvey would have been sorry as he also knew enough to recognise when the musical chemistry worked and, with their current lineup, that was indisputable. Webster, the new reed man, was pulling his weight but landing Lee had been the clincher. Harvey remembered him being good when they played together in Dover, and there'd been improvements since. After swapping the cornet for a trumpet, the Yank's technique fully developed while his film star looks always went down well with the ladies. This might even be the time for them to find an agent, one who could sort out a recording contract. They'd need a gimmick, these days that was expected; something memorable to identify them with the public, and he might have chanced upon the very thing.

Recently he'd been working on an arrangement of *Honeysuckle Rose*; taking it slower and in a lower key – to make full use of Nichole's husky tenor, while the more relaxed pace would allow her to emphasise the undeniably erotic lyrics. A few more charts like that and the band would have real identity and there was no telling where it might go.

He'd been happy to help out with Thompson, a mate was a mate after all, although the main point of that morning's activities was to keep their residency. Nichole must be there now, and probably singing, even if it would not be the same without him. But tomorrow night he'd be back; back with the band, back with Nichole, and Harvey wanted nothing more.

In the engine room, Pickering wasn't feeling particularly greedy either. There was no trace of envy when Newman was promoted to the post of Chief Motor Mechanic, although he found the problems his new boss encountered with the youngster, Kipling, more than annoying. Thankfully all that was over; the three of them were working as a team, and just as smoothly as any of the Packards currently rumbling at modest revs in their small space. He cared little about the club, though did accept and respect what it had done to bond the entire gunboat's crew, and for that reason alone was glad to have saved it.

And, on the bridge, Morgan knew nothing of any club and

nor did he wish to. Being at sea gave him the only satisfaction he craved and, after a lifetime spent so, knew he had finally found the organisation and respectability he needed. Though relatively untrained, his captain was not without talent as a seaman while the youngster who supported him had more academic knowledge and was steadily acquiring the necessary sensitivities. So, in Morgan's mind at least, he became the last piece in the jigsaw; his experience and knowledge bonding them into a single unit, while he was also no novice when it came to avoiding an enemy.

The crew continued to improve with every trip; even that evening he noticed instances of them truly pulling together, which was good to see. Yet the most important element was something that must remain personal – something Morgan would probably not have mentioned even to Marjorie, had the opportunity presented.

His private study was beginning to take effect; already he was starting to think and behave like a true RN man and that pleased him more than anything else. The war that called him back to the sea would not last forever; eventually he must return to the beach to spend the rest of his days in retirement. After a lifetime of tapping the glass and dodging all forms of authority, it would be a surprisingly honest one with the respectability of being a former Royal Naval officer. And though he told himself it meant little to him, Marjorie would have been delighted.

* * *

By the time the French coast was in plain sight the rain was falling with a vengeance. If anything, the conditions were worse than when *320* last put to sea and, though no one now mentioned their private doubts, all on the bridge were unusually tense. Both gunboats were running on their auxiliary V8s, main engines having been cut some time before, and their hulls – so solid at high-speed, so unsteady at low – wallowed in the heavy swell.

"That's Santagno." Morgan pointed at the dull shape barely visible off their port bow; a perfect landfall. Anderson turned and looked back at Castle's boat.

"She's moving in," Milner announced, and that was surely the case. The Fairmile C's larger hull might have been slightly more steady, though she still made heavy weather of it.

"The island's less than a mile off, and she'll be able to anchor close by," Morgan said, and Anderson nodded. They all knew the procedure well enough; once secured – using a grass line that could be cut in an instant – Castle would send in his fourteen-foot surf boat with a crew of two. Santagno offered a shallow, but steep, beach which was preferable as it could be accessed at all states of the tide. The latter had started to rise though there was no way of knowing the state of the agent and whether a stretcher was necessary. If so, it would need to be secured, then the dinghy – a clumsy affair that rode high – could return to her mother ship and they might all start for home. Providing everything went well, the whole procedure should take no more than thirty minutes with less than five on shore. But if an enemy appeared during that time the boat, her crew, and the agent were likely to be lost. That had yet to happen on any mission Anderson was involved in, though remained a possibility and one 15 Flotilla suffered in the past.

He raised his binoculars away from the Fairmile and swept the horizon. The weather was still closing in; little could be seen in any direction apart from the occasional balls of squall that rolled with the growing wind. To seaward it was marginally better, but facing the island, and the mainland beyond, was a different matter. Anything might be lurking in that portentous darkness; whoever agreed to take the small boat in was brave indeed.

"369 appears to be anchoring." This was Milner, and Anderson's focus returned to the Fairmile. She was ideally placed though it was not the first time Castle had used this particular pinpoint.

"Any sign of a signal from the shore?" Anderson asked.

Both men shook their heads with Milner adding, "None that I have seen."

That was not unusual, the light would come from a hooded torch – a modern-day equivalent of the smugglers' spout lamp – and be pointed directly at 369.

"The surf boat's going in."

Again, Anderson was unsurprised. Considering the importance time had in such an operation, those manning her might even have set off before 369 was totally secure. They watched as the tiny vessel made slow progress until the gloom swallowed her up.

"Now all we can do is wait," Milner said. 320 was facing the current, the auxiliary V8 keeping her roughly stationary, and she had definitely been in worse situations. But remaining so for any length of time went against the instincts of everyone on the bridge and they soon began to grow restless.

"I could send down for some kye," Milner suggested, and Anderson was about to reply when another voice cut in.

"Vessel, red 10 and closing!" It was Peters, at the Vickers, and all eyes stared out over their port bow.

Where nothing could be seen other than driving rain interspersed with the occasional rolling bundle of storm...

Anderson drew breath; Peters might play the fool at times, but could be trusted when sighting an enemy.

"Fire her up," he ordered, and the almost immediate rumble from their centre Packard told him Newman was expecting just such a command. The outer wing engines soon followed yet still nothing was in sight and the tension rose further.

Then a flash of white slightly off their bow drew everyone's attention; a deeper squall lay in that direction and from it, traveling at what must have been close to her maximum speed, came the ghostly outline of an oncoming E-boat.

* * *

"Hard a starboard, bring her up to fifteen hundred," Anderson yelled. "And tell Harvey to report an enemy sighting to Southern Command!"

Castle, aboard *369*, should pick up on the W/T transmission even if he failed to spot the E-boat, though he must also see – and hear – *320* turning away while she reared up onto the plane. Anderson had no idea what the other captain would do and didn't care: there were other problems.

"Meet her, midships – up to full speed!"

It was now a straightforward chase, with *320* less than a mile ahead of the speeding enemy the patches of storm suddenly became a potential benefit. Unless there was something decidedly wrong with her, the E-boat would gain while *320* must already be within range of her forward cannon. Should the danger become too great, he could shelter in one of the squalls but for now there was good reason to expose his command. Once more Anderson's job was to protect the Fairmile and every foot they covered must lure the enemy that much further from her.

Green tracer began to whip past; at a shout from his captain, Milner slammed his fist down on the firing gongs and Bridger, at the Oerlikon, immediately sent a wave of red in return.

"Starboard ten – midships!"

The weaving would throw their own gunners as much, but the enemy mounted heavier weapons and Anderson had no choice. He stared forward, suddenly keen for a patch of bad weather large enough to hide them, if only temporarily.

"To starboard!" Morgan was shouting in his ear, while pointing off their beam. Anderson looked across; yes, that was a likely contender.

"Starboard ten – meet her – starboard five," a pause, "meet her, starboard ten."

Now Bridger would have to contend with an erratic turn along with the inevitable disturbance as they crossed the current, although the gunner was making better practice than his counterpart aboard the E-boat.

A straight run of several seconds, then the squall lay ahead. He could just make out Castle's boat to starboard; still anchored and presumably trusting in him to keep the E-boat occupied.

"Bring her down, eighteen hundred!"

Nolan duly repeated the order while his gloved hand eased the triple throttles back.

"Port five!" – a slight adjustment. And then they were in the centre of the storm and all else was hidden.

"Hard a port, full speed, and silence the guns!"

320 tore through the black rain, her hull bouncing over the rising waves.

"Meet her – midships!"

Flashes of green flew passed; the German must have followed them into the squall though clearly had no fix and was firing blind. With further effort and not a little luck, they might escape, though Anderson's aim was more subtle and a good deal harder. Like any parent distracting a hunter that might otherwise discover his young, he must entice the enemy away from a far tastier, far more important prey. And even if it meant *320* were ultimately lost, continue to do so for as long as it was physically possible.

* * *

No one greeted the sudden loss of visibility as much as Thompson. As soon as the E-boat came into sight he'd known they were in for one hell of a battle and unlikely to come out on top. In the past, with at least the illusion of security from his turret, he could be more dispassionate, but being stuck out at the stern, with an unshielded gun and only a scrap of canvas for protection, was very different.

And there was another feeling, one he did not expect or even truly understand. Thompson had been no angel in the past; not so very long ago he was in the same line of work as Ted and Charlie, and only now could appreciate the misery he must have caused. Of course, nothing could be done about that, but there was something in acknowledging the previous wrong that made him feel even more vulnerable.

A few shells came their way as they entered the storm cloud, but none fell close; Jerry must have been firing wildly, yet a stray round was as lethal as any carefully aimed. And before that there had only been fleeting glimpses of his opponent, with no chance of him returning fire.

He looked across to where Daly could be made out. The Irishman would be just as wet and miserable as everyone else on deck; once this present danger was over, Thompson would make for the galley. And not just for shelter; apart from the sandwiches hurriedly wolfed down before departure, the men's stomachs were empty. There was nothing more solid on board, but a mug of hot soup always went down well, and looking after others brought a sense of satisfaction to Thompson which came as yet another surprise.

A flash of white from astern; that might be the enemy and it might not. The gongs had sounded; no firing was permitted, but he shouldered his weapon to be on the safe side. Then, out of the gloom and barely visible, came the German's prow.

And with it, gunfire; the briefest of bursts. Green tracer swept towards them, seeming to accelerate as it drew near. But the enemy's aim was off, and Thompson was breathing a sigh of relief when he felt the hot pain of a hit.

Daly seemed to be with him before he even struck the deck.

"Alright, pal, I got you."

283

Thompson blinked. "It were the wind, Pad'," he said. "Carried the tracer further, I weren't allowin' for that."

"Sure, but don't give it another thought," Daly told him. "We'll get you for'ard."

"Never make a gunner, me," Thompson added sadly. The pain was growing, though remained bearable while it carried an air of punishment that was almost welcome.

"There's worse things," Daly told him. "Now grab hold of me arm."

* * *

Visibility was clearing, they were at the end of the storm cloud. *320* had met with the enemy while sheltered, but Anderson was unaware of any damage or casualties.

"To port!" This was Morgan, and Anderson followed his pointing finger. Yes, there was a slightly denser patch; they must make for that next.

"Port ten!"

320 turned as the E-boat reappeared once more and a barrage of green landed squarely off her starboard beam.

"Meet her, midships!"

The fresh squall was nowhere near as large; they would be through in seconds while the E-boat was definitely back on their tail. Further streaks of green – they had nothing more to lose.

"Firing gongs!"

Yet again the Oerlikon opened up at once and this time they could see actual hits on the enemy's bridge.

"Hard a starboard!"

There was still a fair amount of squall remaining, so the command was mainly based on instinct, but Anderson reckoned his opponent would have other things to consider and not notice the sudden, and irrational turn. And this time he held it for longer, until *320* had gone completely about and would soon be passing the speeding enemy on a reciprocal course.

The forward Vickers began to speak, casting further bolts of red and *320* almost had an advantage. But that could not last, Anderson must turn again before the German's heavier aft ordnance came into play.

"Port fifteen."

They were free of all storm clouds now and in the closest that night could offer to clear air. And there was the Fairmile, though no longer anchored; presumably her cargo was safely aboard – that or abandoned, along with the surf boat and its crew.

"Another – to larboard!" Morgan's language lapsed in his excitement, but Anderson could follow a pointing finger and the prospect – a particular dense storm cloud – appeared perfect.

More green flashes but they could almost be ignored; it was important not to give the game away and Anderson continued to weave, bearing slightly from the squall before turning directly into it, and silencing the guns once more.

And there it was dark indeed while the rain, now being blown almost horizontal, meant those on the bridge could barely make out one another. Morgan, to Anderson's right, was pointing off the gunboat's starboard quarter as if keeping track of a man overboard, though his target was far more sinister.

"Bring her to fifteen hundred," Anderson bellowed, "and port ten."

If the elderly midshipman's bearing was correct, that would place the E-boat directly astern; the best place for her while they continued to head away from the Fairmile.

There was a whistle from the voice pipe, and Milner bent forward to answer.

"It's Tel'," he shouted. "*369*'s reporting a successful collection."

That was good to hear, Castle must know they would intercept the message and realise he was heading for home; Anderson need only entertain the E a few minutes longer.

"Weather's clearing."

Yes, they were coming to the end of the squall, but it had been excellent cover.

"Take her back up to twenty hundred." Anderson spoke just as they burst from the storm cloud. And then they were through once more and all began to search for the enemy.

There remained several patches of heavy weather with those between hardly any clearer. But though they scoured the area until their eyes were raw, there was no sign of the E-boat.

"Done a runner," Nolan muttered.

285

"She must still be close," Morgan said.

That was indisputable, but with their vision measured in hundreds of yards they could continue searching for hours and not find her.

"We'd better meet up with Castle," Anderson said. It was possible – likely even – the German had left to go in search of the larger gunboat, in which case their duty was to pair up as soon as possible. However, Anderson sensed they had seen the last of that particular enemy. "Can anyone give me a course?" It was almost a rhetorical question, but Morgan responded by instantly raising his arm and pointing out into the darkness.

"Can't be certain, mind," he said, "and I'm only guessin' at her speed. But we know what direction she'll be heading. If you steer so, I reckon we'll meet up."

"Very good." Anderson gave a nod of thanks. And then, to Nolan, "Starboard fifteen."

Chapter Twenty-Six

Now alone at the furthest station aft, Daly was feeling distinctly uncomfortable. They had first glimpsed the Fairmile fifteen minutes before and, once properly identified, *320* pulled alongside. But there was no let-up in the wind, and the rain continued to fall, while the swell might even have increased with every other wave seemingly intent on knocking him from his perch. However, the E-boat was gone and only the most determined enemy would put out on such a night; surely any remaining fight could only be with the elements.

Of course, that might turn out a vain hope, but it comforted Daly as he gripped the lifeline and gained what shelter he could. Though no expert, he'd fixed up Thumper right enough. The only thing the Irishman knew about wounds was they should be avoided, though he and Harvey had done their best with a pressure dressing and several lengths of webbing. After a bit of manoeuvring and not a little mess, Thompson was trussed up like a turkey on Christmas Eve, and now should be sleeping the sleep of the just; the syrette of morphine would see to that. Whether he survived or not was probably still in the balance, but Daly doubted anyone on board could have done much better.

And, if nothing else, he should be reasonably dry, which was more than the Irishman could say for himself. The other gunboat still lay close by, with the two skippers bellowing at each other through loud hailers. But Daly wasn't listening; at that point all he cared about was getting home and being warm once more: nothing else mattered.

* * *

Anderson had more immediate concerns. A worrying report had come through from Southern Command; *369* still lay close by and the heavy swell was making both gunboats reel and heave with sickening regularity as their captains conferred.

"Convoy was spotted by bombers returning from an aborted mission," Castle said.

"If it *is* a convoy," Anderson replied. "They just said substantial enemy shipping." One hand held a guard rail, the other gripped the Tannoy's microphone while his voice, oddly distorted, was being reflected by the storm, although the other captain had no difficulty hearing him.

"Unless the Germans are planning to invade," he said.

It was probably good that Castle had kept his sense of humour, although Anderson could have wished otherwise. A major convoy route was crossing their path; he must decide between stooging about for several hours while the danger passed or making a run for it. But first he needed more information.

"What of your patient?"

"Not good."

The heavily cloaked figures on the Fairmile's bridge were swaying and staggering in the atrocious weather; Anderson wondered if his lot looked quite so comical.

"He's currently heavily sedated though needs proper attention," Castle continued. "We're keeping him warm, but this motion won't be helping any."

"Then I suggest we make a run for it."

It was an awkward situation; both captains were of equal rank and almost identical in seniority. As the escort responsible for the safety of both vessels, Anderson should have the final say although Castle was caring for a sick passenger. Were he to object, or insist on another course of action, it could be tricky, and this was not the time, the place, or the conditions for an argument. But it seemed they were on the same wavelength.

"I'm with you in that," came the reply. "Will you take the lead?"

"What speed can you make?" Anderson asked.

"In this?" Castle paused. "Probably no more than sixteen."

"Very well, I'll pull back if you start to fall behind."

"What about RDF?"

"I'm going to use it," Anderson said. They were still close enough to enemy territory to make this a risk, to say nothing of directly contradicting standing orders, but he clearly had the other man's approval.

"Absolutely." Despite the atrocious conditions, Castle's enthusiasm was obvious. "Better than having to feel our way!"

288

Yet when they tried the equipment, it proved a disappointment.

"Tel's done all he can," Milner told his captain a few minutes later, "but the set's completely dead."

"Nothing to do with water ingress?" Anderson asked – even after this long in the storm, the fear remained.

"No, sir. There's power, just no screen; he thinks it must be all this jigging about."

That seemed most likely. RDF was new technology and had been rushed through, though to be let down in such a way felt like the last straw.

"Very well, tell him to keep a close check on all wireless traffic; first hint of a convoy nearby, I want to hear about it."

Anderson glanced back to where *369* was making heavy weather in the storm. With each yard that brought them deeper into the Channel the waves grew larger, most regularly broke over both ships' foredecks while their own bridge was remaining dry due only to the constant flow of rainwater draining under the duck boards. The Fairmile's passenger would hardly be comfortable in such conditions although it was difficult to consider the welfare of one – unknown – man who was putting over thirty lives at risk.

He turned to Morgan.

"How long before we raise our coast?"

It was an impossible question, and unfair, considering the various currents that would have to be taken into consideration. Yet Anderson felt he had to ask, and the old man seemed surprisingly unphased.

"At this speed, sir? Roughly four hours," he said. "That's if we can avoid diversions."

In which case it would be starting to get light, which was some consolation, Anderson supposed. And four hours he could probably manage, as might the ship; he just hoped there would be no diversions.

* * *

The first came less than fifteen minutes later. Milner remained on the bridge and *320* was continuing to slice her way through the devilish waves when a cry came from forward.

"Vessel in sight, port bow!"

289

It was Peters again; the lad had excellent eyes and, even as he stared out into the filthy weather, Anderson made a mental note to commend him later.

"I see it!" Milner was pointing into the storm and Anderson – who had failed to – breathed a sigh of relief.

He stared some more, and slowly, mockingly, the form of a large fishing vessel came into view.

"Armed trawler," Anderson announced and there were nods from the other two officers.

Quite what they might do about it was another matter. Such an enemy was nothing like the neutral it appeared and could be carrying anything from Oerlikons to 88mm cannon, all of which would be fired from a far firmer platform. And if this was indeed a convoy, it would not be the only escort; there may also be R-boats, VPs and possibly E-boats hereabouts.

"Port ten!" Anderson ordered and the trawler quickly faded from sight. The Germans would not be expecting an approach from the south; providing Castle was on his toes and followed, they might avoid detection.

"If it weren't for the weather..." Milner began, and Anderson could only agree. Although deep in the Channel and far to the west, Southern Command would normally have despatched a force of gun and torpedo boats to deal with such a tempting target. But no Flotilla SO could justify putting out in such conditions: they were on their own.

Until then their course had been predominantly westerly, relying on the steady but powerful current to sweep them back to Weymouth, while also avoiding the wind and waves striking directly onto their beam. Turning to port, and into the stream, might prove dangerous to the slower Fairmile, but any change to starboard would effectively set them on a race against the convoy. And, even if it was one they could win, they must then make for a more easterly harbour.

The motion aboard *320* changed as she nosed into the current, then altered some more, forcing Anderson to up the revs slightly to maintain their previous pace. He glanced back; Castle might not have sufficient power in reserve, and it was more important than ever they stayed together.

But the Fairmile remained on station throughout the turn, the only worry now was whether the German escort had spotted them and, if so, what action they might take.

This last point was definitely in doubt. Whenever he attacked an enemy convoy, the accompanying warships always put up an excellent defence, though usually proved reluctant to leave their charges unprotected for any length of time. With this in mind, and provided he and Castle avoided further contact, running in with the convoy should mean no more than a slight delay in their return to Weymouth; annoying, but by no means a disaster. At least that's what he hoped.

"No sign of anything now," Milner bellowed as *320* settled on her new course.

"Much will depend on exactly how we caught them," Anderson shouted back.

"If that were the head, the convoy will stretch back a fair distance," Morgan agreed, and Anderson was struck by how quickly the three had grown used to working as a team.

"I intend giving it at least a mile," he announced and received nods of agreement in reply.

All good; Castle was remaining in touch and, even with a powerful enemy so close, there was time to draw breath. Experience taught him this should soon be nothing more than a bad memory; within a few hours they'd be back on British soil and probably safe and warm in their beds. And there was even room for optimism; the mission had been brought forward, so he would be free the following evening; a chance to meet up with Eve, which was a pleasant thought in itself. Then a cry went up from Nolan that brought them all back to reality.

"Vessel dead ahead and closing!"

"Hard a port!" The order came instinctively, and Anderson knew it less than ideal. They were effectively turning back and must shortly take the full force of both wind and current on their beam. But the alternative, turning to starboard, was far more dangerous and would trap them between two fires: this new sighting and the German convoy.

"It's an E!" Milner's shout came as his hand automatically edged towards the firing gongs and, at a nod from Anderson, the alarm was given. Almost immediately Peters, at their forward two-pounder, opened up, sending a hail of red in the speeding German's path. The barrage continued throughout the turn and was soon answered by a stream of green that peppered the waters about them. Anderson glanced back; Castle had been alert enough to follow them round, but would he pick up on what must happen next? Or, to be exact, would he continue heading south when *320* turned back to take on the E-boat?

"Starboard fifteen!"

Nolan gave a brief acknowledgement although Milner and Morgan remained silent. Once more, Anderson was allowing instinct to take over; he might appreciate their support, but there were times when a captain's duty was to make the decisions. And *320*'s mission remained the same; to protect the Fairmile. If he could distract the enemy for long enough, and maybe drive her back towards its convoy, Castle should be able to make his escape in the darkness and storm.

Anderson had already decided the E-boat would be one of the stern escorts, probably summoned by the armed trawler previously encountered. There was even a moment to appreciate the irony in it protecting a convoy he had no intention of attacking. The E-boat altered course at *320*'s first turn with the obvious intent of bearing down on a fleeing enemy; now they would discover how keen their opponent was on facing a direct attack.

The question was answered remarkably quickly. Despite Anderson effectively aiming his gunboat in their direction, the E-boat turned further to attack the Fairmile.

"*369*'s the larger target!" Milner's remark might have been reasonable enough, although it didn't solve Anderson's dilemma. The E-boat remained some distance off but was traveling fast; Unless something happened quickly, *320* would pass her and lose any chance of blocking an approach on Castle's boat.

"Hard a port – bring her down to twelve hundred – meet her!"

Now he was effectively throwing *320* in the German's path, although it did allow her aft Oerlikon to come into action. Between them, the British guns would create a veritable wall of fire for their attacker to penetrate.

But it did not dissuade the E-boat in any way: the very reverse. A line of green snaked through the red, finding *320*'s foredeck and instantly silencing her two-pounder.

"Port fifteen."

With his forward armament inoperative, Anderson must now fight a rearguard action, and much would depend on how far from its convoy the enemy was prepared to stray.

"Increase to twenty hundred."

This was not *320*'s maximum speed, though fast enough to prevent their minimal lead disappearing entirely. Protecting the Fairmile remained Anderson's primary objective; he was still determined not to run from the E-boat.

* * *

It had taken no more than a second to turn the forward-mounted Vickers into a mass of tangled steel while Peters, who was firing at the time, now appeared to have become a part of it.

"Hey, matie!" Hickman said. "Hang on, we'll soon have you out."

"Save your breath." Peters' voice was almost lost in the din of high-revving engines and driving rain. "And get below."

"Not leavin' you like this," Hickman replied. "Wait a while, I'll bring help."

"I ain't movin'." Now Peters spoke with urgency and, from the little Hickman could see, he could guess at his pain.

"Well I ain't either," he said. Pure chance dictated what had struck the Vickers missed him, yet Hickman could not shake the feelings of guilt; the least he could do was stick by his partner.

"Stay if you want, it'll soon be over."

Hickman sensed that to be true.

"Looks like we made the wrong choice," Peters continued.

"Coastal Forces?" Hickman chanced.

"Gunboats," Peters corrected. "You was right all along; we should have gone for gumboots."

Hickman gave a grim chuckle but there were no more jokes from Peters and soon he realised there never would be.

* * *

Turning aft, Anderson could see Bridger and Mitchel were sending up a reasonable barrage on the pursuing boat, and even Daly could now reach with his Lewis. Of Thompson there was no sign, though equally no time to pursue that particular thought; the enemy were proving annoyingly obstinate and paying them little attention, preferring instead to target the Fairmile, now less than a quarter

293

of a mile off.

And the shots were beginning to tell. Despite Castle's vessel returning fire, she was soon hit, and flames started to appear at her stern while the steering must also have been damaged as she was turning with the current. Then, seemingly satisfied, the E-boat switched her attention to *320*.

Shells ripped into the gunboat's topsides and hull, sending splinters, fittings, and men flying in all directions and silencing both the Oerlikon and two of her engines. Had the attack continued for many more seconds, she would have sunk or exploded; as it was, the risk of either remained. And, when the German finally turned away, her mission apparently accomplished, Anderson knew the chances of their raising Weymouth again were slight.

Chapter Twenty-Seven

"*369* ahoy!"

Anderson was having to bellow through cupped hands, power to *320*'s Tannoy having been lost. And it felt like wasted effort; the Fairmile was wallowing heavily about twenty feet off their starboard beam. Low in the water and listing to port, her empty decks lacked several major fittings and were pockmarked with shot holes.

"Can you hear me, *369*?"

"Looks a proper mess," Milner said.

"Indeed." Anderson wiped water from his face, yet the weather was turning in their favour. The wind remained as strong, but the rain had started to ease, and it felt like the storm itself might pass before long.

Movement caught his eye; *369*'s port wheelhouse door must have buckled and someone was forcing it open. Three seamen appeared; one apparently shaken or wounded, was being supported by another, and then came a taller figure dressed in an ursula but bare headed. The group regarded *320* as if she were some form of apparition and only after several seconds did one of the ratings raise a hand in acknowledgement.

"Is your captain there?" Anderson bellowed.

"Captain's dead." It was the tall figure, probably an officer. "And we lost the cox'n – everyone on the bridge is gone."

"Very well. Can you stay afloat?"

There was no answer, and Anderson drew breath. It was likely the fellow was in shock, though his craft looked to be settling fast. "I shall come alongside," he said.

Closing with a vessel likely to blow at any moment was a risky business, but *369* could not stay afloat much longer, and transferring what was left of her crew by boat would be a hazardous and slow operation.

Another seaman appeared through the wheelhouse door, then two more clambered out of a hatchway further aft. One caught a line thrown by Hickman, and slowly the two vessels were drawn together.

"Better go and supervise, Number One," Anderson said. "And..."

Milner flashed a smile. "Don't worry, sir, I won't hang about."

* * *

Bridger and Mitchel were fine, their gun was only abandoned when the hydraulics failed in the Oerlikon's powered mount. And they had not been idle, with Mitchel taking up Thompson's Lewis towards the end of the action. And now, with *320* in such a sorry state, the pair set to with a will, clearing debris and patching holes in the deck and upper hull with tacks and rolls of webbing.

And below them, in the engine room, Newman was equally occupied. Several shells had penetrated his cramped space silencing both the central and starboard Packards along with their auxiliary V8. Even their remaining engine was misfiring badly, while a constant stream of fumes leaked from one of the exhaust manifolds. Two of the bulkhead lamps were also smashed while rain poured in from a dozen minor holes in the deckhead. And Kipling was dead.

"Asbestos strapping," Newman ordered, but Pickering already held a roll of the grey, flaky cloth and was approaching the bubbling engine.

With so much to attend to, the fact of the lad's death did not trouble him greatly, though it remained in the back of his mind and, as Newman already knew, would haunt him for some time to come.

The air was thick with fumes, though at least one of the extractor fans still operated and, if they were even mildly successful in blocking the exhaust, the problem should be solved for the next few hours.

With Pickering making good progress with the asbestos, Newman decided he would attend to the central engine. Even in *320*'s darkened hell hole he could tell the storm was easing, though there would still be many miles to cover before they reached land; getting another mill back could make all the difference.

He raised himself up and inspected the central engine more carefully. As he had thought, the damage was mainly

296

electrical and relatively straightforward. He'd simply replace everything that appeared faulty or burnt out, starting with the low tension circuit. And it was a shame really, this was just the sort of job he'd like to have shown Kipling.

* * *

Despite the heavy swell, evacuating *369* was carried out relatively quickly. Even transferring the stretcher bearing the reason for their mission went well and, when Anderson could finally cast off, the larger gunboat settled further, before disappearing beneath the waves as if to order.

Then, while those able did what they could to make his own command watertight, Anderson met with the Fairmile's young officer on *320*'s battered mess deck.

His guess had been correct; the lad turned out to be *369*'s first lieutenant and was barely in his twenties.

"In the present conditions my CMM reckons he might get ten knots from our remaining engine," Anderson told the youngster. "But as to where we strike land, or precisely when, is a mystery."

"Very good, sir."

That was hardly the case, though there would be little point in saying so; from the look on the young face Anderson wondered if his words had even registered.

"Where were you when your boat was hit?" he asked, and this time there was more of a reaction.

"Below, sir, in the wheelhouse. I was plotting our course back – or trying to."

Anderson nodded. He supposed Morgan, currently on the bridge and in nominal charge of *320*, might have more of an idea of their position, though it seemed irrelevant; simply heading north should do; any patch of land would be welcome.

"Can I ask, sir, did you report our running in with the convoy?"

"I did not," Anderson said; there was no point in hiding it. "At the time it would have been dangerous. With that amount of enemy shipping close by, at least one German radio op. was likely to be on a listening brief."

"I understand, sir." The young man was quick to agree.

"You don't mind my asking only..."

"No, of course not."

"Maybe Southern Command was tracking them, and us, on RDF?"

Anderson felt that unlikely. When based at *Wasp*, it was reassuring to know much of what happened would be monitored by those ashore. But they were far deeper into the Channel now and the science was still relatively new.

"It doesn't look good, does it, sir?"

"It doesn't," Anderson agreed. "But there's still a lot we can do, and the storm appears to be easing." Milner's hurried fabric reports, though serious, were not insurmountable and they had already done much to make the hull watertight. "Providing we avoid further contact with the enemy I'd say we have a fair chance of making it home."

"I'll see my chaps give all the assistance they can."

"I'm sure that'll be welcome, and, once more, I'm sorry for the loss of your ship – and your captain, of course."

"He taught me so much." The young man's eyes were growing moist.

"I understand," Anderson said.

"No, I don't think you do." Sorrow was turning to anger now and the face flushed red. "Begging your pardon, sir, Lieutenant Castle was a brilliant commander, probably the best. I owe him so much." He faltered for a moment, then recovered. "We understood each other – it was a special relationship, I suppose you might say, yet I never got the chance to thank him, not properly."

Anderson nodded. "I'm afraid that is often the case."

* * *

"You must be Harvey."

The telegraphist turned to see a young man of roughly his own age standing in the W/T office doorway.

"Name's Stone, Paul Stone; I was the radio op. on *369*. They said you might need a hand."

Harvey nodded toward the small desk, now filled with the chassis from two wireless units. "I could certainly use another

298

eye," he said.

The air was already sweet with the fumes of past soldering as the visitor dragged a stool next to Harvey and sat down.

"Both sets are blown," Harvey continued. "I'm cannibalising parts; at least if we can get the transmitter working..."

"Makes sense," Stone agreed. "Though we won't know if we've been heard."

"I'm a long way from even trying." Harvey passed an AVOmeter across. "Maybe if you check out some resistances?"

"Glad to, though it might take a while."

"I expect so," Harvey agreed, "but then, what else would we be doing?"

* * *

"Below!"

The cry came from the engine room's entrance hatch and was followed by a cascade of water as it opened fully. Two overall-clad figures slipped down, landing squarely in front of Newman.

"We're from the Fairmile," one announced. "Come to see if you needed an 'and."

"This one's my main concern." Newman indicated the central engine where he had been working. "Get her going and we'll have hydraulics back as well as the main generator."

"HTs are a mess," one said, looking over his shoulder. "What say I attend to those on t'other side?"

"And the distributor," the other added. "Providin' there's room."

"Very well, do what you can." Being one man down, Newman welcomed any assistance, though was already missing Kipling for something other than his help.

"There's a body down 'ere." The second mechanic pointed to the boy's remains. "Be easier if we got that out of the way an' all. Move it, shall I?"

"No, leave him," Newman said. "He can stay where he is."

* * *

299

If what lay before him was the reason for that night's mission, it was a pretty poor one and hardly worth the loss of so many men, not to mention one of His Majesty's gunboats or the partial destruction of another.

Anderson only intended looking in at the wardroom briefly, but the sick berth attendant had a minor wound that needed dressing, and he agreed to cover him.

Once alone with the heavily blanketed form, he drew closer. The patient had been strapped to the sofa and his face was that of one who had already been through much. Lines from past pain were deeply entrenched, the skin, stretched white across bone, was tissue thin, and what life remained had only a tenuous hold. As if alerted by his presence, one eye opened, forcing Anderson to suppress feelings of guilt for his own healthiness.

"Is there anything you need?" The question was foolish; *320* carried minimal medical equipment and might still sink before reaching land. Besides, how could a former geography teacher, now masquerading as a naval officer, help such a pathetic specimen?

"Where are we?"

"Aboard a British gunboat; we're heading for England and safety." It was a relief to have an answer to hand.

"How long?"

Not quite so simple.

"An hour or two, maybe more. Try and get some sleep; would you like me to leave?"

"No, I will not sleep." The eye opened wider. "It will not come until..."

"We cannot give you more morphine." The sick berth attendant had emphasised this before leaving.

"I will be fine for a while and able to talk. Please stay." It was more a plea than a request. "It helps."

Despite *320*'s condition, there was little for him, as captain, to do and, since Newman's success in starting the central engine, they were making better progress. Anderson supposed a few minutes' company was something he could provide, especially when they might turn out to be the man's last.

"It is good to hear we will soon be in England."

Now he felt awkward about having given reassurance when so much could still go wrong. "You will be well treated," Anderson said.

"I am sure of it, and grateful for the sacrifices that have been made."

"And what will you do there?" Anderson was keen to change the subject.

"First they must remove my leg." The man raised one eyebrow. "And then... Then I don't know." There was a faint smile. "Hopefully I will live."

"Is there anyone to care for you?"

"Oh yes." The eye was closing now; pain must be returning. "There has been excellent assistance." The patient's voice was definitely fading, and Anderson regretted his question. "One in particular has helped me so much and I must thank her properly."

"I understand the support SOE gives is very good." A noise made him turn and he looked up to see the sick berth attendant, now sporting a bandage that covered most of his head, at the wardroom door.

"But she was special, very special: very kind," the agent continued. "Eve Newman is an angel."

Anderson stood to leave. "He's awake and been talking," he told the rating.

"Very good, sir; you didn't give him any more morphine?"

"I did not."

"Thank you; I'll take over from here."

"I hope she will continue to care for me," the patient continued, "through the operation and after."

"I'm sure she will." Anderson was turning to go when a thought occurred, and he stopped. "What did you say her name was?"

* * *

Morgan had been on the bridge for several hours and, despite being cold, wet, stiff, and – in places – numb, he had no wish to move. The storm was continuing to ease, with far less rain and a considerable reduction in wind, though the swell, and current, was as strong. For the first hour the gunboat's remaining engine struggled to give them steerage but when the second came online, running smoother and at higher revs, all that changed and for some while they had been making proper progress. Dawn would

301

soon be breaking and must reveal land of some description though he remained uncertain of their exact location.

Though a rare occurrence, it was not the first time such a thing had happened, and the extenuating circumstances definitely excused him. And equally, Morgan had nursed badly damaged vessels in the past, although this was one of the few occasions when the objective, and his part in it, could be regarded as worthy. Admittedly once, when hired to transport a shipment of stolen artwork to the continent, they'd chanced upon a sinking fisher and were able to rescue her crew, and another time he picked up a solitary swimmer swept out on the rip, though Morgan's activities were normally less than laudable. He supposed some might consider the violence and killing of the last few hours dishonourable, though he would argue otherwise. And, equally rarely, the law would back him; however lowly the rank, he was now a King's Officer and had been fighting for something other than personal gain.

"All well up top?"

The first lieutenant appeared at the head of the wheelhouse ladder. Milner was a fellow Royal Navy man and, though less than half his age and superior in rank, the youngster obviously held him in respect; something Morgan found more than gratifying.

"All well," he replied.

"And how is it with you, 'Swain?" Milner enquired as he pulled himself fully onto the bridge.

"Sound, thank you, sir," Nolan replied. "Not much happenin', just waitin' for land." That was obviously the case, and all three stared out into the darkness.

Though that was no longer the correct term; Morgan glanced at his watch. Dawn might not be imminent, yet, with the storm all but spent, there was a definite lightening in the sky. The Germans had a word for it, but Morgan's attention was solely on a horizon that seemed to be deepening even as he looked. And then, almost to taunt him, came what might be a faint line in the far distance. He closed his eyes and waited, then opened them once more. Yes, it was land, he was sure of it.

"Reckon that'll be England, gents." Nolan's comment was offhand, and even Milner, who could be expected to show a little more enthusiasm, appeared less than elated.

"You might be right at that, 'Swain," he said. "Any idea

where we are, Mid?"

Morgan considered for a moment. "I'm not exactly sure," he finally admitted, and neither man seemed surprised, nor concerned.

"Well maybe they'll know more." This time Nolan was pointing to starboard.

Morgan looked and immediately drew breath.

There, several points off the starboard bow and less than two miles away he could see another vessel. More than one, in fact; trailing behind a stately tug lay another gunboat. And a British one, her silhouette unmistakable in the growing light. He went to speak, but mercifully held back. Morgan had already learned much about being a naval officer, and this was definitely an occasion when overt enthusiasm would not be necessary.

"Looks like the cavalry've shown up." Milner was equally cool.

"Maybe Tel' was able to get a signal off after all," Morgan suggested.

Milner pursed his lips and nodded. "Still, they did well to find us. Anyone know where the skipper might be?"

"Last I heard he was with Newman in the engine room." It was a tough call, but Morgan felt he was matching the younger man's composure and might even be behaving like a regular Navy man.

"Right oh," Milner said. "We'd better inform him."

"I'm sure he'd like to know," Morgan agreed.

Epilogue

"You goose, you silly goose!"

Anderson shook his head. "I'm only telling you what he said."

"Yet you clearly believe him!"

They were back in the Weymouth tearoom though it was busier than before. A pair of middle-aged women were at a distant table and the waitress – younger than the last and far more severe – was keeping a predatory eye over all as she prowled about.

"I don't know what to believe," Anderson said. "Frankly there's not been much chance to sleep since we got back. I did think you'd be a little more understanding."

She reached past the two plates of untouched cake and took his hand.

"I met him the once," Eve said, "for no more than an hour, just before he went away, and there's been no contact since."

"Not even..."

"Not even a postcard," she smiled.

"But you've been following his progress?"

"Yes, I've been following his progress, we all have. I've said it before, we're like a family." Her expression fell for a moment. "Though in this instance there was little to go on."

The two women were preparing to leave; the waitress rang up their bill, giving them slightly more privacy.

"Actually, Ian, we lost touch for quite a while," Eve looked away and continued as if in thought, "which made it all the harder."

"So, you were worried about him?"

"We were *all* worried about him." She turned back.

"Then why?" Anderson prompted.

Now down to only the strange young couple at the end who seemed more interested in talking than eating, the waitress retreated to the kitchen.

"People say strange things when they're ill," Eve continued, "it must just have been that."

"But he knew your name."

304

"And I know his, but it doesn't mean anything." She sighed and let go of his hand momentarily before returning and taking a firmer grip. "You have to believe me, Ian. Poor chap's up in London now and not expected to live. And even if he does, he'll be little use to us; I doubt we'll ever hear from him again."

"He called you an angel," Anderson told her.

"Did he?" She smiled again, apparently pleased. "No one's ever done that before."

"What, called you an angel?"

"No." Again, she was suddenly serious and, again, took hold of his hand. "Ian," she said, her face now a mask of concern. "You don't think it's true, do you?"

"What, that you're an angel?"

For a moment they shared a look of mock horror, before giving way to laughter loud enough to make the kitchen door open once more.

* * *

Harvey knew he'd be late; having to arrange for replacement wirelesses was bad enough, but the mess he and Stone made of the RDF set got them into all sorts of trouble. Though unable to salvage any parts, even opening the case annoyed a lot of top brass and it had taken the skipper's intervention, backed by some pipe-smoking commander, to see he wasn't put up on a charge. The bickering took much of the day and, after no sleep the previous night, Harvey was on his uppers. Yet he remained keen to get back to the club and, in particular, Nichole. If his luck was in, he might even be in time for their duet at the start of the second set.

But as he opened the front door and stepped inside, automatically acknowledging greetings from some at the already full tables, fortune was definitely not smiling, and it was obvious he had missed the boat on several counts.

Nichole was there, on the small stage Nolan had rigged for her, and lit only by the glow of a dozen table candles, yet that black satin dress never failed to make her shine. And her voice was just as good, slightly husky, perhaps, but then the room was more smoke than air; besides a little throatiness always suited her. What

305

he didn't like quite so much was the figure alongside.

Lee, the Yank trumpeter, always came over well on stage, but when standing next to Nichole something extra was added, and he definitely appeared very much at home. They were in the middle of a popular number from the States, one Harvey had been asked for countless times and, though always happy to play, never greatly rated. Lipstick-stained cigarettes, fairground swings, used airline tickets; all the detritus of a failed relationship set to a sweet enough tune; no more. But the couple's obvious chemistry was adding so much, turning a mediocre crowd pleaser into true Jazz.

As Nichole sang, Lee added bluesy phrases under and above the melody, his horn blending perfectly with her voice with a result that was both musically pleasing and oddly sensuous.

The audience were spellbound; even the musical side of Harvey's brain was carried away, although sufficient reason remained to suggest something very wrong was panning out before him. Then, as if in a form of synaesthesia, his thoughts began to blend with their phrasing, although to very different lyrics.

The lights, the candles, and the dark location. The sense of nearness and their shared affection. The song, deceptively sweet, yet wickedly sharp, cut straight to the bone.

The way they melded and the loaded glances. The unplanned touch, a smile, her silent promise. The look that filled his dreams, directed elsewhere, another to own.

The golden trumpet and her dusky tenor, the blend of energies, their understanding. And as the climax rose, he watched from below, no longer involved.

The number came to an end with universal applause, while she leant into Lee's chest, holding him in a way Harvey knew only too well. The pair paused, exchanged further knowing looks, and then began another number, but Harvey did not stay to watch. Instead, unnoticed and ignored, he turned and was soon outside, in the dark once more and, once more, alone.

* * *

"Kind of you, Joycie," Thompson told her, and she shrugged.

"Apples is everywhere this time of year," she said, eyeing the brown paper bag. "Weren't no bother."

It was a military hospital and part of the Weymouth barracks. Most of his fellow patients were squaddies either injured in training or having tonsils or appendixes removed. And though there was a bit of interservice ribbing, they got on all right, although Thompson especially looked forward to Joyce's daily visits.

"Nurse said you won't be here much longer," she told him.

"That's right, they need the bed or something. Though the old chest is healing up nicely."

"So, where'll you be going then?"

"Convalescent home, more'n likely; soon as they can find me a place," Thompson said. "But not for long; they reckons I should be back to active service by Christmas."

"Seems a long time away, though it'll go soon enough," she said and for a moment there was silence. Then, "Frank, I was thinkin', you could always come back to the flat."

"What, your flat?" he blinked. "Over the club?"

"If it were allowed. I couldn't look after you in the evenings so much, but daytime would be okay. That's if you fancy it."

Finally their eyes met in complete understanding.

"I'd like that very much," he said.

Author's Notes

The BPB MkV gunboat **MGB320** is totally fictitious, the number actually belonging to a Fairmile C of the 12th Flotilla. She survived the war and, when last heard of, had been converted to a houseboat and moored in Bembridge on the Isle Of Wight.

HMS *Bee* was a working up base for Coastal Forces craft. Commonly known as Swinley's Circus after its senior training officer Commander (later Captain) RFB Swinley, a WW1 veteran. Opening in 1942, it remained in Weymouth until October 1943 when it was moved to Holyhead to make space for preparations for Operation Overlord.

The 15th Motor Gun Boat Flotilla was formed in 1942 under the direction of Captain Frank Slocum then known at the Admiralty as Deputy Director Operations Division [Irregular] or DDOD[I]. With its base on the River Dart, and using an elderly paddle steamer as depot ship, the flotilla carried out numerous clandestine missions to the Britany coast supporting the various escape networks then active; delivering supplies, ferrying or collecting agents, and rescuing downed airmen and escaping POWs. Manned mainly by RNVR officers and 'hostilities only' ratings, it was to become the most highly decorated Royal Naval unit of the Second World War

Vera Atkins *(1908-2000)* was born in Galați, then in the Kingdom of Romania. After studying modern languages at the Sorbonne, she attended secretarial college in London, finally emigrating to England in 1937. Shortly afterwards Atkins was recruited by Canadian spymaster Sir William Stephenson of British Security Co-ordination and sent on several missions to Europe to gauge the threat posed by the strengthening Nazi party. In February 1941, Atkins joined the newly formed SOE initially as a secretary in F (French) section, though she was soon appointed assistant to section head, Colonel Maurice Buckmaster and later became the section's intelligence officer (F-Int). Though nominated for an MBE at the end of hostilities, this was never awarded. She did, however, receive a CBE in the 1997 Birthday

Honours, was awarded the Croix de Guerre in 1948, and made a Knight of the Legion of Honour by the French government in 1987.

Viginia Hall DSC, Croix de Guerre, MBE *(1906-1982)* was an American Office of Strategic Services agent who worked extensively for the SOE despite the loss of her left leg. Known variously as Marie Monin, Germaine, Diane, Camille, (and 'The Limping Lady' by the Gestapo), she was the first female agent to arrive in Vichy France where she set up the Heckler network. During her considerable time in enemy-occupied territory, she continued to organise and maintain networks and safe houses, arranged prisoner escapes, and recruited supporters.

Selected Glossary

Abwehr: The German Military Intelligence Service.

Aldis: A form of signalling lamp.

Amatol: A high-explosive mixture of TNT and ammonium nitrate.

Andrew: *(Slang)* The Royal Navy.

AVOmeter: Brand name for a prominent electronic multimeter.

AWOL: Absent without leave.

Bandstand: A type of guard made from bars supporting splinter mattresses that encompassed an Oerlikon or other small ordnance.

Bezzie: *(Slang)* Scouse term for a cheer.

Bint: *(Slang)* A female.

Blancoed: To whiten straps, webbing etc, usually with a proprietary product (available since 1880).

Blighty: *(Slang)* Britain.

Blow the gaff: *(Slang)* Literally reveal a secret or give the game away.

Bob: *(Slang)* A shilling (twelve pennies). A tanner was sixpence, florin two shillings, and a quid was (and still is) one pound.

Bonkers: *(Slang)* Mad (usually happily so).

Brown job: *(Slang)* A soldier.

Builders' tea: *(Slang)* Any blend that is cheap and strong.

China (plate): *(Rhyming Slang)* Mate.

CMB: Coastal motor boat (usually WW1 era).

CMM: Chief motor mechanic.

CO: Commanding officer.

Cornet: Similar to a trumpet and pitched in the same key, though its conical (as opposed to the trumpet's cylindrical) bore gives a more mellow sound.

Commissioned lovely: *(Slang)* A Wren (WRNS) officer.

Comms: *(Abbreviation)* Communications.

CPO: Chief petty officer.

Deckhead: Effectively a vessel's ceiling.

Dibs: *(Slang)* Shares.

Drum: *(Rhyming slang)* Drum and bass: place.

Flyboy: *(Slang)* Member of the RAF.

Geddes Axe: In 1922, a committee chaired by Sir Eric Geddes recommended financial cuts to the Royal Navy that saw a dramatic reduction in the service's ships, weaponry, and manpower.

Geordie: *(Slang)* One from Tyneside, North East England.

German Sea: Alternative (and antiquated) name for the North Sea.

Gestapo: The German secret police.

Goebbels: Joseph Goebbels was initially chief propagandist for the Nazi party and became Minister of Propaganda for the Reich.

Goon suit: *(Slang)* A kapok-lined, one-piece suit similar to a boiler or flying suit. See ursula.

Grey class: A type of steam-powered gunboat (SGB) 145' in length. Only 9 of the 52 planned were built.

Gumboots: Working boots usually made of rubber and rising to the knee. Also known as Wellingtons.

Hard lying (money): Additional allowance made to men of Coastal Forces and some other divisions of the RN.

HMS *Badger*: Royal Navy base in Harwich.

HMS *Ganges*: Royal Navy training base for "Hostilities Only New Entry Training".

HMS *Hornet*: Coastal Forces base at Gosport.

HMS *St Christopher*: Coastal Forces training base at Fort William, Scotland.

Howay marra: Geordie greeting; literally 'hello, friend'.

Hog Out: *(Slang)* Clean up.

Holman projector: A weapon using pneumatic power to fire an explosive charge. Mainly intended for anti-aircraft use, it proved ineffective and was eventually withdrawn.

Jimmy (the One): *(Slang)* The first lieutenant.

Jimmy (riddle): *(Rhyming slang)* Urination.

Khazi: *(Slang)* A toilet (supposedly from the corruption of the Cockney-Italian word casa for house).

Kickers: *(Slang)* Boots.

Kye: *(Slang)* A drink made from shavings of chocolate

mixed with boiling water and usually heavily sweetened.

Lyons: In 1894, Jo Lyons established one of the first chains of teashops.

Matriculate: To be admitted into a university, usually by examination.

MGB: Motor gun boat.

ML: Motor launch.

Mutt and Jeff: *(Rhyming slang)* Deaf.

NAAFI: (Pronounced NAAFI) The acronym for Navy, Army and Air Force Institutes, an organisation set up in 1920 to cater for servicemen and their families.

Narrow Seas: Colloquial name for the English Channel.

Neb: *(Slang)* Scouse for nose.

Necker: *(Slang)* A measure of spirit taken with beer. Also chaser.

Nutty: *(Slang)* Seaman's term for chocolate (whether it contained nuts or not).

Old Bill: *(Slang)* Civil police. See also Rozzers.

Pens: Mooring area at HMS *Wasp.*

Phiz: *(Slang)* Face.

Pilot: In nautical terminology a person, or manual, that guides a vessel through difficult passages.

Pinpoint: Site chosen for the delivery or collection of agents, arms, mail, or materiel.

PMO: Principal medical officer.

PO: Petty officer.

Prep school: Preparatory, or primary school; a forerunner to secondary education and usually privately funded.

Pussy: *(Slang)* Soft.

Quid: *(Slang)* One pound Sterling. (See Bob.)

RASC: Royal Army Service Corps, a former unit of the British Army responsible for logistics and administration. The initials were often jokingly claimed to stand for **R**un **A**way **S**omeone's **C**oming.

Ready room: Area used for (often less formal) pre-and post-mission briefings.

R-boat: *(Räumboote)* German launch originally intended as a mine sweeper. 130' length, 19' beam, crew of 30-40. Twin diesel engines, heavily armed.

Rissole:　Small patty made with meat, fish and/or vegetables which was baked or fried. During wartime, the poorest ingredients were often used.

Rozzers:　*(Slang)* Civil police. See also Old Bill.

RNVR:　Royal Naval Volunteer Reserve, formed from the Royal Naval Volunteer Supplementary Reserve. A force made up of amateur (or in the case of the **RNR** professional) seamen.

R/T:　Radio telegraphy (voice).

Safari jar:　A large vacuum flask that could keep several pints of fluid hot for many hours.

Salt horse:　*(Slang)* A regular sea officer without specific training in a technical field, and often taken to mean one with an old-fashioned (usually pre-WW1) approach.

Scrambled egg:　*(Slang)* Usually referring to the gold decoration on the caps of Naval commanders and above.

Scrumpy:　Strong homemade cider.

Scouser:　*(Slang)* Liverpudlian.

SK C/30:　German 37mm anti-aircraft and general-purpose, semi-automatic cannon.

S-Craft:　German designation for what the British called E-boats.

Sitrep:　*(Slang)* Situation report, a brief record of recent events.

SIS:　Secret Intelligence Service (**MI6**). Early in 1939, the SIS reported Germany intended to invade the Netherlands with the aim of using the Dutch airfields to destroy England. The intelligence this was based on turned out to be manufactured by the *Deuxième Bureau* to encourage Britain in its defence of France.

Slate:　A basic form of credit: bills are literally chalked up on a slate for later settlement.

Smoko:　*(Slang)* A short, informal, (and often unauthorised) break from work.

Special (Constable):　A volunteer police officer.

S-pipes:　Method of reducing exhaust noise in high-speed launches.

Spiv:　*(Slang)* One who deals in black market goods.

Spout lamp:　Lantern that was closed on three sides with a tube connected to the fourth that only allowed light to be shown in one direction. An early smuggler's tool.

SOE: Special Operations Executive. Formed by Hugh Dalton in 1940, SOE was responsible for organising sabotage, espionage, and reconnaissance in occupied Europe.

SO: Senior officer.

Spray rail: Raised ledge fitted along and above the chine of a high-speed launch to reduce extraneous spray.

Straight striper: *(Slang)* A regular RN officer. Due to the stripes denoting rank being straight (rather than wavy for RNVR officers).

Suck eggs: Part of a colloquial expression: "Don't teach your grandmother to suck eggs," meaning those who already know don't need to be taught.

Survivor leave: It was customary to allow RN officers and ratings two weeks' paid leave following the loss of their ship. This contrasted with the crews of merchant shipping; before the Emergency Work Order of May 1941 was implemented, wages ceased the moment their vessel was sunk.

Syrette: Single-use syringe usually containing a strong analgesic.

Tapping the glass: *(Slang)* To hasten the end of a watch, trick or work period. From earlier times when the hourglass would be tapped to speed the flow of sand.

Tea and a wad: *(Slang)* A tea break/refreshment, the wad being cake or a bun of some description.

TO: Training officer.

Toad in the hole: A dish of sausages cooked in a thick batter pudding.

Tod (on your): *(Rhyming slang)* Alone. On Your Tod Sloan. Tod Sloan was a 19th-century American jockey. Despite being abandoned by his parents, he went on to be successful in his field and became the subject of the song *Yankey Doodle Dandy*.

Trilby: A hat similar to a fedora but with a narrower brim.

Ursula: Heavy, waxed cotton clothing originally derived from motorcycle racing wear.

VP: *(Vorpostenboote)*. German patrol boats usually converted from fishery, or similar, vessels. Heavily armed with medium to light calibre weapons (usually 88, 40, and

20mm) which could be used against aircraft or shipping. Crewed by up to seventy men and with reinforced gun emplacements, they were a formidable, if slow, opponent to Coastal Forces' craft.

Vosper: A prominent maker of high-speed launches that was also responsible for Malcolm Campbell's record-breaking *Bluebird K4*.

Wavy (Wavy Navy): RNVR officers' stripes denoting rank were wavy, (rather than straight for regular officers).

Welsh rarebit: A hot dish of cheese sauce served on toast.

Wet Nelly: Traditional Liverpudlian fruitcake made from white bread, sugar, eggs, spices, and dried fruit. Usually served with custard.

Whaleback: Distinctive feature in the lines of certain high-speed launches.

Whale Island: Royal Navy gunnery school.

Woolly Pully: *(Slang)* Woolen pullover beloved by all UK armed forces, usually with cotton reinforcements to sleeve and shoulders.

W/T: Wireless telegraphy (Morse).

WVS: Women's Voluntary Services; founded in 1938 the WVS recruited women to assist in air raid precautions and with general civilian support. It was noted for having no hierarchy; all members being considered of equal rank and value.

About the Author

Alaric Bond has written for various markets including television, radio and the stage but currently focuses on historical nautical fiction with nineteen published novels, fifteen of which being in his acclaimed 'Fighting Sail' series. *Glory Boys* is the second instalment in the 'Coastal Forces' series that centres around the small ship navy of high-speed launches used during ww2.

He lives in Sussex, is married, and has two far taller sons. Apart from researching nautical history he enjoys cycling (in gumboots, rather than lycra), sailing and carpentry as well as jazz, blues, swing, and dance band music from the thirties onwards. He also plays a variety of musical instruments and collects 78 rpm records.

www.alaricbond.com

About Old Salt Press

Old Salt Press is an independent press catering to those who love books about ships and the sea. We are an association of writers working together to produce the very best of nautical and maritime fiction and non-fiction. We invite you to join us as we go down to the sea in books.

www.oldsaltpress.com

The Latest Great Reading from Old Salt Press

Rick Spilman
Evening Gray Morning Red

A young American sailor must escape his past and the clutches of the Royal Navy, in the turbulent years just before the American Revolutionary War. In the spring of 1768, Thom Larkin, a 17-year-old sailor newly arrived in Boston, is caught by Royal Navy press gang and dragged off to HMS *Romney*, where he runs afoul of the cruel and corrupt First Lieutenant. Years later, after escaping the Romney, Thom again crosses paths with his old foe, now in command HMS *Gaspee*, cruising in Narragansett Bay. Thom must finally face his nemesis and the guns of the *Gaspee*, armed only with his wits, an unarmed packet boat, and a sand bar.

Joan Druett
Tupaia, Captain Cook's Polynesian Navigator

Tupaia sailed with Captain Cook from Tahiti, piloted the *Endeavour* about the South Pacific, and was the ship's translator. Lauded by Europeans as "an extraordinary genius", he was also a master navigator, a brilliant orator, an artist and mapmaker, and a devious politician. Winner of the New Zealand Post General Non-Fiction Prize.

V E Ulett
Blackwell's Homecoming

In a multigenerational saga of love, war and betrayal, Captain Blackwell and Mercedes continue their voyage in Volume III of Blackwell's Adventures. The Blackwell family's eventful journey from England to Hawaii, by way of the new and tempestuous nations of Brazil and Chile, provides an intimate portrait of family conflicts and loyalties in the late Georgian Age. Blackwell's Homecoming is an evocation of the dangers and rewards of desire.

317

Seymour Hamilton
Ellie: A Story from the World of The Astreya Trilogy
Ellie is a story about losing your way and finding it again.
Ellie, the youngest navigator in the fleet, challenges the authority of her uncle Astreya, the Grand Commander. Only hours later, cannon shots cripple her boat, she falls overboard and is lost ashore. Ellie tries to return home to Matris, but unexpected friends and threatening foes intervene. As her uncle, sister, and cousins search for her, Ellie is forced to travel by foot, horseback, and land crawler to the Castle, where the Governor is fomenting war.
Ellie is the sixth book set in the world of The Astreya Trilogy.

Antoine Vanner
Britannia's Morass: The Dawlish Chronicles September - December 1884
1884: Florence Dawlish remains in Britain when her husband, Captain Nicholas Dawlish, leaves for service in the Sudan. She faces months of worry about him but she'll cope by immersing herself in welfare work for Royal Navy seamen's families at Portsmouth. It'll be a dull but worthy time . . .
. . . until the suicide of a middle-aged widow whom Florence respects. Left wealthy by her husband, this lady died a pauper, beggared within a few months, how and by whom, is not known. The widow's legal executor isn't interested and the police have other concerns. Lacking close family, she'll be soon forgotten. But not by Florence. Someone was responsible and there must be retribution. And getting justice will demand impersonation, guile and courage.

Linda Collison
Water Ghosts
Fifteen-year-old James McCafferty is an unwilling sailor aboard a traditional Chinese junk, operated as adventure-therapy for troubled teens. Once at sea, the ship is gradually taken over by the spirits of courtiers who fled the Imperial court during the Ming Dynasty, more than 600 years ago. One particular ghost wants what James has and is intent on trading places with him. But the teens themselves are their own worst enemies in the struggle for life in the middle of the Pacific Ocean. A psychological story set at sea, with historical and paranormal elements.

Alaric Bond
On the Barbary Coast
(The Fighting Sail Series)

Spring 1814 and, after four exhausting years on the North American Station, HMS *Tenacious* is finally heading home. With the war in Europe drawing to a close, it is even doubtful whether she will be needed again while her captain has his own reasons to reach England.

But their journey is broken by a strange encounter, and many are soon robbed of the peace they have earned as a new and particularly wicked enemy emerges, one that threatens far more than their personal safety.

With engrossing naval action and intense personal dynamics, *On the Barbary Coast* is a thriller in the best tradition of Historical Nautical Fiction.

Printed in Great Britain
by Amazon

49761063R00181